Gripping Novels of
Intrigue and Suspense

SIGNET DOUBLE MYSTERIES:

ONE
LONELY NIGHT

and

THE
TWISTED THING

SIGNET Mysteries by Mickey Spillane

One
Lonely
Night

and

The
Twisted
Thing

By

MICKEY SPILLANE

A SIGNET BOOK

NEW AMERICAN LIBRARY

TIMES MIRROR

NAL BOOKS ARE AVAILABLE AT QUANTITY DISCOUNTS WHEN USED TO PROMOTE PRODUCTS OR SERVICES. FOR INFORMATION PLEASE WRITE TO PREMIUM MARKETING DIVISION, THE NEW AMERICAN LIBRARY, INC., 1633 BROADWAY, NEW YORK, NEW YORK 10019.

 SIGNET TRADEMARK REG. U.S. PAT. OFF. AND FOREIGN COUNTRIES
REGISTERED TRADEMARK—MARCA REGISTRADA
HECHO EN CHICAGO, U.S.A.

SIGNET, SIGNET CLASSICS, MENTOR, PLUME, MERIDIAN AND NAL BOOKS *are published by The New American Library, Inc., 1633 Broadway, New York, New York 10019*

FIRST PRINTING (Double Mickey Spillane edition), OCTOBER, 1980

1 2 3 4 5 6 7 8 9

PRINTED IN THE UNITED STATES OF AMERICA

One
Lonely
Night

To Marty

CHAPTER ONE

NOBODY ever walked across the bridge, not on a night like this. The rain was misty enough to be almost fog-like, a cold gray curtain that separated me from the pale ovals of white that were faces locked behind the steamed-up windows of the cars that hissed by. Even the brilliance that was Manhattan by night was reduced to a few sleepy, yellow lights off in the distance.

Some place over there I had left my car and started walking, burying my head in the collar of my raincoat, with the night pulled in around me like a blanket. I walked and I smoked and I flipped the spent butts ahead of me and watched them arch to the pavement and fizzle out with one last wink. If there was life behind the windows of the buildings on either side of me, I didn't notice it. The street was mine, all mine. They gave it to me gladly and wondered why I wanted it so nice and all alone.

There were others like me, sharing the dark and the solitude, but they huddled in the recessions of the doorways not wanting to share the wet and the cold. I could feel their eyes follow me briefly before they turned inward to their thoughts again.

So I followed the hard concrete footpaths of the city through the towering canyons of the buildings and never noticed when the sheer cliffs of brick and masonry diminished and disappeared altogether, and the footpath led into a ramp then on to the spidery steel skeleton that was the bridge linking two states.

I climbed to the hump in the middle and stood there leaning on the handrail with a butt in my fingers, watching the red and green lights of the boats in the river below. They winked at me and called in low, throaty notes before disappearing into the night.

Like eyes and faces. And voices.

I buried my face in my hands until everything straightened itself out again, wondering what the judge would say if he could see me now. Maybe he'd laugh because I was supposed to be so damn tough, and here I was with hands that wouldn't stand still and an empty feeling inside my chest.

He was only a little judge. He was little and he was old with eyes like two berries on a bush. His hair was pure white and wavy and his skin was loose and wrinkled. But he had a voice like the avenging angel. The dignity and knowledge behind his face gave him the stature of a giant, the poise of Gabriel reading your sins aloud from the Great Book and condemning you to your fate.

He had looked at me with a loathing louder than words, lashing me with his eyes in front of a courtroom filled with people, every empty second another stroke of the steel-tipped whip. His voice, when it did come, was edged with a gentle bitterness that was given only to the righteous.

But it didn't stay righteous long. It changed into disgusted hatred because I was a licensed investigator who knocked off somebody who needed knocking off bad and he couldn't get to me. So I was a murderer by definition and all the law could do was shake its finger at definitions.

Hell, the state would have liquidated the gun anyway . . . maybe he would have pronounced sentence himself. Maybe he thought I should have stayed there and called for the cops when the bastard had a rod in his hand and it was pointing right at my gut.

Yeah, great.

If he had let it stay there it would have been all right. I'd been called a lot of things before. But no, he had to go and strip me naked in front of myself and throw the past in my face when it should have stayed dead and buried forever. He had to go back five years to a time he knew of only secondhand and tell me how it took a war to show me the power of the gun and the obscene pleasure that was brutality and force, the spicy sweetness of murder sanctified by law.

That was me. I could have made it sound better if I'd said it. There in the muck and slime of the jungle, there in the stink that hung over the beaches rising from the bodies of the dead, there in the half-light of too many dusks and dawns laced together with the crisscrossed patterns of bullets, I had gotten a taste of death and found it palatable to the extent that I could never again eat the fruits of a normal civilization.

Goddamn, he wouldn't let me alone! He went on and on cutting me down until I was nothing but scum in the gutter, his fists slamming against the bench as he prophesied a rain of purity that was going to wash me into the sewer with the other scum leaving only the good and the meek to walk in the cleanliness of law and justice.

One day I would die and the world would be benefited by my death. And to the good there was only the perplexing question: Why did I live and breathe now . . . what could possibly be the reason for existence when there was no good in me? None at all.

So he gave me back my soul of toughness, hate and bitterness and let me dress in the armor of cynicism and dismissed me before I could sneer and make the answer I had ready.

He had called the next case up even before I reached the side of the room. It had all the earmarks of a good case, but nobody seemed to be interested. All they watched was me and their eyes were bright with that peculiar kind of horrified disgust that you see in people watching some nasty, fascinating creature in a circus cage.

Only a few of them reflected a little sympathy. Pat was there. He gave me a short wave and a nod that meant everything was okay because I was his friend. But there were things the judge had said that Pat had wanted to say plenty of times too.

Then there was Pete, a reporter too old for the fast beats and just right for the job of picking up human interest items from the lower courts. He waved too, with a grimace that was a combination grin for me and a sneer for the judge. Pete was a cynic too, but he liked my kind of guy. I made bonus stories for him every once in a while.

Velda. Lovely, lovely Velda. She waited for me by the door and when I walked up to her I watched her lips purse into a ripe, momentary kiss. The rows and rows of eyes that had been following me jumped ahead to this vision in a low-cut dress who threw a challenge with every motion of her body. The eyes swept from her black pumps to legs and body and shoulders that were almost too good to be real and staggered when they met a face that was beauty capable of the extremes of every emotion. Her head moved just enough to swirl her black page-boy hair and the look she sent back to all those good people and their white-haired guardian of the law was something to be remembered. For one long second she had the judge's eye and outraged justice flinched before outraged love.

That's right, Velda was mine. It took a long time for me to find out just how much mine she was, much too long. But now I knew and I'd never forget it. She was the only decent thing about me and I was lucky.

She said, "Let's get out of here, Mike. I hate people with little minds."

We went outside the building to the sidewalk and climbed in my car. She knew I didn't want to talk about it and kept still. When I let her out at her apartment it was dark and starting to rain. Her hand went to mine and squeezed it. "A good drunk and you can forget about it, Mike. Sometimes people are too stupid to be grateful. Call me when you're loaded and I'll come get you."

That was all. She knew me enough to read my mind and didn't care what I thought. If the whole damn world climbed on my back there would still be Velda ready to yank them off and stamp on their faces. I didn't even tell her good-by. I just shut the door and started driving.

No, I didn't get drunk. Twice I looked in the mirror and saw me. I didn't look like me at all. I used to be able to look at myself and grin without giving a damn how ugly it made me look. Now I was looking at myself the same way those people did back there. I was looking at a big guy with an ugly reputation, a guy who had no earthly reason for existing in a decent, normal society. That's what the judge had said.

I was sweating and cold at the same time. Maybe it did happen to me over there. Maybe I did have a taste for death. Maybe I liked it too much to taste anything else. Maybe I was twisted and rotted inside. Maybe I would be washed down the sewer with the rest of all the rottenness sometime. What was stopping it from happening now? Why was I me with some kind of lucky charm around my neck that kept me going when I was better off dead?

That's why I parked the car and started walking in the rain. I didn't want to look in that damn mirror any more. So I walked and smoked and climbed to the hump in the bridge where the boats in the river made faces and spoke to me until I had to bury my face in my hands until everything straightened itself out again.

I was a killer. I was a murderer, legalized. I had no reason for living. Yeah, he said that!

The crazy music that had been in my head ever since I came back from those dusks and dawns started again, a low steady beat overshadowed by the screaming of brassier, shriller instruments that hadn't been invented yet. They shouted and pounded a symphony of madness and destruction while I held my hands over my ears and cursed until they stopped. Only the bells were left, a hundred bells that called for me to come closer to the music, and when I wouldn't come they stopped, one by one, all except one deep, persistent bell with a low, resonant voice. It wouldn't give up. It called me to it, and when I opened my eyes I knew the bell was from a channel marker in the river, calling whenever it swayed with the tide.

It was all right once I knew where it came from. At least it was real. That judge, that damn white-headed son-of-a-bitch got me like this. I wasn't so tough after all. It wouldn't have been so bad . . . but maybe he was right. Maybe he was dead right and I'd never be satisfied until I knew the answer myself. If there was an answer.

I don't know how long I stood there. Time was just the ticking of a watch and a blend of sound from the ramp behind me. At some point after the sixth cigarette the cold mist had turned into a fine snow that licked at my face and clung to my coat. At first it melted into damp patches on the steel and concrete, then took hold and extended itself into a coverlet of white.

Now the last shred of reality was gone completely. The girders became giant trees and the bridge an eerie forest populated by whitecapped rubber-tired monsters streaking for the end of the causeway that took them into more friendly surroundings. I leaned back into the shadow of a girder and watched them to get my mind off other things, happy to be part of the peace and quiet of the night.

It came at last, the lessening of tension. The stiffness went out of my fingers and I pulled on a smoke until it caught in my lungs the way I liked it to do. Yeah, I could grin now and watch the faces fade away until they were onto the port and starboard lights of the ships again, and the bell that called me in was only a buoy some place off in the dark.

I ought to get out of it. I ought to take Velda and my office and start up in real estate in some small community where murder and guns and dames didn't happen. Maybe I would, at that. It was wonderful to be able to think straight again. No more crazy mad hatred that tied my insides into knots. No more hunting the scum that stood behind a trigger and shot at the world. That was official police business. The duty of organized law and order. And too slow justice. No more sticks with dirty ends on them either.

That's what the snow and the quiet did for me. It had been a long time since I had felt this good. Maybe the rottenness wasn't there at all and I was a killer only by coincidence. Maybe I didn't like to kill at all.

I stuck another Lucky in my mouth and searched my pockets for matches. Something jerked my head up before I found them and I stood there listening.

The wind blew. The snow hissed to the street. A foghorn sounded. That was all.

I shrugged and tore a match out of the book when I heard it again. A little, annoying sound that didn't belong on the bridge in the peace and quiet. They were soft, irregular sounds that faded when the wind shifted, then came back stronger. Footsteps, muted by the inch or so of snow on the walk.

I would have gotten the butt lit if the feet weren't trying to run with the desperate haste that comes with fatigue. The sound came closer and closer until it was a shadow fifty feet away that turned into a girl wrapped in a coat with a big woolly collar, her hands reaching for the support of a girder and missing.

She fell face down and tried to pull herself up to run again, but she couldn't make it. Her breathing was a long, racking series of sobs that shook her body in a convulsion of despair.

I'd seen fear before, but never like this.

She was only a few steps away and I ran to her, my hands hooking under her arms to lift her to her feet.

Her eyes were like saucers, rimmed with red, overflowing with tears that blurred her pupils. She took one look at me and choked, "Lord . . . no, please!"

"Easy, honey, take it easy," I said. I propped her against the girder and her eyes searched my face through the tears unable to see me clearly. She tried to talk and I stopped her. "No words, kid. There's plenty of time for that later. Just take it easy a minute, nobody's going to hurt you."

As if that stirred something in her mind, her eyes went wide again and she turned her head to stare back down the ramp. I heard it too. Footsteps, only these weren't hurried. They came evenly and softly, as if knowing full well they'd reach their objective in a few seconds.

I felt a snarl ripple across my mouth and my eyes went half shut. Maybe you can smack a dame around all you want and make her life as miserable as hell, but nobody has the right to scare the daylights out of any woman. Not like this.

She trembled so hard I had to put my arm around her shoulder to steady her. I watched her lips trying to speak, the unholy fear spreading into her face as no sound came.

I pulled her away from the girder. "Come on, we'll get this straightened out in a hurry." She was too weak to resist. I held my arm around her and started walking toward the foot-steps.

He came out of the wall of white, a short, pudgy guy in a

heavy belted ulster. His homburg was set on the side of his head rakishly, and even at this distance I could see the smile on his lips. Both his hands were stuck in his pockets and he walked with a swagger. He wasn't a bit surprised when he saw the two of us. One eyebrow went up a little, but that was all. Oh yes, he had a gun in one pocket.

It was pointing at me.

Nobody had to tell me he was the one. I wouldn't even have to know he had a rod in his hand. The way the kid's body stiffened with the shock of seeing him was enough. My face couldn't have been nice to look at right then, but it didn't bother the guy.

The gun moved in the pocket so I'd know it was a gun. His voice fitted his body, short and thick. He said, "It is not smart to be a hero. Not smart at all." His thick lips twisted into a smile of mingled satisfaction and conceit. It was so plain in his mind that I could almost hear him speak it. The girl running along, stumbling blindly into the arms of a stranger. Her pleas for help, the guy's ready agreement to protect her, only to look down the barrel of a rod.

It didn't happen like that at all, but that's what he thought. His smile widened and he said harshly, "So now they will find the two of you here tomorrow." His eyes were as cold and as deadly as those of a manta ray.

He was too cocky. All he could see was his own complete mastery of the situation. He should have looked at me a little harder and maybe he would have seen the kind of eyes I had. Maybe he would have known that I was a killer in my own way too, and he would have realized that I knew he was just the type who would go to the trouble of taking the gun out of his pocket instead of ruining a good coat.

I never really gave him a chance. All I moved was my arm and before he had his gun out I had my .45 in my fist with the safety off and the trigger back. I only gave him a second to realize what it was like to die then I blew the expression clean off his face.

He never figured the hero would have a gun, too.

Before I could get it back in the holster the girl gave a lunge and backed up against the railing. Her eyes were clear now. They darted to the mess on the ground, the gun in my hand and the tight lines that made a mask of kill-lust of my face.

She screamed. Good God, how she screamed. She screamed as if I were a monster that had come up out of the pit! She screamed and made words that sounded like, "You . . . one of them . . . no more!"

I saw what she was going to do and tried to grab her, but the brief respite she had was enough to give her the strength she needed. She twisted and slithered over the top of the rail and I felt part of her coat come away in my hand as she tumbled headlong into the white void below the bridge.

Lord, Lord, what happened? My fingers closed over the handrail and I stared down after her. Three hundred feet to the river. The little fool didn't have to do that! She was safe! Nothing could have hurt her, didn't she realize that? I was shouting it at the top of my lungs with nobody but a dead man to hear me. When I pulled away from the rail I was shaking like a leaf.

All because of that fat little bastard stretched out in the snow. I pulled back my foot and kicked what was left of him until he rolled over on his face.

I did it again, I killed somebody else! Now I could stand in the courtroom in front of the man with the white hair and the voice of the Avenging Angel and let him drag my soul out where everybody could see it and slap it with another coat of black paint.

Peace and quiet, it was great! I ought to have my head examined. Or the guy should maybe; his had a hell of a hole in it. The dirty son-of-a-bitch for trying to get away with that. The fat little slob walks right up to me with a rod in his hand figuring to get away with it. The way he strutted you'd think he didn't have a care in the world, yet just like that he was going to kill two people without batting an eye. He got part of what he wanted anyway. The girl was dead. He was the kind of a rat who would have gotten a big laugh out of the papers tomorrow. Maybe he was supposed to be the rain of purity that was going to wash me down the gutter into the sewer with the rest of the scum. Brother, would that have been a laugh.

Okay, if he wanted a laugh, he'd get it. If his ghost could laugh I'd make it real funny for him. It would be so funny that his ghost would be the laughingstock of hell and when mine got there it'd have something to laugh at too. I'm nothing but a stinking no-good killer but I get there first, Judge. I get there first and live to do it again because I have eyes that see and a hand that works without being told and I don't give a damn what you do to my soul because it's so far gone nothing can be done for it! Go to hell yourself, Judge! Get a real belly laugh!

I tore his pockets inside out and stuffed his keys and wallet in my coat. I ripped out every label on his clothes right down to the laundry marks then I kicked the snow off the pavement and rubbed his fingertips against the cold concrete until there weren't any fingertips left. When I was finished he looked like the remains of a scarecrow that had been up too many seasons. I grabbed an arm and a leg and heaved him over the rail, and when I heard a faint splash many seconds later my mouth split into a grin. I kicked the pieces of the cloth and his gun under the rail and let them get lost in the obscurity of the night and the river. I didn't even have to worry about the bullet. It was lying right there in the snow, all flattened out and glistening wetly.

I kicked that over the side too.

Now let them find him. Let them learn who it was and how it happened. Let everybody have a laugh while you're at it!

It was done and I lit a cigarette. The snow still coming down put a new layer over the tracks and the dark stain. It almost covered up the patch of cloth that had come from the girl's coat, but I picked that up and stuck it in with the rest of the stuff.

Now my footsteps were the only sound along the ramp. I walked back to the city telling myself that it was all right, it had to happen that way. I was me and I couldn't have been anything else even if there had been no war. I was all right, the world was wrong. A police car moaned through the pay station and passed me as its siren was dying down to a low whine. I didn't even give it a second thought. They weren't going anywhere, certainly not to the top of the hump because not one car had passed during those few minutes it had happened. Nobody saw me, nobody cared. If they did the hell with 'em.

I reached the streets of the city and turned back for another look at the steel forest that climbed into the sky. No, nobody ever walked across the bridge on a night like this.

Hardly nobody.

CHAPTER TWO

I DIDN'T GO HOME that night. I went to my office and sat in the big leather-covered chair behind the desk and drank without getting drunk. I held the .45 in my lap, cleaned and reloaded, watching it, feeling in it an extension of myself. How many people had it sent on the long road? My mind blocked off the thought of the past and I put the gun back in the sling under my arm and slept. I dreamt that the judge with the white hair and eyes like two berries on a bush was pointing at me, ordering me to take the long road myself, and I had the .45 in my hand and my finger worked the trigger. It clicked and wouldn't go off, and with every sharp click a host of devilish voices would take up a dirge of laughter and I threw the gun at him, but it wouldn't leave my hand. It was part of me and it stuck fast.

The key turning in the lock awakened me. Throughout that dream of violent action I hadn't moved an inch, so that when I brought my head up I was looking straight at Velda. She didn't know I was there until she tossed the day's mail on the desk. For a second she froze with startled surprise, then relaxed into a grin.

"You scared the whosis out of me, Mike." She paused and bit her lip. "Aren't you here early?"

"I didn't go home, kid."

"Oh. I thought you might call me. I stayed up pretty late."

"I didn't get drunk, either."

"No?"

"No."

Velda frowned again. She wanted to say something, but during office hours she respected my position. I was the boss and she was my secretary. Very beautiful, of course. I loved her like hell, but she didn't know how much and she was still part of the pay roll. She decided to brighten the office with a smile instead, sorted the things on my desk, and started back to the reception room.

"Velda . . ."

She stopped, her hand on the knob and looked over her shoulder. "Yes, Mike?"

"Come here." I stood up and sat on the edge of the desk tapping a Lucky against my thumbnail. "What kind of a guy am I, kitten?"

Her eyes probed into my brain and touched the discontent. For a moment her smile turned into an animal look I had seen only once before. "Mike . . . that judge was a bastard. You're an all-right guy."

"How do you know?" I stuck the butt between my lips and lit it.

She stood there spraddle-legged with her hands low on her hips like a man, her breasts rising and falling faster than they should, fighting the wispy thinness of the dress. "I could love you a little or I could love you a lot, Mike. Sometimes it's both ways but mostly it's a lot. If you weren't all right I couldn't love you at all. Is that what you wanted me to say?"

"No." I blew out a stream of smoke and looked at the ceiling. "Tell me about myself. Tell me what other people say."

"Why? You know it as well as I do. You read the papers. When you're right you're a hero. When you're wrong you're kill-happy. Why don't you ask the people who count, the ones who really know you? Ask Pat. He thinks you're a good cop. Ask all the worms in the holes, the ones who have reason to stay out of your way. They'll tell you too . . . if you can catch them."

I chucked the butt into the metal basket. "Sure, the worms'll tell me. You know why I can't catch them, Velda? Do you know why they're scared to death to tangle with me? I'll tell you why. They know damn well I'm as bad as they are . . . worse, and I operate legally."

She reached out a hand and ran it over my hair. "Mike, you're too damn big and tough to give a hang what people say. They're only little people with little minds, so forget it."

"There's an awful lot of it."

"Forget it."

"Make me," I said.

She came into my arms with a rush and I held her to me to get warm and let the moist softness of her lips make me forget. I had to push to get her away and I stood there holding her arms, breathing in a picture of what a man's woman should look like. It was a long time before I could manage a grin, but she brought it out of me. There's something a woman does without words that makes a man feel like a man and forget about the things he's been told.

"Did you bring in the paper?"

"It's on my desk."

She followed me when I went out to get it. A tabloid and a full-sized job were there. The tab was opened to a news account of the trial that was one column wide and two inches long. They had my picture, too. The other rag gave me a good spread and a good going over and they didn't have my picture. I could start picking my friends out of the pack now.

Instead of digesting the absorbing piece of news, I scanned the pages for something else. Velda scowled at my concentration and hung over my shoulder. What I was looking for wasn't there. Not a single thing about two bodies in the river.

"Something, Mike?"

I shook my head. "Nope. Just looking for customers."

She didn't believe me. "There are some excellent prospects in the letter file if you're interested. They're waiting for your answer."

"How are we fixed, Velda?" I didn't look at her.

I put the paper down and reached in my pocket for a smoke.

"We're solvent. Two accounts paid up yesterday. The money has been banked and there's no bills. Why?"

"Maybe I'll take a vacation."

"From what?"

"From paid jobs. I'm tired of being an employee."

"Think of me."

"I am," I said. "You can take a vacation too if you want to."

She grabbed my elbow and turned me around until I was fencing with her eyes again. "Whatever you're thinking isn't of fun on some beach, Mike."

"It isn't?" I tried to act surprised.

"No." She took the cigarette from my mouth, dragged on it and stuck it back. She never moved her eyes. "Mike, don't play with me, please. Either tell me or don't, but quit making up excuses. What's on your mind?"

My mouth felt tight. "You wouldn't believe it if I told you."

"Yes I would." There was nothing hidden in her answer. No laughter, no scorn. Just absolute belief in me.

"I want to find out about myself, Velda."

She must have known what was coming. I said it quietly, almost softly, and she believed me. "All right, Mike," she said. "If you need me for anything you know where to find me."

I gave her the cigarette and went back to the office. How

deep can a woman go to search a man's mind? How can they know without being told when some trival thing can suddenly become so important? What is it that gives them that look as if they know the problem and the answer too, yet hold it back because it's something you have to discover for yourself?

I sat down in the swivel chair again and pulled all the junk out of my pockets; the keys, the wallet and the change. Two of the keys were for a car. One was an ordinary house key, another for a trunk or suitcase, and another for either a tumbler padlock or another house.

If I expected to find anything in the wallet I was mistaken. There were six fives and two singles in the bill compartment, a package of three-cent stamps and a card-calendar in one pocket, and a plain green card with the edges cut off at odd angles in the other pocket. That was all.

That was enough.

The little fat boy didn't have his name in print anywhere. It wasn't a new wallet either. Fat boy didn't want identification. I didn't blame him. What killer would?

Yeah, that was enough to make me sit back and look at the scuffed folder of calfskin and make me think. It would make you think too. Take a look at your own wallet and see what's in it.

I had the stuff spread out on the desk when I remembered the other pocket of my raincoat and pulled out the huge tweed triangle that had come from the girl's coat. I laid it out on my lap with the night before shoved into some corner of my brain and looked at it as though it were just another puzzle, not a souvenir of death.

The cloth had come apart easily. I must have grabbed her at the waist because the section of the coat included the right-hand and pocket and part of the lining. I rubbed the fabric through my fingers feeling the soft texture of fine wool, taking in the details of the pattern. More out of curiosity than anything else, I stuck my hand inside the pocket and came up with a crumpled pack of cigarettes.

She didn't even have time for a last smoke, I thought. Even a condemned man gets that. She didn't. She took one look at me and saw my eyes and my face and whatever she saw there yanked a scream from her lungs and the strength to pull her over the rail.

What have I got locked up inside me that comes out at times like that? What good am I alive? Why do I have to be the one to pull the trigger and have my soul torn apart afterwards?

The cigarettes were a mashed ball of paper in my hand, a little wad of paper, cellophane and tinfoil that smelt of tobacco and death. My teeth were locked together and when I looked down at my hand my nail ripped through the paper and I saw the green underneath.

Between the cigarettes and the wrapper was another of those damnable green cards with the edges cut off at odd angles.

Two murders. Two green cards.

It was the same way backwards. Two green cards and two murders.

Which came first, the murders or the cards?

Green for death.

Murder at odd angles. Two murders. Eight odd angles. Yes, two murders. The fat boy got what he was after. Because of him the girl was murdered no matter how. So I got him. I was a murderer like they said, only to me it was different. I was just a killer. I wondered what the law would say and if they'd make that fine difference now. Yeah. I could have been smart about it; I could have done what I did, called the police and let them take over then take the dirty medicine the papers and the judge and the public would have handed me. No, I had to be smart. I had to go and mix it up so much that if those bodies were found and the finger pointed at me all I could expect was a trip on that long road to nowhere.

Was that why I did it . . . because I felt smart? No, that wasn't the reason. I didn't feel smart. I was mad. I was kill crazy mad at the bastards the boy with the scythe pointed out to me and goddamn mad at all the screwy little minds and the screwy big minds that had the power of telling me off later. They could go to hell, the judge and the jury and all the rest of them! I was getting too sick and disgusted of fighting their battles for them anyway! The boy with the scythe could go to hell with the rest and if he didn't like it he could come after me, personally. I'd love that. I wish there *was* a special agency called Death that could hear what I was thinking and make a try for me. I'd like to take that stinking black shadow and shove his own scythe down his bony throat and disjoint him with a couple of .45's! Come on, bony boy, let's see you do what you can! Get your white-haired judge and your good people tried and true and let's see just how good you are! I think I'm better, see? I think I can handle any one of you, and if you get the idea I'm kidding, then come and get me.

And if you're afraid to come after me, then I'm going after

you. Maybe I'll know what I'm like then. Maybe I'll find out what's going on in my mind and why I keep on living when fat cold-blooded killers and nice warm-blooded killers are down there shaking hands with the devil!

I pulled the green card out of the cigarettes and matched it to the one from the wallet. They fitted—Twins. I put them in my shirt pocket, grabbed my coat and hat and slammed the door after me when I left the office.

At a little after ten I pulled up outside the brick building that was the house of the law. Here was where the invisible processes went on that made cops out of men and murderers out of clues. The car in front of mine was an official sedan that carried the D.A.'s sticker and I smoked a butt right down to the bottom before I decided to try to reach Pat even if the fair-haired boy of the courts was around.

I should have waited a minute longer. I had my hand on the door when he pushed through and it looked like a cold wind hit him in the face. He screwed his mouth up into a snarl, thought better of it and squeezed a smile out.

Strictly an official smile.

He said, "Morning."

I said, "Nice day."

He got in his car and slammed the door so hard it almost fell off. I waved when he drove by. He didn't wave back. The old guy on the elevator took me upstairs and when I walked into Pat's office I was grinning.

Pat started, "Did you . . ."

I answered with a nod. "I did. We met at the gate. What got into the lad, is he sore at me?"

"Sit down, Mike." Pat waved his thumb at the straight-back wooden chair reserved for official offenders about to get a reprimand. "Look, pal, the District Attorney is only an elected official, but that's a mighty big 'only.' You put him over a barrel not so long ago and he isn't going to forget it. He isn't going to forget who your friends are, either."

"Meaning you."

"Meaning me exactly. I'm a Civil Service servant, a Captain of Homicide. I have certain powers of jurisdiction, arrest and influence. He supersedes them. If the D.A. gets his hooks into you just once, you'll have a ring through your nose and I'll be handed the deal of whipping you around the arena just to give him a little satisfaction. Please quit antagonizing the guy for my sake if not for your own. Now what's on your mind?"

Pat leaned back and grinned at me. We were still buddies.

"What's new on the dockets, chum?"

"Nothing," he shrugged. "Life has been nice and dull. I come in at eight and go home at six. I like it."

"Not even a suicide?"

"Not even. Don't tell me you're soliciting work."

"Hardly. I'm on a vacation."

Pat got that look. It started behind the pupils where no look was supposed to be. A look that called me a liar and waited to hear the rest of the lie. I had to lie a little myself. "Since you have it so easy, how about taking your own vacation with me? We could have some fun."

The look retreated and disappeared altogether. "Hell, I'd love to, Mike, but we're still scratching trying to catch up on all the details around here. I don't think it's possible." He screwed up his forehead. "Don't you feel so hot?"

"Sure, I feel fine, that's why I want a vacation while I can enjoy it." I slapped my hat back on my head and stood up. "Well, since you won't come I'll hit the road alone. Too bad. Ought to be lots doing."

He rocked his chair forward and took my hand. "Have fun, Mike."

"I will." I gave it a pause, then: "Oh, by the way. I wanted to show you something before I left." I reached in my shirt pocket and took out the two green cards and tossed them on the desk. "Funny, aren't they?"

Pat dropped my hand like it had been hot. Sometimes he gets the damnedest expression on his face you ever saw. He held those cards in his fingers and walked around the desk to close and lock the door. What he said when he sat down makes dirty reading.

"Where'd you get these?" His voice had an edge to it that meant we were close to not being buddies any more.

"I found 'em."

"Nuts. Sit down, damn it." I sat down easy again and lit a smoke. It was hard to keep a grin off my mouth. "Once more, Mike, where'd they come from?"

"I told you I found them."

"Okay, I'll get very simple in my questioning. *Where* did you find them?"

I was getting tired of wearing the grin. I let it do what it wanted to do and I felt the air dry my teeth. "Look, Pat, remember me? I'm your friend. I'm a citizen and I'm a stubborn jerk who doesn't like to answer questions when he doesn't know why. Quit the cop act and ask right. So tell me I handed you a line about a vacation when all I wanted to get was some information. So tell me something you haven't told me before."

"All right, Mike, all right. All I want to know is where you got them."

"I killed a guy and took it off his body."

"Stop being sarcastic."

I must have grinned the dirtiest kind of grin there was. Pat watched me strangely, shook his head impatiently and tossed the cards back on the desk. "Are they so important I can't hear about it, Pat?"

He ran his tongue across his lips. "No, they're not so important in one way. I guess they could be lost easily enough. They're plenty of them in circulation."

"Yeah?"

He nodded briefly and fingered the edge of one. "They're Communist identification cards. One of the new fronts. The Nazi bund that used to operate in this country had cards just like 'em. They were red though. Every so often they change the cuts of the edges to try to trip up any spies. When you get in the meeting hall your card has to match up with a master card."

"Oh, just like a lodge." I picked one up and tucked it in my coat pocket.

He said, "Yeah," sourly.

"Then why all the to-do with the door. We're not in a meeting hall."

Pat smacked the desk with the flat of his hand. "I don't know, Mike. Damn it, if anybody but you came in with a couple of those cards I would have said what they were and that's all. But when it's you I go cold all over and wait for something to happen. I know it won't happen, then it does. Come on, spill it. What's behind them?" He looked tired as hell.

"Nothing, I told you that. They're curious and I found two of them. I'd never seen anything like it before and thought maybe you'd know what they were."

"And I did."

"That's right. Thanks."

I put my hat back on and stood up. He let me get as far as the door. "Mike . . ." He was looking at his hand.

"I'm on vacation now, pal."

He picked up a card and looked at the blank sides of it. "Three days ago a man was murdered. He had one of these things clutched in his hand."

I turned the knob. "I'm still on vacation."

"I just thought I'd tell you. Give you something to think about."

"Swell. I'll turn it over in my mind when I'm stretched out on a beach in Florida."

"We know who killed him."

I let the knob slip through my fingers and tried to sound casual. "Anybody I know?"

"Yes, you and eight million others. His name is Lee Deamer. He's running for State Senator next term."

My breath whistled through my teeth. Lee Deamer, the people's choice. The guy who was scheduled to sweep the state clean. The guy who was kicking the politicians all over the joint. "He's pretty big," I said.

"Very."

"Too big to touch?"

His eyes jumped to mine. "Nobody is that big, Mike. Not even Deamer."

"Then why don't you grab him?"

"Because he didn't do it."

"What a pretty circle *that* is. I had you figured for a brain, Pat. He killed a guy and he didn't do it. That's great logic, especially when it comes from you."

A slow grin started at the corner of his eyes. "When you're on vacation you can think it over, Mike. I'll wrap it up for you, just once. A dead man is found. He has one of these cards in his hand. Three people positively identified the killer. Each one saw him under favorable conditions and was able to give a complete description and identification. They came to the police with the story and we were lucky enough to hush it up.

"Lee Deamer was identified as the killer. He was described right to the scar on his nose, his picture was snapped up the second it was shown and he was identified in person. It's the most open-and-shut case you ever saw, yet we can't touch him because when he was supposed to be pulling a murder he was a mile away talking to a group of prominent citizens. I happened to be among those present."

I kicked the door closed with my foot and stood there. "Hot damn."

"Too hot to handle. Now you know why the D.A. was in such a foul mood."

"Yeah," I agreed. "But it shouldn't be too tough for you, Pat. There's only four things that could have happened."

"Tell me. See if it's what I'm thinking."

"Sure, kid. One: twins. Two: a killer disguised as Deamer. Three: a deliberate frame-up with witnesses paid to make the wrong identification. Four: it was Deamer after all."

"Which do you like, Mike?"

I laughed at his solemn tone. "Beats me, I'm on vacation." I found the knob and pulled it open. "See you when I get back."

"Sure thing, Mike." His eyes narrowed to slits. "If you run across any more cards, tell me about them, will you?"

"Yeah, anything else?"

"Just that one question. Where did you get them?"

"I killed a guy and took it off his dead body."

Pat was swearing softly to himself when I left. Just as the elevator door closed he must have begun to believe me because I heard his door open and he shouted, "Mike . . . damn it, Mike!"

I called the *Globe* office from a hash house down the street. When I asked the switchboard operator if Marty Kooperman had called in yet she plugged into a couple of circuits, asked around and told me he was just about to go to lunch. I passed the word for him to meet me in the lobby if he wanted a free chow and hung up. I wasn't in a hurry. I never knew a reporter yet who would pass up a meal he wasn't paying for.

Marty was there straddling a chair backwards, trying to keep his eyes on two blondes and a luscious redhead who was apparently waiting for someone else. When I tapped him on the shoulder he scowled and whispered, "Hell, I almost had that redhead nailed. Go away."

"Come on, I'll buy you another one," I said.

"I like this one."

The city editor came out of the elevator, said hello to the redhead and they went out together. Marty shrugged. "Okay, let's eat. A lousy political reporter doesn't stand a chance against that."

One of the blondes looked at me and smiled. I winked at her and she winked back. Marty was so disgusted he spit on the polished floor. Some day he'll learn that all you have to do is ask. They'll tell you.

He tried to steer me into a hangout around the corner, but I nixed the idea and kept going up the street to a little bar that put out a good meal without any background noise. When we had a table between us and the orders on the fire, Marty flipped me a cigarette and the angle of his eyebrows told me he was waiting.

"How much about politics do you know, Marty?"

He shook the match out. "More than I can write about."

"Know anything about Lee Deamer?"

His eyebrows came down and he leaned on his elbows.

"You're an investigator, Mike. You're the lad with a gun under his coat. Who wants to know about Deamer?"

"Me."

"What for?" His hand was itching to go for the pad and pencil in his pocket.

"Because of something that's no good for a story," I said. "What do you know about him?"

"Hell, there's nothing wrong with him. The guy is going to be the next senator from this state. He packs a big punch and everybody likes him including the opposition. He's strictly a maximum of statesman and a minimum of politician. Deamer has the cleanest record of anybody, probably because he has never been mixed up in politics too much. He is independently wealthy and out of reach as far as bribery goes. He has no use for chiselers or the spoils system, so most of the sharp boys are against him."

"Are you against him, Marty?"

"Not me, feller. I'm a Deamer man through and through. He's what we need these days. Where do you stand?"

"I haven't voted since they dissolved the Whig party."

"Fine citizen you are."

"Yeah."

"Then why the sudden curiosity?"

"Suppose I sort of hinted to you . . . strictly off the record . . . that somebody was after Deamer. Would you give me a hand? It may be another of those things you'll never get to write about."

Marty balled his hands into fists and rubbed his knuckles together. His face wasn't nice to look at. "You're damn right I'll help. I'm just another little guy who's sick of being booted around the block by the bastards that get themselves elected to public office and use that office to push their own wild ideas and line their own pockets. When a good thing comes along those stinking pigs go all out to smear it. Well, not if I can help it, and not if about nine tenths of the people in this burg can help it either. What do you need, kid?"

"Not much. Just a history on Deamer. All his background from as far back as you can go. Bring it right up to date. Pictures too, if you have any."

"I have folders of the stuff."

"Good," I said. Our lunch came up then and we dug into it. Throughout the meal Marty would alternately frown at his plate then glance up at me. I ate and kept my mouth shut. He could come to his own decision. He reached it over the apple pie he had for dessert. I saw his face relax and he let out a satisfied grunt.

"Do you want the stuff now?"

"Any time will do. Stick it in an envelope and send it to my office. I'm not in a hurry."

"Okay." He eyed me carefully. "Can you let me in on the secret?"

I shook my head. "I would if I could, pal. I don't know what the score is yet myself."

"Suppose I keep my ears to the ground. Anything likely to crop up that you could use?"

"I doubt it. Let's say that Deamer is a secondary consideration to what I actually want. Knowing something about him might help both of us."

"I see." He struck a match under the table and held it to a cigarette. "Mike, if there is a news angle, will you let me in on it?"

"I'd be glad to."

"I'm not talking about publishable news."

"No?"

Marty looked through the smoke at me, his eyes bright. "In every man's past there's some dirt. It can be dirt that belongs to the past and not to the present. But it can be dirty enough to use to smear a person, smear him so good that he'll have to retreat from the public gaze. You aren't tied up in politics like I am so you haven't got any idea how really rotten it is. Everybody is out for himself and to hell with the public. Oh, sure, the public has its big heroes, but they do things just to make the people think of them as heroes. Just look what happens whenever Congress or some other organization uncovers some of the filthy tactics behind government . . . the next day or two the boys upstairs release some big news item they've been keeping in reserve and it sweeps the dirt right off the front page and out of your mind.

"Deamer's straight. Because he's straight he's a target. Everybody is after his hide except the people. Don't think it hasn't been tried. I've come across it and so have the others, but we went to the trouble of going down a little deeper than we were expected to and we came across the source of the so-called 'facts.' Because it was stuff that was supposed to come to light during any normal compilation of a man's background the only way it could reach the public without being suspected of smear tactics by the opposition was through the newspapers.

"Well, by tacit agreement we suppressed the stuff. In one way we're targets too because the big boys with the strings know how we feel. Lee Deamer's going to be in there, Mike. He's going to raise all kinds of hell with the corruption we have in our government. He'll smoke out the rats that live on the public and give this country back some of the strength that it had before we were undermined by a lot of pretty talk and pretty faces.

"That's why I want to get the story from you . . . if there is one. I want to hold a conference with the others who feel like I do and come to an honest conclusion. Hell, I don't know why I've become so damn public-spirited. Maybe it's just that I'm tired of taking all the crap that's handed out."

I put a light to my butt and said, "Has there been anything lately on the guy?"

"No. Not for a month, anyway. They're waiting until he gets done stumping the state before they pick him apart."

Pat was right then. The police had kept it quiet, not because they were part of the movement of righteousness, but because they must have suspected a smear job. Deamer couldn't have been in two places at once by any means.

"Okay, Marty. I'll get in touch with you if anything lousy comes up. Do me a favor and keep my name out of any conversation, though, will you?"

"Of course. By the way, that judge handed you a dirty one the other day."

"What the hell, he could be right, you know."

"Sure he could, it's a matter of opinion. He's just a stickler for the letter of the law, the exact science of words. He's the guy that let a jerk off on a smoking-in-the-subway charge. The sign said NO SMOKING ALLOWED, so he claimed it allowed you not to smoke, but didn't say anything about not smoking. Don't give him another thought."

I took a bill from my wallet and handed it to the waiter with a wave that meant to forget the change. Marty looked at his watch and said he had to get back, so we shook hands and left.

The afternoon papers were out and the headlines had to do with the Garden fight the night before. One of the kids was still out like a light. His manager was being indicted for letting him go into the ring with a brain injury.

There wasn't a word about any bodies being found in the river. I threw the paper in a waste barrel and got in my car.

I didn't feel so good. I wasn't sick, but I didn't feel so good. I drove to a parking lot, shoved the car into a corner and took a cab to Times Square and went to a horror movie. The lead feature had an actor with a split personality. One was a man, the other was an ape. When he was an ape he killed people and when he was a man he regretted it. I could imagine how he felt. When I stood it as long as I could I got up and went to a bar.

At five o'clock the evening editions had come out. This time the headlines were a little different. They had found one of the bodies.

Fat boy had been spotted by a ferryboat full of people and the police launch had dragged him out of the drink. He had no identification and no fingerprints. There was a sketch of what he might have looked like before the bullet got him smack in the kisser.

The police attributed it to a gang killing.

Now I was a one-man gang. Great. Just fine. Mike Hammer, Inc. A gang.

CHAPTER THREE

THE RAIN. The damned never-ending rain. It turned Manhattan into a city of deflections, a city you saw twice no matter where you looked. It was a slow, easy rain that took awhile to collect on your hat brim before it cascaded down in front of your face. The streets had an oily shine that brought the rain-walkers out, people who went native whenever the sky cried and tore off their hats to let the tears drip through their hair.

I buttoned my coat under my neck and turned the collar up around my ears. It was good walking, but not when you were soaking wet. I took it easy and let the crowd sift past me, everybody in a hurry to get nowhere and wait. I was going south on Broadway, stopping to look in the windows of the closed stores, not too conscious of where my feet were leading me. I passed Thirty-fourth still going south, walked into the Twenties with a stop for a sandwich and coffee, then kept my course until I reached the Square.

That was where my feet led me. Union Square. Green cards and pinched-faced guys arguing desperately in the middle of little groups. Green cards and people listening to the guys. What the hell could they say that was important enough to keep anybody standing in the rain? I grinned down at my feet because they had the sense that should have been in my head. They wanted to know about the kind of people who carried green cards, the kind of people who would listen to guys who carried green cards.

Or girls.

I ambled across the walk into the yellow glare of the lights. There were no soapboxes here, just those little knots of people trying to talk at once and being shouted down by the one in the middle.

A cop went by swinging his night stick. Whenever he passed a group he automatically got a grip on the thing and looked over hopefully.

I heard some of the remarks when he passed. They weren't nice.

Coming toward me a guy who looked like a girl and a girl who looked like a guy altered their course to join one group. The girl got right into things and the guy squealed with pleasure whenever she said something clever.

Maybe there were ten groups, maybe fifteen. If it hadn't been raining there might have been more. Nobody talked about the same thing. Occasionally someone would drop out of one crowd and drift over to another.

But they all had something in common. The same thing you find in a slaughterhouse. The lump of vomit in the center of each crowd was a Judas sheep trying to lead the rest to the ax. Then they'd go back and get more. The sheep were asking for it too. They were a seedy bunch in shapeless clothes, heavy with the smell of the rot they had asked for and gotten. They had a jackal look of discontent and cowardice, a hungry look that said you kill while we loot, then all will be well with the world.

Yeah.

Not all of them were like that, though. Here and there in the crowd was a pin-striped business suit and homburg. An expensive mink was flanked by a girl in a shabby gray cloth job and a guy in a hand-me-down suit with his hands stuck in the pockets.

Just for the hell of it I hung on the edge of the circle and listened. A few latecomers closed in behind me and I had to stand there and hear just why anybody that fought the war was a simple-minded fool, why anybody who tolerated the foreign policy of this country was a Fascist, why anybody who didn't devote his soul and money to the enlightenment of the masses was a traitor to the people.

The goddamn fools who listened agreed with him, too. I was ready to reach out and pluck his head off his shoulders when one of the guys behind me stood on his toes and said, "Why don't you get the hell out of this country if you don't like it?" The guy was a soldier.

I said, "Attaboy, buddy," but it got lost in the rumble from the crowd and the screech the guy let out. The soldier swore back at him and tried to push through the crowd to get at the guy, only two guys in trench coats blocked him.

Lovely, lovely, it was just what I wanted! The soldier went to shove the two guys apart and one gave him an elbow. I was just going to plant a beauty behind his ear when the cop stepped in. He was a good cop, that one. He didn't lift the night stick above his waist. He held it like a lance and when it hit it went in deep right where it took all the sound out of your body. I saw two punks fold up in the middle and one of the boys in the raincoats let out a gasp. The other one stepped back and swore.

The cop said, "Better move on, soldier."

"Ah, I'd like to take that pansy apart. Did you hear what he said?"

"I hear 'em every night, feller," the cop told him. "They got bats in their heads. Come on, it's better to let 'em talk."

"Not when they say those things!"

The cop grinned patiently. "They gotta right to say 'em. You don't *have* to listen, you know."

"I don't give a hoot. They haven't got a right to say those things. Hell, the big mouth probably was too yeller to fight a war and too lazy to take a job. I oughta slam 'im one."

"Uh-huh." The cop steered him out of the crowd. I heard him say, "That's just what they want. It makes heroes of 'em when the papers get it. We still got ways of taking care of 'em, don't worry. Every night this happens and I get in a few licks."

I started grinning and went back to listening. One boy in a trench coat was swearing under his breath. The other was holding on to him. I shifted a little to the side so I could see what I thought I had seen the first time. When the one turned around again I knew I was right the first time.

Both of them were wearing guns under their arms.

Green cards, loud-mouthed bastards, sheep, now guns.

It came together like a dealer sweeping in the cards for shuffling. The game was getting rough. But guns, why guns? This wasn't a fighting game. Who the devil was worth killing in this motley crowd? Why guns here when there was a chance of getting picked up with them?

I pulled back out of the crowd and crossed the walk into the shadows to a bench. A guy sat on the other end of it with a paper over his face, snoring. Fifteen minutes later the rain quit playing around and one by one the crowd pulled away until only a handful was left around the nucleus. For guys who were trying to intimidate the world they certainly were afraid of a little water. All of a sudden the skies opened up and let loose with everything in sight. The guy on the end of the bench jumped up, fighting the paper that wrapped itself around his face. He made a few drunken animal noises, swallowed hard when he saw me watching him and scurried away into the night.

I had to sit through another five minutes of it before I got up. The two men in the trench coats waited until the loose-jointed guy in the black overcoat had a fifty-foot start, then they turned around and followed him. That gave them a good reason for the rods under their arms.

Bodyguards.

Maybe it was the rain that made my guts churn. Maybe it was those words beating against my head, telling me that I was only scum. Maybe it was just me, but suddenly I wanted to grab that guy in the overcoat and slam his teeth down his throat and wait to see what his two boys would do. I'd like to catch them reaching for a gun! I'd like them to move their hands just one inch, then I'd show them what practice could do when it came to snagging a big, fat gun out of a shoulder sling! So I was a sucker for fighting a war. I was a sap for liking my country. I was a jerk for not thinking them a superior breed of lice!

That cop with the round Irish face should have used a knife in their bellies instead of the butt end of a night stick.

I waited until they were blurs in the rain then tagged along in the rear. They were a fine pair, those two, a brace of dillies. I tailed them into the subway and out again in Brooklyn. I was with them when they walked down Coney Island Avenue and beside them when they turned into a store off the avenue and they never knew I was there.

Down at the corner I crossed the street and came back up the other side. One of the boys was still in the doorway playing watchdog. I wanted to know how smart the people were who wanted to run the world. I found out. I cut across the street and walked right up to the guy without making any fuss about it. He gave me a queer look and drew his eyebrows together in a frown, trying to remember where he had seen me before. He was fumbling for words when I pulled out the green card.

He didn't try to match them up. One look was enough and he waved his head at the door. I turned the knob and went in. I'd have to remember to tell Pat about that. They weren't being so careful at all.

When I closed the door I changed my mind. The light went on, just like a refrigerator, and I saw the blackout shades on the windows and door, the felt padding beneath the sill so no light could escape under the door. And the switch. A home-made affair on the side of the door that cut the light when the door opened and threw it back on again when it closed.

The girl at the desk glanced up impatiently and held out her hand for the card. She matched them. She matched them damn carefully, too, and when she handed them back she had

sucked hollows into her cheeks trying to think of the right
thing to say.

"You're from . . . ?"

"Philly," I supplied. I hoped it was a good answer. It
was. She nodded and turned her head toward a door in the
back of the anteroom. I had to wait for her to push a button
before it opened under my hand.

There were twenty-seven people in the other room. I
counted them. They were all very busy. Some of them were at
desks clipping things from newspapers and magazines. One
guy in a corner was taking pictures of the things they clipped
and it came out on microfilm. There was a little group around
a map of the city over against one wall, talking too earnestly
and too low for me to catch what they were saying.

I saw the other boy in the trench coat. He still had it on
and he was sticking close with the guy in the overcoat. Evidently the fellow was some kind of a wheel, checking on ac-
tivities here and there, offering sharp criticism or curt words
of approval.

When I had been there a full five minutes people began
to notice me. At first it was just a casual glance from odd
spots, then long searching looks that disappeared whenever I
looked back. The man in the overcoat licked his lips nervously
and smiled in my direction.

I sat down at a table and crossed my legs, a smoke dangling
from my mouth. I smoked and I watched, trying to make
some sense out of it. Some of them even looked like Commies, the cartoon kind. There were sharp eyes that darted
from side to side, too-wise women dazzled by some meager
sense of responsibility, smirking students who wore their hair
long, tucked behind their heads. A few more came in while
I sat and devoted themselves to some unfinished task. But
sooner or later their eyes came to mine and shifted away hurriedly when I looked at them.

It became a game, that watching business. I found that if I
stared at some punk who was taking his time about doing
things he became overly ambitious all of a sudden. I went
from one to the other and came at last to the guy in the overcoat.

He was the head man here, no doubt about it. His word
was law. At twenty minutes past eleven he started his rounds
of the room, pausing here and there to lay a mimeographed
sheet on a desk, stopping to emphasize some obscure point.

Finally he had to pass me and for a split second he hesitated, simpered and went on. I got it and played the game
to the hilt. I walked to a desk and picked up one of the

sheets and read it as I sat on the edge of the desk. The scrag-gly blonde at the desk couldn't keep her hands from shaking.

I got the picture then. I was reading the orders for the week; I was in on the pipeline from Moscow. It was that easy. I read them all the way through, tossed the sheet down and went back to my chair.

I smiled.

Everybody smiled.

The boy in the trench coat with the gun under his arm came over and said, "You will like some coffee now?" He had an accent I couldn't place.

I smiled again and followed him to the back of the room. I didn't see the door of the place because it was hidden be-hind the photography equipment.

It led into a tiny conference room that held a table, six chairs and a coffee urn. When the door closed there were seven of us in the room including two dames. Trench Coat got a tray of cups from the closet and set them on the table. For me it was a fight between grinning and stamping some-body's face in. For an after-office-hours coffee deal it cer-tainly was a high-tension deal.

To keep from grinning I shoved another Lucky in my mouth and stuck a light to it. There they were, everyone with a coffee cup, lined up at the urn. Because I took my time with the smoke I had to join the end of the line, and it was a good thing I did. It gave me time enough to get the pitch.

Everybody had been watching me covertly anyway, saying little and satisfied with me keeping my mouth shut. When they took their coffee black and wandered off to the table the two women made a face at the bitter taste. They didn't like black coffee. They weren't used to black coffee. Yet they took black coffee and kept shooting me those sidewise glances.

How simple can people get? Did they take everybody for dummies like themselves? When I drew my cup from the urn Trench Coat stood right behind me and waited. He was the only one that bothered to breathe and he breathed down my neck.

I took my sugar and milk. I took plenty of it. I turned around and lifted my cup in a mock toast and all the jerks started breathing again and the room came to life. The two women went back and got sugar and milk.

The whole play had been a signal setup a kid could have seen through.

Trench Coat smiled happily. "It is very good you are here, comrade. We cannot be too careful, of course."

"Of course." It was the first time I had said anything, but

you might have thought I gave the Gettysburg Address. Overcoat came over immediately, his hand reaching out for mine.

"I am Henry Gladow, you know. Certainly you know." His chuckle was nervous and high-pitched. "We had been expecting you, but not so quickly. Of course we realize the party works quickly, but this is almost faith-inspiring! You came with incredible speed. Why, only tonight I picked up the telegram from our messenger uptown announcing your arrival. Incredible."

That was the reason for the bodyguards and the guns. My new chum was receiving party instructions from somebody else. That was why the Trench Coats closed in around the soldier, in case it had been a trap to intercept the message. Real cute, but dumb as hell.

". . . happy to have you inspect our small base of operation, comrade." I turned my attention back to him again and listened politely. "Rarely do we have such an honor. In fact, this is the first time." He turned to Trench Coat, still smiling. "This is my, er, traveling companion, Martin Romberg. Very capable man, you know. And my secretary," he indicated a girl in thick-lensed glasses who was just out of her teens, "Martha Camisole."

He went around the room introducing each one and with every nod I handed out I got back a smile that tried hard to be nice but was too scared to do a good job of it.

We finished the coffee, had another and a smoke before Gladow looked at his watch. I could see damn well he had another question coming up and I let him take his time about asking it. He said, "Er, you are quite satisfied with the operation at this point, comrade? Would you care to inspect our records and documents?"

My scowl was of surprise, but he didn't know that. His eyebrows went up and he smiled craftily. "No, comrade, not written documents. Here, in the base, we have experts who commit the documents . . ." he tapped the side of his head, "here."

"Smart," I grunted. "What happens if they talk?"

He tried to seem overcome with the preposterous. "Very funny, comrade. Quite, er . . . yes. Who is there to make them talk? That is where we have the advantage. In this country force is never used. The so-called third degree has been swept out. Even a truthful statement loses its truth if coercion is even hinted at. The fools, the despicable fools haven't the intelligence to govern a country properly! When the party is in power things will be different, eh, comrade?"

"Much, much different," I said.

Gladow nodded, pleased. "You, er, care to see anything of special importance, comrade?" His voice had a gay tone.

"No, nothing special. Just checking around." I dragged on the butt and blew a cloud of smoke in his face. He didn't seem to mind it.

"Then in your report you will state that everything *is* satisfactory here?"

"Sure, don't give it another thought."

There was more sighing. Some of the fear went out of their eyes. The Camisole kid giggled nervously. "Then may I say again that we have been deeply honored by your visit, comrade," Gladow said. "Since the sudden, untimely death of our former, er, compatriot, we have been more or less uneasy. You understand these things of course. It was gratifying to see that he was not identified with the party in any way. Even the newspapers are stupid in this country."

I had to let my eyes sink to the floor or he would have seen the hate in them. I was an inch away from killing the bastard and he didn't know it. I turned my hand over to look at the time and saw that it was close to midnight. I'd been in the pigsty long enough. I set the empty cup down on the table and walked to the door. The crumbs couldn't even make good coffee.

All but two of the lesser satellites had left, their desks clear of all papers. The guy on the photography rig was stuffing the microfilm in a small file case while a girl burned papers in a metal wastebasket. I didn't stop to see who got the film. There was enough of it that was so plain that I didn't need any pictures drawn for me.

Gladow was hoping I'd shake hands, but he got fooled. I kept them both in my pockets because I didn't like to handle snakes, not of their variety.

The outside door slammed shut and I heard some hurried conversation and the girl at the desk say, "Go right in." I was standing by the inside door when she opened it.

I had to make sure I was in the right place by taking a quick look around me. This was supposed to be a Commie setup, a joint for the masses only, not a club for babes in mink coats with hats to match. She was one of those tall, willowy blondes who reached thirty with each year an improvement.

She was almost beautiful, with a body that could take your mind off beauty and put it on other things. She smiled at Gladow as soon as she saw him and gave him her hand.

His voice took on a purr when he kissed it. "Miss Brighton,

it is always a pleasure to see you." He straightened up, still smiling. "I didn't expect you to come at this hour."

"I didn't expect you to be here either, Henry. I decided to take the chance anyway. I brought the donations." Her voice was like rubbing your hand on satin. She pulled an envelope out of her pocketbook and handed it to Gladow unconcernedly. Then, for the first time, she saw me.

She squinted her eyes, trying to place me.

I grinned at her. I like to grin at a million bucks.

Ethel Brighton grinned back.

Henry Gladow coughed politely and turned to me. "Miss Brighton is one of our most earnest comrades. She is chiefly responsible for some of our most substantial contributions."

He made no attempt to introduce me. Apparently nobody seemed to care. Especially Ethel Brighton. A quick look flashed between them that brought the scowl back to her face for a brief moment. A shadow on the wall that came from one of the Trench Coats behind me was making furious gestures.

I started to get the willies. It was the damnedest thing I had ever seen. Everybody was acting like at a fraternity initiation and for some reason I was the man of the moment. I took it as long as I could. I said, "I'm going uptown. If you're going back you can come along."

For a dame who had her picture in most of the Sunday supplements every few weeks, she lost her air of sophistication in a hurry. Her cheeks seemed to sink in and she looked to Gladow for approval. Evidently he gave it, for she nodded and said, "My car . . . it's right outside."

I didn't bother to leave any good nights behind me. I went through the receptionist's cubicle and yanked the door open. When Ethel Brighton was out I slammed it shut. Behind me the place was as dark as the vacant hole it was supposed to be.

Without waiting to be asked I slid behind the wheel and held out my hand for the keys. She dropped them in my palm and fidgeted against the cushions. That car . . . it was a beauty. In the daylight it would have been a maroon convertible, but under the street lights it was a mass of mirrors with the chrome reflecting every bulb in the sky.

Ethel said, "Are you from . . . New York?"

"Nope. Philly," I lied.

For some reason I was making her mighty nervous. It wasn't my driving because I was holding it to a steady thirty to keep inside the green lights. I tried another grin. This time she smiled back and worried the fingers of her gloves.

I couldn't get over it, Ethel Brighton a Commie! Her old man would tan her hide no matter how old she was if he ever heard about it. But what the hell, she wasn't the only one with plenty of rocks who got hung up on the red flag. I said, "It hasn't been too easy for you to keep all this under your hat, has it?"

Her hands stopped working the glove. "N-no. I've managed, though."

"Yeah. You've done a good job."

"Thank you."

"Oh, no thanks at all, kid. For people with intelligence it's easy. When you're, er, getting these donations, don't people sorta wonder where it's going?"

She scowled again, puzzled. "I don't think so. I thought that was explained quite fully in my report."

"It was, it was. Don't get me wrong. We have to keep track of things, you know. Situations change." It was a lot of crap to me, but it must have made sense to her way of thinking.

"Usually they're much too busy to listen to my explanations, and anyway, they can deduct the amounts from their income tax."

"They ought to be pretty easy to touch, then."

This time she smiled a little. "They are. They think it's for charity."

"Uh-huh. Suppose your father finds out what you've been doing?"

The way she recoiled you'd think I smacked her. "Oh . . . please, you wouldn't!"

"Take it easy, kid. I'm only supposing."

Even in the dull light of the dash I could see how pale she was. "Daddy would . . . never forgive me. I think . . . he'd send me some place. He'd disinherit me completely." She shuddered, her hands going back to the glove again. "He'll never know. When he does it will be too late!"

"Your emotions are showing through, kid."

"So would yours if . . . oh . . . oh, I didn't mean . . ." Her expression made a sudden switch from rage to that of fear. It wasn't a nice fear, it was more like that of the girl on the bridge.

I looked over slowly, an angle creeping into the corner of my mind. "I'm not going to bite. Maybe you can't say things back there in front of the others, but sometimes I'm not like them. I can understand problems. I have plenty of my own."

"But you . . . you're . . ."

"I'm what?"

"You know." She bit into her lip, looking at me obliquely. I nodded as if I did.

"Will you be here long?"

"Maybe," I shrugged. "Why?"

The fear came back. "Really, I wasn't asking pointed questions. Honest I wasn't. I just meant . . . I meant with the . . . other being killed and all, well . . ."

Damn it, she let her sentence trail off as if I was supposed to know everything that went on. What the hell did they take me for anyway? It was the same thing all night!

"I'll be here," I said.

We went over the bridge and picked a path through the late traffic in Manhattan. I went north to Times Square and pulled into the curb. "This is as far as I go, sugar. Thanks for the ride. I'll probably be seeing you again."

Her eyes went wide again. Brother, she could sure do things with those eyes. She gasped, "Seeing me?"

"Sure, why not?"

"But . . . you aren't . . . I never supposed . . ."

"That I might have a personal interest in a woman?" I finished.

"Well, yes."

"I like women, sugar. I always have and always will."

For the first time she smiled a smile she meant. She said, "You aren't a bit like I thought you'd be. Really. I like you. The other . . . agent . . . he was so cold that he scared me."

"I don't scare you?"

"You could . . . but you don't."

I opened the door. "Good night, Ethel."

"Good night." She slid over under the wheel and gunned the motor. I got one last quick smile before she pulled away.

What the hell. That's all I could think of. What the hell. All right, just what the hell was going on? I walked right into a nest of Commies because I flashed a green card and they didn't say a word, not one word. They played damn fool kids' games with me that any jerk could have caught, and bowed and scraped like I was king.

Not once did anyone ask my name.

Read the papers today. See what it says about the Red Menace. See how they play up their sneaking, conniving ways. They're supposed to be clever, bright as hell. They were dumb as horse manure as far as I was concerned. They were a pack of bugs thinking they could outsmart a world. Great. That coffee-urn trick was just great.

I walked down the street to a restaurant that was still open and ordered a plate of ham and eggs.

It was almost two o'clock when I got home. The rain had stopped long ago, but it was still up there, hanging low around the buildings, reluctant to let the city alone. I walked up to my apartment and shoved the key in the lock. My mind kept going back to Gladow, trying to make sense of his words, trying to fit them into a puzzle that had no other parts.

I could remember his speaking about somebody's untimely death. Evidently I was the substitute sent on in his place. But whose death? That sketch in the paper was a lousy one. Fat boy didn't look a bit like that sketch. All right then, who? There was only one other guy with a green card who was dead, the guy Lee Deamer was supposed to have killed.

Him. He's the one, I thought. I was his replacement. But what was I supposed to be?

There was just too much to think about; I was too tired to put my mind to it. You don't kill a fat man and see a girl die because of the look on your face and get involved with a Commie organization all in two days without feeling your mind sink into a soggy ooze that drew it down deeper and deeper until it relaxed of its own accord and you were asleep.

I sat slumped in the chair, the cigarette that had dropped from my fingers had burned a path through the rug at right angles with another. The bell shrilled and shrilled until I thought it would never stop. My arm going out to the phone was an involuntary movement, my voice just happened to be there.

I said hello.

It was Pat and he had to yell at me a half-dozen times before I snapped out of it. I grunted an answer and he said, "Too late for you, Mike?"

"It's four o'clock in the morning. Are you just getting up or just going to bed?"

"Neither. I've been working."

"At this hour?"

"Since six this evening. How's the vacation?"

"I called it off."

"Really now. Just couldn't bear to leave the city, could you? By the way, did you find any more green cards with the ends snipped off?"

The palms of my hands got wet all of a sudden. "No."

"Are you interested in them at all?"

"Cut the comedy, Pat. What're you driving at? It's too damn late for riddles."

"Get over here, Mike," his voice was terse. "My apartment, and make it as fast as you can."

I came awake all at once, shaking the fatigue from my brain. "Okay, Pat," I said, "give me fifteen minutes." I hung up and slipped into my coat.

It was easier to grab a cab than wheel my car out of the garage. I shook the cabbie's shoulder and gave him Pat's address, then settled back against the cushions while we tore across town. We made it with about ten seconds to spare and I gave the cabbie a fin for his trouble.

I looked up at the sky before I went in. The clouds had broken up and let the stars come through. Maybe tomorrow will be nice, I thought. Maybe it will be a nice normal day without all the filth being raked to the top. Maybe. I pushed Pat's bell and the door buzzed almost immediately.

He was waiting outside his apartment when I got off the elevator. "You made it fast, Mike."

"You said to, didn't you?"

"Come on in."

Pat had drinks in a shaker and three glasses on the coffee table. Only one had been used so far. "Expecting company?" I asked him.

"Big company, Mike. Sit down and pour yourself a drink."

I shucked my coat and hat and stuck a Lucky in my mouth. Pat wasn't acting right. You don't go around entertaining anybody at this hour, not even your best friends. Something had etched lines into his face and put a smudge of darkness under each eye. He looked tight as a drumhead. I sat there with a drink in my hand watching Pat trying to figure out what to say.

It came halfway through my drink. "You were right the first time," he said.

I put the glass down and stared at him. "Do it over. I don't get it."

"Twins."

"What?"

"Twins," Pat repeated. "Lee Deamer had a twin brother." He stood there swirling the mixture around in his glass.

"Why tell me? I'm not in the picture."

Pat had his back to me, staring at nothing. I could barely hear his voice. 'Don't ask me that, Mike. I don't know why I'm telling you when it's official business, but I am. In one way we're both alike. We're cops. Sometimes I find myself waiting to know what you'd do in a situation before I do it myself. Screwy, isn't it?"

"Pretty screwy."

"I told you once before that you have a feeling for things that I haven't got. You don't have a hundred bosses and a lot of sidelines to mess you up once you get started on a case. You're a ruthless bastard and sometimes it helps."

"So?"

"So now I find myself in one of those situations. I'm a practical cop with a lot of training and experience, but I'm in something that has a personal meaning to me too and I'm afraid of tackling it alone."

"You don't want advice from me, chum. I'm mud, and whatever I touch gets smeared with it. I don't mind dirtying myself, but I don't want any of it to rub off onto you."

"It won't, don't worry. That's why you're here now. You think I was taken in by that vacation line? Hell. You have another bug up your behind. It has to do with those green cards and don't try to talk your way out of it."

He spun around, his fact taut. "Where'd you get them, Mike?"

I ignored the question. "Tell me, Pat. Tell me the story."

He threw the drink down and filled the glass again. "Lee Deamer . . . how much do you know about him?"

"Only that he's the up-and-coming champ. I don't know him personally."

"I do, Mike. I know the guy and I like him. Goddamn it, Mike, if he gets squeezed out this state, this country will lose one of its greatest assets! We can't afford to have Deamer go under!"

"I've heard that story before, Pat," I said, "a political reporter gave it to me in detail."

Pat reached for a cigarette and laid it in his lips. The tip of the flame from the lighter wavered when he held it up. "I hope it made an impression. This country is too fine to be kicked around. Deamer is the man to stop it if he can get that far.

"Politics never interested you much, Mike. You know how it starts in the wards and works itself right up to the nation. I get a chance to see just how dirty and corrupt politics can be. You should put yourself in my shoes for a while and you'd know how I feel. I get word to lay off one thing or another . . . or else. I get word that if I do or don't do a certain thing I'll be handed a fat little present. You'd think people would respect the police, but they don't. They try to use the department to push their own lousy schemes and it happens more often than you'd imagine."

"And you, Pat, what did you do?" I leaned forward in my chair, waiting.

"I told them to go to hell. They can't touch an honest man until he makes a mistake. Then they hang him for it."

"Any mistakes yet?"

Two streams of smoke spiraled from his nostrils. "Not yet, kid. They're waiting though. I'm fed up with the tension. You can feel it in the air, like being inside a storage battery. Call me a reformer if you want to, but I'd love to see a little decency for a change. That's why I'm afraid for Deamer."

"Yeah, you were telling me about him."

"Twins. You were right, Mike. Lee Deamer was at that meeting the night he was allegedly seen killing this Charlie Moffit. He was talking to groups around the room. I was there."

I stamped the butt out in a tray and lit another. "You mean it was as simple as that . . . Lee Deamer had a twin brother?"

Pat nodded. "As simple as that."

"Then why the secrecy? Lee isn't exactly responsible for what his brother does. Even a blast in the papers couldn't smear him for that, could it?"

"No . . . not if that was all there was to it."

"Then . . ."

Pat slammed the glass down impatiently. "The brother's name was Oscar Deamer. He was an escaped inmate of a sanitarium where he was undergoing psychiatric treatment. Let that come out and Lee is finished."

I let out a slow whistle. "Who else knows about this, Pat?"

"Just you. It was too big. I couldn't keep it to myself. Lee called me tonight and said he wanted to see me. We met in a bar and he told me the story. Oscar arrived in town and told Lee that he was going to settle things for him. He demanded money to keep quiet. Lee thinks that Oscar deliberately killed this Charlie Moffit hoping to be identified as Lee, knowing that Lee wouldn't dare reveal that he had a lunatic for a brother."

"So Lee wouldn't pay off and he got the treatment."

"It looks that way."

"Hell, this Oscar could have figured Lee would have an alibi and couldn't be touched. It was just a sample, something to get him entangled. That doesn't make him much of a loony if he can think like that."

"Anybody who can kill like that is crazy, Mike."

"Yeah, I guess so."

Before he could answer me, the bell rang, two short burps and Pat got up to push the buzzer. "Lee?" I asked.

Pat nodded. "He wanted more time to think about it. I

told him I'd be at home. It has him nearly crazy himself."
He went to the door and stood there holding it open as he
had done for me. It was so still that I heard the elevator
humming in its well, the sound of the doors opening and
the slow, heavy feet of a person carrying a too-heavy weight.

I stood up myself and shook hands with Lee Deamer. He
wasn't big like I had expected. There was nothing outstand-
ing about his appearance except that he looked like a schoolteacher, a very tired, middle-aged Mr. Chips.

Pat said, "This is Mike Hammer, Lee. He's a very special,
capable friend of mine."

His handshake was firm, but his eyes were too tired to
take me in all at once. He said to Pat very softly, "He knows?"

"He knows, Lee. He can be trusted."

I had a good look at warm gray eyes then. His hand tightened just a little around mine. "It's nice to find people that
can be trusted."

I grinned my thanks and Pat pulled up a chair. Lee Deamer
took the drink Pat offered him and settled back against the
cushions, rubbing his hand across his face. He took a sip of
the highball, then pulled a cigar from his pocket and pared
the end off with a tiny knife on his watch chain.

"Oscar hasn't called back," he said dully. "I don't know
what to do." He looked first at Pat, then to me. "Are you a
policeman, Mr. Hammer?"

"Just call me Mike. No, I'm not a city cop. I have a Private
Operator's ticket and that's all."

"Mike's been in on a lot of big stuff, Lee," Pat cut in. "He
knows his way around."

"I see." He was talking to me again. "I suppose Pat told
you that so far this whole affair has been kept quiet?" I
nodded and he went on. "I hope it can stay that way, though
if it must come out, it must. I'm leaving it all to the dis-
cretion of Pat here. I—well, I'm really stumped. So much has
happened in so short a time I hardly know where I'm at."

"Can I hear it from the beginning?" I asked.

Lee Deamer bobbed his head slowly. "Oscar and I were
born in Townley, Nebraska. Although we were twins, we were
worlds apart. In my younger days I thought it was because
we were just separate personalities, but the truth was . . .
Oscar was demented. He was a sadistic sort of person, very
sly and cunning. He hated me. Yes, he hated me, his own
brother. In fact, Oscar seemed to hate everyone. He was in
trouble from the moment he ran off from home until he
came back, then he found more trouble in our own state.
He was finally committed to an institution.

"Shortly after Oscar was committed I left Nebraska and settled in New York. I did rather well in business and became active in politics. Oscar was more or less forgotten. Then I learned that he had escaped from the institution. I never heard from him again until he called me last week."

"That's all?"

"What else can there be, Mike? Oscar probably read about me in the papers and trailed me here. He knew what it would mean if I was known to have a brother who wasn't quite . . . well, normal. He made a demand for money and told me he'd have it one way or another."

Pat reached for the shaker and filled the glasses again. I held mine out and our eyes met. He answered my question before I could ask it. "Lee was afraid to mention Oscar, even when he was identified as the killer of Moffit. You can understand why, can't you?"

"Now I can," I said.

"Even the fact that Lee *was* identified, although wrongly, would have made good copy. However, the cop on the beat brought the witnesses in before they could speak to the papers and the whole thing was such an obvious mistake that nobody dared take the chance of making it public."

"Where are the witnesses now?"

"We have them under surveillance. They've been instructed to keep quiet about it. We checked into their backgrounds and found that all of them were upright citizens, plain, ordinary people who were as befuddled as we were about the whole thing. Fortunately, we were able to secure their promise of silence by proving to them where Lee was that night. They don't understand it, but they were willing to go along with us in the cause of justice."

I grunted and pulled on the cigarette. "I don't like it."

Both of them looked at me quickly. "Hell, Pat, you ought to smell the angle as well as I do."

"You tell me, Mike."

"Oscar served his warning," I said. "He'll make another stab at it. You can trap him easily enough and you know it."

"That's right. It leaves one thing wide open, too."

"Sure it does. You'll have another Lee Deamer in print and pictures, this one up for a murder rap which he will skip because he's nuts." Lee winced at the word but kept still.

"That's why I wanted you here," Pat told me.

"Fine. What good am I?"

The ice rattled against the side of his glass. Pat tried to

keep his voice calm. "You aren't official, Mike. My mind works with the book. I know what I should do and I can't think of anything else."

"You mean you want me to tell you that Oscar should be run down and quietly spirited away?"

"That's right." ·

"And I'm the boy who could do it?"

"Right again." He took a long swallow from the glass and set it on the table.

"What happens if it doesn't work out? To you, I mean."

"I'll be looking for a job for not playing it properly."

"Gentlemen, gentlemen." Lee Deamer ran his hand through his hair nervously. "I-I can't let you do it. I can't let you jeopardize your positions. It isn't fair. The best thing is to let it come to light and let the public decide."

"Don't be jerky!" I spat out. Lee looked at me, but I wasn't seeing him. I was seeing Marty and Pat, hearing them say the same thing . . . and I was hearing that judge again.

There were two hot spaces where my eyes should have been. "I'll take care of it," I said. "I'll need all the help I can get." I looked at Pat. He nodded. "Just one thing, Pat. I'm not doing this because I'm a patriot, see? I'm doing it because I'm curious and because of it I'll be on my toes. I'm curious as hell about something else and not about right and wrong and what the public thinks."

My teeth were showing through my words and Pat had that look again. "Why, Mike?"

"Three green cards with the edges cut off, kid. I'm curious as hell about three green cards. There's more to them than you think."

I said good night and left them sitting there. I could hear the judge laughing at me. It wasn't a nice laugh. It had a nasty sound. Thirteen steps and thirteen loops that made the knot in the rope. Were there thirteen thousand volts in the chair too? Maybe I'd find out the hard way.

CHAPTER FOUR

I SLEPT for two hours before Velda called me. I told her I wouldn't be in for a good long while, and if anything important came up she could call, but unless it was a matter of life or death, either hers or mine, to leave me be.

Nothing came up and I slept once around the clock. It was five minutes to six when my eyes opened by themselves and didn't feel hot any more. While I showered and shaved I stuck a frozen steak under the broiler and ate in my shorts, still damp.

It was a good steak; I was hungry. I wanted to finish it but I never got the time. The phone rang and kept on ringing until I kicked the door shut so I wouldn't hear it. That didn't stop the phone. It went on like that for a full five minutes, demanding that I answer it. I threw down my knife with a curse and walked inside.

"What is it?" I yelled.

"It took you long enough to wake up, damn it!"

"Oh, Pat. I wasn't asleep. What's up this time?"

"It happened like we figured. Oscar made the contact. He called Lee and wants to see him tonight. Lee made an appointment to be at his apartment at eight."

"Yeah?"

"Lee called me immediately. Look, Mike, we'll have to go this alone, just the three of us. I don't want to trust anybody else."

The damp on my body seemed to turn to ice. I was cold all over, cold enough to shake just a little. "Where'll I meet you, Pat?"

"Better make it at my place. Oscar lives over on the East Side." He rattled off the address and I jotted it down. "I told Lee to go ahead and keep his appointment. We'll be right behind him. Lee is taking the subway up and we'll pick him up at the kiosk. Got that?"

"I got it. I'll be over in a little while."

We both stood waiting for the other to hang up. Finally, "Mike. . . ."

"What?"

"You sure about this?"

"I'm sure." I set the receiver back in its cradle and stared at it. I was sure, all right, sure to come up with the dirty end of the stick. The dam would open and let the clean water through and they could pick me out of the sewer.

I pulled on my clothes halfheartedly. I thought of the steak in the kitchen and decided I didn't want any more of it. For a while I stood in front of the mirror looking at myself, trying to decide whether or not I should wear the artillery. Habit won and I buckled on the sling after checking the load in the clip. When I buttoned up the coat I took the box from the closet shelf that held the two spare barrels and the extra shells, scooped up a handful of loose .45s and dropped them in my pocket. If I was going to do it I might as well do it right.

Velda had just gotten in when I called her. I said, "Did you eat yet, kitten?"

"I grabbed a light bite downtown. Why, are you taking me out?"

"Yeah, but not to supper. It's business. I'll be right over. Tell you about it then."

She said all right, kissed me over the phone and hung up. I stuck my hat on, picked up another deck of Luckies and went downstairs where I whistled for a cab.

I don't know how I looked when she opened the door. She started to smile then dropped it like a hot rivet to catch her lower lip between her teeth. Velda's so tall I didn't have to bend down far to kiss her on the cheek. It was nice standing there real close to her. She was perfume and beauty and all the good things of life.

She said, "Come into the bedroom, Mike. You can tell me while I'm getting dressed."

"I can talk from out here."

Velda turned around, a grin in her eyes. "You *have* been in a woman's bedroom before, haven't you?"

"Not yours."

"I'm inviting you in to talk. Just talk."

I faked a punch at her jaw. "I'm just afraid of myself, kid. You and a bedroom could be too much. I'm saving you for something special."

"Will it cost three dollars and can you frame it?"

I laughed for an answer and went in after her. She pointed to a satin-covered boudoir chair and went behind a screen. She came out in a black wool skirt and a white blouse. God, but she was lovely.

When she sat down in front of the vanity table and started to brush her hair I caught her eyes in the mirror. They reflected the trouble that was in mine. "Now tell me, Mike."

I told her. I gave her everything Pat gave me and watched her face.

She finished with the brush and put it down. Her hand was shaking. "They want a lot of you, don't they?"

"Maybe they want too much." I pulled out a cigarette and lit one. "Velda, what does this Lee Deamer mean to you?"

This time she wouldn't meet my eyes. She spaced her words carefully. "He means a lot, Mike. Would you be mad if I said that perhaps they weren't asking too much?"

"No . . . not if you think not. Okay, kid. I'll play the hand out and see what I can do with a kill-crazy maniac. Get your coat on."

"Mike . . . you haven't told me all of it yet."

She was at it again, looking through me into my mind. "I know it."

"Are you going to?"

"Not now. Maybe later."

She stood up, a statuesque creature that had no equal, her hair a black frame for her face. "Mike, you're a bastard. You're in trouble up to your ears and you won't let anybody help you. Why do you always have to play it alone?"

"Because I'm me."

"And I'm me too, Mike. I *want* to help. Can you understand that?"

"Yes, I understand, but this isn't another case. It's more than that and I don't want to talk about it."

She came to me then, resting her hands on my shoulders. "Mike, if you *do* need me . . . ever, will you ask me to help?"

"I'll ask you."

Her mouth was full and ripe, warm with life and sparkling with a delicious wetness. I pulled her in close and tasted the fire that smoldered inside her, felt her body mold itself to mine, eager and excited.

My fingers ran into her hair and pulled her mouth away. "No more of it, Velda. Not now."

"Some day, Mike."

"Some day. Get your coat on." I shoved her away roughly, reluctant to let her go. She opened the closet and took the jacket that matched the skirt from a hanger and slipped into it. Over her shoulder she slung a shoulderstrap bag, and when it nudged the side of the dresser the gun in it made a dull clunk.

"I'm ready, Mike."

I pushed the slip of paper with Oscar's address on it into her hand. "Here's the place where he's holed up. The subway is a half-block away from the place. You go directly there and look the joint over. I don't know why, but there's something about it I don't like. We're going to tag after Lee when he goes in, but I want somebody covering the place while we're there.

"Remember, it's a rough neighborhood, so be on your toes. We don't want any extra trouble. If you spot anything that doesn't seem to be on the square, walk over to the subway kiosk and meet us. You'll have about a half-hour to look around. Be careful."

"Don't worry about me." She pulled on her gloves, a smile playing with her mouth. Hell, I wasn't going to worry about her. That rod in her bag wasn't there for ballast.

I dropped her at the subway and waited on the curb until a cab cruised by.

Pat was standing under the canopy of his apartment building when I got there. He had a cigarette cupped in the palm of his hand and dragged on it nervously. I yelled at him from the taxi and he crossed the street and got in.

It was seven-fifteen.

At ten minutes to eight we paid off the cab and walked the half-block to the kiosk. We were still fifty feet away when Lee Deamer came up. He looked neither to the right nor left, walking straight ahead as if he lived there. Pat nudged me with his elbow and I grunted an acknowledgement.

I waited to see if Velda would show, but there wasn't a sign of her.

Twice Lee stopped to look at house numbers. The third time he paused in front of an old brick building, his head going to the dim light behind the shades in the downstairs room. Briefly, he cast a quick glance behind him, then went up the three steps and disappeared into the shadowy well of the doorway.

Thirty seconds, that's all he got. Both of us were counting under our breaths, hugging the shadows of the building. The street boasted a lone light a hundred yards away, a wan, yellow eye that seemed to search for us with eerie tendrils, determined to pull us into its glare. Somewhere a voice cursed. A baby squealed and stopped abruptly. The street was too damn deserted. It should have been running with kids or something. Maybe the one light scared them off. Maybe they had a better place to hang out than a side street in nowhere.

We hit the thirty count at the same time, but too late. A door slammed above our heads and we could hear feet pounding on boards, diminishing with every step. A voice half sobbed something unintelligible and we flew up those stairs and tugged at a door that wouldn't give. Pat hit it with his shoulder, ramming it open.

Lee was standing in the doorway, hanging on to the sill, his mouth agape. He was pointing down the hall. "He ran . . . he ran. He looked out the window . . . and he ran!"

Pat muttered, "Damn . . . we can't let him get away!" I was ahead of him, my hands probing the darkness. I felt the wall give way to the inky blackness that was the night behind an open door and stumbled down the steps.

That was when I heard Velda's voice rise in a tense, "Mike . . . MIKE!"

"Over here, Pat. There's a gate in the wall. Get a light on!"

Pat swore again, yelling that he had lost it. I didn't wait. I made the gate and picked my way through the litter in the alley that ran behind the buildings. My .45 was in my hand, ready to be used. Velda yelled again and I followed her voice to the end of the alley.

When I came to the street through the two-foot space that separated the buildings I couldn't have found anybody, because the street was a funnel of people running to the subway kiosk. They ran and yelled back over their shoulders and I knew that whatever it was happened down there and I was afraid to look. If anything happened to Velda I'd tear the guts out of some son-of-a-bitch! I'd nail him to a wall and take his skin off him in inch-wide strips!

A colored fellow in a porter's outfit came up bucking the crowd yelling for someone to get a doctor. That was all I needed. I made a path through that mob pouring through the exit gates onto the station and battled my way up to the front.

Velda was all right. She was perfectly all right and I could quit shaking and let the sweat turn warm again. I shoved the gun back under my arm and walked over to her with a sad attempt of trying to look normal.

The train was almost all the way in the station. Not quite. It had to jam on the brakes too fast to make the marker farther down the platform. The driver and two trainmen were standing in front of the lead car poking at a bloody mess that was sticking out under the wheels. The driver said, "He's dead as hell. He won't need an ambulance."

Velda saw me out of the corner of her eye. I eased up to her, my breath still coming hard. "Deamer?"

She nodded.

I heard Pat busting through the crowd and saw Lee at his heels. "Beat it, kid. I'll call you later." She stepped back and the curious crowd surged around her to fill the spot. She was gone before Pat reached me.

His pants were torn and he had a dirty black smear across his cheek. He took about two minutes to get the crowd back from the edge and when a cop from the beat upstairs came through the gang was herded back to the exits like cattle, all bawling to be in on the blood.

Pat wiped his hand across his face. "What the hell happened?"

"I don't know, but I think that's our boy down there. Bring Lee over."

The trainmen were tugging the remains out. One said, "He ain't got much face left," then he puked all over the third rail.

Lee Deamer looked over the side and turned white. "My God!"

Pat steadied him with an arm around his waist. They had most of the corpse out from under the train now. "That him?" Pat asked.

Lee nodded dumbly. I could see his throat working hard.

Two more cops from the local precinct sauntered over. Pat shoved his badge out and told them to take over, then motioned me to bring Lee back to one of the benches. He folded up in one like a limp sack and buried his face in his hands. What the hell could I say? So the guy was a loony, but he was still his brother. While Pat went back to talk to the trainmen I stood there and listened to him sob.

We put Lee in a cab outside before I had a chance to say anything. The street was mobbed now, the people crowding around the ambulance waiting to see what was going in on the stretcher. They were disappointed when a wicker basket came up and was shoved into a morgue wagon instead. A kid pointed to the blood dripping from one corner and a woman fainted. Nice.

I watched the wagon pull away and reached for a butt. I needed one bad. "It was an easy way out," I said. "What did the driver say?"

Pat took a cigarette from my pack. "He didn't see him. He thinks the guy must have been hiding behind a pillar then jumped out in front of the car. He sure was messed up."

"I don't know whether to be relieved or not."

"It's a relief to me, Mike. He's dead and his name will get published but who will connect him with Lee? The trouble's over."

"He have anything on him?"

Pat stuck his hand in his pocket and pulled out some stuff. Under the light it looked as if it had been stained with ink. Sticky ink. "Here's a train ticket from Chicago. It's in a bus envelope so he must have taken a bus as far as Chi then switched to rail." It was dated the 15th, a Friday.

I turned the envelope over and saw "Deamer" printed across the back with a couple of schedule notations in pencil. There was another envelope with the stuff. It had been torn in half and used for a memo sheet, but the name Deamer, part of an address in Nebraska and a Nebraska postage mark were still visible. It was dated over a month ago. The rest of the stuff was some small change, two crumpled bills and a skeleton key for a door lock.

It was as nice an answer as we could have hoped for and I didn't like it. "What's the matter now?" Pat queried.

"I don't know. It stinks."

"You're teed off because you were done out of a kill."

"Aw, shaddup, will you!"

"Then what's so lousy about it?"

"How the hell do I know? Can't I not like something without having to explain about it?"

"Not with me you can't, pal. I stuck my neck out when I invited you in."

I sucked in on the cigarette. It was cold standing there and I turned my collar up. "Get a complete identification on that corpse, Pat. Then maybe I can tell you why I think it stinks."

"Don't worry, I intend to. I'm not taking any chances of having him laughing at us from somewhere. It would be like the crazy bastard to push someone else under that train to sidetrack us."

"Would he have time to jam that stuff in his pockets too?" I flipped my thumb at the papers Pat was holding.

"He could have. Just the same, we'll be sure. Lee has both their birth certificates and a medical certificate on Oscar that has his full description. It won't take long to find out if that's him or not."

"Let me know what you find."

"I'll call you tomorrow. I wish I knew how the devil he

spotted us. I nearly killed myself in that damn alley. I thought I heard somebody yelling for you, too."

"Couldn't have been."

"Guess not. Well, I'll see you tomorrow?"

"Uh-huh." I took a last pull on the butt and tossed it at the curb. Pat went back into the station and I could hear his heels clicking on the steps.

The street was more deserted now than ever. All that was left was the one yellow light. It seemed to wink at me. I walked toward it and went up the three steps into the building. The door was still standing open, enough light from the front room seeping into the hall so I could find my way.

It wasn't much of a place, just a room. There was a chair, a closet, a single bed and a washstand. The suitcase on the bed was half filled with well-worn clothes, but I couldn't tell whether it was being packed or unpacked. I poked through the stuff and found another dollar bill stuffed in the cloth lining. Twenty pages of a mail-order catalog were under everything. Part of them showed sporting goods including all sorts of guns. The others pictured automobile accessories. Which part was used? Did he buy a gun or a tire? Why? Where?

I pulled out the shirts and shook them open, looking for any identifying marks. One had "DEA" for a laundry tag next to the label, the others had nothing so he must have done his own wash.

That was all there was to it.

Nothing.

I could breathe a little easier and tell Marty Kooperman that his boy was okay and nothing could hurt him now. Pat would be satisfied, the cops would be satisfied and everything was hunky-dory. I was the only one who still had a bug up my tail. It was a great big bug and it was kicking up a fuss. I was a hell of a way from being satisfied.

This wasn't what I was after, that's why. This didn't have to do with three green cards except that the dead man had killed a guy who carried one. What was his name . . . Moffit, Charlie Moffit. Was he dead because of a fluke or was there more to it?

I kicked at the edge of the bed in disgust and took one last look around. Pat would be here next. He'd find prints and check them against the corpse in his usual methodical way. If there was anything to be found, he'd find it and I could get it from him.

It had only been a few hours since I climbed out of the sack, but for some reason I was more tired than ever. Too much of a letdown, I guessed. You can't prime yourself for something to happen and feel right when it doesn't come off. The skin of my face felt tight and drawn, pulling away from my eyes. My back still crawled when I thought of the alley and that thing under the train.

I went into a shabby drugstore and called Velda's home. She wasn't there. I tried the office and she was. I told her to meet me in the bar downstairs and walked outside again, looking for a cab. The one that came along had a driver who had all the information about the accident in the subway secondhand and insisted on giving me a detailed account of all the gruesome details. I was glad to pay him off and get out of there.

Velda was sitting in a back booth with a Manhattan in front of her. Two guys at the bar had swung halfway around on their stools and were trying out their best leers. One said something dirty and the other laughed. Tony walked down behind the bar, but he saw me come in and stopped. The guy with the dirty mouth said something else, slid off his stool and walked over to Velda.

He set his drink down and leaned on her table, mouthing a few obscenities. Velda moved too fast for him. I saw her arm fly out, knock away the support of his hand and his face went into the table. She gave him the drink right in the eyes, glass and all.

The guy screamed, "You dirty little . . ." then she laid the heavy glass ash tray across his temple and he had it. He went down on his knees, his head almost on the floor. The other guy almost choked. He slammed his drink down and came off his stool with a rush. I let him go about two feet before I snagged the back of his coat collar with a jerk that put him right on his skinny behind.

Tony laughed and leaned on the bar.

I wasn't laughing. The one on the floor turned his head and I saw a pinched weasel face with eyes that had quick death in them. Those eyes crawled over me from top to bottom, over to Velda and back again. "A big tough guy," he said. "A big wise guy."

As if a spring exploded inside him, he came up off the floor with a knife in his hand, blade up.

A .45 can make an awful nasty sound in a quiet room when you pull the hammer back. It's just a little tiny click, but it can stop a dozen guys when they hear it. Weasel Face couldn't take his eyes off it. I let him have a good look and smashed it across his nose.

The knife hit the floor and broke when I stepped on it. Tony laughed again. I grabbed the guy by the neck and hauled him to his feet so I could drag the cold sharp metal of the rod across his face until he was a bright red mask mumbling for me to stop.

Tony helped me throw them in the street outside. He said, "They never learn, do they, Mike? Because there's two of 'em and they got a shiv they're the toughest mugs in the world. It ain't nice to get took, by a woman, neither. They never learn."

"They learn, Tony. For about ten seconds they're the smartest people in the world. But then it's always too late. After ten seconds they're dead. They only learn when they finally catch a slug where it hurts."

I walked back to the booth and sat down opposite Velda. Tony brought her another Manhattan and me a beer. "Very good," I said.

"Thanks. I knew you were watching."

She lit a cigarette and her hands were steadier than mine. "You were too rough on him."

"Nuts, he had a knife. I have an allergy against getting cut." I drained off half of the beer and laid it down on the table where I made patterns with the wet bottom. "Tell me about tonight."

Velda started to tear matches out of the book without lighting them. "I got there about seven-thirty. A light was on in the front window. Twice I saw somebody pull aside the corner of the shade and look out. A car went around the block twice, and both times it slowed down a little in front of the house. When it left I tried the door, but it was locked so I went next door and tried that one. It was locked too, but there was a cellar way under the stairs and I went down there. Just as I was going down the steps I saw a man coming up the block and I thought it might be Deamer.

"I had to take the chance that it was and that you were behind him. The cellar door was open and led through to the back yard. I was trying to crawl over a mound of boxes when I heard somebody in the back yard. I don't know how long it took me to get out there, possibly two minutes. Anyway, I heard a yell and somebody came out the door of the next house. I got through into the back alley and heard him running. He went too fast for me and I started yelling for you."

"That was Oscar Deamer, all right. He saw us coming and beat it."

"Maybe."

"What do you mean . . . 'maybe'?"

"I think there were two people in that alley ahead of me."

"Two people?" My voice had an edge to it. "Did you see them?"

"No."

"Then how do you know?"

"I don't. I just think so."

I finished the beer and waved to Tony. He brought another. Velda hadn't touched her drink yet. "Something made you think that. What was it?"

She shrugged, frowning at her glass, trying to force her mind back to that brief interval. "When I was in that cellar I thought I heard somebody in the other yard. There was a flock of cats around and I thought at the time that I was hearing them."

"Go on."

"Then when I was running after him I fell and while I lay there it didn't sound like just one person going down that alley."

"One person could sound like ten if they hit any of the junk we hit. It makes a hell of a racket."

"Maybe I'm wrong, Mike. I thought there could have been someone else and I wanted you to know about it."

"What the hell, it doesn't matter too much now anyway. The guy is dead and that should end it. Lee Deamer can go ahead and reform all he wants to now. He hasn't got a thing to worry about. As far as two people in that alley . . . well, you saw what the place was like. Nobody lives there unless he has to. They're the kind of people who scare easily, and if Lee started running somebody else could have too. Did you see him go down the subway?"

"No, he was gone when I got there, but two kids were staring down the steps and waving to another kid to come over. I took the chance that he went down and followed. The train was skidding to a stop when I reached the platform and I didn't have to be told why. When you scooted me away I looked for those kids in the crowd upstairs but they weren't around."

I hoisted my glass, turned it around in my hand and finished it. Velda downed her Manhattan and slipped her arms into her coat. "What now, Mike?"

"You go home, kid," I told her. "I'm going to take me a nice long walk."

We said good night to Tony and left. The two guys we had thrown in the street were gone. Velda grinned. "Am I safe?"

"Hell yes!"

I waved a taxi over, kissed her good night and walked off. My heels rapped the sidewalk, a steady tap-tap that kept time with my thoughts. They reminded me of another walk I took, one that led to a bridge, and still another one that led into a deserted store that came equipped with blackout curtains, light switches on the door and coffee urns.

There lay the story behind the green cards. There was where I could find out why I had to killl a guy who had one, and see a girl die because she couldn't stand the look on my face. That was what I wanted to know . . . why it was me who was picked to pull the trigger.

I turned into a candy store and pulled the telephone directories from the rack. I found the Park Avenue Brightons and dialed the number.

Three rings later a somber voice said, "Mr. Brighton's residence."

I got right to the point. "Is Ethel there?"

"Who shall I say is calling, sir?"

"You don't. Just put her on."

"I'm sorry, sir, but . . ."

"Oh, shut up and put her on."

There was a shocked silence and a clatter as the phone was laid on a table. Off in the distance I heard the mutter of voices, then feet coming across the room. The phone clattered again, and, "Yes?"

"Hello, Ethel," I said. "I drove your car into Times Square last night. Remember?"

"Oh! Oh, but . . ." Her voice dropped almost to a whisper. "Please, I can't talk to you here. What is . . ."

"You can talk to me outside, kid. I'll be standing on your street corner in about fifteen minutes. The northeast corner. Pick me up there."

"I-I can't. Honestly . . . oh, please . . ." There was panic in her voice, a tone that held more than fear.

I said, "You'd better, baby." That was enough. I hung up and started walking toward Park Avenue. If I could read a voice right she'd be there.

She was. I saw her while I was still a half block away, crossing nervously back and forth, trying to seem busy. I came up behind her and said hello. For a moment she went rigid, held by the panic that I had sensed in her voice.

"Scared?"

"No—of course not." The hell she wasn't! Her chin was wobbling and she couldn't hold her hands still. This time I was barely smiling and dames don't usually go to pieces when I do that.

I hooked my arm through hers and steered her west where there were lights and people. Sometimes the combination is good for the soul. It makes you want to talk and laugh and be part of the grand parade.

It didn't have that effect on her.

The smile might have been pasted on her face. When she wasn't looking straight ahead her eyes darted to me and back again. We went off Broadway and into a bar that had one empty end and one full end because the television wasn't centered. The lights were down low and nobody paid any attention to us on the empty end except the bartender, and he was more interested in watching the wrestling than hustling up drinks for us.

Ethel ordered an Old Fashioned and I had a beer. She held the fingers of her one hand tightly around the glass and worked a cigarette with the other. There was nothing behind the bar to see, but she stared there anyway. I had to give up carrying the conversation. When I did and sat there as quietly as she did the knuckles of her fingers went white.

She couldn't keep this up long. I took a lungful of smoke and let it come out with my words. "Ethel . . ." She jerked, startled. "What's there about me that has you up a tree?"

She wet her lips. "Really, there's . . . there's nothing."

"You never even asked me my name."

That brought her head up. Her eyes got wide and stared at the wall. "I . . . I'm not concerned with names."

"I am."

"But you . . . I'm . . . please, what have I done? Haven't I been faithful? Must you go on. . . ." She had kept it up too long. The panic couldn't stay. It left with a rush and a pleading tone took its place. There were tears in her eyes now, tears she tried hard to hold back and being a woman, couldn't. They flooded her eyelids and ran down her cheeks.

"Ethel . . . quit being scared of me. Look in a mirror and you'll know why I called you tonight. You aren't the kind of woman a guy can see and forget. You're too damned serious."

Dames, they can louse me up every time. The tears stopped as abruptly as they came and her mouth froze in indignation. This time she was able to look at my eyes clearly. "We have to be serious. You, of all people, should know that!"

This was better. The words were her own, what was inside her and not words that I put there. "Not all the time," I grinned.

"All the time!" she said. I grinned at her and she returned it with a frown.

"You'll do, kid."

"I can't understand you." She hesitated, then a smile blossomed and grew. She was lovely when she smiled. "You were testing me," she demanded.

"Something like that."

"But . . . why?"

"I need some help. I can't take just anybody, you know." It was true. I did need help, plenty of it too.

"You mean . . . you want me to help you . . . find out who . . . who did it?"

Cripes, how I wanted her to open up. I wasn't in the mood for more of those damn silly games and yet I had to play them. "That's right."

It must have pleased her. I saw the fingers loosen up around the glass and she tasted the drink for the first time. "Could I ask a question?"

"Sure, go ahead."

"Why did you choose me?"

"I'm attracted to beauty."

"But my record . . ."

"I was attracted to that too. Being beautiful helped."

"I'm not beautiful." She was asking for more. I gave it to her.

"All I can see are your face and hands. They're beautiful, but I bet the rest of you is just as beautiful, the part I can't see."

It was too dark to tell if she had the grace to blush or not. She wet her lips again, parting them in a small smile. "Would you?"

"What?"

"Like to see the rest of me." No, she couldn't have blushed.

I laughed at her, a slow laugh that brought her head around and showed me the glitter in her eyes. "Yeah, Ethel, I want to. And I will when I want to just a little more."

Her breath came so sharply that her coat fell open and I could see the pulse in her throat. "It's warm here. Can we . . . leave?"

Neither of us bothered to finish our drinks.

She was laughing now, with her mouth and her eyes. I held her hand and felt the warm pressure of her fingers, the stilted reserve draining out of her at every step. Ethel led the way, not me. We walked toward her place almost as if we were in a hurry, out to enjoy the evening.

"Supposing your father . . . or somebody you know should come along," I suggested.

She shrugged defiantly. "Let them. You know how I feel." She held her head high, the smile crooked across her lips.

"There's not one of them I care for. Any feeling I've had for my family disappeared several years ago."

"Then you haven't any feeling left for anyone?"

"I have! Oh, yes I have." Her eyes swung up to mine, half closed, revealing a sensuous glitter. "For the moment it's you."

"And other times?"

"I don't have to tell *you* that. There's no need to test me any longer."

A few doors from her building she stopped me. Her convertible was squatting there at the curb. The cars in front and behind had parking tickets on the windshield wiper. Hers bore only a club insignia.

"I'll drive this time," she said.

We got in and drove. It rained a little and it snowed a little, then, abruptly, it was clear and the stars came in full and bright, framed in the hole in the sky. The radio was a chant of pleasure, snatching the wild symphonic music from the air and offering us orchestra seats though we were far beyond the city, hugging the curves of the Hudson.

When we stopped it was to turn off the highway to a winding macadam road that led beneath the overhanging branches of evergreens The cottage nestled on top of a bluff smiling down at the world. Ethel took my hand, led me inside to the plush little playhouse that was her own special retreat and lit the heavy wax candles that hung in brass holders from the ceiling.

I had to admire the exquisite simplicity of the place. It proclaimed wealth, but in the most humble fashion. Somebody had done a good job of decorating. Ethel pointed to the little bar that was set in the corner of the log cabin. "Drinks are there. Would you care to make us one . . . Then start the fire? The fireplace has been laid up."

I nodded, watched her leave the room, then opened the doors of the liquor cabinet. Only the best, the very best. I picked out the best of the best and poured two straight, not wanting to spoil it with any mixer, sipped mine then drank it down. I had a refill and stared at it.

A Commie. She was a jerky Red. She owned all the trimmings and she was still a Red. What the hell was she hoping for, a government order to share it all with the masses? Yeah. A joint like this would suddenly assume a new owner under a new regime. A fat little general, a ranking secret policeman, somebody. Sure, it's great to be a Commie . . . as long as you're top dog. Who the hell was supposed to be fooled by all the crap?

Yet Ethel fell for it. I shook my head at the stupid asses that are left in this world and threw a match into the fireplace. It blazed up and licked at the logs on the andirons.

Ethel came out of the other room wearing her fur coat. Her hair looked different. It seemed softer. "Cold?"

"In there it is. I'll be warm in a moment."

I handed her the glass and we touched the rims. Her eyes were bright, hot.

We had three or four more and the bottom was showing in the bottle. Maybe it was more than three or four. I wanted to ask her some questions. I wanted the right answers and I didn't want her to think about them beforehand. I wanted her just a little bit drunk.

I had to fumble with the catch to get the liquor cabinet open. There was more of the best of the best in the back and I dragged it out. Ethel found the switch on a built-in phonograph and stacked on a handful of records.

The fireplace was a leaping, dancing thing that threw shadows across the room and touched everything with a weird, demoniac light. Ethel came to me, holding her arms open to dance. I wanted to dance, but there were parts of me trying to do other things.

Ethel laughed. "You're drunk."

"I am like hell." It wasn't exactly the truth.

"Well *I'm* drunk. I'm very, very drunk and I love it!" She threw her arms up and spun around. I had to catch her. "Oo, I want to sit down. Let's sit down and enjoy the fire."

She pulled away and danced to the sofa, her hands reaching out for the black bearskin rug that was draped over the back of it. She threw it on the floor in front of the fire and turned around. "Come on over. Sit down."

"You'll roast in that coat," I said.

"I won't." She smiled slyly and flipped open the buttons that held it together. She shrugged the shoulders off first letting it fall to her waist, then swept it off and threw it aside.

Ethel didn't have anything on. Only her shoes. She kicked them off too and sunk to the softness of the bearskin, a beautiful naked creature of soft round flesh and lustrous hair that changed color with each leap of the vivid red flame behind her.

It was much too warm then for a jacket. I heard mine hit a chair and slide off. My wallet fell out of the pocket and I didn't care. The sling on my gun rack wouldn't come loose and I broke it.

She shouldn't have done it. Damn it, she shouldn't have done it! I wanted to ask her some questions.

Now I forgot what I wanted to ask her.

My fingers hurt and she didn't care. Her lips were bright red, wet. They parted slowly and her tongue flicked out over her teeth inviting me to come closer. Her mouth was a hungry thing demanding to be tasted. The warmth that seemed to come from the flames was a radiation that flowed from the sleek length of her legs and nestled in the hollow of her stomach a moment before rising over the convex beauty of her breasts. She held her arms out invitingly and took me in them.

CHAPTER FIVE

I CAME AWAKE with the dawn, my throat dry and my mind groping to make sense out of what had happened. Ethel was still there, lying curled on her side up against me. Sometime during the night the fire had gone down and she had gotten up to get a blanket and throw it over us.

Somehow I got to my feet without waking her up. I pulled on my clothes, found my gun sling and my jacket on the floor. I remembered my wallet and felt around for it, getting mad when I didn't find it. I sat on the arm of the sofa and shook my head to clear out the spiders. Bending over didn't do me much good. The next time I used my foot and scooped it out from under the end table where I must have kicked it in getting dressed.

Ethel Brighton was asleep and smiling when I left. It was a good night, but not at all what I had come for. She giggled and wrapped her arms around the blankets. Maybe Ethel would quit being mad at the world now.

I climbed into my raincoat and walked out, looking up once at the sky overhead. The clouds had closed in again, but they were thinner and it was warmer than it had been.

It took twenty minutes to reach the highway and I had to wait another twenty before a truck came along and gave me a lift into town. I treated him to breakfast and we talked about the war. He agreed that it hadn't been a bad war. He had gotten nicked too, and it gave him a good excuse to cop a day off now and then.

I called Pat about ten o'clock. He gave me a fast hello, then: "Can you come up, Mike? I have something interesting."

"About last night?"

"That's right."

"I'll be up in five minutes. Stick around."

Headquarters was right up the street and I stepped it up. The D.A. was coming out of the building again. This time he didn't see me. When I rapped on Pat's door he yelled to come in and I pushed the knob.

Pat said, "Where the hell have you been?" He was grinning.

"No place." I grinned back.

"If what I suspect goes on between you and Velda, then you better get that lipstick off your face and shave."

"That bad?"

"I can smell whisky from here too."

"Velda won't like that," I said.

"No dame in love with a dope does," Pat laughed. "Park it, Mike. I have news for you." He opened his desk drawer and hauled out a large manila envelope that had CONFIDENTIAL printed across the back.

When he was draped across the arm of the chair he handed a fingerprint photostat to me. "I took these off the corpse last night."

"You don't waste time, pal."

"Couldn't afford to." He dug in the envelope and brought out a three-page document that was clipped together. It had a hospital masthead I didn't catch because Pat turned it over and showed me the fingerprints on the back. "These are Oscar Deamer's too. This is his medical case history that Lee was holding."

I didn't need to be an expert to see that they matched. "Same guy all right," I remarked.

"No doubt about it. Want to look at the report?"

"Ah, I couldn't wade through all that medical baloney. What's it say?"

"In brief, that Oscar Deamer was a dangerous neurotic, paranoiac and a few other phychiatric big words."

"Congenital?"

Pat saw what I was thinking. "No, as a matter of fact. So rest easy that no family insanity could be passed on to Lee. It seems that Oscar had an accident when he was a child. A serious skull fracture that somehow led to his condition."

"Any repercussions? Papers get any of it?" I handed the sheets back to Pat and he tucked them away.

"None at all, luckily. We were on tenterhooks for a while, but none of the newsboys connected the names. There was one fortunate aspect to the death of Oscar . . . his face wasn't recognizable. If the reporters had seen him there wouldn't have been a chance of covering up, and would some politicians like to have gotten that!"

I pulled a Lucky from my pack and tapped it on the arm of the chair. "What was the medical examiner's opinion?"

"Hell, suicide without a doubt. Oscar got scared, that's all. He tried to run knowing he was trapped. I guess he knew he'd go back to the sanitarium if he was caught . . . if he didn't stand a murder trial for Moffit's murder, and he couldn't take it."

Pat snapped his lighter open and fired my butt. "I guess that washes it up then," I said.

"For us . . . yes. For you, no."

I raised my eyebrows and looked at him quizzically.

"I saw Lee before I came to work. He called," Pat explained. "When he spoke to Oscar over the phone Oscar hinted at something. He seems to think that Oscar might have done other things than try to have him identified for a murder he didn't do. Anyway, I told him you had some unusual interest in the whole affair that you didn't want to speak about, even to me. He quizzed me about you, I told all and now he wants to see you."

"I'm to run down anything left behind?"

"I imagine so. At any rate, you'll get a fat fee out of it instead of kicking around for free."

"I don't mind. I'm on vacation anyway."

"Nuts. Stop handing me the same old thing. Think of something different. I'd give a lot to know what you have on your mind."

"You sure would, Pat." Perhaps it was the way I said it. Pat went into a piece of police steel. The cords in his neck stuck out like little fingers and his lips were just a straight, thin line.

"I've never known you to hang your hat on anything but murder, Mike."

"True, ain't it." My voice was flat as his.

"Mike, after the way I've been pitching with you, if you get in another smear you'll be taking me with you."

"I won't get smeared."

"Mike, you bastard, you have a murder tucked away somewhere."

"Sure, two of 'em. Try again."

He let his eyes relax and forced a grin. "If there were any recent kills on the pad I'd go over them one by one and scour your hide until you told me which one it was."

"You mean," I said sarcastically, "that the Finest haven't got one single unsolved murder on their hands?"

Pat got red and squirmed. "Not recently."

"What about that laddie you hauled out of the drink?"

He scowled as he remembered. "Oh, that gang job. Body still unidentified and we're tracking down his dental work. No prints on file."

"Think you'll tag him?"

"It ought to be easy. That bridgework was unusual. One

false tooth was made of stainless steel. Never heard of that before."

The bells started in my head again. Bells, drums, the whole damn works. The cigarette dropped out of my fingers and I bent to pick it up, hoping the blood pounding in my veins would pound out the crazy music.

It did. That maddening blast of silent sound went away. Slowly.

Maybe Pat never heard of stainless-steel teeth before, but I had.

I said, "Is Lee expecting me?"

"I told him you'd be over some time this morning."

"Okay." I stood up and shoved my hat on. "One other thing, what about the guy Oscar bumped?"

"Charlie Moffit?"

"Yeah."

"Age thirty-four, light skin, dark hair. He had a scar over one eye. During the war he was 4-F. No criminal record and not much known about him. He lived in a room on Ninety-first Street, the same one he's had for a year. He worked in a pie factory."

"Where?"

"A pie factory," Pat repeated, "where they make pies. Mother Switcher's Pie Shoppe. You can find it in the directory."

"Was that card all the identification he had on him?"

"No, he had a driver's license and a few other things. During the scuffle one pocket of his coat was torn out, but I doubt if he would have carried anything there anyway. Now, Mike, . . . why?"

"The green cards, remember?"

"Hell, quit worrying about the reds. We have agencies who can handle them."

I looked past Pat outside into the morning. "How many Commies are there floating around, Pat?"

"Couple hundred thousand, I think," he said.

"How many men have we got in those agencies you mentioned?"

"Oh . . . maybe a few hundred. What's that got to do with it?"

"Nothing . . . just that that's the reason I'm worried."

"Forget it. Let me know how you make out with Lee."

"Sure."

"And Mike . . . be discreet as hell about this, will you? Everybody with a press card knows your reputation and if you're spotted tagging around Lee there might be some questions asked that will be hard to answer."

"I'll wear a disguise," I said.

Lee Deamer's office was on the third floor of a modest building just off Fifth Avenue. There was nothing pretentious about the place aside from the switchboard operator. She was special. She had one of those faces that belonged in a chorus and a body she was making more effort to show than to conceal. I heard her voice and it was beautiful. But she was chewing gum like a cow and that took away any sign of pretentiousness she might have had.

There was a small anteroom that led to another office where two stenos were busy over typewriters. One wall of that room was all glass with a speaking partition built in at waist level. I had to lean down to my belt buckle to talk and gave it up as a bad job. The girl behind it laughed pleasantly and came out the door to see me.

She was a well-tailored woman in her early thirties, nice to look at and speak to. She wore an emerald ring that looked a generation older than she was. She smiled and said, "Good morning, can I do something for you?"

I remembered to be polite. "I'd like to see Mr. Deamer, please."

"Is he expecting you?"

"He sent word for me to come up."

"I see." She tapped her teeth with a pencil and frowned. "Are you in a hurry?"

"Not particularly, but I think Mr. Deamer is."

"Oh, well . . . the doctor is inside with him. He may be there awhile, so . . ."

"Doctor?" I interrupted.

The girl nodded, a worried little look tugging at her eyes. "He seemed to be quite upset this morning and I called in the doctor. Mr. Deamer hasn't been too well since he had that attack awhile back."

"What kind of attack?"

"Heart. He had a telephone call one day that agitated him terribly. I was about to suggest that he go home and at that moment, he collapsed. I . . . I was awfully frightened. You see, it had never happened before, and . . ."

"What did the doctor say?"

"Apparently it wasn't a severe attack. Mr. Deamer was instructed to take it easy, but for a man of his energy it's hard to do."

"You say he had a phone call? That did it?"

"I'm sure it did. At first I thought it was the excitement of watching the Legion parade down the avenue, but Ann told me it happened right after the call came in."

Oscar's call must have hit him harder than either Pat or I thought. Lee wasn't a young man any more, a thing like that could raise a lot of hell with a guy's ticker. I was about to say something when the doctor came out of the office. He was a little guy with a white goatee out of another era.

He nodded to us both, but turned his smile on the girl. "I'm sure he'll be fine. I left a prescription. See that it's filled at once, please?"

"Thank you, I will. Is it all right for him to have visitors?"

"Certainly. Apparently he has been thinking of something that disturbed him and had a slight relapse. Nothing to worry about as long as he takes it easy. Good day."

We said so long and she turned to me with another smile, bigger this time. "I guess you can go ahead in then. But please . . . don't excite him."

I grinned and said I wouldn't. Her smile made her prettier. I pushed through the door, passed the steno and knocked on the door with Deamer's name on it.

He rose to greet me but I waved him down. His face was a little flushed and his breathing fast. "Feeling better now? I saw the doctor when he came out."

"Much better, Mike. I had to fabricate a story to tell him . . . I couldn't tell the truth."

I sat in the chair next to his and he pushed a box of cigars toward me. I said no and took out a Lucky instead. "Best to keep things to yourself. One word and the papers'll have it on page one. Pat said you wanted to see me."

Lee sat back and wiped his face with a damp handkerchief. "Yes, Mike. He told me you were interested somehow."

"I am."

"Are you one of my . . . political advocates?"

"Frankly, I don't know a hoot about politics except that it's a dirty game from any angle."

"I hope to do something about that. I hope I can, Mike, I sincerely hope I can. Now I'm afraid."

"The heart?"

He nodded. "It happened after Oscar called. I never suspected that I have a . . . condition. I'm afraid now the voters must be told. It wouldn't be fair to elect a man not physically capable of carrying out the duties of his office." He smiled wistfully, sadly. I felt sorry for the old boy.

"Anyway, I'm not concerned with the politics of the affair."

"Really? But what . . ."

"Just a loose end, Lee. They bother me."

"I see. I don't understand, but I see . . . if you can make sense of that."

I waved the smoke away from in front of him. "I know what you mean. Now about why you wanted to see me. Pat gave me part of it already, enough so I can see the rest."

"Yes. You see, Oscar intimated that no matter what happened, he was going to see to it that I was broken, completely broken. He mentioned some documents he had prepared."

I crushed the butt out and looked at him. "What kind of documents?"

Lee shook his head slowly. "The only possible thing he could compound would be our relationship as brothers. How, I don't know, because I have all the family papers. But if he could establish that I was the brother of a man committed to a mental institution, it would be a powerful weapon in the hands of the opposition."

"There's nothing else," I asked, "that could stick you?"

He spread his hands apart in appeal. "If there was it would have been brought to light long ago. No, I've never been in jail or in trouble of any sort. I'm afraid that my attention to business precluded any trouble."

"Uh-huh. How come this awful hatred?"

"I don't know, actually. As I told Pat and you previously, it may have been a matter of ideals, or because though we were twins, we weren't at all alike. Oscar was almost, well . . . sadistic in his ways. We had little to do with each other. As younger men I became established in business while Oscar got into all sorts of scrapes. I've tried to help him, but he wouldn't accept help from me at all. He hated me fiercely. I'm inclined to believe that this time Oscar had intended to bleed me for all the money he could, then make trouble for me anyway."

"You were lucky you took the attitude you did. You can't pay off, it only makes matters worse."

"I don't know, Mike; as much as he hated me I certainly didn't want that to happen to him."

"He's better off."

"Perhaps."

I reached for another cigarette. "You want me to find out what he left then, that's it."

"If there is anything to be found, yes."

When I filled my lungs with smoke I let it go slowly, watching it swirl up toward the ceiling. "Lee," I said, "you don't know me so I'll tell you something. I hate phonies. Suppose I *do* find something that ties you up into a nice little ball.

Something real juicy. What do you think I should do with it?"

It wasn't the reaction I expected. He leaned forward across the desk with his fingers interlocked. His face was a study in emotions. "Mike," he said in a voice that had the crisp clarity of static electricity, "if you do, I charge you to make it public at once. Is that clear?"

I grinned and stood up. "Okay, Lee. I'm glad you said that." I reached out my hand and he took it warmly. I've seen evangelists with faces like that, unswerving, devoted to their duty. We looked at each other then he opened his desk drawer and brought out a lovely sheaf of green paper. They had big, beautiful numbers in the corners.

"Here is a thousand dollars, Mike. Shall we call it a retainer?"

I took the bills and folded them tenderly away. "Let's call it payment in full. You'll get your money's worth."

"I'm sure of it. If you need any additional information, call on me."

"Right. Want a receipt?"

"No need of it. I'm sure your word is good enough."

"Thanks. I'll send you a report if anything turns up." I flipped a card out of my pocket and laid it on his desk. "In case you want to call me. The bottom one is my home phone. It's unlisted."

We shook hands again and he walked me to the door. On the way out the cud-chewing switchboard sugar smiled between chomps then went back to her magazine. The receptionist said so-long and I waved back.

* * *

Before I went to the office I grabbed a quick shave, a trim around the ears and took a shower that scraped the hide off me along with the traces of Ethel's perfume. I changed my shirt and suit but kept old Betsy in place under my arm.

Velda was working at the filing cabinet when I breezed in with a snappy hello and a grin that said I had money in my pocket. I got a quick once-over for lipstick stains, whisky aromas and what not, passed and threw the stack of bills on the desk.

"Bank it, kid."

"Mike! What did *you* do?"

"Lee Deamer. We're employed." I gave it to her in short order and she listened blankly.

When I finished she said, "You'll never find a thing, Mike. I know you won't. You shouldn't have taken it."

"You're wrong, chick. It wasn't stealing. If Oscar left anything that will tie Lee up wouldn't you want me to get it?"

"Oh, Mike, you must! How long do we have to put up with the slime they call politics? Lee Deamer is the only one . . . the only one we can look to. Please, Mike, you *can't* let anything happen to him!"

I couldn't take the fear in her voice. I opened my arms out and she stepped into them. "Nobody will hurt the little guy, Velda. If there's anything I'll get it. Stop sniffling."

"I can't. It's all so nasty. You never stop to think what goes on in this country, but I do."

"Seems to me that I helped fight a war, didn't I?"

"You shouldn't have let it stop there. That's the matter with things. People forget, even the ones who *shouldn't* forget! They let others come walking in and run things any way they please, and what are they after—the welfare of the people they represent? Not a bit. All they want is to line their own pockets. Lee isn't like that, Mike. He isn't strong like the others, and he isn't smart politically. All he has to offer is his honesty and that isn't much."

"The hell it isn't. He's made a pretty big splash in this state."

"I know, and it has to stick, Mike. Do you understand?"

"I understand."

"Promise me you'll help him, Mike, promise me your word."

Her face turned up to mine, drawn yet eager to hear. "I promise," I said softly. "I'll never go back on a promise to you, nor to myself."

It made her feel better in a hurry. The tears stopped and the sniffling died away. We had a laugh over it, but behind the laughter there was a dead seriousness. The gun under my arm felt heavy.

I said, "I have a job for you. Get me a background on Charlie Moffit. He's the one Oscar Deamer bumped."

Velda stopped her filing. "Yes, I know."

"Go to his home and his job. See what kind of a guy he was. Pat didn't mention a family so he probably didn't have any. Take what cash you need to cover expenses."

She shoved the drawer in and fingered the bills on the desk. "How soon?"

"I want it by tonight if you can. If not, tomorrow will do."

I could see her curiosity coming out, but there are times when I want to keep things to myself and this was one of them. She knew it and stayed curious without asking questions.

Before she slipped the bills inside the bank book I took out two hundred in fifties. She didn't say anything then, either, but she smelt a toot coming up and I had to kiss the tip of her nose to get the scowl off her puss.

As soon as Velda left I picked up the phone and dialed Ethel Brighton's number. The flunky recognized my voice from last night and was a little more polite. He told me Ethel hadn't come in yet and hung up almost as hard as he could but not quite.

I tapped out a brief history of the case for the records, stuck it in the file and called again. Ethel had just gotten in. She grabbed the phone and made music in it, not giving a damn who heard her. "You beast. You walked right out of the cave and left me to the wolves."

"That bearskin would scare them away. You looked nice wrapped up in it."

"You liked . . . all of me, then. The parts you could see?"

"All of you, Ethel. Soft and sweet."

"We'll have to go back."

"Maybe," I said.

"Please," softly whispered.

I changed the subject. "Busy today?"

"Very busy. I have a few people to see. They promised me sizable . . . donations. Tonight I have to deliver them to Com . . . Henry Gladow."

"Yeah. Suppose I go with you?"

"If *you* think it's all right I'm sure no one will object."

"Why me?" That was one of the questions I wanted an answer to.

She didn't tell me. "Come now," she said. "Supposing I meet you in the Oboe Club at seven. Will that do?"

"Fine, Ethel. I'll save a table so we can eat."

She said so long with a pleasant laugh and waited for me to hang up. I did, then sat there with a cigarette in my fingers trying to think. The light hitting the wall broke around something on the desk making two little bright spots against the pale green.

Like two berries on a bush. The judge's eyes. They looked at me.

Something happened to the light and the eyes disappeared. I picked the phone up again and called the *Globe*. Marty was just going out on a story but had time to talk to me. I asked him, "Remember the Brighton family? Park Avenue stuff."

"Sure, Mike. That's social, but I know a little about them. Why?"

"Ethel Brighton's on the outs with her father. Did it ever make the papers?"

I heard him chuckle a second. "Getting toney, aren't you, kid? Well, part of the story was in the papers some time ago. It seems that Ethel Brighton publicly announced her engagement to a certain young man. Shortly afterwards the engagement was broken."

"Is that all?"

"Nope," he grunted, "the best is yet to come. A little prying by our diligent Miss Carpenter who writes the social chatter uncovered an interesting phase that was handled just as interestingly. The young man in question was a down-and-out artist who made speeches for the Communist Party and was quite willing to become a capitalist by marriage. He was a conscientious objector during the war though he probably could have made 4-F without trouble. The old man raised the roof but there was nothing he could do. When he threatened to cut Ethel off without a cent she said she'd marry him anyway.

"So the old man connived. He worked it so that he'd give his blessing so long as the guy enlisted in the army. They needed men bad so they took him and as soon as he was out of training camp he was shipped overseas. He was killed in action, though the truth was that he went AWOL during a battle and deserved what he got. Later Ethel found out that her father was responsible for everything but the guy's getting knocked off and he had hoped for that too. She had a couple of rows with him in public, then it died down to where they just never spoke."

"Nice girl," I mused.

"Lovely to look at anyway."

"You'll never know. Well, thanks, pal."

He stopped me before I could hang up. "Is this part of what you were driving at the other day . . . something to do with Lee Deamer?" His voice had a rasp.

"Not this," I said. "It's personal."

"Oh, well call me any time, Mike." He sounded relieved.

And so the saga of one Ethel Brighton. Nice girl turned dimwit because her old man did her out of a marriage. She was lucky and didn't know it.

I looked at my watch, remembered that I had meant to buy Velda lunch and forgot, then went downstairs and ate by myself. When I finished the dessert I sat back with a cigarette and tried to think of what it was that fought like the hammers of hell to come through my mind. Something was eating its way out and I couldn't help it. I gave up finally and paid my check. There was a movie poster behind the register advertising the latest show at the house a block over, so I ambled over and plunked in a seat before the show started. It wasn't good enough to keep me awake. I was on the second time around when I glanced at the time and hustled into the street.

The Oboe Club had been just another second-rate saloon on a side street until a wandering reporter happened in and mentioned it in his column as a good place to relax if you liked solitude and quiet. The next day it became a first-rate nightclub where you could find anything but solitude and quiet. Advertising helped plenty.

I knew the headwaiter to nod to and it was still early enough to get a table without any green passing between handshakes. The bar was lined with the usual after-office crowd having one for the road. There wasn't anyone to speak to, so I sat at the table and ordered a highball. I was on my fourth when Ethel Brighton came in, preceded by the headwaiter and a few lesser luminaries.

He bowed her into her seat, then bowed himself out. The other one helped her adjust her coat over the back of the chair. "Eat?" I asked.

"I'll have a highball first. Like yours." I signaled the waiter and called for a couple more.

"How'd the donations come?"

"Fine," she said, "even better than I expected. The best part is, there's more where that came from."

"The party will be proud of you." She looked up from her drink with a nervous little smile.

"I . . . hope so."

"They should. You've brought in a lot of mazuma."

"One must do all one can." Her voice was a flat drone, almost machine-like. She picked up her glass and took a long pull. The waiter came and took our orders, leaving another highball with us.

I caught her attention and got back on the subject. "Do you ever wonder where it all goes to?"

"You mean . . . the money?" I nodded between bites. "Why . . . no. It isn't for me to think about those things. I only do as I'm told." She licked her lips nervously and went back to her plate.

I prodded her again. "I'd be curious if I were in your shoes. Give a guess, anyway."

This time there was nothing but fear in her face. It tugged at her eyes and mouth, and made her fork rattle against the china. "Please . . ."

"You don't have to be afraid of me, Ethel. I'm not entirely like the others. You should know that."

The fear was still there, but something else overshadowed it. "I can't understand you . . . you're different. It's well. . . ."

"About the money, give a guess. Nobody should be entirely ignorant of party affairs. After all, isn't that the principle of the thing . . . everybody for everybody? Then you'd have to know everything about everybody to be able to really do the party justice."

"That's true." She squinted and a smile parted her lips. "I see what you mean. Well, I'd guess that most of the money goes to foster the schools we operate . . . and for propaganda, of course. Then there are a lot of small things that come up like office expenses here and there."

"Pretty good so far. Anything else?"

"I'm not too well informed on the business side of it so that's about as far as I can go."

"What does Gladow do for a living?"

"Isn't he a clerk in a department store?"

I nodded as if I had known all along. "Ever see his car?" Ethel frowned again. "Yes. He has a new Packard, why?"

"Ever see his house?"

"I've been there twice," she said. "It's a big place up in Yonkers."

"And all that on a department store clerk's salary."

Her face went positively white. She had to swallow hard to get her drink down and refused to meet my eyes until I told her to look at me. She did, but hesitantly. Ethel Brighton was scared silly . . . of me. I grinned but it was lost. I talked and it went over her head. She gave all the right answers and even a laugh at one of my jokes, but Ethel was scared and she wasn't coming out of it too quickly.

She took the cigarette I offered her. The tip shook when she bent into the flame of my lighter. "What time do you have to be there?" I asked.

"Nine o'clock. There's . . . a meeting."

"We'd better go then. It'll take time getting over to Brooklyn."

"All right."

The waiter came over and took away a ten spot for his trouble while the headboy saw us to the door. Half the bar turned around to look at Ethel as she brushed by. I got a couple of glances that said I was a lucky guy to have all that mink on my arm. Real lucky.

We had to call the parking lot to get her car brought over

then drove the guy back again. It was a quarter after eight before we pointed the car toward the borough across the stream. Ethel was behind the wheel, driving with a fixed intensity. She wouldn't talk unless I said something that required an answer. After a while it got tiresome so I turned on the radio and slumped back against the seat with my hat down over my eyes.

Only then did she seem to ease up. Twice I caught her head turning my way, but I couldn't see her eyes nor read the expression on her face. Fear. It was always there. Communism and Fear. Green Cards and Fear. Terror on the face of the girl on the bridge; stark, unreasoning fear when she looked at my face. Fear so bad it threw her over the rail to her death.

I'd have to remember to ask Pat about that, I thought. The body had to come up sometime.

The street was the same as before, dark, smelly, unaware of the tumor it was breeding in its belly. Trench Coat was standing outside the door seemingly enjoying the night. Past appearance didn't count. You showed your card and went in the door and showed it again. There was the same girl behind the desk and she made more of me than the card I held. Her voice was a nervous squeak and she couldn't sit still. Deliberately, I shot her the meanest grin I could dig up, letting her see my face when I pulled my lip back over my teeth. She didn't like it. Whatever it was scared her, too.

Henry Gladow was a jittery little man. He frittered around the room, stopped when he saw us and came over with a rush. "Good evening, good evening, comrades." He spoke directly to me. "I am happy to see you again, comrade. It is an honor."

It had been an honor before, too.

"There is news?" I screwed my eyebrows together and he pulled back, searching for words until he found them. "Of course. I am merely being inquisitive. Ha, ha. We are all so very concerned, you know."

"I know," I said.

Ethel handed him another of those envelopes and excused herself. I watched her walk to a table and take a seat next to two students where she began to correct some mimeographed sheets. "Wonderful worker, Miss Brighton," Gladow smiled. "You would scarcely think that she represents all that we hate."

I made an unintelligible answer.

"You are staying for the meeting?" he asked me.

"Yeah, I want to poke around a little."

This time he edged close to me, looking around to see if there was anyone close enough to hear. "Comrade, if I am not getting too inquisitive again, is there a possibility that . . . the person could be here?"

There it was again. Just what I wanted to know and I didn't dare ask the question. It was going to take some pretty careful handling. "It's possible," I said tentatively.

He was aghast. "Comrade! It is unthinkable!" He reflected a moment then: "Yet it had to come from somewhere. I simply can't understand it. Everything is so carefully screened, every member so carefully selected that it seems impossible for there to be a leak anywhere. And those filthy warmongers, doing a thing like that . . . so cold-blooded! It is simply incredible. How I wish the party was in power at this moment. Why, the one who did that would be uncovered before the sun could set!"

Gladow cursed through his teeth and pounded a puny, carefully tended fist into his palm. "Don't worry," I said slowly.

It took ten seconds for my words to sink in. Gladow's little eyes narrowed in pleasure like a hog seeing a trough full of slops. The underside of his top lip showed when he smiled. "No, comrade. I won't worry. The party is too clever to let a direct representative's death go unpunished. No, I won't worry because I realize that the punishment that comes will more than equal the crime." He beamed at me fatuously. "I am happy to realize that the higher echelon has sent a man of your capacity, comrade."

I didn't even thank him. I was thinking and this time the words made sense. They made more than sense . . . they made murder! Only death is cold-blooded, and who was dead? Three people. One hadn't been found. One was found and not identified, even by a lousy sketch. The other was dead and identified. He was cold-bloodedly murdered and he was a direct representative of the party and I was the guy looking for his killer.

Good Lord, the insane bastards thought I was an MVD man!

My hands started to shake and I kept them in my pockets. And who was the dead man but Charlie Moffit! My predecessor. A goddamned Commie gestapo man. A hatchetman, a torpedo, a lot of things you want to call him. Lee ought to be proud of his brother, damn proud. All by himself he went out and he knocked off a skunk.

But I was the prize, I was the MVD guy that came to take

his place and run the killer down. Oh, brother! No wonder the jerks were afraid of me! No wonder they didn't ask my name! No wonder I was supposed to know it all.

I felt a grin trying to pull my mouth out of shape because so much of it was funny. They thought they were clever as hell and here I was right in the middle of things with an *in* that couldn't be better. Any good red would give his shirt to be where I was right this minute.

Everything started to come out right then, even the screwy test they put me through. A small-time setup like this was hardly worth the direct attention of a Moscow man unless something was wrong, so I had to prove myself.

Smart? Sure, just like road apples that happen behind horses.

Now I knew and now I could play the game. I could be one of the boys and show them some fun. There were going to be a lot of broken backs around town before I got done.

There was only one catch I could think of. Someplace was another MVD laddie, a real one. I'd have to be careful of him. At least careful that he didn't see me first, because when I met up with that stinkpot I was going to split him right down the middle with a .45!

I had been down too deep in my thoughts to catch the arrival of the party that came in behind me. I heard Gladow extending a welcome that wasn't handed out to just everybody. When I turned around to look I saw one little fat man, one big fat man and a guy who was in the newspapers every so often. His name was General Osilov and he was attached to the Russian Embassy in Washington. The big and little fat men were his aides and they did all the smiling. If anything went on in the head of the bald-headed general it didn't show in is flat, wide face.

Whatever it was Henry Gladow said swung the three heads in my direction. Two swung back again fast leaving only the general staring at me. It was a stare-down that I won. The general coughed without covering his mouth and stuck his hands in the pockets of his suitcoat. None of them seemed anxious to make my acquaintance.

From then on there was a steady flow of traffic in through the door. They came singly and in pairs, spaced about five minutes apart. Before the hour was out the place was packed. It was filled with the kind of people you'd expect to find there and it would hit you that when the cartoonists did a caricature of a pack of shabby reds lurking in the shadow of democracy they did a good job.

A few of them dragged out seats and the meeting was on.

I saw Ethel Brighton slide into the last chair in the last row and waited until she was settled before I saw down beside her. She smiled, let that brief look of fear mask her face, then turned her head to the front. When I put my hand over hers I felt it tremble.

Gladow spoke. The aides spoke. Then the general spoke. He pulled his tux jacket down when he rose and glared at the audience. I had to sit there and listen to it. It was propaganda right off the latest Moscow cable and it turned me inside out. I wanted to feel the butt of an M-1 against my shoulder pointing at those bastards up there on the rostrum and feel the pleasant impact as it spit slugs into their guts.

Sure, you can sit down at night and read about the hogwash they hand out. Maybe you're fairly intelligent and can laugh at it. Believe me, it isn't funny. They use the very thing we build up, our own government and our own laws, to undermine the things we want.

It wasn't a very complicated speech the general made. It was plain, bitter poison and they cheered him noiselessly. He was making plain one thing. There were still too many people who didn't go for Communism and not enough who did and he gave a plan of organization that had worked in a dozen countries already. One armed Communist was worth twenty capitalists without guns. It was Hitler all over again. A powerful Communist government already formed would be there to take over when the big upset came, and according to him it was coming soon. Here, and he swept the room with his arm, was one phase of that government ready to go into action.

I didn't hear the rest of it. I sat there fiddling with my fingernails because I was getting ready to bust loose and spoil their plans. If I let any more words go in my ears there was going to be blood on the floor and it wasn't time for that yet. I caught snatches of things that went on, repeated intimations of how the top men were already in the core of the present government eating its vitals out so the upset would be an easy one.

For a long time I sat there working up more hatred than I had ever had at any time and I wasn't conscious of how tightly Ethel Brighton was squeezing my hand. When I looked at her tears were running down her face. That's the kind of thing the general and his party could do to decent people.

I took a long look at him, making sure that I wouldn't forget his face, because some day he'd be passing a dark alley or forget to lock his door when he went to bed. That's when he'd catch it. And I didn't want to get tagged for it either. That would be like getting the chair for squashing a spider.

The meeting ended with handshakes all around. The audience lined up along the walls taking handfuls of booklets and printed sheets to distribute later, then grouped in bunches around the room talking things over in excited murmurs. Henry Gladow and Martin Romberg were up on the rostrum having their own conference. The general said something to Henry and he must have ordered his bodyguard down into the crowd to look for his trench coat or something. Martin Romberg looked hurt. Tough.

While the seats were folded and stacked I lost track of Ethel. I saw her a few minutes later coming from the washroom and she looked a little better. She had a smile for me this time, a big one. I would have made something of it if a pimply-faced kid about twenty didn't come crawling over and tell me that the general wanted to know if I had time to speak to him.

Rather than answer I picked a hole in the crowd that had started to head for the door and walked up to the rostrum. The general stood alone, his hands behind his back. He nodded briefly and said something in a guttural tongue.

I let my eyes slide to the few who remained near by. There wasn't any respect in my tone when I said, "English. You know better than that."

The general paled a little and his mouth worked. "Yes . . . yes. I didn't expect to find anyone here. Do you have a report for me?"

I shook a cigarette out of the pack and stuck it in my mouth. "When I have you'll know about it."

His head bobbed anxiously and I knew I had the bull on him. Even a general had to be leery of the MVD. That made it nice for me. "Of course. But there should be some word to bring back to the committee."

"Then tell 'em things are looking up. It won't be long."

The general's hands came out in front where he squeezed them happily. "Then you *do* have word! The courier . . . he did have the documents? You know where they are?"

I didn't say a word. All I did was look at him and he got that same look on his face as the others had. He was thinking what I thought he was thinking, that he had taken me for granted and it was his mistake and one word to the right sources and he'd feel the ax.

He tried his first smile. "It is very all right, you know. Comrade Gladow told me."

I dragged on the cigarette and blew it in his face wishing

it was some mustard gas. "You'll know soon enough," I said. I left him standing there and walked back to Ethel. She was slipping into her mink and nobody seemed to care a hoot what she wore.

"Going home?"

"Yes . . . are you?"

"I don't mind."

One of the men paused to have a word with her before she left. She excused herself to talk to him and I used the time to look around and be sure there weren't any faces there that I'd ever forget. When the time came I wanted to be able to put the finger on them and put it on good.

Maybe it was the way I stared at the babe from the desk at the door or maybe it was because I looked at her too long. Her lashes made like bird's wings for a second and everything in the room seemed to get interesting all of a sudden. Her eyes jerked around but kept coming back to mine and each time there was a little more of a blush crowding her hairline.

I kept my grin hidden because she thought I was on the make. It could have been pathetic if it wasn't so damn funny. She wasn't the kind of woman a guy would bother with if there was anything else around. Strictly the last resort type. From the way she wore her clothes you couldn't tell what was underneath and suspected probably nothing. Her face looked like nature had been tired when it made it and whatever she did to her hair certainly didn't improve things any.

Plain was the word. Stuffy was the type. And here she thought a man saw something interesting in her.

I guessed that all women were born with some conceit in them so I put on a sort of smile and walked over to her casually. A little flattery could make a woman useful sometimes.

I held out my deck of butts. "Smoke?"

It must have been her first cigarette. She choked on it, but came up smiling. "Thank you."

I said, "You've, er . . . belonged some time, Miss . . ."

"Linda Holbright." She got real fluttery then. "Oh, yes, for years, you know. And I . . . try to do anything I can for the party."

"Good, good," I said. "You seem to be . . . very capable. Pretty, too."

Her first blush had been nothing. This one went right down to her shoes. Her eyes got big and blue and round and gave me the damnedest look you ever saw. Just for the hell of it I gave one back with a punch in it. What she made of it stopped her from breathing for a second.

I heard Ethel finish her little conversation behind me and I said, "Good night, Linda. I'll see you soon." I gave her that look again. "Real soon."

Her voice sounded a little bit strained. "I . . . meant to ask you. If there is anything . . . important you should know . . . where can I reach you?"

I ripped the back off a book of matches and wrote down my address. "Here it is. Apartment 5B."

Ethel was waiting for me, so I said good night again and started for the door behind the mink coat. It made nice wiggles when she walked. I liked that.

I let her go out first then followed her. The street was empty enough so you wouldn't think anything unusual about the few couples who were making their way to the subways. Trench Coat was still at the door holding a cigarette in his mouth. His belt was too tight and the gun showed underneath. One day a cop would spot that and there'd be more trouble.

Yeah, they sure were smart.

Going back was better than going down. This time Ethel turned into a vivid conversationalist, commenting on everything she saw. I tried to get in a remark about the meeting and she brushed it off with some fast talk. I let her get it out of her system, sitting there with my mouth shut, grinning at the right places and chiming in with a grunt whenever she laughed.

About a block from my apartment I pointed to the corner and said, "I'll get off under the light, kid."

She edged into the curb and stopped. "Good night, then," she smiled. "I hope you enjoyed the meeting."

"As a matter of fact, I thought they stunk." Ethel's mouth dropped open. I kissed it and she closed it, fast. "Do you know what I'd do if I were you, Ethel?"

She shook her head, watching me strangely.

"I'd go back to being a woman and less of a dabbler in politics."

This time her eyes and mouth came open together. I kissed her again before she could get it shut. She looked at me as if I were a puzzle that couldn't be solved and let out a short, sharp laugh that had real pleasure in it.

"Aren't you a bit curious about my name, Ethel?"

Her face went soft. "Only for my own sake."

"It's Mike. Mike Hammer and it's a good name to remember."

"Mike . . ." very softly. "After last night . . . how could I forget?"

I grinned at her and opened the door. "Will I be seeing you again?"

"Do you want to?"

"Very much."

"Then you'll be seeing me again. You know where I live."

I couldn't forget her, either. On that bearskin rug with the fire behind her she was something a man never forgets. I stuck my hands in my pockets and started to whistle my way down the street.

I got as far as the door next to mine when the sedan across the street came to life. If the guy at the wheel hadn't let the clutch out so fast I wouldn't have looked up and seen the snout of the rifle that hung out the back window. What happened then came in a blur of motion and a mad blasting of sound. The long streak of flame from the rifle, the screaming of the ricocheted slug, the howl of the car engine. I dove flat out. Rolling before I hit the concrete, my hand pulling the gun out, my thumb grabbing for the hammer. The rifle barked again and gouged a hunk out of the sidewalk in front of my face, but by that time the .45 in my hand was bucking out the bullets as fast as my finger could pull the trigger, and in the light of the street lamp overhead I saw the dimples pop into the back of the car and the rear window spiderweb suddenly and smash to the ground. Somebody in the car screamed like a banshee gone mad and there were no more shots. Around me the windows were slamming up before the car had made the turn at the corner.

I kept saying it over and over to myself. "Those goddamned bastards. They got wise! Those goddamn bastards!"

A woman shrieked from a window that somebody was dead and when I looked up I saw she was pointing to me. When I climbed back on my feet she shrieked again and fell away from the window.

It hadn't been a full twenty seconds since that car had started up, and a police car was wheeling around the corner. The driver slammed on the brakes and the two of them came out with Police Specials in their hands, both of them pointed at me. I was trying to shove a fresh load into the clip when the cop snarled, "Drop that gun, damn it!"

I wasn't doing any arguing with them. I tossed the gun so it landed on my foot then shoved it away gently. The other cop picked it up. Before they told me to put my hands on my head and stood there while they flashed the beam of light in my face.

"There's a ticket for that rod in my wallet along with a Private Operator's license."

The cop didn't lose any time frisking me for another rod before yanking my wallet out. He had a skeptical look on his face until he saw the ticket. "Okay, put 'em down," he said. I dropped my hands and reached for my .45. "I didn't say to pick that up yet," he added. I let it stay there. The cop who drove the buggy looked the ticket over then looked at me. He said something to his partner and motioned for me to get the gun.

"All clear?" I blew the dust off old Betsy and stowed it away. A crowd was beginning to collect and one of the cops started to herd them away.

"What happened?" He wasn't a man of many words.

"There you got me, feller. I was on my way home when the shooting started. Either it's the old yarn of mistaken identity which isn't too probable or somebody whom I thought was a friend, isn't."

"Maybe you better come with us."

"Sure, but in the meantime a black Buick sedan with no back window and a few bullets in its behind is making tracks to the nearest garage. I think I got one of the guys in the car and you can start checking the doctors."

The cop peered at me under his visor and took my word for it. The call went out on the police wires without any more talk. They were all for dragging me with them until I had a call put in to Pat and his answer relayed back to the squad car. Pat told them I was available at any time and they gave me the green light through the crowd.

I got a lot of unfriendly looks that night.

When I stood in front of my door with the key in my hand it hit me just like that. My little love scene with Ethel Brighton had had repercussions. My wallet on the floor. It wasn't in the same place in the morning. When she had gotten up for that blanket she had seen it, and my P.I. card in the holder. Tonight she passed the word.

I was lucky to get out of there with a whole skin.

Ethel, I thought, you're a cute little devil. You looked so nice in your bare skin with the fire behind you. Maybe I'll see you stripped again. Soon. When I do I'm going to take my belt off and lash your butt like it should have been lashed when you first broke into this game.

In fact, I looked forward to doing it.

CHAPTER SIX

I FINISHED A QUART bottle of beer before calling Velda. I got her at home and asked her what she'd found. She said, "There wasn't much *to* find, Mike. His landlady said he was on the quiet side because he was too stupid to talk. He never complained about a thing and in all the time he was living there he never once had company."

No, he wouldn't talk too much if he was an M.V.D. agent. And he wouldn't have company for that matter, either. His kind of company was met at night and in the dark recesses of a building somewhere.

"Did you try the pie factory where he worked?"

"I did but I didn't get anywhere. The last few months he had been on deliveries and most of the guys who knew him were out selling pies. The manager told me he was a stupid egg who had to write everything down in order to remember it, but he did his job fairly well. The only driver I did see said something nasty when I mentioned Moffit and tried to date me."

The boy put on a good act. People aren't likely to get too friendly with somebody who's pretty stupid. I said. "When do the drivers leave the plant?"

"Eight A.M., Mike. Are you going back?"

"I think I'd better. Supposing you come along with me. I'll meet you on the street in front of the office about seven and that'll give us time to get over there and see some of them."

"Mike . . . what's so important about Charlie Moffit?"

"I'll tell you tomorrow."

Velda grunted her displeasure and said good night. I had hardly hung up when I heard the feet in the hall and my doorbell started to yammer. Just in case, I yanked the .45 out and dropped it in my pocket where I could keep my hand around it.

The gun wasn't necessary at all. It was the boys from the papers, four of them. Three were on the police beat and the fourth was Marty Kooperman. He wore a faint, sardonic smile that was ready to disbelieve any lie I told.

85

"Well, the Fourth Estate. Come on in and don't stay too long." I threw the door open.

Bill Cowan of the *News* grinned and pointed to my pocket. "Nice way to greet old friends, Mike."

"Isn't it. Come on in."

They made a straight line for the refrigerator, found it empty, but uncovered a fresh bottle of whisky that I had been saving and helped themselves. All but Marty. He closed the door himself and stood behind me.

"We hear you got shot at, Mike."

"You heard right, friend. They missed."

"I'm thinking that I could say 'too bad' and mean it."

"What's your bitch, Marty! I've been shot at before. How come you're on the police run?"

"I'm not. I came along for the ride when I heard what happened." He paused. "Mike . . . for once come clean. Has this got to do with Lee Deamer?"

The boys in the kitchen were banging their first drinks down. I had that much time at least. I said, "Marty, don't worry about your idol. Let's say that this happened as a result of my poking into something that I *thought* was connected with Deamer. He doesn't figure into it in any way."

Marty took in a breath and let it out slowly. He twisted his hat in his hands then flipped it on the coat rack. "Okay, Mike, I'll take your word for it."

"Suppose it had to do with Lee, what then, chum?"

His lips tightened over a soft foice. "We'd have to know. They're out to get Lee any way they can and there aren't many of us who can stop them."

I scowled at him. "Who's us?"

"Your Fourth Estate, Mike. Your neighbors. Maybe even you if you knew what we knew."

That was all we had time for. The boys came charging back with fresh drinks and pencils ready. I led them inside to the living room and sat down. "Shoot, laddies. What's on your mind?"

"The shooting, Mike. Good news item, ya know."

"Yeah, great news. Tomorrow the public gets my picture and another lurid account of how that Hammer character conducts a private war on a public thoroughfare and I'll get an eviction notice from my landlord and a sudden lack of clients."

Bill laughed and polished his drink off. "Just the same, it's news. We got some of it from headquarters but we want the story straight from you. Hell, man, look how lucky you are. You get to tell your side of it while the others can't say a word. Come on, give."

"Sure, I'll give." I lit up a Lucky and took a deep drag on it. "I was walking home and . . ."

"Where were you?"

"Movies. So just as I . . ."

"What movie?"

I showed him my teeth in a lopsided grin. That was an easy one. "Laurance Theatre. Bum show."

Marty showed me his teeth back. "What was playing, Mike?" He was the only one not ready to take notes.

I started in on as much of the picture as I had seen and he stopped me with his hand. "That's enough. I saw it myself. Incidentally, have you still got your stub?"

Marty should have been a cop. He knows damn well that most men have an unconscious habit of dropping the things in their pockets. I pulled out an assortment and handed him one. He took it while the other boys watched, wondering what the hell it was all about. He picked up the phone, called the theatre and gave them the number on the ticket, asking if it had been sold that day. They said it had been and Marty hung up sheepishly. I let go my breath, glad that he hadn't asked what time. He wasn't such a good detective after all.

"Go on," he said.

"That's all. I was coming home when the punks in the car started to blast. I didn't get a look at any of 'em."

Bill said, "You on a case now?"

"If I was I wouldn't say so anyhow. What else?"

One of the boys from a tabloid wrinkled his nose at my story. "Come on, Mike, break down. Nobody took a shot at you without a reason."

"Look, pal, I have more enemies than I have friends. The kind of enemies I make go around loaded. Take a check on most known criminals and you'll find people who don't like me."

"In other words, we don't get a story," Bill said.

"In other words," I told him, ". . . yes. Want another drink?"

At least that was satisfactory. When they had the bottom of the bottle showing I whistled to stop their jabbering and got them together so I could get in a last word. "Don't any of you guys try tagging me around hoping for a lead about this. I'm not taking anything without paying it back. If a story crops up I'll let you in on it, meantime stick to chasing ambulances."

"Aw, Mike."

"No, 'Aw,' pally. I'm not kidding around about it, so stay out of my way."

As long as the bottle was empty and I wouldn't give with a yarn, they decided that there wasn't much sense in sticking around. They went out the door in a bunch with Marty trailing along in the rear. He said so long ruefully, his eyes warning me to be careful.

I spread the slats of the blinds apart and watched them all climb into a beat-up coupé and when I was sure they were gone for the night I took off my clothes and climbed into the shower.

I took a hot and a cold, brushed my teeth, started to put away my tools and the bell rang again. I damned a few things in general and the Fourth Estate in particular for not making sure all the boys were there when they started their inquisition. Probably a lone reporter who got the flash late and wanted to know all about it. I wrapped a towel around my lower half and made wet tracks from the bathroom to the front door.

She stood there in the dim light of the hall not knowing whether to be startled, surprised or shocked. I said, "Goddamn!"

She smiled hesitantly until I told her to come in and made a quick trip back for a bathrobe. Something had happened to Linda Holbright since the last time I had seen her and I didn't want to stand there in a towel while I found out what it was.

When I got back to the living room she was sitting in the big chair with her coat thrown over the back. This time she didn't have on a sack suit and you knew what was underneath it. It wasn't "probably nothing" either. It was a whole lot of something that showed and she wasn't making any bones about it. The angles seemed to be gone from her face and her hair was different. Before it was hair. Now it was a smooth wavy mass that trailed across her shoulders. She still wasn't pretty, but a guy didn't give a damn about that when there was a body like hers under her face.

Because of a smile she had gone to a hell of a lot of trouble. She must have taken her one asset to a perfectionist and let him build a dress around it. I think it was a dress. Paint would have done the same thing. There wasn't anything on underneath to spoil the effect and that showed. She was excited as hell and that showed too.

I was thinking that it could be very nice if she had only come a little sooner before I knew that Ethel had told what she had found in my wallet. Linda smiled at me tentatively as I sat down opposite her and lit up a smoke. I smiled back and started thinking again. This time there was a different answer. Maybe they were playing real cute and sent her in for the kicker. Maybe they had figured that their little shooting deal might get messed up and sent her around to get the score on me.

It made nice thinking because that was the way they worked and I didn't feel sorry for her any more. I got up and moved to the couch and told her to come over. I made her a drink and it must have been her first drink because she choked on it.

I kissed her and it must have been her first kiss, but she didn't choke on it. She grabbed me like the devil was inside her, bit me twice on the neck then pushed back to look at me to be sure this was happening to her.

There was no softness to her body. It was tense with the pain that was pleasure, oddly resilient under my hands. She closed her eyes, smothering the leaping fire to glowing coals. She fought to open them halfway and when she saw that I had been burnt by their flame she smiled a twisted smile as if she was laughing at herself.

If she was going to, she should have asked me then. Any woman should know when a man is nothing but a man and when he'll promise or tell anything. I knew all those things too and it didn't do me any good because I was still a man.

She asked nothing. She said, "This . . . is the first time . . . I ever . . ." and stopped there with the words choking to a hoarse whisper in her throat. She made me feel like a goddam heel. She hadn't known about Ethel's little stunt because she had been too busy getting prettied up for me.

I was going to make her put her coat on and tell her to get the hell out of there and learn more about being a woman before she tried to act like one. I would have done just that until I thought a little further and remembered that she was new to the game and didn't know when to ask the questions but figured on trying anyway. So I didn't say a damn thing.

Her hand did something at her back and the dress that looked like paint peeled off like paint with a deliberate slowness that made me go warm all over.

And she still asked nothing except to be shown how to be a woman.

She wouldn't let me go to the door with her later. She wanted to be part of the darkness and alone. Her feet were a soft whisper against the carpet and the closing of the door an almost inaudible click.

I made myself a drink, had half of it and threw the rest

away. I had been right the first time and went back to feeling like a heel. Then it occurred to me that now that she had a little taste of life maybe she'd go out and seek some different company for a change.

I stopped feeling like a heel, made another drink, finished it and went to bed.

The alarm woke me up at six, giving me time to shower and shave before getting dressed. I grabbed a plate of bacon and eggs in a diner around the corner then hopped in my car and drove downtown to pick up Velda. She was standing in front of the building tucked inside a dark gray business suit, holding her coat open with her hand on her hip.

A newsboy was having trouble trying to watch her and hawk his editions too. I pulled in at the curb and tooted the horn. "Let's go, sugar."

When she climbed in next to me the newsboy sighed. "Early, isn't it?" she grinned.

"Too damned."

"You were going to tell me something today, Mike."

"I didn't say when."

"One of those deals. You're a fine one." She turned her head and looked out the window.

I tugged at her arm and made her look back at me. "I'm sorry, Velda. It doesn't make nice conversation. I'll give it to you all at once when we get back. It's important to me not to talk about it right now. Mind?"

Maybe she saw the seriousness in my eyes. She smiled and said all right, then turned on the radio so we could have some music on our way across the bridge to Brooklyn where Mother Switcher had her pie factory.

Mother Switcher turned out to be a short, squat guy with long handlebar whiskers and eyebrows that went up and down like window shades. I asked him if I could speak to a few of his drivers and he said, "If you're a union organizer it's no good. All my boys already belong to a union and get paid better'n union wages besides."

I said I was no organizer. "So what is it then?"

"I want to find out about a guy named Moffit. He worked for you."

"That dope! He owe you money?"

"Not exactly."

"Sure. Go talk to the boys, only don't stop their work."

I said thanks and took Velda with me when I went around behind the building where the trucks were lined up for their quota of pies. We waited until the first truck was filled then buttonholed the driver. He gave Velda a big smile and tipped his cap.

She took it from there. "You knew Charlie Moffit, didn't you?"

"Yeah, sure, lady. What's he done now, crawled out of his grave?"

"I imagine he's still there, but tell me, what was he like?"

The guy frowned and looked at me for the first time. "I don't get it," he grunted.

I flashed my buzzer. So did Velda. "Now I get it," he said. "Was he in trouble?"

"That's what we want to find out. What was he like?"

He leaned against his truck and chewed on a match. "Well, I'll tell ya. Charlie was a queer duck." He tapped his head and made a screwy face. "Not all there, ya know. We were forever playing all kinds of gags on him. The dope would fall for 'em too. He was always losing something. Once it was his change bag and once it was a whole load of pies. He said some kids got him in a ball game and while he played they swiped his pies. Ever hear of anything like that?"

"No, I didn't," Velda laughed.

"That wasn't all, either. He was a mean bast . . . son-of-a-gun. Once we caught him trying to set fire to a cat. One of the boys slugged him."

It didn't sound right, that picture of Charlie Moffit. I was thinking while Velda popped the questions. Some of the other men came over and added a little something that distorted the picture even more. Charlie liked women and booze. Charlie molested kids in the street. Charlie was real bright for long periods then he'd get drunk and seem to fall into a conscious coma when he'd act like a kid. He wasn't right in his dome. He had rocks in his head. He sure liked the women, though.

I took Velda out of there and started back to Manhattan, my head aching from thoughts that were too big for it. I had to squint to watch the traffic and hunch over the wheel to be sure I knew where I was going. Away in the back of my mind that devilish unseen conductor was warming up his orchestra for another of those wild symphonies. I must be mad, I thought, I must be mad. I don't think like I used to. The little things won't come through anymore and it was the little things falling into place that made big things.

My mind rambled on until Velda said, "We're here."

The attendant was waving me into the parking lot. I took my ticket and handed him the keys while she flagged a cab. All the way to the office I sat with my eyes closed and kept the curtains down on the orchestra that was trying so hard to play. Whoever was at the drums wouldn't give up. He kept up a steady beat, thumping his drum with a muted stick, trying to make me open the curtain.

Velda brought out the bottle and handed it to me. I stared at the glass, filled it and drank it down. She offered me another and I shook my head. I had to sit down. I wanted to sit down and pull something over my head to shut out the light and the sound.

"Mike." Velda ran her fingers through my hair.

"What is it, kid?" My voice didn't sound right.

"If you tell me I might be able to help you." I opened my eyes and looked at her. She had her coat off and her breasts rose high against the folds of the blouse. She pulled up the big chair and sat down, her legs flashing in the light that streamed through the window. They were beautiful legs, long, alive with smooth muscles that played through the tight fabric of her dress as she moved. It was so easy to love that woman. I ought to try it more often. It was mine whenever I wanted it.

I closed my eyes again.

There wasn't any answer or any special way to tell her. I sat there with my eyes closed and gave it to her as it happened, bit by bit. I told her how I killed on the bridge. I told her about Marty and almost all about Ethel. I told her everything that happened and waited to see what she would say.

A minute went by. I opened my eyes and saw that Velda was watching me and there was no shame, no terror in her face. She believed in me. She said, "It doesn't make sense, Mike."

"It doesn't at that," I said tiredly. "There's a flaw in it that I can see. Do you see it too?"

"Yes. Charlie Moffit."

"That's right. The man with a present and no past. Nobody knows him or knows where he comes from. He's just a present."

"Almost ideal for an MVD operative."

"That's right again. Almost. Where's the flaw?"

Velda's fingers made a little tap-tap against the arm of the chair. "The act was too nearly perfect. It was too good to be anything but true."

"Roger. Charlie Moffit was anything but MVD. I thought those Reds were figuring me to be the man who took his place. I was wrong. I was impersonating the wrong dead man. The boy on the bridge was MVD. Pat handed it to me on a platter but I let it slip by. His only identifiable mark was his bridge-work because he had a stainless-steel tooth. There's only one country where they use stainless steel for teeth . . . the U.S.S.R. Fat boy was an imported killer, a checkrein on other agents in this country. Do you know how they knew he was dead?"

"Not from the sketch in the papers. He didn't have any fingerprints, either."

"They wouldn't have found them if he did. I forgot to tell you, but I wore his fingertips to the bone on the concrete before I threw him over."

Velda bit her lip and shuddered. She said "Mike!" too softly.

"No, the reason they knew he was dead was because he dropped out of sight. I don't think they got the connection until later when some smart apple started to check the unidentified bodies in the morgue. Pat said they sent dental charts out. One of those that received them could have recognized what that stainless-steel tooth meant and there it was."

"But they knew he was dead the next night . . . or so you supposed."

"Uh-huh. Fat boy didn't check in. They must have a system for those things. There was only one answer if he didn't check in. He was dead. The dental charts only verified it."

"What must they think? Why . . ."

I kept my voice low so I wouldn't get boiling mad again. "They think it was a dirty democratic conspiracy. It was all too secret to be normal. They think it was our government playing them dirty. They're the only ones who are supposed to be able to kick you under the table."

Velda said something dirty and she wasn't smiling.

I went on: "The other night there was a new note in the party. Something happened to a courier of theirs, something about documents. They are missing. The party is very upset, the poor devils."

Velda came up out of her seat, her face tight as a drumhead. "They're at it again, Mike. Government documents and double-dealing. Damn it, Mike, why do these things have to happen?"

"They happen because we're soft. We're honorable."

"Did they say what they were?"

"No. I gathered they were pretty important."

"They must be."

"Velda, there's a lot of things that are important that we give away for free. Do you know what they were doing one night? They had a pile of technical journals and flying mags you can pick up on any newsstand. They were photographing the stuff onto microfilm for shipment back. A good intelligence man can pick out a lot of data from photos. They take a bit here and a bit there until the picture is complete and bingo, they have something we're trying to keep under the hat."

"But documents, Mike. That's government stuff! That's something the FBI should know about."

"I know, I know. Maybe they do. Maybe they know they're missing and suspect where they've gone. Maybe they don't know because the documents were photostats. They're gone and that's what counts. I'm in a muddle because they found me out and now I can't do any more snooping. They'll be looking for me with a vengeance now. They tried to kill me last night and . . ."

"Mike!"

"Oh, you didn't hear about that. You should read the papers. There's six lines about it on page four. They didn't even print my picture. Yeah, they know me now and it's every man for himself. The next time I'll start the shooting and I won't miss."

Velda had her hand over her mouth, her teeth clamped on a fingernail. "God, you get into some of the most horrible scrapes! I do wish you'd be careful." Her eyes got a little wet and she got mad at herself. "You won't tell anybody anything and you won't ask for help when you need it most. Mike . . . please . . . there are times when you have to let somebody else in on things."

I could feel my lip curling. "Sure, Velda, sure. I'll tell everybody that I go around killing people just like that. It's easy to say, but I'm the guy who's supposed to be a menace to society. Hell, I'll take it my way and the public can lump it."

She wiped away a tear that was feeling its way down her cheek. "He shouldn't have done that to you, Mike."

"Who?"

"The judge."

I swore violently and my voice was hoarse.

"Are you . . . going to keep looking?"

I nodded my head. "Indirectly, yes. I'm still on a case for Lee Deamer."

Velda's head snapped up. "Mike . . . that's it!"

"What?"

"The documents! Charlie Moffit was the courier they spoke about! He was carrying those documents the night Oscar attacked and killed him! Oscar must have taken them from him."

"Damn!" The word exploded out of me. Of course, of course! the pocket that was ripped out of his coat! I shot Velda a grin that had "thanks" written on it. "It comes clear, kid, real clear. Oscar came to town to bleed Lee and he wouldn't bleed. So he goes out and kills a guy hoping to be identified as Lee, knowing damn well Lee would have an alibi and it would just make sensational reading for the public. He figured that would bring Lee to heel when he asked for money again. The gimmick came when he killed the guy. The papers must have stuck out of his pocket and Oscar grabbed them. When he realized what they were he saw the ideal way to bring Lee around. That's what he hinted at to Lee over the phone. If Lee brought in the cops and anything happened to him, the presence of those papers was to be attributed to Lee."

Velda was white, dead-white and her breathing came too fast. "It's rotten, Mike. Good heavens, if it ever gets out . . ."

"Yeah, Lee is finished even if he *can* prove himself innocent."

"Oh, no!"

"Beautiful. No matter what happens the Commies win. If they get the documents they probably have something juicy for cruddy Uncle Joe. If they don't and somebody else finds them, their worst enemy is yanked off their necks."

"Mike . . . it can't happen!"

"Now do I go it alone, Velda? Now do I take it by myself?"

"Yes. You . . . and me. The bastards. The dirty, filthy red bastards!" They should see her now, I was thinking. Gladow, the general, the boys in the Kremlin should see her now and they'd know what they were getting into. They'd see the face of beauty that had a kill-lust in every beautiful line and they'd stick inside their cold, walled-in city and shake in their shoes!

"When do we start, Mike?"

"Tonight. Be here at nine sharp. We'll see if we can find what Oscar did with those papers." She sat back in the chair and stared at the wall.

I picked up the phone and dialed Pat's number. He came on with, "Homicide, Captain Chambers speaking."

"Mike, pal. Any new corpses today?"

"Not yet. You didn't shoot straight enough. When are you coming in to explain about last night? I went to bat for you and I want a report and not a lot of subterfuge."

"I'm practically on my way now. I'll drop by your office and pick you up for lunch."

"Okay. Make it snappy."

I said I would and cradled the receiver. Velda was waiting for orders. "Stay here," I told her. "I have to see Pat and I'll call you when I'm finished. In case I don't call or come back, be here at nine."

"That's all?"

"That's all," I repeated. I tried to look stern like a boss should, but she grinned and spoiled it. I had to kiss her good-by before she'd let me go. "There's no telling if I'll see you alive again," she laughed. Then she slapped her hand over her mouth and her eyes went wide. "What am I saying?"

"I still have a couple of lives left, kid. I'll save one for you, so don't worry." I grinned again and went out the door.

Downstairs I got tired of waiting for a cab so I walked the half mile to the lot. A car in the city could be a pain in the butt sometimes. But what the hell, it was a nice day for a change and the air felt fairly fresh if a bus or something didn't go by.

I picked up my keys when I handed over the ticket and found my heap. I was in second and heading toward the gate when I saw that the boy had cleaned off my windows, and jammed on my brakes to flip him a quarter. That two-bits saved my skin. The truck that had been idling up the street had jumped ahead to intercept me broadside, saw I was stopping and tried to get me by swerving onto the driveway and off again.

Metal being ripped out by the roots set up a shriek and the car leaped ahead before there was a nasty snap that disengaged it from the body of the truck. I let out a string of curses because the jolt had wedged me up against the wheel and I couldn't get my rod out. By the time I was back in the seat the truck was lost in the traffic.

The attendant yanked the door open, his face ashen. "Gawd, mister, you hurt?"

"No, not this time."

"Them crazy fools! Gawd, they coulda killed ya!" His teeth started to chatter violently.

"They sure coulda." I got out of the car and walked around the front. One side of the bumper had been ripped clear off the frame and stuck out like an oversize L.

"Boy, that was close, awright. I seen 'em come up the street but I never give 'em a thought. Them crazy fools musta been fooling around the cab and hit the gas. They never stopped. You want I should call a cop?"

I kicked the bumper and it all but fell loose. "Forget it. They got away by now. Think you can get this bumper off?"

"Sure, I got some tools. Only two bolts holding it on anyway."

"Okay, take it off and pick one up for this model at a garage somewhere. I'll fix you up for your trouble."

He said, "Yessir, mister. Sure," and ran after his tools. I sat on the fender and smoked a cigarette until he finished then passed him two bucks and told him not to forget a new bumper. He said he wouldn't forget.

When I pulled away I looked up and down the one-way street just to be sure. It happened twice. I said it wouldn't but it happened again anway. They must have had a tail on me when I came out of the office and saw a beautiful chance to nail me cold. That truck would have made hash of me if it had connected right.

They were going to all kinds of trouble, weren't they? That made me important. You have to be important if you were better off dead. The judge should like that.

Pat was sitting with his back to the door looking out the window at the city when I came in. He swung around in his chair and nodded hello. I pulled a chair up and sat down with my feet propped up on his desk. "I'm all set, Captain. Where are the bright lights?"

"Cut it out, Mike. Start talking."

"Pat, so help me, you know almost everything right now."

"Almost. Give me the rest."

"They tried again a little while ago. This time it was a truck and not bullets."

The pencil in Pat's hand tapped the desk. "Mike, I'm not a complete fool. I play along with you because we're friends, but I'm a cop, I've been a cop a long time, and I know my business. You're not telling me people are shooting you up in the streets without a reason."

"Hell, they gotta have a reason."

"Do you know what it is?" He was drawing to the end of his patience.

I took my feet off the desk and leaned toward him. "We've been through this before, Pat. I'm not a complete fool either. In your mind every crime belongs to the police, but there are times when an apparent crime is a personal affront and it isn't very satisfying not to take care of it yourself. That's how I feel about it."

"So you know then."

"I think I know. There's nothing you can do about it so quit being a cop and let's get back to being friends."

Pat tried to grin, but didn't put it over too well. "Are you straightened out with Lee?"

My feet went up on the desk again. "He gave me a tidy sum to poke around. I'm busy at it."

"Good, Mike. Be sure you make a clean sweep." He dropped his head and passed his hand over his hair. "Been reading the papers lately?"

"Not too much. I noticed one thing . . . they're pulling for Deamer in nearly every editorial column. One sheet reprints all his speeches."

"He's giving another tonight. You should go hear him."

"I'll leave that stuff up to you, chum. There's too much dribble and not enough pep talk at those meetings."

"The devil there isn't! Take the last one I was at. We had supper with the customary speeches afterward, but it was the small talk later that counted. Lee Deamer made the rounds speaking to small groups and he gave them the real stuff. It was easier for him to talk that way. Most of us had never met him until that time, but when he spoke we were sold completely. We have to have that guy in, Mike. No two ways about it. He's strong. He can't be pushed or bullied. You wouldn't know it to look at him, but he's the strength that this nation will be relying on some day."

"That was the same night Oscar pulled the stops out, wasn't it?"

"That's right. That's why we didn't want any of it to reach the public. Even a lie can be told to give the people the wrong impression."

"You've sure gotten a big interest in politics, Pat."

"Hell, why not? I'll be glad to go back to being a cop again instead of a tool in some politician's workshop. Lee gave a talk over the radio last night. You know what he did?"

I said no. I had been too busy to listen.

"He's brought some of his business sense into politics. He sat down with an adding machine and figured things up. He wanted to know why it cost the state ten million for it to have a job done when any private contractor could do it for six. He quoted names and places and figures and told the public that if he was elected his first order would be to sign warrants of arrest for certain political joes who are draining the state dry."

"And?"

Pat looked at the desk and glared. "And today I heard that

the big push comes soon. Lee has to be smeared any way at all."

"It won't happen, Pat."

I shouldn't have used that tone. His head jerked up and his eyes were tiny bright spots watching me from tight folds of skin. His hand closed into a fist slowly and tightened until the cords bulged out. "You know something, Mike, by God, you know something!"

"I do?" I couldn't make it sound funny.

Pat was ready to split wide open. "Mike, you're in on it. Damn it, you went and found something. Oh, I know you . . . no talking until you're ready, but this isn't a murder that involved only a handful of people . . . this is something that takes in a whole population and you better not tip the apples over."

He stood up, his hands on the edge of the desk for support. He spat the words out between his teeth and meant every one. "We've been friends, Mike. You and I have been in and out of a lot of things together and I've always valued your friendship. And your judgment. Just remember this, if I'm guessing right and you're in on something that might hurt Lee and won't talk about it, and if that something *does* hurt Lee, then we can forget about being friends. Is that clear?"

"That's clear, Pat. Would it make you feel better if I told you that your line of reasoning is a little off? You're getting teed off at me when you ought to be teeing off on some of the goddamn Commies we got loose in this city."

His face had a shrewd set to it. "So they're part of it too." Muscles stuck out in lumps along his jaws. Let him think how he liked.

"Nothing will happen to Lee," I said. "At least nothing that I'm concerned with." This time I got some conviction in my voice. Pat stopped glaring and sat down.

He didn't forget the subject. "You still have those green cards on your mind?"

"Yeah, I have. I don't like what they mean, and you shouldn't either."

"I hate everything they stand for. I'm sorry we have to tolerate it. We ought to do what they would have done a hundred years ago."

"Stop talking nonsense. You're in America now."

"Sure I am, and I want to stay here. If you want a democracy you have to fight for it. Why not now before it's too late? That's the trouble, we're getting soft. They push us all around the block and we let them get away with it!"

"Calm down, will you." I hadn't realized that I was banging on his desk until he rapped my knuckles. I sat down.

"What did you do about Oscar?" I asked.

"What could we do? Nothing. It's over, finished."

"And his personal effects?"

"We went through them and there was nothing to be found. I posted a man to check his place in case any mail came in. I had the idea that Oscar might have mailed something to himself. I took the man off today when nothing showed."

I had to struggle to hold my face straight. Pat had the place watched! Neat, very neat. If we weren't the only ones who wanted to go through that apartment then we wouldn't be going in on a cold deal. Nobody else could have gotten there either!

I reached for a butt and lit it. "Let's go out to eat, Pat."

He grabbed his coat off the rack and locked the door to the office. On the way out I thought of something I should have thought of before and had him open it up again. I picked up the phone and called the office. Velda answered with a silky hello.

I said, "Mike, honey. Look, have you emptied the wastebasket by my desk yet?"

"No, there wasn't anything to empty."

"Go look if there's a cigarette pack there. Don't touch it."

She dropped the phone and I heard her heels clicking along the floor. In a moment she was back. "It's there, Mike."

"Swell. Take it out of there without touching it if you can. Put it in a box and have a boy run it down to Pat right away."

Pat watched me curiously. When I hung up he said, "What is it?"

"An almost empty pack of butts. Do me a favor and lift the prints off it. You'll find a lot of mine on them and if I'm lucky you'll find some others too."

"Whose?"

"Hell, how do I know? That's why I want you to get the prints. I need an identification. That is, if we're still friends."

"Still friends, Mike," he grinned. I socked him on the arm and started for the door again.

CHAPTER SEVEN

THAT NIGHT the nation got the report on the 6:15 P.M. news broadcast. There had been a leak in the State Department and the cat was out of the bag. It seemed that we had had a secret. Somebody else was in on it now. The latest development in the process for the annihilation of man had been stolen. Supposedly secret files had been rifled and indications pointed to the duplication of the secret papers. The FBI was making every effort to track down the guilty parties.

I threw my cigarette against the wall and started swearing until I ran out of words. Then I started over again. The commentator droned on repeating what he had already said and I felt like screaming at him to tell the world who took those damn papers. Tell 'em it was the same outfit who tried to make a mockery of our courts and who squirmed into the government and tried to bring it down around our necks. Tell everybody who did it. You know you want to say it; what are you afraid of?

There wasn't any doubt of it now, those documents the general had been so anxious to get hold of were the ones we were looking for ourselves! My guts were all knoted up in a ball and my head felt like a machineshop was going on inside it. Here I had the whole lousy situation right in my hands and I had to keep it there.

Me. Mike Hammer. I was up in the big leagues now. No more plain and simple murders. I was playing ball with the big boys and they played rough. The end justified the means, that was their theory. Lie, steal, kill, do anything that was necessary to push a political philosophy that would enslave the world if we let it. Great!

Nice picture, Judge, a beautiful picture of a world in flames. You must be one of the normal people who get the trembles when they read the papers. A philosophy like that must give you the willies. What are you thinking now . . . how that same secret that was stolen might be the cause of your death? And what would you say if you knew that I was the only one who might be able to stop it in time? Okay,

*Judge, sit your fanny in a chair and relax. I have a little
philosophy of my own. Like you said, it's as bad as theirs.
I don't give a damn for a human life any more, even my own.
Want to hear that philosophy? It's simple enough. Go after the
big boys. Oh, don't arrest them, don't treat them to the
dignity of the democratic process of courts and law . . .
do the same thing to them that they'd do to you! Treat 'em to
the unglorious taste of sudden death. Get the big boys and
show them the long road to nowhere and then one of those
stinking little people with little minds will want to get big.
Death is funny, Judge, people are afraid of it. Kill 'em left
and right, show 'em that we aren't so soft after all. Kill, kill,
kill, kill! They'll keep away from us then!*

Hell, it was no use trying to smoke. I'd light up a butt and
take a drag then throw it away because my fingers weren't
steady enough to hold it. I went inside to the bedroom and
took my .45 off the top of the dresser to clean it for the
second time. It felt good, feeling the cold butt setting up
against the palm of my hand. The deadly noses of the slugs
showing in the clip looked so nice and efficient.

They liked to play dirty, I was thinking. Let's make it real
dirty. I thumbed the slugs out, laying them in a neat row,
then took a penknife and clipped the ends off the noses. That
was real dirty. They wouldn't make too much of a hole
where they went in, but the hole on the other side would be
a beaut. You could stick your head in and look around without getting blood on your ears. I put the gun together, shoved
the slugs back in the clip and strapped on the sling. I was
ready.

It was a night to give you the meemies. Something happened to the sky and a slow, sticky fog was rolling in
from the river. The cold was penetrating, indecisive as to
whether to stay winter or turn into spring. I turned the collar
of my coat up around my ears and started walking down the
street. I didn't lose myself in any thoughts this time. My eyes
looked straight ahead, but they saw behind me and to either
side. They picked up figures hurrying to wherever it was they
were going, and the twin yellow eyes of the cars that rolled in
the street, boring holes in the fog. My ears picked up footsteps,
timed their pace and direction, then discarded them for other
sounds.

I was waiting for them to try again.

When I reached the corner I crossed over to my car, passed
it, then walked back again. I opened the door, felt for the
handle that unlocked the hood and took a quick check of the
engine. I wasn't in the mood to get myself blown all over

the neighborhood when I started the car. The engine was clean. So was the rest of the heap.

A car came by and I drew out behind it, getting in line to start the jaunt downtown to the office. The fog was thicker there and the traffic thinner. The subways were getting a big play. I found a place to park right outside the office and scraped my wheels against the curb then cut the engine. I sat there until a quarter to nine trying to smoke my way through a deck of Luckies. I still had a few to go when I went inside, put my name in the night register and had the elevator operator haul me up to my office floor.

At exactly nine P.M. a key turned in the lock and Velda came in. I swung my feet off the desk and walked out to the outside office and said hello. She smiled, but her heart wasn't in it. "Did you catch the news broadcast, kid?"

Her lips peeled back. "I heard it. I didn't like it."

"Neither did I, Velda. We have to get them back."

She opened her coat and perched on the edge of the desk. Her eyes were on the floor, staring at a spot on the carpet. She wasn't just a woman now. An aura of the jungle hung around her, turning her into a female animal scenting a game run and anxious to be in on the kill. "It can't stop there, Mike."

I dropped my butt and ground it into the carpet. "No, it can't." I knew what she was thinking and didn't like it.

"The papers aren't all. As far as they can go is to checkmate us. They'll try again."

"Will they?"

Her eyes moved up to meet mine, but that was all. "We can stop them, Mike."

"I can, sugar. Not you. I'm not shoving you into any front lines."

Her eyes still held mine. "There's somebody in this country who directs operations for them. It isn't anyone we know or the FBI knows or the party knows. It's somebody who can go and come like anybody else and not be interfered with. There are others who take orders and are equally dangerous because they represent the top of the chain of command and can back up their orders with force if necessary. How long will it take us to get them all, the known and the unknown?"

"It might take *me* a long time. Me, I said."

"There's a better way, Mike. We can get all those we know and any we suspect and the rest will run. They'll get the hell out of here and be afraid to come back."

It was almost funny, the way her reasoning followed mine. "Just me, Velda," I said.

Her head came up slowly and all I could think of was a big cat, a great big, luxurious cat leaning against the desk. A cat with gleaming black hair darker than the night and a hidden body of smooth skin that covered a wealth of rippling, deadly muscles that were poised for the kill. The desk light made her teeth an even row of merciless ivory, ready to rip and tear. She was still grinning, but a cat looks like it's grinning until you see its ears laid flat back against its head.

"Mike, there are men and women in this country. They made it together even when it was worse than now. Women learned how to shoot and shoot straight. They learned fast, and knew how to use a gun or a knife and use it right when the time came. I said we'd do it together. Either that or I take the whole thing to Pat."

I waited a long minute before I said, "Okay, it's us. I want it that way anyhow."

Velda slid off the desk and reached for my hand. I squeezed it hard, happy as hell I had the sense to realize that I knew what I wanted at last. She said it very simply. "I love you, Mike."

I had her in my arms, searched for her mouth and found it, a warm mouth with full, ripe lips that burned into my soul as they fused with mine. I tasted the love she offered and gave it back with all I had to give, crushing her until her breath came in short, quick jerks.

I held her face in my hands and kissed her eyes and her cheeks, listened to her moan softly and press herself closer and closer. I was lucky as hell and I knew it.

She opened her eyes when I held her off. I dropped my hand in my pocket and took out the box that I had picked up that afternoon. When I pressed the button the lid flew up and the sapphire threw back a perfect star. My fingers felt big and clumsy when I took it out and slipped it over her finger.

You don't have to speak at a time like that. Everything has been said and if anything remains it's written there in a silent promise your heart makes and that's all there is to it. Velda looked at it with a strange wonder for a long time before she kissed me again.

It was better than the last time.

It told her everything she wanted to know and no matter what happened now nothing would ever change.

"We have to go," I said.

She snapped out the lights while I waited at the door and

we went down the elevator together. The watchman gave me the okay sign, so I knew nobody had been near my car while I was gone. When we were back in the fog I told her about Pat's having kept a man on Oscar's house and she picked it right up.

"Maybe . . . maybe we'll be the first."

"I'm hoping that," I said.

"What will they look like?"

"I don't know. If Moffit had them in his pocket, then they were in a package or an envelope big enough to fit in there. It may be that we're barking up the wrong tree. They might have been on microfilm."

"Let's hope we're right."

About two blocks away I ran the car in between a couple of parked trucks and waved her out. "We're taking the long way around this time."

"Through the alley?"

"Uh-huh. I don't like the idea of using the front door. When we reach the opening between the buildings duck in and keep on going."

Velda felt for my hand and held on to it. For all the world we might have been just a couple of dopes out for a walk. The fog was a white tube all around us, but it could be hiding a lot of things beside us. We crossed the street, came up around the subway kiosk and walked in the protection of the wall, the two of us searching for the narrow passageway that led behind the buildings.

As it was, we almost passed it. I stepped in holding Velda's hand and the darkness swallowed us up. For two or three minutes we stood there letting our eyes accustom themselves to this deeper gloom, then edged forward slowly, picking our way through the trash that had accumulated over the years. Animals and people had made a barely perceptible path through the center of the litter and we followed it until we stood behind the building and could feel our way along the alley by sticking close to the rotted planking that formed the wall of the yards behind the houses.

Velda was fishing in her handbag and I told her, "No lights. Just keep looking for a pile of bottles. There's a door in the wall behind it and that's the place."

I tried to judge the distance from that other night and found little to remember. Soft furry things would squeal and run across our feet whenever we disturbed the junk lying around. Tiny pairs of eyes would glare at us balefully and retreat when we came closer. A cat moved in the darkness and trapped a pair of eyes that had been paying too much attention to us and the jungle echoed with a mad death cry.

Velda tugged my hand and pointed to the ground. "Here're the bottles, Mike." She dropped my hand to walk around them. "The door is still open."

I pushed her through into the yard and we held still, taking in the black shadow of the building. The back door still swung open on one hinge. How many people lived here, I thought. How long ago was it when this dirty pile of brick and mortar was a home besides being a house? I went up the short flight of steps and took the flashlight from my pocket.

Velda flashed hers on the wall beside the door, illuminating a printed square of cardboard tacked to the framework. It read, THIS BUILDING HAS BEEN CONDEMNED FOR OCCUPANCY. A paragraph explained why and a rubber stamp signature made it official.

Ha.

The air had a musty odor of decay that collected in the long hall and clung to the walls. There was a door that led to the cellar, but the stairs were impenetrable, piled high with an unbelievable collection of scrap. Velda opened the door to the room that faced the backyard and threw her spot around the walls. I looked in over her shoulder and saw a black, charred mass and the remains of some furniture. It must have been a year or more since that room had started to burn, and nobody had been in it since. It was amazing to me that the house still stood.

Halfway down the hall there was a doorframe but no door and the room was stacked with old bedframes, a few mattresses left to the fleas and nothing worth stealing. The next room was, or had been, Oscar's. I had my hand on the knob when Velda grabbed me and we froze there.

From somewhere in the upper recesses of the house came a harsh, racking cough and the sound of someone vomiting.

I heard Velda take a deep breath of relief. "Drunk," she said.

"Yeah." I went back to the door. A plain skeleton key unlocked it and we stepped inside, locking it again behind us. Velda went to the windows, and tucked the shade in so there would be no chance of our lights being seen from the outside. Then we started to take that room apart.

Oscar's effects were collecting dust in the police storeroom, but it was unlikely that they had been in his bag or among his clothes. If they had been I would have found them the first time. We peeled the covers off the bed, found nothing and put them back. We felt in the corners and under things. I even tore the molding off the wall and shoved my hand behind it. There was nothing there, either.

Velda was working her way along the rear wall. She called softly, "Mike, come here a minute."

I followed the track of light to where she was fiddling with some aged draperies that had been tacked to the wall in a vain attempt to give a tapestry effect. She had one side pulled away and was pointing to it. "There used to be a door here. It led to that storeroom on the other side."

"Umm. This house was a one-family job at one time."

"Do you suppose. . . ."

"That it's in there?" I finished. She nodded. "We better look. This room is as bare as a baby's spanked tail."

The two of us wormed out into the hall and shut the door. Velda led the way with her light and took a cautious step over the sill into the room beyond. From upstairs the coughing came again. I banged my shin against an iron bedpost and swore softly.

It only took ten minutes to go over that room, but it was long enough to see that nothing had been put in or taken out in months. A layer of dust covered everything; the junk was attached to the walls with thousands of spider webs. The only prints in the grime on the floor were those we had made ourselves.

I hated to say it; Velda hated to hear it. "Not a damn thing. Oscar never had those papers."

"Oh, Mike!" There was a sob in her voice.

"Come on, kid, we're only wasting time now."

The flashlight hung in her hand, the penny-sized beam a small, lonely spot on the floor, listlessly trying to add a bit of brightness to a night that was darker than ever now.

"All right, Mike," she said. "There must be other places for it to be."

The guy upstairs coughed again. We would have paid no attention to him except that we heard the thump of his feet hitting the floor then the heavy thud as he fell. The guy started cursing then was still.

It wasn't a conscious thing that held us back; we just stood there and listened, not scared, not worried, just curious and cautious. If we hadn't stopped where we were at the moment we did we would have walked right into the mouth of hell.

The front door opened and for a brief interval the Trench Coats were dimly silhouetted against the gray of the fog outside. Then the door closed and they were inside, motionless against the wall.

I did two things fast. I grabbed Velda and pulled out the .45.

Why did I breathe so fast? I hadn't done a thing and yet I wanted to pant my lungs out. They were on fire, my throat was on fire, my brain was on fire. The gun that I used to be able to hold so still was shaking hard and Velda felt it too. She slid her hand over mine, the one that squeezed her arm so hard it must have hurt, and I felt some of the tension leave me.

Velda wasn't shaking at all. Trench Coats moved and I heard a whispered voice. Something Velda did made a metallic snap. My brain was telling me that now it had come, the moment I had waited for. Trench Coats. Gladow and Company. The hammer and sickle backed up with guns. The general's boys.

They came for me! Even in the fog they had managed to follow me here and now they were ready to try again. *The third time they won't miss.* That was the common superstition, wasn't it? It was to be at close quarters and a crossfire with me in the middle.

I could feel my teeth grinding together. A hot wave of hate, so violent that it shook me from top to bottom, swept through my body. Who the hell were they supposed to be? Did they expect to come in and find me with my back to the door? Was I supposed to be another sap . . . the kind of guy who'd give people like them the old fighting chance . . . a gesture of sportsmanship? I should take a chance on dying like that?

They went in the room then, softly, but not so softly that my ears couldn't follow every step they took. I could hear their breathing coming hard, the scuffle of leather against wood. I even heard the catch of the flashlight when it snapped on.

Very slowly I jacked the hammer of the .45 back. My hand told Velda to stay there. Just stay there and shut up. I bent down and unlaced my shoes, stepped out of them and into the hall. I lay on my stomach looking into the room, the .45 propped on my forearm. The light of the flash made a circuit of the wall then stopped on the draperies that covered up the opening to the other room. Trench Coat who didn't have a flash stepped forward to pull the drapes down.

And Velda was in there waiting for me.

I said, "Looking for me, Martin?" The sudden shift of the flash and the lance of flame that spit from his gun came at the same time. I heard the bullets smack the wall over my head. He fired at the door where my belly should have been, mouthing guttural, obscene curses.

Then I shot him. I aimed a little below and inside the red eye of his gun barrel and over the blast of the .45 I heard his breath leave him in a wheezing shriek that died in a bubble of blood that came to his mouth. His rod went off once, a bullet ripped into the floor, and Trench Coat dropped.

The other one didn't stay in the room. I heard cloth rip, feet stumble and a heavy body slam against the wood. The other killer had gone into the room with Velda!

I was on my feet trying to decide. I had to decide! Good God, I had to get him before he saw her. If I went in through either door he'd get me and I had to go! I could feel him waiting for me, the darkness screening him completely. He knew I'd come and he knew he'd get me.

I walked toward the door. I didn't bother trying to be quiet.

I stepped into the doorway.

The crack of the gun was a flat noise that echoed once and was gone. There was no steak of flame, only that sudden, sharp sound and a peculiar hiss that seemed out of place. I felt no shock, no pain, only a sudden tensing of the muscles and a stillness that was nearly audible.

I must have caught it, I thought. It wasn't like this before. The last time it hurt. I tried to raise my hand and it came up slowly, effortlessly. In the room a gun clattered on the bare planking and was followed immediately by a soft thunk.

She seemed far away, so far away. "Mike?"

I couldn't get the breath out of my lungs at first. "You . . . all right, Velda?"

"I killed him, Mike."

Dear God, what was there to say? I reached for her and folded her against my chest feeling her sob softly. I grabbed her flash and threw it on Trench Coat. Martin Romberg lay on his face with a hole in his back. She must have held it right against his spine when she pulled the trigger. That's why I didn't see the flash.

I straightened Velda up and pulled her toward the door. "Come on. We can't stay here." I found my shoes and yanked them on without bothering to tie them.

It was easier going out. It always is. The fog was still there, rolling in over the walls, sifting down between the buildings. Our eyes, so long in the dark, could see things that were hidden before and we raced down that back alley heading for that narrow slit a block away from the house.

The curious had already started their pilgrimage toward the sound of the shooting. A police car whined through the night, its light a blinking eye that cleared the way. We lost ourselves in the throng, came out of it and found the car. Two more police cars passed us as we started to cut back to the land of the living on the other side of town.

Velda sat stiff and straight staring out the window. When I looked down she still held the gun in her hand. I took it away from her and laid it on the seat. "You can file another notch on it, kid. That makes two."

I gave it to her brutally hoping it might snap her out of it. She turned her head and I saw that her mouth had taken on a smile. She picked up that nasty little .32 automatic and dropped it in her handbag. The snap catch made the same metallic sound that I had heard back there in the room. "My conscience doesn't hurt me, Mike," she said softly.

I patted her hand.

"I was afraid I wouldn't be quick enough. He never saw me. He stood in the center of the room covering both entrances and I knew what he was waiting for and I knew you'd come after him. He would have killed you, Mike."

"I know, honey."

"He was standing close enough so I could reach out and put my gun right against him." Her lips tightened. "Is this how . . . you feel, Mike? Is it all right for me to feel like this? Not having a sensation of guilt?"

"I feel happy."

"So do I. Perhaps I shouldn't, Mike. Maybe I should feel ashamed and sinful, but I don't. I'm glad I shot him. I'm glad I had the chance to do it and not you. I wanted to, do you understand that?"

"I understand completely. I know how you feel because it's how I feel. There's no shame or sin in killing a killer. David did it when he knocked off Goliath. Saul did it when he slew his tens of thousands. There's no shame to killing an evil thing. As long as you have to live with the fact you might as well enjoy it."

This time Velda laughed easily. My mind turned to the judge and I could picture his face, disappointed and angry that my time still hadn't come. And we had the best alibi in the world. Self-defense. We had a gun license and they didn't. If it reached us we were still clear.

Velda said, "They were there after the same thing, weren't they?"

"What?"

She repeated it. I slammed the wheel with my hand and said something I shouldn't have. Velda looked at me, her forehead furrowed. "They were . . . weren't they?"

I shook my head in disgust at myself. "What a sap I am. Of course they were! I thought they were after me again and they were searching for those damn documents!"

"Mike! But how would they know? The papers never carried any news of Charlie Moffit's murder. They reported it, but that was all. How could they know?"

"The same way the public knew the documents were stolen. Look, it's been a good time since he was knocked off. Just about long enough for somebody to get a loose tongue and spill something. That's how they knew . . . there was a leak. Somebody said something they shouldn't have!"

"The witnessess. They'd be the ones. Didn't Pat say they were warned to keep quiet about it?"

" 'Advised' is the word," I said. "That doesn't make them liable to any official action. Damn it, why can't people keep their big mouths shut!"

Velda fidgeted in her seat. "It was too big to keep, Mike. You don't witness a murder and just forget about it."

"Ah, maybe you're right. Maybe I give people credit for having more sense than they actually have. Hell, the leak could just as well have come out of police headquarters too. It's too late now to worry about it. The damage is done."

Velda lost herself in her thoughts for a good five minutes. I stayed hunched over the wheel trying to see through the fog. "It wasn't there, Mike. If it wasn't there then it has to be somewhere else."

"Yeah."

"You looked around the place right after Oscar died. It wasn't among his things. The police must have looked too. Then we looked again. Do you think it could possibly be that Oscar didn't have them?"

"What else is there to think? Either that or he hid them outside his room."

"Doubtful, Mike. Remember one thing, if Oscar showed himself anywhere he would have been mistaken for Lee. He couldn't have done much fooling around."

I had to grin because the girl who was wearing my ring was so smart I began to feel foolish around her. I did pretty good for myself. I picked a woman who could shoot a guy just like that and still think straight. "Go on, Velda."

"So maybe Oscar never got those documents. Charlie's ripped pocket just happened when he fell. If Charlie was the courier, and if the documents he was carrying are missing, then Charlie must have them tucked away somewhere. Remember what the men at the pie factory said . . . that he was dopey for certain periods of time? He was forgetful? Couldn't he have. . . ."

I stopped her and took it from there myself. She had tapped it right on the nose.

"When, Mike?"

I glanced at her quickly. "When what?"

"When do we go trough his apartment?"

She was asking for more! Once in a night wasn't enough. "Not now," I told her. "Tomorrow's another day. Our dead friends won't be making a report tonight and the party won't be too anxious to make any more quick moves until they figure this one out first. We have time, plenty of time."

"No we don't."

I convinced her that we had by talking my head off all the way up to her apartment. When I let her out I only had one more thing to say. She waited, knowing well enough what was coming. "In case anyone asks, I was with you in your place all night, understand?"

"Can't we partially tell the truth?"

"Nope, we're engaged."

"Oh. Now I have to wait some more."

"Not long, kid, not too long. When this is all finished there'll be time for other things."

"I can wait."

"Good. Now hop upstairs and get to bed, but first, take that gun of yours and hide it somewhere. Put it where it can't be found until I tell you to take it out."

She leaned over and kissed me, a soft, light kiss that left my mouth tingling with the thought of what lay behind this girl who could be so completely lovable and so completely deadly. There were fires burning in her eyes that nothing could ever quench, but they asked me to try . . . to try hard.

I looked at her legs as she got out of the car and decided that I'd never see enough of them. They had been there all the time, mine any time I had wanted to ask and until now I never had the sense to ask. I had been stupid, all right. I was much smarter now. I waited until she was in the door before I turned the car around and crawled back to my own place.

It was late and I was tired. There had been too much in this one night again, I thought to myself. You get wound up like a watch spring, tighter and tighter until the limit is reached and you let go with a bang that leaves you empty and gasping.

When I locked the door I went directly to the closet and took down the box of parts and shells for the gun. I laid them out on the kitchen table and took the .45 apart piece by piece, cleaning and oiling every bit of it. I unwrapped the new barrel and put it in place, throwing the rest of the gun together around it. On second thought I changed the firing pin too. A microscope could pick up a lot of details from empty shell cases.

It took a half-hour to get the gun ready to go again. I shoved the old barrel and pin in a quart beer can, stuffed in some paper to keep it from rattling and dumped the works down the incinerator.

I was feeling pretty good when I crawled into the sack. Now let's see what would happen.

The alarm was about to give up when I finally woke up. There was nothing I wanted more than staying in bed, but I forced myself into a sitting position, fought a brief battle with the sheets and got my feet on the floor. A cold shower took the sleep out of my eyes and a plate of bacon and eggs put some life into my body.

I dressed and called Velda. She wasn't at home so I tried the office. She was there. I said, "How the devil do you do it?"

She laughed and came right back at me. "I'm still a working girl, Mike. Office hours are from eight to five, remember?"

"Any customers?"

"Nope."

"Any bills?"

"Nope."

"Love me?"

"Yup. Love me?"

"Yup. What a conversation. Any calls?"

"Yup. Pat called. He wants to see you. Lee Deamer called. He wants to see you, too."

I brightened up fast. "If they call back, tell them I'll check in. How about the papers?"

"Headlines, Mike. Big black headlines. It seems that a couple of rival gangs met up with each other in an old building over on the East Side. They forgot to carry their dead off when the battle was finished."

"Don't sound so smug. Did Pat mention anything about it?"

"No, but he will. He was pretty edgy with me."

"Okay, give him my love. I'll see you shortly." I hung up and laid out my working suit for the day. When I finished dressing I looked out the window and swore to myself. The

fog was gone, but a drizzle had come in on its heels and the
people on the street were bundled into coats trying to keep
warm. The winter was dying a hard death.

On the way to the office I stopped off at a saloon and saw
a friend of mine. I told him I wanted an unlicensed automatic of a certain make and .32 caliber, one that hadn't done
anything except decorate somebody's dresser drawer since it
was bought. My friend went to the phone and made two calls.
He came back, told me to wait a few minutes, served a few
customers at the bar, then went into the kitchen in the rear
and I heard his voice arguing for a while. He came back with
a package in his hand and said, "Twenty bucks, Mike."

I peeled off twenty, took the gun apart and removed the
barrel and the pin. The rest I told my friend to dump in with
his trash, thanked him and left. I stopped off at the office long
enough to hand the two parts to Velda and tell her to slip
them in her gun during her lunch hour. Then I went down
to see Pat.

As Velda said, he wasn't happy. He said, "Hell, Mike,"
but his eyes raked me up and down. "Sit," he said.

I sat down and picked the paper off his desk. The headlines
were big and black. There was a picture of the outside of the
house with an interior shot in the middle section with white
dotted lines to indicate where the bodies had been found.
"Real trouble, huh, Pat?"

"Yeah, I thought maybe you could explain some of it."

"Don't be silly."

"Been shooting your gun lately?"

"Yesterday, as a matter of fact. I fired one into some waste
right in my own apartment to check the ejector action.
Why?"

"A paraffin test is out of order then. Mind if I see your
gun?"

I said no and handed it over. Pat pressed a button on his
desk and one of the technicians came in. Pat handed him
the gun. "Get me a photograph of one of the slugs, Art."

"You're assuming a lot, aren't you, Pat?"

"I think so. Want to talk about it?"

"No, wait until you get your photograph."

He sat back and smiled and I read the papers. The two
men were identified as Martin Romberg and Harold Valleck.
They were good and dead. Both had prison records for various crimes and were suspected of being killed in a gang
brawl. The police were expecting early developments in the
crime. The reporters didn't have much to go on.

Art came back before I finished the funnies and handed

Pat an enlarged sheet that was covered with angle shots of the slug. He laid the gun on the desk. Pat smiled again and pulled another sheet from his desk drawer. There wasn't anything funny about the way he smiled. I looked at him with a frown covering up the grin that was trying to break through, lit a butt and went back to the paper and finished the funnies.

Pat said, "You're too smart to be dumb, Mike. That or you're clean and I'm stupid as hell." His face looked empty.

I had a nice speech all ready to take him down a peg or two when I realized that he was on the spot. "You mean they were supposed to match, is that it?"

He nodded. "Something like that. A .45 killed one of them. There were only three of us who knew about Oscar's being there."

"Were they after Oscar or just there?"

"Hell, I don't know, Mike. Murder isn't uncommon in that neighborhood. Ordinarily I wouldn't give a hoot about it, but this isn't an ordinary thing. I feel about as effective as a clam right now."

"What for? Cripes, you can't help yourself if somebody gets shot. The place was empty. It was a good place for a hideout. Maybe those two eggs were holed up in there when they got caught up with."

Pat leaned back and rubbed his hands across his eyes. "Look, Mike, I'm not too dumb. Anybody can change barrels in a gun. I'll bet you the shell cases won't match your pin either."

"How'd you guess?"

"You're treating me like a kid now, feller. You're the one who's forgetting that we're friends. I know you like a book and I don't want to tear any pages out of that book because if I do I'm afraid of what the ending will be like. I know it was you, I don't know who handled the .32, I'm scared to ask questions and I hate to have you lie to me. Little lies I don't like."

I folded the paper and put it back on his desk. Pat wouldn't look at me. "Why the finger pointing at me, Pat?"

"Nuts. Just plain nuts. You should know why."

"I don't."

"One of those boys had a green Commie card on him. Now do you know why?"

"Yeah," I said. I had forgotten all about that. I lifted the cigarette and dragged the smoke down into my chest. "Now what?"

"I want to know what you're after. I want to know everything, Mike. Whenever I think about things I get cold all over and want to smash things. You've been playing cute and there's no way I can touch you. I have to absorb myself in police work and routine detail when I know I'm on the outside hoping for a look in."

"That's the trouble with the police. They have to wait until something happens. A crime has to be committed before they can make a move."

Pat watched me thoughtfully, his hands locked behind his head. "Things have happened."

"Roger, but, as you stated, they have been played very cute."

"I'm still on the outside looking in."

I snubbed the butt out and stared at the shreds of tobacco hanging out the end. "Pat . . . more things are going to happen. I know you like a book, too, but there's something else I have to know."

"Go on."

"How far can I trust you?"

"It depends on a lot of things. Never forget that I'm still a cop."

"You're still a plain citizen who likes his country and likes to see it stay the way it is, aren't you?"

"Naturally."

"All right. You're all snagged up in the ritual of written law and order. You have to follow the rules and play it square. There's a weight around your neck and you know it. If I told you what I knew you'd bust a gut trying to get something done that couldn't be done and the rats would get out of the trap.

"I'm only one guy, Pat, but I'm quite a guy and you know it. I make my own rules as I go along and I don't have to account to anybody. There's something big being kicked around and it's exactly as you said . . . it's bigger than you or me or anybody and I'm the only one who can handle it. Don't go handing me the stuff about the agencies that are equipped to handle every conceivable detail of this and that. I'm not messing with detail . . . I'm messing with people and letting them see that I'm nobody to mess with and there are a lot more like me if you want to look for them.

"What's going on isn't a case for the crime laboratory and it isn't a case for the police. The whole thing is in the hands of the people, only they don't know it yet. I'm going to show it to them because I'm the only one who has the whole works wrapped up tight trying to bring it together so we can see what it is. You can stop worrying about your law and your order and about Lee Deamer, because when I'm finished

Lee can win his election and go ahead and wipe out the corruption without ever knowing that he had a greater enemy than crime plain and simple."

I picked up my gun and stuck it in the sling. Pat hadn't moved. His head bobbed slightly when I said so long, but that was all.

I was still seeing the tired smile on Pat's face, telling me that he understood and to go ahead, when I called Lee Deamer's office. His secretary told me that he was speaking at a luncheon of U.N. delegates in a midtown hotel and had already left. I got the name of the hotel, thanked her and hung up.

He must be getting anxious and I didn't blame him a bit. It was a little before noon, so I hopped in the heap and tooled it up Broadway and angled over to the hotel where it cost me a buck to park in an unloading zone with a guy to cover for me.

The clerk at the desk directed me to the hall where the luncheon was to be held and had hardly finished before I saw Lee come in the door. He swung a brief case at his side and one of the girls from his office trailed behind him carrying another. Before I could reach him a swarm of reporters came out of nowhere and took down his remarks while the photogs snapped his picture.

A covey of important-looking joes stood on the outside of the circle impatient to speak to Deamer, yet unwilling to offend the press by breaking up the party. It was Lee himself who told the boys to see him after the luncheon and walked through their midst. He had spotted me leaning against the desk and went directly into the manager's office. That little man went in after him, came out in a minute and scanned the desk. I didn't have to be told that he was looking for me.

I nodded and strode in as casually as I could. The manager smiled at me, then took up a position near the door to give us a few minutes in private. Lee Deamer was sitting in a leather-covered chair next to the desk and his face was a study in anxiety.

"Hello, Lee."

"Mike, how are you? I've been worried sick ever since I saw the papers this morning."

I offered him a butt and he shook his head. "There's nothing to worry about, Lee. Everything is fine."

"But last night. I . . . you mean you weren't connected with the doings in Oscar's place?" I grinned and lit the smoke.

"I don't know what to think. I called Captain Chambers and he led me to believe that he thought the same thing."

"He did. I talked him out of it." I raked another chair up with my foot and sat down. Murder is murder. It can be legal and it can't. No matter what it is it's still murder and the less people know about it the better. I said, "I went through Oscar's place right after the accident. Pat went through it himself. Later I took another check and I'm satisfied that if Oscar *did* leave any incriminating junk lying around, he didn't leave it in his room."

Lee sighed, relieved. "I'm glad to hear that, Mike, but I'm more than glad to hear that you didn't have anything to do with those . . . deaths. It's ugly."

"Murder is always ugly."

"Then there's nothing further to be said, I imagine. That takes a great load off my mind. Truly, Mike, I was terribly worried."

"I should think so. Well, keep your mind at rest. I'm going to backtrack on Oscar a little bit and see what comes up. It's still my opinion that he was bluffing. It's not the easiest thing in the world to frame somebody who can't be framed. If anything comes up I'll let you know, meanwhile, no news is good news, so they say."

"Fine, Mike, I'll leave everything to you. Captain Chambers will co-operate as he sees possible. I want nothing hanging over my head. If it becomes necessary I would rather the public knew about my relationship with Oscar and the facts of the case before the election."

"Forget that stuff," I told him brusquely, "there's plenty the public shouldn't know. If you went into George Washington's background you'd probably kick up a lot of dirt too. You're the one that counts, not Oscar. Remember that."

I put the chair back in place and doused the butt in a flower pot. I told Lee to give me a few minutes before he left, said so-long and took off. Lee looked ten years younger than he had when he came in. I liked that guy.

There was a public phone in the lobby and I called Velda to ask her if she had switched parts in her gun. She said she had, then told me Pat had just been on the wire. I said, "But I just saw him a little while ago."

"I know, but he told me to have you contact him right away if I could reach you."

"Okay, I'll call him back. Look, I'll probably be out most of the day, so I'll pick you up sometime tonight at your place."

"Charlie Moffit?"

"Yeah, we'll take in his joint."

"I'll be ready, Mike."

I hung up, threw in another nickel and spun Pat's number when I got the dial tone. The last time I had seen him he looked tired. This time his voice was dancing.

Like on hot coals.

"Pat, feller, why the sudden rush?"

"I'll tell you later. Get your tail down here chop-chop. I have things to talk over with you. Privately."

"Am I in trouble?"

"There's a damn good chance that you'll be in jail if you don't hurry."

"Get off my back, Pat. Get a table in Louie's and I'll be down for lunch. The check is yours this time."

"I'll give you fifteen minutes."

I made it just in time. Louie was behind the bar and thumbed me toward the booths in the rear. Pat was in the last one on the aisle sucking on a cigarette as hard as he could.

Did you ever see a guy who was burned up at his wife? He was like a bomb trying hard to go off and couldn't because the powder was wet. That's what Pat reminded me of. Police efficiency was leaking out his ears and his usual suavity hung on him like a bag. If he could call those narrow slits eyes then you could say he was looking at me with intent to kill.

I walked back to the bar and had Louie make me up a drink before the session started.

He waited until I was comfortable against the back of the booth and started on my drink before he yanked an envelope out of his pocket and flipped it across the table at me. I slid the contents out and looked at him.

They were photographs of fingerprints. Most were mine. Four weren't.

Attached to the four that weren't was a typewritten sheet, single spaced and carefully paragraphed. "They came off that cigarette pack," Pat said.

I nodded and read through the report.

Her name was Paula Riis. She was thirty-four years old, a college grad, a trained nurse and a former employee in a large Western insane asylum. Since it was a state job her prints were on file there and in Washington.

Pat let me stuff the sheets back in the envelope before he spoke. I hardly heard him say unnecessarily, "She worked in the same place that Oscar had been assigned to." A cloud of smoke circled his head again.

The music started in my head. It was different this time. It wasn't loud and it had a definite tune and rhythm. It was soft, melodious music that tried to lullaby me into drowsiness with subtle tones. It tried to keep me from thinking and I fought it back into the obscurity from which it came.

I looked at his eyes and I looked deep into twin fires that had a maddening desire to make me talk and talk fast. "What, Pat?"

"Where is she?" His voice sounded queer.

I said, "She's dead. She committed suicide by jumping off a bridge into the river. She's dead as hell."

"I don't believe you, Mike."

"That's tough. That's just too damn bad because you have to believe me. You can scour the city or the country from now to doomsday and you won't find her unless you dredge the river and by now maybe even that's too late. She's out at sea somewhere. So what?"

"I'm asking the same thing. So what, Mike? She isn't an accident, a freak coincidence that you can explain off. I want to know why and how. This thing is too big for you to have alone. You'd better start talking or I'm going to have to think one thing. You aren't the Mike Hammer I knew once. You used to have sense enough to realize that the police are set up to handle these things. You used to know that we weren't a bunch of saps. If you still want to keep still then I'm going to think those things and the friendship I had for a certain guy is ended because that guy isn't the same guy any more."

That was it. He had me and he was right. I took another sip of the drink and made circles with the wet bottom on the table.

"Her name was Paula. Like I said, she's dead. Remember when I came to you with those green cards, Pat? I took them from her. I was walking across the bridge one night when this kid was going into her dutch act. I tried to stop her. All I got was the pocket of her coat where she had the pack of butts and the cards.

"It made me mad because she jumped. I had just been dragged over the coals by that damned judge and I was feeling sour enough not to report the thing. Just the same, I wanted to know what the cards meant. When I found out she was a Commie, and that Charlie Moffit was a Commie I got interested. I couldn't help it.

"Now the picture is starting to take form. I think you've put it together already. Oscar was insane. He had to be. He and that nurse planned an escape and probably went into hiding in their little love nest a long time ago. When money became scarce they saw a way to get some through using Oscar's physical similarity to Lee.

"The first thing that happened was that Oscar killed a guy,

a Commie. Now: either he took those cards off Moffit's body for some reason, or he and this Paula Riis actually were Commies themselves. Anyway when Oscar killed Moffit, Paula realized that the guy was more insane than she thought and got scared. She was afraid to do anything about it so she went over the bridge."

It was a wonderful story. It made a lot of sense. The two people that could spoil it were dead. It made a lot of sense without telling about the fat boy on the bridge and setting myself up for a murder charge.

Pat was on the last of his smokes. The dead butts littered the table and his coat was covered with ashes. The fires in his eyes had gone down . . . a little anyway. "Very neat, Mike. It fits like a glove. I'm wondering what it would fit like if there was more to it that you didn't tell me."

"Now you're getting nasty," I said.

"No, just careful. If it's the way you told it the issue's dead. If it isn't there will be a lot of hell coming your way."

"I've seen my share," I grunted.

"You'll see a lot more. I'm going to get some people on this job to poke around. They're other friends of mine and though it won't be official it will be a thorough job. These boys carry little gold badges with three words you can condense to FBI. I hope you're right, Mike. I hope you aren't giving me the business."

I grinned at him. "The only one who can get shafted is me. You . . . hell, you're worried about Lee. I told you I wouldn't line him up for a smear. He's my client and I'm mighty particular about clients. Let's order some lunch and forget about it."

Pat reached for the menu. The fires were still in his eyes.

CHAPTER EIGHT

I LEFT Pat at two o'clock and picked up a paper on the corner. The headlines had turned back to the cold war and the spy trials going on in New York and Washington. I read the sheet through and tossed it in a basket then got in my car.

I made a turn at the corner and cut over to an express street to head back to my place when I noticed the blue coupé behind me. The last time I had seen it it had been parked across from mine outside Pat's office. I turned off the avenue and went down a block to the next avenue and paralleled my course. The blue coupé stuck with me.

When I tried the same thing again it happened all over This time I picked out a one-way street, crept along it behind a truck until I saw room enough at the curb to park the car. I went into the space head first and sat there at the wheel waiting. The coupé had no choice, it had to pass me.

The driver was a young kid in a pork-pie hat and he didn't give me a glance. There was a chance that I could be wrong, but just for the hell of it I jotted down his license number as he went by and swung out behind him. Only once did I see his eyes looking into his mirror, and that was when he turned on Broadway. I stuck with him a way to see what he'd do.

Five minutes later I gave it up as a bad job. He wasn't going anywhere. I made a left turn and he kept going straight ahead. I scowled at my reflection in the dirty windshield.

I was getting the jumps, I thought. I never used to get like that. Maybe Pat had put his finger on it . . . I'd changed.

When I stopped for the red light I saw the headlines on the papers laid out on a stand. More about the trials and the cold war. Politics. I felt like an ignorant bastard for not knowing what it was all about. There's no time like the present then. I swung the wheel and cut back in the other direction. I parked the car and walked up to the gray stone building where the pickets carried banners protesting the persecution of the "citizens" inside.

One of the punks carrying a placard was at the meeting in Brooklyn the other night. I crossed the line by shoving him almost on his fanny. An attendant carried my note in to Marty Kooperman and he came out to lead me back to the press seats.

Hell, you read the papers, you know what went on in there. It made me as sick to watch it as it did you to read about it. Those damned Reds pulled every trick they knew to get the case thrown out of court. They were a scurvy bunch of lice who tried to turn the court into a burlesque show.

But there was a calm patience in this judge and jury, and in the spectators too that told you what the outcome would be. Oh, the defendants didn't see it. They were too cocksure of themselves. They were The Party. They were Powerful. They represented the People.

They should have turned around and seen the faces of the people. They would have had their pants scared off. All at once I felt good. I felt swell!

Then I saw the two guys in the second row. They were dressed in ordinary business suits and they looked too damn smug. They were the boys who came in with General Osilov that night. I sat through two more hours of it before the judge broke it up for the day. The press boys made a beeline for the phones and the crowd started to scramble for the doors.

A lot of the people covered it up, but I had time to see the general's aides pass a fat brief case to another guy who saw that it reached one of the defendants.

All I could think of was the nerve they had, the gall of them to come into a court of law and directly confirm their relationship with a group accused of a crime against the people. Maybe that's why they could get ahead so fast. They were brazen. That brief case would hold one thing. Money. Cash in bills. Dough to support the trial and the accompanying propaganda.

Nuts.

I waited until they went through the doors and stayed on their heels. At least they had the sense not to come in an official car; that would have been overdoing it. They walked down a block, waved a cab to the curb and climbed in. By that time I was in a cab myself and right behind them. One nice thing about taking a taxi in New York. There're so many cabs you can't tell if you're being followed or not.

The one in front of us pulled to a stop in front of the hotel I had left not so long before. I paid off my driver and tagged after them into the lobby. The place was still jammed with reporters and the usual collection of the curious. General Osilov was standing off in a corner explaining things to four reporters through an interpreter. The two went directly up to him, interrupted and shook his hand as if they hadn't seen him in years. It was all very clubby.

The girl at the newsstand was bored. I bought a pack of Luckies and held out my hand for the change. "What's the Russky doing?"

"Him? He was a speaker at the luncheon upstairs. You should have heard him. They piped all the speeches into the lobby over the loud-speaker and he had to be translated every other sentence."

Sure, he couldn't speak English. Like hell!

I said, "Anything important come out?"

She handed me my change. "Nah, same old drivel every time. All except Lee Deamer. He jumped on that Cossack for a dozen things and called him every name that could sneak by in print. You should have heard the way the people in the lobby cheered. Gosh, the manager was fit to be tied. He tried to quiet them down, but they wouldn't shut up."

Good going, Lee. You tear the bastards apart in public and I'll do it in private. Just be careful, they're like poisonous snakes . . . quiet, stealthy and deadly. Be careful, for Pete's sake!

I opened the Luckies and shook one out. I hung it in my mouth and fumbled for a match. A hand draped with mink held a flame up to it and a voice said, "Light, mister?"

It was a silly notion, but I wondered if I could be contaminated by the fire. I said, "Hello, Ethel," and took the light.

There was something different about her face. I didn't know what it was, but it wasn't the same any more. Fine, nearly invisible lines drew it tight, giving an Oriental slant to her eyes. The mouth that had kissed so nice and spoke the word that put the finger on me seemed to be set too firm. It pulled the curve of her lips out of shape.

She had a lesson coming to her, this one. Bare skin and a leather belt. Either she was playing it bold or she didn't think I had guessed. Maybe she thought she couldn't have made it out the door without my seeing her and decided to make the first move herself. Whatever her reason, I couldn't read it in her voice or her face.

I was going to ask her what she was doing here and I saw why. The reputable Mr. Brighton of Park Avenue and Big Business was holding court next to a fluted column. A lone reporter was taking notes. A couple of big boys whose faces I recognized from newspapers were listening intently, adding a word now and then. They all smiled but two.

The sour pusses were General Osilov and his interpreter. The little guy beside the general talked fast and gesticulated freely, but the general was catching it all as it came straight from Brighton himself.

A couple hundred words later Ethel's old man said something and they all laughed, even the general. They shook hands and split up into new groups that were forming every time a discussion got started.

I took Ethel's arm and started for the door. "It's been a' long time, kid. I've missed you."

She tried a smile and it didn't look good on her. "I've missed you too, Mike. I halfway expected you to call me."

"Well, you know how things are."

"Yes, I know." I threw my eyes over her face, but she was expressionless.

"Were you at the luncheon?" I asked.

"Oh . . ." she came out of it with a start. "No, I stayed in the lobby. Father was one of the speakers, you know."

"Really? No need for you to stick around, is there?"

"Oh no, none at all. I can . . . oh, Mike, just a moment. I forgot something, do you mind?"

We paused at the door and she glanced back over her shoulder. I turned her around and walked back. "Want me to go with you?"

"No, I'll be right back. Wait for me, will you?"

I watched her go and the girl at the counter smiled. I said, "There's a ten in it if you see what she does, sister." She was out of there like a shot and closed up on Ethel. I stood by the stand smoking, looking at the mirrors scattered around the walls. I could see myself in a half dozen of them. If Ethel watched to see whether or not I moved she must have been satisfied.

She was gone less than a minute. Her face looked tighter than ever.

I walked up to meet her and the girl scrambled behind her counter. I took out a dime, flipped it in my hand and went over and got a pack of gum. While the girl gave me my nickel change I dropped the ten on the counter. "She spoke to a couple of guys back in the hall. Nothing else. They were young."

I took my gum pack and offered Ethel a piece. She said she didn't want any. No wonder she looked so damned grim. She had fingered me again. Naked skin and ten extra lashes. She was going to be a sorry girl.

When we got in the cab two boys in almost identical blue suits opened the doors of a black Chevvy sedan and came out behind us. I didn't look around again until we had reached the lot where I left my car. The black Chevvy was down the street. Ethel kept up a running conversation that gave me a chance to look at her, and back over my shoulder occasionally.

If I had been paying any attention I would have gotten what she was driving at. She kept hinting for me to take her up to my place. MAN MURDERED IN OWN APARTMENT. More nice headlines. I ignored her hints and cruised around Manhattan with the black sedan always a few hundred feet behind.

Dusk came early. It drove in with the fog that seemed to like this town, a gray blind that reduced visibility to a minimum. I said to her, "Can we go back to your cabin, kid? It was pretty nice there."

I might have been mistaken, but I thought I saw the glint of tears. "It *was* nice there, wasn't it?"

"It was you, not the cabin, Ethel."

I wasn't mistaken, the tears were there. She dropped her eyes and stared at her hands. "I had forgotten . . . what it was like to live." She paused, then: "Mike . . ."

"What?"

"Nothing. We can go to the cabin if you'd like to."

The Chevvy behind us pulled around a car and clung a little closer. I loosened the .45 with my forearm and a shrug. The dusk deepened to dark and it was easy to watch the lights in the mirror. They sat there, glowering, watching, waiting for the right moment to come.

How would it be? Ethel wanted it in my apartment. Why? So she would be out of the line of fire? Now what. They'd draw alongside and open up and they wouldn't give a hoot whether they got the both of us or not. It was a question of whether I was important enough to kill at the same time sacrificing a good party worker. Hell, there were always suckers who could rake in the dough for them. Those two headlights behind me trying to act casual said that.

We were out of the city on a wide open road that wound into the dark like a beckoning finger. The houses thinned out and there were fewer roads intersecting the main drag.

Any time now, I thought. It can happen any time. The .45 was right where I could get at it in a hurry and I was ready to haul the wheel right into them. The lights behind me flicked on bright, back to dim and on bright again, a signal they were going to pass.

I signaled an okay with my lights and gripped the wheel. The lights came closer.

I didn't watch the mirror. I had my eyes going between
the road and the lightbeams on the outside lane that got
brighter as they came closer when all of a sudden the beams
swerved and weren't there any more. When I looked they
were going in a crazy rolling pattern end over end into the
field alongside the road.

I half whispered, "Cripes!" and slammed on the brakes. A
handful of cars shot by the accident and began to pull in to
a stop in front of me.

Ethel was rigid in her seat, her hands pushing her away
from the windshield where the quick stop had thrown her.
"Mike! What . . ."

I yanked the emergency up. "Stay here. A car went over
behind us."

She gasped and said something I didn't catch because I
was out and running back toward the car. It was upside down
and both doors were open. The horn blasted, a man screamed
and the lights still punched holes in the night. I was the first
one there, a hundred yards ahead of anyone else.

I had time to see the tommy gun on the grass and the
wallet inside the car. So that was it. That was how it was to
be pulled off. One quick blast from a chatter gun that would
sweep my car and it was all over. Somebody groaned in the
darkness and I didn't bother to see who it was. They deserved everything they got. I grabbed that tommy gun and
the wallet and ducked behind the car in the darkness and
ran back down the road. The others had just reached the
wreck and were hollering for somebody to get a doctor.

Ethel screamed when I threw the trunk open and I yelled
for her to shut up. I tossed the tommy gun on the spare tire
and shut the lid. There were more cars coasting up, threading
through the jam along the road. A siren screamed its way up
and two state cops started the procession moving again. I
joined the line and got away from there.

"Who was it, Mike? What happened back there?"

"Just an accident," I grinned. "A couple of guys were going
too fast and they rolled over."

"Were they . . . hurt?"

"I didn't stay to look. They weren't dead . . . yet." I
grinned again and her face tightened. She looked at me with
an intense loathing and the tears started again.

"Don't worry, baby. Don't be so damn soft-hearted. You
know what the Party policies are. You have to be cold and
hard. You aren't forgetting, are you?"

The "no" came through her teeth.

"Hell, the ground was soft and the car wasn't banged up

much. They were probably just knocked out. You know, you have to get over being squeamish about such things."

Ethel shifted in her seat and wouldn't look at me again. We came to the drive and the trees that hung over it. We pulled up to the front of the cabin that nestled on the bluff atop the river and sat there in the dark watching the lights of the river boats.

Red and green eyes. No, they were boats. From far away came a dull booming, like a giant kettledrum. I had heard it once before, calling that way. It was only a channel marker, only a steel bell on a float that clanged when the tide and the waves swung it. I felt a shudder cross my shoulders and I said, "Shall we go in?"

She answered by opening the door. I went into the cabin behind her.

I closed the door and reached behind my back and turned the key in the lock. Ethel heard the ominous click and stopped. She looked over her shoulder at me once, smiled and went on. I watched her throw her mink on the sofa then put a match to the tapers in the holders.

She thought it was a love nest. We were locked in against the world where we could practice the human frailties without interruption. She thought I didn't know and was going to give her all for the party so as not to arouse my suspicions. She was crying softly as if the sudden passion was too much for her.

I put the key in my pocket and crossed the room to where she was and put my hands on her shoulders. She spun around, her hands locking behind my waist, her mouth reaching up for mine. I kissed her with a brutal force she'd remember and while I kissed her my fingers hooked in the fabric of her dress.

She ripped her mouth away from mine and pressed it against my cheek. She was crying hard and she said, "I love you, Mike. I never wanted to love again and I did. I love you." It was so low I hardly heard it.

My teeth were showing in a grin. I raised my hand until it was against her breast and pushed. Ethel staggered back a step and I yanked with the hand that held her dress and it came off in one piece with a quick loud tear, leaving her gasping and hurt with vivid red marks on her skin where the fabric had twisted and caught.

She gasped, pressed the back of her hand to her mouth and looked at me through eyes wide with fear. "Mike . . . you didn't have to . . ."

"Shut up." I took a step forward and she backed off, slowly, slowly, until the wall was at her back and she could retreat no more. "Am I going to rip 'em right off your hide, Ethel?"

Her head shook, unbelieving what was happening to her. It only lasted a moment, and her hands that trembled so bent up behind her back and the bra fell away and landed at her feet. Her eyes were on mine as she slid her hands inside the fragile silk of the shorts and pushed them down.

When she stepped out of them I slid my belt off and let it dangle from my hand. I watched her face. I saw the gamut of emotions flash by in swift succession, leaving a startled expression of pure animal terror.

"Maybe you should know why you're getting this, Ethel. It's something you should have gotten a long time ago. Your father should have given it to you when you started fooling around one of those Commie bastards who was after the dough you could throw his way instead of yourself. I'm going to lace the hell out of you and you can scream all you want, and nobody will be around to hear you but me and that's what I want to hear.

"You put the finger on me twice now. You fingered me when you saw the badge inside my wallet and the party put a man on my back. They put a lot of men, I guess. Two of 'em are dead already. It didn't go so good and you saw a chance to finger me again in the lobby back there. What did you expect for it, a promotion or something?"

I started to swing the belt back and forth very gently. Ethel pressed against the wall, her face a pale oval. "Mike ... it wasn't ..."

"Keep quiet," I said.

A naked woman and a leather belt. I looked at her, so bare and so pretty, hands pressed for support against the paneling, legs spread apart to hold a precarious balance, a flat stomach hollowed under the fear that burned her body a faint pink, lovely smooth breasts, firm with terrible excitement, rising and falling with every gasping breath. A gorgeous woman who had been touched by the hand of the devil.

I raised the belt and swung it and heard the sharp crack of the leather against her thighs and her scream and that horrible blasting roar all at once. Her body twisted and fell while I was running for the window with the .45 in my hand pumping slugs into the night and shouting at the top of my voice.

And there in the darkness I heard a body crashing through the brush, running for the road. I ran to the door that I had locked myself and cursed my own stupidity while I fumbled for the key in my pocket.

The door came open, but there was only silence outside, a dead, empty silence. I jammed a fresh clip into the gun and held it steady, deliberately standing outlined in the light of the door asking to be made a target.

I heard it again, the heavy pounding of feet going away. They were too far to catch. When they stopped a motor roared into life and he was gone. My hands had the shakes again and I had to drop the rod back in the sling. The prints of his feet were in the grass, winding around the house. I followed them to the window and bent over to pick up the hat.

A pork-pie hat. It had a U-shaped nick taken out of the crown. The boy in the blue Chevvy. Mr. MVD himself, a guy who looked like a schoolboy and could pass in a crowd for anything but what he was. I grinned because he was one thing he shouldn't have been, a lousy shot. I was duck soup there in that room with my back toward him and he missed. Maybe I was supposed to be his first corpse and he got nervous. Yeah. I turned and looked in the window.

Ethel was still on the floor and a trickle of red drained from her body.

I ran back to her, stumbling over things in the darkness. I turned her over and saw the hole under her shoulder, a tiny blue thing that oozed blood slowly and was beginning to swell at the edges.

I said, "Ethel . . . Ethel honey!"

Her eyes came open and she looked tired, so tired. "It . . . doesn't hurt, Mike."

"I know. It won't for a while. Ethel . . . I'm sorry. God, I feel awful."

"Mike . . . don't."

She closed her eyes when I ran my hand over her cheek. "You said . . . a badge, Mike. You're not one of them, are you?"

"No. I'm a cop."

"I'm . . . glad. After . . . I met you I saw . . . the truth, Mike. I knew . . . I had been a fool."

"No more talking, Ethel. I'm going for a doctor. Don't talk."

She found my hand and hung on. "Let me, Mike . . . please. Will I die?"

"I don't know, Ethel. Let me go for a doctor."

"No . . . I want to tell you . . . I loved you. I'm glad it happened. I had to love somebody . . . else."

I forced her fingers off my hand and pushed her arm away gently. There was a phone on the bar and I lifted it to my ear. I dialed the operator and had a hard time keeping my voice level. I said I wanted a doctor and wanted one quick. She told me to wait and connected me with a crisp voice that sounded steady and alert. I told him where we were and to get here fast. He said he would hurry and broke the connection.

I knelt beside her and stroked her hair until her eyes came open, silently protesting the pain that had started. Her shoulder twitched once and the blood started again. I tried to be gentle. I got my arms under her and carried her to the couch. The wound was a deeper blue and I prayed that there was no internal hemmorrhage.

I sat beside her holding her hand. I cursed everything and everybody. I prayed a little and I swore again. I had thoughts that tried to drive me mad.

It was a long while before I realized that she was looking at me. She struggled to find words, her mind clouding from the shock of the bullet. I let her talk and heard her say, "I'm not . . . one of them any more. I told . . . everything . . . I told . . ."

Her eyes had a glazed look. "Please don't try to talk, kid, please."

She never heard me. Her lips parted, moved. "I never . . . told them about you . . . Mike. I never saw . . . your badge. Tonight . . . those men . . ." It was too much for her. She closed her eyes and was still, only the cover I had thrown over her moved enough to tell that she was still alive.

I never heard the doctor come in. He was a tall man with a face that had looked on much of the world. He stepped past me and leaned over her, his hand opening the bag he carried. I sat and waited, smoking one cigarette after another. The air reeked with a sharp chemical smell and the doctor was a tall shadow passing back and forth across my line of vision, doing things I wasn't aware of, desperate in his haste.

His voice came at me several times before I answered him. He said, "She will need an ambulance."

I came out of the chair and went to the phone. The operator said she would call and I hung up. I turned around. "How is she, doc?"

"We won't know for a while yet. There's a slight chance that she'll pull through." His whole body expressed what he felt. Disgust. Anger. His voice had a demanding, exasperated tone. "What happened?"

Perhaps it was the sharpness of his question that startled me into a logical line of reasoning. There was a sudden clarity about the whole thing I hadn't noticed before I heard

Ethel telling me that she had pulled out of the party and it left me with an answer that said this time it wasn't me they were after . . . it was her . . . and Pork Pie *had* been a good shot. He would have been a dead shot, only Ethel had twisted when I laid the strap across her and the bullet that was intended for her heart had missed by a fraction and might give her life back to her.

The soft kill-music that I always hear at the wrong times took up a beat and was joined by a multitude of ghostly instruments that plucked at my mind to drive away any reason that I had left.

I walked to the doctor and stared at his eyes so he could see that I had looked on the world too, and could see the despair, the lust, the same dirty thoughts that he had seen in so many others and said, "Do you know who I am, doctor?"

He looked long this time, searching me. "Your face is familiar."

"It should be, doctor. You've seen it in the papers. You've read about it many times. It's been described a hundred different ways and there's always that reference to a certain kill-look that I have. My name is Mike Hammer. I'm a private detective. I've killed a lot of people."

He knew me then; his eyes asked if I were trying to buy his silence with the price of death. "Did you do that to her too?"

"No, doctor. Somebody else did that, and for it that somebody is going to die a thousand times. It wasn't just one person who wanted that girl dead. One person ordered it, but many demanded it. I'm not going to tell you the story of what lies behind this, but I will tell you one thing. It's so damned important that it touches your life and mine and the lives of everyone in this country and unless you want to see the same thing happen again and again you'll have to hold up your report.

"You know who I am and I can show you my papers so there will never be any trouble in finding me if you think it should be done. But listen . . . if ever you believed anything, believe this . . . if I get connected with this I'll be tied up in that crazy web of police detail and a lot of other people will die. Do you understand me?"

"No." Just like that, no. I tried to keep from grabbing his neck in my hands and forcing my words down his throat. My face went wild and I couldn't control it. The doctor didn't scare, he just stood there and watched me make myself keep from killing him too.

"Perhaps I do after all." His face became sober and stern.

I swallowed hard with the relief I felt. "I don't understand it at all," he said. "I'll never understand these things. I do know this though, a powerful influence motivates murder. It is never simple enough to understand. I can't understand war, either. I'll do what I can, Mr. Hammer. I do have a good understanding of people and I think that you are telling me a truth that could have some very unpleasant aspects, whatever they are."

I squeezed his hand hard and got out of there. So much to be done, I thought, so much that's still left to do. My watch said it was after ten and Velda would be waiting. Tonight we had a mission planned and after that another and another until we found the ending.

I touched the starter and the engine caught with a roar. The night had sped by and there never was enough time to do what I wanted. First Pork-Pie Hat, then those men, then Ethel. I stopped and retraced my thoughts. Ethel and those men. She was going to tell me about them; she almost did. I reached in my pocket and took out the wallet.

The card was behind some others in one of the pockets. It was an official card with all the works. The words I saw stood out as though they were written in flame. FEDERAL BUREAU OF INVESTIGATION. Good Lord, Ethel had fingered me to the FBI! She had turned on the party and even on me! Now it *was* clear . . . Those two Feds had tailed me hoping to be led to my apartment and perhaps a secret cache of papers that could lead to those missing documents! They tailed me but they in turn were being tailed by somebody else who knew what had happened. Pork-Pit Hat ran them off the road and came after us with the intention of killing Ethel before she could spill anything else she knew!

I let the music in my head play. I laughed at it and it played harder than ever, but this time I didn't fight it. I sat back and laughed, enjoying the symphony of madness and cheered when it was done. So I *was* mad. I *was* a killer and I *was* looking forward to killing again. I wanted them all, every one of them from bottom to top and especially the one at the top even if I had to go to the Kremlin to do it. The time for that wouldn't be now . . . I'd only get a little way up the ladder if one of the rungs didn't break first and throw me to my death.

But some day, maybe, some day I'd stand on the steps of the Kremlin with a gun in my fist and I'd yell for them to come out and if they wouldn't I'd go in and get them and when I had them lined up against the wall I'd start shooting until all I had left was a row of corpses that bled on the cold

floors and in whose thick red blood would be the promise
of a peace that would stick for more generations than I'd
live to see.

The music gave up in a thunder of drums and I racked my
wheels against the curb outside Velda's apartment house. I
looked up at her floor when I got out and saw the lights on
and I knew she was ready and waiting.

I went on in.

She said hello and knew that something was wrong with me.
"What happened, Mike?"

I couldn't tell her the whole thing. I said simply, "They
tried again."

Her eyes narrowed down and glinted at me. They asked the
question.

I said, "They got away again, too."

"It's getting deeper, isn't it?"

"It'll go deeper before we're through. Get your coat on."

Velda went inside and reappeared with her coat on and her
handbag slung over her shoulder. It swung slowly under the
weight of the gun. "Let's go, Mike."

We went downstairs to the car and started driving. Broadway was a madhouse of traffic that weaved and screamed,
stopped for red lights and jumped away at the green. I let
the flow take me past the artificial daylight of the marquees
and the signs and into the dusk of uptown. When we came
to the street Velda pointed and I turned up it, parking in
the middle of the block under a street light.

Here was the edge of Harlem, that strange no-man's-land
where the white mixed with the black and the languages over-
flowed into each other like that of the horde around the
Tower of Babel. There were strange, foreign smells of cooking and too many people in too few rooms. There were the
hostile eyes of children who became suddenly silent as you
passed.

Velda stopped before an old sandstone building. "This is
it."

I took her arm and went up the stairs. In the vestibule I
truck a match and held it before the name plates on the
mailboxes. Most were scrawled in childish writing on the backs
of match books. One was an aluminum stamp and it read C. C.
LOPEX, SUPT.

I pushed the button. There was no answering buzz of the
door. Instead, a face showed through the dirty glass and the
door was pulled open by a guy who only came up to my

chest. He smoked a smelly cigar and reeked of cheap whisky. He was a hunchback. He said, "Whatta ya want?"

He saw the ten bucks I had folded in my fingers and got a greedy look on his face. "There ain't but one empty room and ya won't like that. Ya can use my place. For a tenner ya can stay all night."

Velda raised her eyebrows at that. I shook my head. "We'll take the empty."

"Sure, go ahead. Ya coulda done whatcha wanted in my place but if ya want the empty go ahead. Ya won't like it, though."

I gave him the ten and he gave me the key, telling me where the room was. He leered and looked somewhat dissatisfied because he wouldn't be able to sneak a look on something he probably never had himself. Velda started up the stairs using her flashlight to pick out the snags in the steps.

The room faced on a dark corridor that was hung heavy with the smell of age and decay. I put the key in the lock and shoved the door open. Velda found the lone bulb that dangled from the ceiling and pulled the cord to throw a dull yellow light in the room. I closed the door and locked it.

Nobody had to tell us what had happened. Somebody had been here before us. The police had impounded Charlie Moffit's personal belongings, but they hadn't ripped the room up doing it. The skinny mattress lay in the center of the floor ripped to shreds. The hollow posts of the bed had been disemboweled and lay on the springs. What had been a rug at one time lay in a heap in the corner under the pile of empty dresser drawers.

"We're too late again, Mike."

"No we're not." I was grinning and Velda grinned too. "The search didn't stop anywhere. If they found it we could have seen where they stopped looking. They tore the place apart and never came to the end. It never was here."

I kicked at the papers on the floor, old sheets from weeks back. There was a note pad with pencil sketches of girls doing things they shouldn't. We roamed around the room poking into the remains doing nothing but looking out of curiosity. Velda found a box of junk that had been spilled under the dresser, penny curios from some arcade.

There was no place else to look that hadn't already been searched. I took the dresser drawers off the rug and laid them out. They were lined with newspapers and had a few odds and ends rolling on the bottoms. There was part of a fountain pen and a broken harmonica. Velda found a few pictures of girls in next to nothing that had been cut from a magazine.

Then I found the photographs. They were between the paper lining and the side of the drawer. One was of two people, too fuzzy to identify. The other was that of a girl and had "To Charlie, with love from P." written on the bottom. I held it in my hand and looked at the face of Paula Riis. She was smiling. She was happy. She was the girl that had jumped off the bridge and was dead. I stared at her face that smiled back at me as if there never had been anything to worry about.

Velda peered over my shoulder, took the picture from me and held it under the light. "Who is she, Mike?"

"Paula Riis," I said finally. "The nurse. Charlie Moffit's girl friend. Oscar Deamer's nurse and the girl who chose to die rather than look at my face. The girl who started it all and left it hanging in mid-air while people died and killed."

I took out a cigarette and gave her one. "I had it figured wrong. I gave Pat a bum steer, then when I thought it over I got to thinking that maybe I told the truth after all. I thought that Paula and Oscar planned his escape and Oscar killed a guy . . . just any guy . . . in order to squeeze Lee. Now it seems that it wasn't just any guy that Oscar killed. It wasn't an accident. Oscar killed him for a very good reason."

"Mike . . . could it be a case of jealousy? Could Oscar have been jealous because Paula played up to Charlie?"

I dragged the smoke down, held it and let it go into the light. "I wish it happened that simply. I wish it did, sugar. I started out with a couple of green cards and took it from there. I thought I had a coincidental connection but now it looks like it wasn't so damn coincidental after all. We have too many dead people carrying those green cards."

"The answer, Mike . . . what can it be?"

I stared at the wall thoughtfully. "I'm wondering that too. I think it lies out West in an asylum for the insane. Tomorrow I want you to take the first plane out and start digging."

"For what?"

"For anything you can find. Think up the questions and look for the answers. The part we're looking for may be there and it may be here, but we haven't the time to look together. You'll have to go out alone while I plod along this end of the track."

"Mike . . . you'll be careful, won't you?"

"Very careful. Velda. I won't ask questions if I think a gun will do the job quicker. This time I'm going to live up to my reputation. I've been thinking some things I don't like and to satisfy myself I'm going to find out whether or not they're true."

"Supposing they make another try for you?"

"Oh, they will, they will. In fact, they have to. From now on I'll be sleeping with my gun in my fist and my eyes open. They'll make the play again because I know enough and think too much. I might run into a conclusion that will split things wide open. They'll be looking for me and possibly you because they know there were two guns that killed those boys in Oscar's room. They'll know I wasn't alone and they may think of you.

"I'll have to keep my apartment and the office covered while I'm away. They'll get around it somehow, but I'll try anyway."

Velda took my shoulder and made me look at her. "You aren't sending me out West just so I won't be there if there's trouble, are you?"

"No, I wouldn't do that to you. I know how much it means to be in on a thing like this."

She knew I was telling the truth for a change and dropped her hand into mine. "I'll do a good job, Mike. When I get back I won't take any chance on their finding any information I have. I'll tuck it in that trick wall lamp in the office so you can get to it without waking me from the sleep I'll probably need."

I pulled the cord and the light did a slow fade-out. Velda held her flash on the floor and stared down the corridor. A little brown face peeked out of a door and withdrew when she threw the spot on it. We held on to the banister and went down the steps that announced our descent with sharp squeals and groans.

The hunchback opened his door at the foot of the landing and took the key back. "That was quick," he said. "Pretty quick for your age. Thought ya'd take longer."

I wanted to rap him in the puss, only that would have shut him up when I had a question to ask him. "We woulda stayed only the room was a mess. Who was in there before us?"

"Some guy died who lived there."

"Yeah, but who was in there next?"

"Young kid. Said he wanted a bunk for a night. Guess he was hot or something. He gimme a ten too, plus a five for the room. Yeah, I remember him 'counta he wore a nice topcoat and one of them flat pork-pie hats. Sure woulda like to get that topcoat."

I pushed Velda outside and down to the car. The MVD had been there. No wonder the search was so complete. He looked and never looked hard enough. In his hurry to find some documents he overlooked the very thing that might have told him where they were.

I drove Velda home and went up for coffee. We talked and we smoked. I laughed at the way she looked at the ring on her finger and told her the next thing she knew there'd be a diamond to match. Her eyes sparkled brighter than the stone.

"When will it be, Mike?" Her voice was a velvet glove that caressed every inch of me.

I squirmed a little bit and managed a sick grin. "Oh, soon. Let's not go too fast, kid."

The devil came into her eyes and she pushed away from the table. I had another smoke and finished it. I started on another when she called me. When I went into the living room she was standing by the light in a gown that was nothing at all, nothing at all. I could see through it and saw things I thought existed only in a dream and the sweat popped out on my forehead and left me feeling shaky all over.

Her body was a milky flow of curves under the translucent gown and when she moved the static current of flesh against sheer cloth made it cling to her in a way that made me hold my breath to fight against the temptation I could feel tugging at my body. The inky blackness of the hair falling around her shoulders made her look taller, and the gown shrouded what was yet to come and was there for me alone.

"For our wedding night, Mike," she said. "When will it be?"

I said, "We're . . . only engaged to be engaged, you know."

I didn't dare move when she came to me. She raised herself on her toes to kiss me with a tongue of fire, then walked back to the light and turned around. I could see through that damned gown as though it weren't there at all.

She knew I'd never be able to wait long after that.

I stumbled out of the room and down to my car. I sat there awhile thinking of nothing but Velda and the brief glimpse of heaven she had showed me. I tried thinking about something else and it didn't work.

I couldn't get her out of my mind.

CHAPTER NINE

I SLEPT with a dream that night. It was a dream of nice things and other things that weren't so nice. There were a lot of people in the dream and not all of them were alive. There were faces from the past that mingled with those of the present, drawn silent faces turned toward me to see when I would become one of them, floating in that limbo of nonexistence.

I saw the bridge again, and two people die while the stern face of the judge looked on disapproving, uttering solemn words of condemnation. I saw flashes of fire, and men fall. I saw Ethel hovering between the void that separates life from death, teetering into the black while I screamed for her not to and tried to run to catch her, only to have my feet turn into stumps that grew from the very soil.

There were others too, bodies of dead men without faces, waiting for me to add that one missing part, to identify them with their brother dead in one sweeping blast of gunfire. I was there with them. They didn't want me because I wasn't dead, and the living didn't want me either. They couldn't figure out why I was still alive when I dwelt in the land of the dead men.

Only Velda wanted me. I could see her hovering above the others, trailing the gown of transparent fabric, her finger beckoning me to come with her where nothing would matter but the two of us.

The dead pushed me out and the living pushed me back. I tried to get up to Velda and I couldn't reach her. I screamed once for them all to shut up before there was only the land of the dead and none of the living.

Then I woke up. My head throbbed and the shout was still caught in my throat. My tongue felt thick and there was an ache across my shoulders. I staggered into the bathroom where I could duck myself under a cold shower whose stinging chill would wash away the dream.

I glanced at the clock, seeing that the morning had come and gone, leaving me only the afternoon and night. I picked up the phone, asked for long distance, then had myself connected with the hospital outside the city. I hung on for ten minutes waiting for the doctor, told him who I was when he came on and asked him how she was.

The doctor held his hand over the receiver and his voice was a slight mumble of sound. Then: "Yes, Mr. Hammer, I can talk now. The patient has passed the crisis and in my opinion she will live."

"Has she talked, doc?"

"She was conscious a few minutes but she said nothing, nothing at all. There are quite a few people waiting to hear her words." I sensed the change in his voice. "They are police, Mr. Hammer . . . and Federal men."

"I figured they'd be there. Have you said anything?"

"No. I rather believe that you told me the truth, especially since seeing those Federal men. I told them I received an anonymous call to go to the cabin and when I did I found her."

"Good. I can say thanks but it won't mean much. Give me three days and you can say what you like if it hasn't already been explained."

"I understand."

"Is Mr. Brighton there?"

"He has been here since the girl was identified. He seems considerably upset. We had to give him a sedative."

"Just how upset is he?"

"Enough to justify medical attention . . . which he won't have."

"I see. All right, doctor, I'll call you again. Let me have those three days."

"Three days, Mr. Hammer. You may have less. Those Federal men are viewing me somewhat suspiciously." We said our good-bys and hung up. Then I went out and ate breakfast.

I got dressed and went straight to the office. Velda had left a note in her typewriter saying that she had taken the morning plane out and for me to be careful. I pulled the sheet out of the roller and tore it up. There was no mail to look at so I gave Pat a ring and caught him just as he was coming in from lunch.

He said, "Hello, Mike. What's new?"

If I told him he would have cut my throat. "Nothing much. I wanted to speak to somebody so I called. What're you doing?"

"Right now I have to go downtown. I have to see the medical examiner and he's out on a case. A suicide, I think. I'm going to meet him there and if you feel like coming along you're welcome."

"Well, I don't feel like it, but I will. Be down in a few minutes. We'll use my car."

"Okay, but shake it up."

I dumped a pack of Luckies out of the carton in my desk and shoved it in my pocket, went downstairs and took off for Pat's. He was waiting for me on the curb, talking earnestly to a couple of uniformed cops. He waved, made a final point to the cops and crossed the street.

"Somebody steal your marbles, Mike? You don't look happy."

"I'm not. I didn't get but eleven hours' sleep."

"Gosh, you poor guy. That must hurt. If you can keep awake, drive down to the foot of Third Avenue. How're you making out with Lee?"

"I'll have a definite report for him in a couple of days."

"Negative?"

I shrugged.

Pat looked at me querulously. "That's a hell of a note. What else could it be?"

"Positive."

Pat got mad. "Do you think Oscar left something behind him, Mike? By damn, if he did I want to know about it!"

"Simmer down. I'm checking every angle I know of and when my report is made you'll be able to depend on its answer. If Oscar left one thing that could frame Lee I'll be sure nobody sees it who shouldn't see it. That's the angle I'm worried about. A smear on Lee now will be fatal . . . and Pat, there's a lot of wrong guys out to smear him. If you only knew."

"I will know soon, sonny boy. I've already had a few initial reports myself and it seems that your name has cropped up pretty frequently."

"I get around," I said.

"Yeah." He relaxed into a silence he didn't break until I saw the morgue wagon and a prowl ahead of me. "Here's the place. Stop behind the car."

We hopped out and one of the cops saluted Pat and told him the medical examiner was still upstairs. Pat lugged his brief case along and met him on the stairs. I stood in the background while they rambled along about something and Pat handed him a manila folder. The M.E. tucked it under his arm and said he'd take care of it.

Pat waved his thumb toward the top of the stairs. "What is it this time?"

"Another suicide. Lieutenant Barner is on the case. Some

old duck took the gas pipe. They're always doing it in this neighborhood. Go up and take a look."

"I see enough of that stuff. Let Barner handle it."

He would have followed the M.E. down the stairs if I hadn't been curious enough to step up to the landing and peer in the door. Pat came up behind me and laughed. "Curious?"

"Can't help it."

"Sure. Then let's go in and see somebody who died by their own hand instead of yours."

"That's not funny, pal. Can it." Pat laughed again and walked in.

The guy was a middle-aged average man. He had a shock of white hair and a peculiar expression and color that come from breathing too much gas. He stunk of whisky and lay in a heap on the floor with his head partially propped up against the cushioned leg of a chair.

Barner was slipping into his coat. "Damn good thing there wasn't a pilot light on that stove. Would have blown the block to bits."

Pat knelt down and took a close look at the body. "How long has he been dead?"

"Few hours, at least. There hasn't been anybody home in this building all morning. The landlady came in around noon and smelt the gas. The door was closed, but not locked, and she smashed a couple of windows out and called a doctor. There wasn't anything he could do so he called us."

"Any note?"

"Nah. The guy was tanked up. He probably got disgusted with himself and turned on the gas. He used to be an actor. Name's Jenkins, Harvey Robinson Jenkins. The landlady said he was pretty good about thirty years ago, a regular matinee idol. He dropped into character parts, got wiped out when vaudeville went out and picked up a few bucks working in small road shows now and then."

I looked around the room and took stock of his things. There was a good leather chair by the window and a new floor lamp, but the rest of the furnishings had lost their shape and luster with age. There were two rooms, a combination sitting-room-bedroom and a kitchenette. A stack of old theater posters were neatly stacked behind the bed and a new military kit decorated the top of the dresser. The kitchen was big enough to hold one person at a time. A faint odor of gas still hung up high and clung to the curtains. The refrigerator didn't work, but then it didn't have to because it was empty. A jar of jam was on the table next to an empty bottle of whisky. There were a dozen other empties under the table in a cardboard carton.

So this is death. This is the way people die if you don't help them. He was on the long road and glad of it. Too bad he had to leave his most prized possessions behind. The make-up kit was old and battered, but it was clean, unlike everything else, and the tubes and jars inside it were all neatly arranged and labeled. The mirror fastened to the back of the lid was polished clear by a careful hand. I could picture the little guy sitting there night after night playing all the great roles of history, seeing his hand transform him to the glories of his youth.

They were taking the body out in the basket when the landlady came in to see that that was all they took out. Barner said so long and left us watching the procession down the stairs. The landlady was a chubby woman whose scraggly hair fell down past her ears. Her hands were calloused and red from work and she kept rubbing them together as though they were cold.

She turned to me, clucking through her teeth. "There you see the evil of drink, young man. I lost me two husbands that way and now I lose a boarder."

"Tough. Did he owe you any money?"

"No, not one red cent. Oh, he was an honorable one was Mr. Jenkins. Lived here over three years he did but always paid his rent somehow. Too bad he got that inheritance. It was too much for him who never had any real money. He spent it all on drink and now look at him."

"Yeah."

"Well, I warned him, you can't say I didn't try. He was always making those speeches like an actor does and he told me that drink was food for the soul. Food for the soul! He never went hungry then."

Pat grunted, anxious to leave. "Let that be a lesson to you, Mike." He looked at the landlady pointedly. "How long was he on that binge?"

"Oh, for quite a while. Let me see, the letter with the money came a week after the Legion Parade. That was a Wednesday, the 13th. Yes, that's it, a week later he got the money. He paid me the three months he owed me and for two more months in advance, then he started drinking. I never did see a man drink so much. Every night he'd get carried in still mumbling one of them silly parts of his and messing up my floor."

Pat nodded thoughtfully. "See, Mike, that's what you're heading for. An untimely end."

"Nuts, I don't drink that much. Anyway, I'll shoot myself before I try to get charged up on gas. Come on, let's get out of here."

The landlady showed us to the door and watched from the stoop as we pulled away. I hunched behind the wheel when I began thinking of the old coot who took the easy way out.

I thought about it for a long time.

I let Pat out at his office, found a saloon that was half empty and perched on a stool where I could think about it some more. The rows of whisky bottles behind the bar gleamed with reflected light. They were like women. Bait. They lured you in where you forget what you were doing then sprung the trap and kicked you out.

The bartender filled my glass again, scooping up the rest of my change. I watched myself in the back mirror, wondering if I was as ugly to others as I was to myself. I grinned and the bartender scowled my way. I scowled and the bartender started grinning because my scowl isn't as pretty as most. I swirled the drink around in my glass, slopping it over the top so I could make patterns on the bar.

I made rings, ovals, faces, then overlaid the whole picture with a bridge that towered high at both ends. I stared at the hump in the middle and drained the glass in a hurry to get my mind off it.

A lot of it had fallen into place, piece by piece. Things I didn't see before were suddenly clear. It was a gigantic puzzle that only started here in Manhattan . . . the rest of it reached down to Washington, across to San Francisco, then on across the ocean. And onward still until it encompassed the world and came back to where it started.

It was a picture of hate, terror and death that had no equal in history and it was here with us now. I was the only one who could see it. There were still parts of the puzzle missing, but it had a broad, recognizable outline now. I could make up parts that would fit, but that wouldn't do. *I had to know. I had to be sure!*

This time I wasn't dealing in murder, I was dealing in war!

It was a curious puzzle that had two solutions. Every part could fit in different places, fooling you into thinking you had it. They were clever, I thought. They were clever, crafty, cunning, anything you wanted to call it.

They had a slogan that the end justified the means.

They would kill to accomplish a purpose.

They would wreck everything to gain their ends, even if they had to build again on the wreckage.

They were here and they were smart as hell. Even the Nazis were like schoolchildren as compared to them.

But that was the catch. They were smart . . . for them! I could laugh now and think rings around them all because I was smarter than the best they could offer. Torture, Death, and Lies were their brothers, but I had dealt with those triplets many times myself. They weren't strangers to me. I gave them my orders and they took them because they had to.

I was a ruthless bastard with a twisted mind who could look on death and find it pleasant. I could break an arm or smash in a face because it was easier that way than asking questions. I could out-fox the fox with a line of reasoning that laughed at the truth because I was the worst of the lot and never did deserve to live. That's what that damned judge thought anyway.

This time I got back in the car and drove over to the building that had the radio antenna projecting up from the roof. There were two police cars parked in front of it and I nodded to the drivers. For once I was glad to have been seen around so much with Pat. I went in and leaned on the railing that separated the room and waited until the cop in the faded alpaca coat and the eyeshade came over to me.

He nodded too.

I said, "Hello, George. I need a favor done."

"Sure, Mike. That is, if I can do it."

"You keep a record of incoming calls, don't you?"

"Yeah, why?"

"Look one up for me. A few days ago a New York prowl car crossed the George Washington bridge." I gave him the date and the approximate time. "See if it was on a call."

He went back to a stall where he rummaged around in a filing cabinet. When he returned he carried a sheet, reading from it. He looked up and raised his eyeshade farther on his forehead. "Here it is. Unidentified girl called and asked to have a police car meet her. I think I remember this one. She was in a hurry and instead of giving her address she said on the walk of the bridge. A car was dispatched to see what went on and called in that it was a wild-goose chase."

"That's all?"

"Yeah. Anything to it?"

"I don't know yet. Thanks a lot, George."

"Sure, Mike, any time. So long."

I went out and sat in the car with a cigarette drooping from my lips. Unidentified girl. That car on the bridge wasn't there by chance. I had just missed things. Too bad, too damn bad in one way that the boys in the car had gotten there late. The weather, no doubt. Then again it was lucky they didn't make it.

The engine came to life under my feet and I drove away from the curb. I took the notebook from my pocket and thumbed the pages while I was stalled in traffic, picking up Paula Riis's address from the jumble of notes. I hoped I had it right, because I had jotted it down after coming from Pat's the time he had thrown her identity at me.

It was a number in the upper Forties just off Eighth Avenue, a four-story affair with three apartments above a shoddy beauty parlor that took up the first floor. A sedan with United States Post Office Department inscribed in the door was double parked outside it. I found a place to leave my heap and got back just as two men came down the stairs and got into the car. I had seen the taller guy before; he was a postal inspector.

A dark, swarthy woman stood in the door with her hands on chunky hips muttering to herself. I took the steps two at a time and said hello to her.

She looked me up and down first. "Now what you want? You not from Post Office."

I looked past her shoulder into the vestibule and knew why those men had been here. A good-sized rectangle had been torn out of the wall. The mailbox that had been there had been ripped out by the roots and the marks of the crowbar that did it still showed in the shattered lath and plaster.

I got that cold feeling again, of being just a little bit too late. I palmed my buzzer and held it out where she could see it.

"Oh, you the police. You come about the room. Whassa matter with other police? He see everything. These crooks! When that girl comes back she be one mad cookie, you bet!"

"That's right, I came about the room. Where is it?"

"Upstairs, what's left of it. Now there's nothing but junk. Thassall, just junk. Go look."

I went and looked. I saw the same thing that had happened to Charlie Moffit's room. This was a little worse because there was more to it. I cursed softly and backed out of the room. I cursed because I was pleased that the room *was* like Charlie Moffit's room, a room ripped apart by a search that didn't have an end. They were still looking. They tore the room up then stole the mailbox because they thought that Charlie had mailed his girl friend the stuff.

Then I stopped cursing because I knew then that they did have it after all. Charlie mailed the stuff and it lay in the mailbox because she was dead. They couldn't get it out so they took the whole works. This time I cursed because I was mad, mad as hell.

I made a circuit of the room, kicking at the pieces with a frenzied futility. Clothes that had been ripped apart at the seams were everywhere. The furniture was broken, disemboweled and scattered across the floor. The bottom had been taken out of the phone and lay beneath the stand by the window. I picked it up, turned it over then chucked it away.

They had come in through the window and gouged hunks out of the sill when they pried up the sash. I threw it up and looked around, saying damn to myself because it had been so easy. There was an overturned ashcan on the ground below. They had stepped on that, then on to the roof of the extension below and right into the room.

Too bad Mr. MVD couldn't have tripped over the phone line and broken his lousy neck. I picked up the strand of wire that ran out the window to the pole and switched it out of the way. It was slack, too damn slack. I saw why in a minute. The insulator that had held it to the wall had been pulled out. I climbed out on the roof and ran my hand along the wire and the answer was in the slit that was in the insulation.

Somebody had a tap on that wire and when they pulled it off they yanked too hard and it came right off the wall. Damn! Damn it all to hell and back again! I climbed back in the room and slammed the window shut, still swearing to myself.

The woman still stood in the doorway. "You see, you see?" Her voice went higher on each word. "These damn crooks. Nobody is safe. What for are the police? What that girl going to say, eh? You know! She give me hell, you betcha. She was all paid up, too. Now whatcha think?"

"Don't get excited. Whoever searched her room took the mailbox too. They were looking for a letter."

She made a sour mouth. "Huh. They don't get it, I tell you that, for sure. She's a lose her key a month ago and I always get her mail personal. The postman he's give it to me every day and I take it inside."

My heart hammered against my ribs and I heard it send the blood driving into my head. I licked my lips to get the words out. "Maybe I better take it all along then. She can call for it when she returns."

She squinted, then bobbed her head. "That is good. I don't have to worry no more about it. From now on till I get a new mailbox I have to take everybody's mail anyhow. Come inside, I give it to you."

We went into the beauty parlor on the first floor and I waited with my hat in my hand. She came back with a handful of envelopes and one of them was a heavy job stuffed so full the flap had torn a little. I thanked her and left.

Just like that.

How simple could it get?

The murder and the wreckage that had been caused by this one fat envelope, and she drops it in my hand just like that. No trouble. No sneaking around with a gun in your hand. No tight spots that left you shaken and trembling. She hands it to me and I take it and leave.

Isn't that the way life is? You fight and struggle to get something and suddenly you're there at the end and there's nothing left to fight for any longer.

I threw the works in the glove compartment and drove back to my office. From force of habit I locked the door before I sat down to see what it was all about. There were nine letters and the big one. Of the nine three were bills, four were from female friends and had nothing to say, one was an answer to a letter she sent an employment agency and the other enclosed a Communist Party pamphlet. I threw it in the wastebasket and opened the main one.

They were photostats, ten in all, both negatives and positives, on extra thin paper. They were photos of a maze of symbols, diagrams and meaningless words, but there was something about them that practically cried out their extreme importance. They weren't for a mind like mine and I knew it.

I folded them up into a compact square and took them to the lamp on the wall. It was a tricky little job that came apart in the middle and had been given to me by a friend who dabbled in magic. At one time a bird flew out of the hidden compartment when you snapped the light on and scared the hell out of you. I stuck the photostats in there and shut it again.

There was an inch of sherry left on the bottom of the bottle in my desk and I put the mouth to my lips.

It was almost over. I had come to the pause before the end. There was little left to do but sort the parts and make sure I had them straight. I sat down again, pulling the phone over in front of me. I dialed headquarters and asked for Pat.

He had left for the weekend.

The next time I dialed Lee Deamer's office. The blonde at the switchboard was still chewing gum and threw the connection over to his secretary. She said, "I'm sorry, but Mr. Deamer has left for Washington."

"This is Mike Hammer. I was there once before. I'd like to get a call in to him."

"Oh, yes, Mr. Hammer. He's registered at the Lafayette. You can call him there. However, you had better call before six because he's speaking at a dinner meeting tonight."

"I'll call him now, and thanks."

I got long distance, gave the number and she told me the lines were all busy and I would have to wait. I hung up and went to the filing cabinet where I had the remains of another bottle of sherry stashed away. There was a box of paper cups with it and I put the makings on my desk and settled back to enjoy the wait.

After the third half-cup of sherry I snapped the radio on and caught the broadcast. The boy with the golden voice was snapping out the patter in a tone so excited that he must have been holding on to the mike to stay on his feet. It was all about the stolen documents. Suspicions were many and clues were nil. The FBI had every available man on the case and the police of every community had pledged to help in every way.

He went off and a serious-voiced commentator took his place. He told the nation of the calamity that had befallen it. The secret of our newest, most powerful weapon was now, most likely, in the hands of agents of an unfriendly power. He told of the destruction that could be wrought, hinted at the continuance of the cold war with an aftermath of a hotter one. He spoke and his voice trembled with the rage and fear he tried so hard to control.

Fifteen minutes later another commentator came on with a special bulletin that told of all ports being watched, the roundup of suspected aliens. The thing that caused the roundup was still as big a mystery as ever, but the search had turned up a lot of minor things that never would have been noticed. A government clerk was being held incommunicado. A big shot labor leader had hanged himself. A group of Communists had staged a demonstration in Brooklyn with the usual scream of persecution and had broken some windows. Twenty of them were in the clink.

I sat back and laughed and laughed. The world was in an uproar when the stuff was safe as hell not five feet away from me. The guardians of our government were jumping through hoops because the people demanded to know why the most heavily guarded secret we ever had could be swiped so easily. There were shakeups from the top to bottom and the rats were scurrying for cover, pleading for mercy. Investigations were turning up reds in the damnedest spots imaginable and the senators and congressmen who recommended them for the posts were on the hot spots in their bailiwicks. Two had already sent in resignations.

Oh, it was great. Something was getting done that should have been done years ago. The heat was on and the fire was burning a lot of pants. The music I had on the radio was interrupted every five minutes now with special newscasts that said the people were getting control of the situation at last.

Of the people, for the people, by the people. We weren't so soft after all. We got pushed too far once too often and the backs were up and teeth bared.

What were the Commies doing! They must be going around in circles. The thing that would have tipped the balance back to them again had been in their hands and they'd dropped it. Was the MVD out taking care of those who had been negligent? Probably. Very probably. Pork-Pie Hat would have himself a field day. They were the only ones who knew where those documents *weren't*. Our own government knew where they started to go and still thought they were in their hands. I was the only one who knew where they *were*.

Not five feet away. Safe as pie, I thought.

The phone rang and I picked it up. The operator said, "I have your party, sir."

I said thanks, waited for the connection and heard Lee saying, "Hello, hello . . ."

"Mike Hammer. Lee."

"Yes, Mike, how are you?"

"Fine. I hear Washington is in an uproar."

"Quite. You can't imagine what it's like. They tell me the hall is filled to the rafters already, waiting to hear the speeches. I've never seen so many reporters in my life."

"Going to give 'em hell tonight?"

"I'll do my best. I have an important topic to discuss. Was there something special you wanted, Mike?"

"Yeah, sort of. I just wanted to tell you that I found it."

"It?"

"What Oscar left behind. I found it."

His voice held a bitter ring. "I knew it, I knew it! I knew he'd do something like that. Mike . . . is it bad?"

"Oh no. In fact it's pretty good. Yeah, pretty good."

He paused, and when he spoke again he sounded tired. "Remember what I told you, Mike. It's in your hands. Authenticate what you found, and if you believe that it would be better to publish the facts, then make them public."

I laughed lightly. "Not this, Lee. It isn't something you can print in a paper. It isn't anything that you nor Pat nor I expected to find. It doesn't tie you into a damn thing so you can blast 'em tonight and make it good because what I have can push you right up there where you can do a good housecleaning job."

The surprise and pleasure showed in his voice. "That *is* fine news, Mike. When can I see it?"

"When will you be back in New York?"

"Not before Monday night."

"It'll keep. I'll see you then."

I pushed the phone back across the desk and started working on the remainder of the sherry. I finished it in a half-hour and closed up the office. It was Saturday night and time to play. I had to wait until Velda came back before I made my decision. I ambled up Broadway and turned into a bar for a drink. The place was packed and noisy, except when the news bulletin came on. At seven o'clock they turned on the TV and all heads angled to watch it. They were relaying in the pics of the dinner in Washington that was to be followed by the speeches. The screen was blurred, but the sound was loud and clear.

I had a good chance to watch Mr. and Mrs. Average People take in the political situation and I felt good all over again. It was no time to come up with the documents. Not yet. Let the fire stay on full for a while. Let it scorch and purify while it could.

The bartender filled my glass and I leaned forward on my elbows to hear Lee when he spoke.

He gave them a taste of hell. He used names and quotations and pointed to the big whiskers in the Kremlin as the brother of the devil. He threw the challenge in the faces of the people and they accepted it with cheers and applause that rocked the building.

I shouted the way I felt louder than anybody and had another drink.

At midnight I walked back to my car and drove home slowly, my mind miles away from my body. Twice I patted the .45 under my arm and out of force of habit I kept a constant check on the cars behind me.

I put the car in the garage, told the attendant to service it fully and went out the side door that led to the street. When I looked both ways and was satisfied that I wasn't going to run into another ambush I stepped out to the sidewalk and walked to my building.

Before I went upstairs I checked the little panel of lights behind the desk in the lobby. It was a burglar alarm and one of the lights was connected to the windows and doors in my apartment. They were all blank so I took the stairs up and shoved the key in the lock.

For safety's sake I went through the place and found it as empty as when I left it. Maybe Pork-Pie was afraid of a trap. Maybe he was waiting to get me on the street. He and the others had the best reason in the world to get me now. It wouldn't be too long before they figured out where the documents went to, and that was the moment I was hoping for.

I wanted them, every one of the bastards. I wanted them all to myself so I could show the sons-of-bitches what happened when they tried to play rough with somebody who likes that game himself!

The late news broadcast was on and I listened for further developments. There weren't any. I shoved the .45 under my pillow and rolled into the sack.

CHAPTER TEN

I SLEPT all day Sunday. At six-fifteen P.M. I got up to answer the persistent ringing of my doorbell and a Western Union messenger handed me a telegram. He got a buck for his persistence and I went into the living room where I opened it up.

The telegram was from Velda. It was very brief, saying the mission was accomplished and she was carrying the papers out on the first plane. I folded the yellow sheet and stuck it in the pocket of my coat that was draped on the back of the chair.

I had a combination meal, sent down for the papers and read them in bed. When I finished I slept again and didn't wake up until twelve hours later. The rain was beating against the windows with a hundred tiny fingers and the street was drenched with an overflow too great to be carried off by the sewers at the end of the block.

For a few minutes I stood at the window and looked out into the murk of the morning, not aware of the people that scurried by on the sidewalks below, or of the cars whose tires made swishing sounds on the wet pavement. Across the street, the front of the building there wavered as the water ran down the glass, assuming the shape of a face moulded by ghostly hands. The face had eyes like two berries on a bush and they turned their stare on me.

This is it, Judge. Here is your rain of purity. You're a better forecaster than I thought. Now, of all times, it should rain. Cold, clear rain that was washing away the scum and the filth and pulling it into the sewer. It's here and you're waiting for me to step out into it and be washed away, aren't you? I could play it safe and stay where I am, but you know I won't. I'm me, Mike Hammer, and I'll be true to form. I'll go down with the rest of the scum.

Sure, Judge, I'll die. I've been so close to death that this time the scythe can't miss me. I've dodged too often, now I've lost the quick-step timing I had that made me duck in time. You noticed it and Pat noticed it . . . I've changed, and now I notice it myself. I don't care any more.

The hell of it is, Judge . . . your question won't get an-swered. You'll never know why I was endowed with the ability to think and move fast enough to keep away from the man with the reaper. I kept breaking his hour-glass and dull-ing his blade and he couldn't do a thing about it.

Your rain of purity has come, and out there in it is the grim specter who is determined that this time he will not miss. He'll raise his vicious scythe and swing at me with all the fury of his madness and I'll go down, but that one wild swing will take along a lot of others before it cuts me in half.

Sorry, Judge, so sorry you'll never know the answer. I was curious myself. I wanted to know the answer too. It's been puzzling me a long, long time.

I showered and dressed, packing the automatic away in the oiled leather holster under my arm. When I finished I called long distance and was connected with the hospital. Again I was lucky and got the doctor while he was there. I told him my name and that was enough.

"Miss Brighton is out of danger," he said. "For some rea-son she is under police guard."

"Studious young men?"

"Yes."

"How about her father?"

"He visits her daily. His own doctor is prescribing for him."

"I see. My time is up, you know. You can talk if you like."

"For some reason I prefer not to, Mr. Hammer. I still don't understand, but I still believe that there is more to this than I can see. Miss Brighton asked me if you had called and I repeated our conversation. She has taken the same attitude of silence."

"Thanks, doc. It's going to be rough when it starts, but thanks. Tell Miss Brighton I was asking for her."

"I will. Good day."

I put the phone back and shrugged into my raincoat. Downstairs I got my car out of the garage and backed out into the rain. The windshield wipers were little demons working furiously, fighting to keep me from being purified. I drove downtown hoping to see Pat, but he had called in that his car was stuck somewhere along the highway and he might not make it in at all.

The morning went by without my noticing its passing. When my stomach tightened I went in and had lunch. I bought a paper and parked the car to read it through. The headlines hadn't changed much. There were pages devoted to the new aspect of the cold war; pages given to the coming election, pages that told of the shake-up in Washington, and of the greater shake-up promised by the candidates running for election.

Lee had given 'em hell, all right. The editorial quoted excerpts from his speech and carried a two-column cut of him shaking his fist at the jackals who were seeking the protection of the same government they had tried to tear down. There was another Communist demonstration, only this one was broken up by an outraged populace and ten of the reds had landed in the hospital. The rest were sweeping out corridors in the city jail.

The rain let up, but it was only taking a breather before it came down even harder. I took advantage of the momentary lull to duck into a drugstore and put in a call to Lee's office. His secretary told me that he wasn't expected in until evening and I thanked her. I bought a fresh pack of Luckies and went back to the car and sat. I watched the rain and timed my thoughts to its intensity.

I took all the parts and let them drop, watching to see how they fit in place. They were all there now, every one. I could go out any time and show that picture around and anybody could tell that it was a big red flag with a star and a hammer and sickle. I could show it to them but I'd have to have the last piece of proof I needed and I'd have that when Velda got back. I went over it time after time until I was satisfied, then I reached for a butt.

There was only one left. I had just bought a pack and there was only one left. My watch was a round little face that laughed at me for thinking the afternoon away and I stared at it, amazed that the night had shifted in around the rain and I hadn't noticed it. I got out and went back to the same drugstore and looked up the number of the terminal.

A sugar-coated voice said that all the planes were on schedule despite the rain and the last one from the Midwest had landed at two o'clock. I smacked my hand against my head for letting time get away from me and called the office. Velda didn't answer so I hung up. I was about to call her apartment when I remembered that she'd probably be plenty tired and curled up in the sack, but she said she'd leave anything she had in the lamp if I wasn't in the office when she got in.

I started the car up and the wipers went back into action. The rain of purity was starting to give up and here I was still warm and dry. For how long?

The lights were on in the office and I practically ran in. I yelled, "Hey, Velda!" the smile I had ready died away because she wasn't there. She *had* been there, though. I smelled the faintest trace of the perfume she used. I went right to the lamp and opened the little compartment. She had laid it right on top of the other stuff for me.

I pulled it out and spread it across my desk, feeling the grin come back slowly as I read the first few lines.

It was done. Finished. I had it all ready to wrap up nice and legal now. I could call Pat and the studious-looking boys with the FBI badges and drop it in their laps. I could sit back in a ringside seat and watch the whole show and laugh at the judge because this time I was free and clear, with my hands clean of somebody's blood. The story would come out and I'd be a hero. The next time I stepped into that court of law and faced the little judge his voice would be quiet and his words more carefully chosen because I was able to prove to the world that I wasn't a bloodthirsty kill-happy bastard with a mind warped by a war of too many dawns and dusks laced by the crisscrossed patterns of bullets. I was a normal guy with normal instincts and maybe a temper that got a little out of hand at times, but was still under control when I wanted it that way.

Hell, Pat should be back now. I'll let him get the credit for it. He won't like it, but he'll have to do it. I reached for the phone.

That's when I saw the little white square of cardboard that had been sitting there in front of me all the time. I picked it up, scowling at the brief typewritten message. CALL LO 3-8099 AT EXACTLY NINE P.M. That was all. The other side was blank.

I didn't get it. Velda was the only one to have been here and she would have left more of an explanation, at least. Besides, we had memo pads for stuff like this. I frowned again and threw it back on the desk. It was ten to eight now. Hell, I wasn't going to wait another hour. I dialed the number and heard the phone ring a dozen times before I hung up.

A nasty taste was in my mouth. My shoulders kept hunching up under my coat as if I were cold. I went to the outer office to see if she had left a note in her desk typewriter and found nothing.

It wasn't right. Not at a moment like this. Nothing else could come up now. Hell, I was on my way to being a hero. The door of the washroom was standing open a little and I went to close it. The light from the lamp on the wall darted in the crack and bounced back at me with bright sparkle. I shoved the door open and every muscle in my body pulled tight as a bowstring and my breath caught in my throat.

There beside the faucet was Velda's ring . . . the sapphire ring I had given her and her wrist watch!

Velda wasn't here but her ring was and no girl is going to go off and forget her ring! No girl will wash her hands and not dry them, either . . . But Velda apparently had, for there was no crumpled paper towel in the basket under the sink!

Somehow I staggered back to my chair and sat down, the awful realization of it hitting me hard. I buried my face in my hands and said, "Oh, God . . . oh, God!" I knew what had happened now . . . *they* had her! They walked in on her and took her away.

I thought I was clever. I thought they'd try for me. But they *were* clever when the chips were down and now they had something they could trade. That's what they'd say . . . trade, that was a laugh. They'd take the documents and when I asked them to give her back I'd get a belly full of slugs. Nice trade. A stupid ass like me ought to get shot anyway.

Goddamn 'em anyway! Why couldn't they act like men and fight with me! Why did they have to pick on women! The dirty yellow bastards were afraid to tangle with me so they decided to do it the easy way. They knew the score, they knew I'd have to play ball. They seemed to know a lot of things.

All right, you conniving little punks, I'll play ball, but I'm going to make up a lot of rules you never heard of. You think I'm cornered and it'll be a soft touch. Well, you won't be playing with a guy who's a hero. You'll be up against a guy with a mind gone rotten and a lust for killing! That's the way I was and that's the way I like it!

I grabbed the phone and dialed Pat's home number. When I got him I said hello and didn't give him a chance to interrupt me. "I need a favor as fast as you can do it, kid. Find out where the phone with the number Longacre 3-8099 is located and call me right back. Shake it because I need it right away."

Pat let out a startled answer that I cut off by slamming the phone back. Five minutes later the phone rang and I picked it up.

"What goes on with you, Mike? That number is a pay station in the Times Square subway station."

"Fine," I answered, "that's all I need to know. See you later."

"Mike . . . hey . . ." I cut him off again and picked up my coat.

They thought they were smart but they forgot I had a fast brain and a lot of connections. Maybe they thought I wouldn't take the chance.

I was downstairs and in the car like a shot. Going up Broadway I pulled out all the stops and forgot there was such a thing as a red light. When I turned off Broadway onto Times Square I saw a patrolman standing in front of the subway entrance idly swinging his stick in his hands.

Tonight was my night and I was going to play it all the way to the hilt. I yanked out the wallet I had taken from that overturned car the other night, plucked the FBI card from the pocket and fitted it into mine. The cop was coming out into the rain to tell me I couldn't park there when I stepped out and shoved the wallet under his nose.

I didn't let him have more than a peek at it, but it was enough. I said, "Stay here and watch that car. I don't want it gone when I come back."

He drew himself all the way up with a look that only public servants old in the service can get and passed me a snappy salute. With the headlines blaring from all the papers he didn't have to ask questions to know what was up. "I'll take care of it," he shot back.

I ran down the stairs and slipped a dime in the turnstile. I had fifteen minutes to find the right booth, fifteen short minutes. I made a tour of the place poking my head into the empties hoping the one I was looking for wouldn't be occupied.

It wasn't. I found it over near the steps that led to the BMT line, the last one on the end of five booths. I stepped into one and shut the door. The light above my head was too dàmn bright, but one crack with the nose of the .45 took care of that. I lifted the receiver off the hook without dropping a nickel in and started conversation with an imaginary person on an imaginary phone.

At five minutes to nine he walked up to the end booth, obviously ignoring the others, and closed the door. I let the minutes tick off until the hands of my watch were at right angles to each other, then shoved a nickel in the slot and dialed LO 3-8099.

It rang just once. "Yes?"

I forced a bluff into my voice, keeping it low. "This is Mike Hammer. Who the hell are you and what's this business with the card?"

"Ah, yes, Mr. Hammer. You got our card. That is very fortunate indeed. Need I tell you who is speaking?"

"You damn well better, friend."

"No, certainly not a friend. Just the opposite, I would think. I'm calling about a matter of documents you have, Mr. Hammer. They're very important documents, you know. We have taken a hostage to insure their safe delivery to us."

"What. . . ."

"Please, Mr. Hammer. I'm speaking about your very lovely secretary. A very obstinate woman. I think we can force her to talk if you refuse, you know."

"You bastard!"

"Well?"

My voice changed pitch and stuttered into the mouthpiece. "What can I say? I know when I'm licked. You . . . can have them."

"I was sure you'd see the light, Mr. Hammer. You will take those documents to the Pennsylvania Station on Thirty-fourth Street and deposit them in one of the pay lockers at the end of the waiting room. You will then take the key and walk about on the streets outside until someone says, 'Wonderful night, friend,' and give that person the key. Keep your hands in plain sight and be absolutely alone. I don't think I have to warn you that you will be under constant observation by certain people who will be armed."

"And the girl . . . Velda?" I asked.

"Provided you do as you are told, and we receive the documents, the girl shall be released, of course."

"Okay. What time do I do all this?"

"Midnight, Mr. Hammer. A fitting hour, don't you think?"

He hung up without waiting for an answer. I grinned and watched him squirm out of the booth, a guy who fitted his voice to perfection. Short, soft and fat, wearing clothes that tried without success to make him look tall, hard and slim.

I grinned again and gave him a good lead, then climbed out of the booth and stayed on his tail. He hesitated at the passages, settled on the route that led up the northwest corner of the block and started up the stairs. My grin like to have split my face open. The famous Hammer luck was riding high, wide and handsome. I could call his shots before he made them and I knew it.

When he reached the street I brushed by him and gave him the elbow for luck. He was so intent upon waving to a cab that he never gave me a tumble. I waited for him to get in then started my car. The cop waved me off with his night stick and I was on my way.

Three hours before the deadline.

How much time was that? Not much, yet plenty when it counted. The cab in front of me weaved around the traffic and I stayed right with it. I could see the back of his head in the rear window and I didn't give a hoot whether or not he turned around.

He didn't. He was so sure that I was on the end of the stick that it never occurred to him that he was being tailed. He was going to get that stick up the tail himself when the time came.

So the judge was right all the while. I could feel the madness in my brain eating its way through my veins, chewing the edges of my nerves raw, leaving me something that resembled a man and that was all. *The judge had been right!* There *had* been too many of those dusks and dawns; there *had* been pleasure in all that killing, an obscene pleasure that froze your face in a grin even when you were charged with fear. Like when I cut down that Jap with his own machete and laughed like hell while I made slices of his scrawny body, then went on to do the same thing again because it got to be fun. The little bastards wanted my hide and I gave them a hard time when they tried to take it. Sure, my mind was going rotten even then. I remember the ways the guys used to look at me. You'd think I had fangs. *And it hung on and rotted even further!* How long had it been since I had taken my face out of the ground? How long had it been since they handed me the paper that said it was over and we could go back to being normal people again? And since . . . how many had died while I backed up the gun? Now who was I trying to fool—me? I enjoyed that killing, every bit of it. I killed because I had to and I killed things that needed killing. But that wasn't the point. *I enjoyed killing those things and I knew the judge was right!* I was rotten right through and I knew that at that moment my face was twisted out of shape into a grin that was half sneer and my heart beat fast because it was nice sitting back there with a rod under my arm and somebody was going to hurt pretty quick now, then die. And it might even be me and I didn't give a good damn one way or another.

I tried to figure out where the hell we were. We had passed over a viaduct and a few other things that were vague outlines, but I couldn't tell where we were. If I didn't see the name on the movie house I would have been screwed up, but I caught it in time along with the smell of the river and knew we were some place in Astoria heading down toward the water where the people gave way to the rats and the trash that littered the shore.

There wasn't much more to the block. I cut my lights and drifted in to the curb, snatching the keys out of the ignition as I opened the door. Ahead of me the tail light of the cab was a red dot getting smaller and for one second I thought I had been too soon.

The red dot stopped moving away from me.

Of all the fates who were out for my skin, only one backed me up. It was a lovely fate that turned over a heap and spilled the pair of studious-looking boys out, the ones who had the FBI cards and that gorgeous black tommy gun that was still in the trunk of my car. I held the lid open and yanked it out, shucking the case on the pavement. It nestled in my hands like a woman, loaded and cocked, with two spare clips that made a pleasant weight in my pocket.

I got in close to the buildings and took off at a half-trot. A drunk watched me go by, then scurried back into his doorway. The dot up front disappeared, turned into two headlights on dim and came back and past me.

I ran faster. I ran like a guy with three feet and reached the corner in time to see the guy angling up the rutted street that paralleled the river.

How nice it is when it gets dark. It's all around you, a black coat that hides the good and the bad, and lets you stay shouting distance behind somebody else and never gives you away. My little man stepped right along as if he knew where he was going.

There weren't any houses now. There was a smell of decay, noises that didn't belong to a city. Far away the lights of cars snaked along a bridge happily unaware of this other part of New York.

Then the rain began again. The glorious rain of purity was nothing but light tears . . . the sky protesting because I was walking and thinking when I should be dead. Long dead. I spit on the ground to show what I thought of it.

My little man was gone. The constant, even grinding of his shoes in the gravel had stopped and now there was a silence that shut out all other noises, even the rain.

I was alone in the darkness and my time had come. It had to come, there was only an hour left and never time to undo it if it had all been a mistake! For about ten seconds I stood still, watching those cars in the distance. They wormed ahead, they disappeared as if going into a tunnel, emerging again many seconds later. I knew where my little man was now.

Not far off was a building. That was what stopped those

lights. There was a building and I saw it when I took a dozen more steps. It was the remains of a building, anyway. Three floors staggered up from the ground in uneven rows of bricks. Only the windows on the top floors showed a few panes whole and unbroken, most likely because they were beyond stone's throw. The rest were plastered with boards that seemed to be there to keep things in rather than out.

I was back in the jungle again. I had that feeling. There was a guy at my shoulder in deeper black than the night and he carried a scythe and a map to point out the long road. I didn't walk, I stalked and the guy stalked with me, waiting patiently for that one fatal misstep.

He was death and I knew him well. I had seen him plenty of times before and I laughed in his face because I was me, see? I was Mike Hammer and I could laugh because what did I give a damn about death? He could laugh back at me with his grisly, bony laugh, and even if we didn't make any sound at all my laugh was louder than his. Stick with me, man in black. Stick close because some customers are going to be made that should have been made a long time ago. You thought I was bad when there was a jungle around me for cover and I learned how to kill and kill and kill and walk away and remind myself that killing was nice. Yeah, you thought I was a wise guy. Stick around, old man, maybe you'll see me for the first time doing something I really enjoy. Maybe some day I'll pick on you and we'll have it out, a hot .45 against that blade of yours.

All the instincts came back. The chatter gun was slung just right for easy carrying and quick action. Without me telling it to, my hand had scooped up gobs of mud and daubed my face and hands, even blanking out the luminous dial of my watch.

The pleasure of the hunt, the wonderful knowledge that you're hot and right! The timing was there, that sense of alertness that gets bred into you when there's blood in the air. I liked it!

I stood in the shadow of the building, melting into the wall with the rain, watching the two men. One was there at the doorway, an invisible figure I sensed rather than saw. The other was coming toward me just as I planned it. It had taken a long while just to get this far. I knew without looking that the hands of my watch would be overlapping. Somewhere back in Manhattan a guy would be looking for me to call me friend. Somewhere inside Velda would be sitting, a hostage who would never talk.

The guy came nearer and I knew he had a gun in his hand. I let him come.

Now I could see him plainly. He stopped three feet away and looked back uncertainly. I had the tommy gun in one hand and the nose of the .45 in the other. I let him look back again and this time I let him see me.

No, it wasn't me he saw, it was the other guy, the one with the cowl and the scythe. I swung that gun butt so hard it made a wet smack and almost twisted out of my hand. The guy didn't have any forehead left. There was nothing but a black hole from his eyes to his hair and I was grinning. I eased him down without a sound and picked up the tommy gun. Then I started around the building.

It goes that way. One guy makes one lousy error and everybody falls into the trap. The guy at the door thought it was the other one when I walked out of the murk. He grunted the last sound he ever made because I wrapped my arm under his neck and started bending him over backwards. I had my knee in his spine, pulling him into a living bow that clawed at my hands to release the scream that sudden fear had driven into his throat.

The goddamn grin wouldn't come off my face even when I heard his spine snap and felt that sickening lurch that comes when the bow is bent too far. Two of them. A pair of bastards who had wanted to play in the Big Game. Slimy, squirmy worms who had visions of being on top where they could rule with the whip.

I went into the building with death at my shoulder and he was mad because I was giving the orders. He was waiting for the mistake he knew I'd have to make sooner or later.

My breath wasn't coming easy now. It was hot and coarse in my throat, rasping into my lungs. I stood inside the door, listening, waiting, letting my eyes use precious seconds to orient themselves to this new gloom. My watch made a mad ticking to remind me that now it had to be quick. Time, it had gone. There was nothing left!

I saw the empty packing boxes that had been smashed and left to rot. I saw the welter of machinery, glazed with rust, lying in heaps under the high, vaulted roof. Long ago it had been a factory of some sort. I wondered incongruously what had been made here. Then the smell of turpentine gave it to me. Paint. There was three hundred feet of length to it, almost that in width. I could make out the partitions of wood and brick separating it into compartments.

But I didn't have time to look through it all, not all three floors of it!

The sons-of-bitches had picked the best spot on earth, not a sound would penetrate these walls! In that maze of partitions and cubicles even the brightest beam of light that could escape would be dulled and unseen. I wanted to pull the trigger of the gun and blast the whole dump to bits and wade into the wreckage with my bare hands. I wanted to scream just like the guys outside wanted to scream and I couldn't.

Another minute to make myself cool off. Another minute to let instinct and training take over.

Another minute for my eyes to see and they picked out the path that led through the rubbish, a path I should have seen sooner because it had been deliberately made and often used. Old paint cans had been pushed aside and spilled their thick, gooey mess on the floor. The larger drums had been slop pails for left-over stuff and marked the turns in the trail.

My eyes saw it, my feet followed it. They took me around the bend and through a hall then up the stairs.

And the path that was cleared through the dirt on the floor led to the middle, then the top story. It led to rooms that reeked of turpentine so strong it almost took my breath away. It led to a corridor and another man who stepped out of the shadows to die. It led to a door that swung open easily and into a room that faced on other rooms where I was able to stand in my invisible cloak of blackness with barely the strength to hold the gun.

I stood there and looked at what I was, hearing myself say, "Good God, no, please . . . no!" I had to stand there for a moment of time that turned into eternity while I was helpless to intervene and see things my mind wanted to shut out . . . hear things my ears didn't want to hear.

For an eternal moment I had to look at them all, every one. General Osilov in a business suit leaning on his cane almost casually, an unholy leer lighting his face. My boy of the subway slobbering all over his chin, puking a little without noticing it, his hands pressed against his belly while his face was a study in obscene fascination.

And the guy in the pork-pie hat!

Velda.

She was stark naked.

She hung from the rafters overhead by a rope that chewed into her wrists, while her body twisted slowly in the single light of the electric lantern! The guy in the pork-pie hat waited until she turned to face him then brought the knotted rope around with all the strength of his arm and I heard it bite into her flesh with a sickening sound that brought her

*head up long enough for me to see that even the pain was
dulling under the evil of this thing.*

He said, "Where is it? You'll die if you don't tell me!"

She never opened her mouth. Her eyes came open, but she
never opened her mouth!

*Then there was only beauty to the nakedness of her body.
A beauty of the flesh that was more than the sensuous curve
of her hips, more than the sharp curve of breasts drawn high
under the weight of her body, more than those long, full
legs, more than the ebony of her hair. There was the beauty
of the flesh that was the beauty of the soul and the guy in
the pork-pie hat grimaced with hate and raised the rope to
smash it down while the rest slobbered with the lust and
pleasure of this example of what was yet to come, even
drooled with the passion that was death made slow in the
fulfillment of the philosophy that lived under a red flag!*

And in that moment of eternity I heard the problem asked
and knew the answer! I knew why I was allowed to live while
others died! I knew why my rottenness was tolerated and
kept alive and why the guy with the reaper couldn't catch me
and I smashed through the door of the room with the tommy
gun in my hands spitting out the answer at the same time
my voice screamed it to the heavens!

*I lived only to kill the scum and the lice that wanted to
kill themselves. I lived to kill so that others could live. I lived
to kill because my soul was a hardened thing that reveled in
the thought of taking the blood of the bastards who made
murder their business. I lived because I could laugh it off and
others couldn't. I was the evil that opposed other evil, leaving the good and the meek in the middle to live and inherit
the earth!*

They heard my scream and the awful roar of the gun
and the slugs tearing into bone and guts and it was the last
they heard. They went down as they tried to run and felt
their insides tear out and spray against the walls.

I saw the general's head splinter into shiny wet fragments
and splatter over the floor. The guy from the subway tried
to stop the bullets with his hands and dissolved into a night-
mare of blue holes.

There was only the guy in the pork-pie hat who made a
crazy try for a gun in his pocket. I aimed the tommy gun for
the first time and took his arm off at the shoulder. It dropped
on the floor next to him and I let him have a good look at it.
He couldn't believe it happened. I proved it by shooting
him in the belly. They were all so damned clever!

They were all so damned dead!

I laughed and laughed while I put the second clip in the gun. I knew the music in my head was going wild this time, but I was laughing too hard to enjoy it. I went around the room and kicked them over on their backs and if they had faces left I made sure they didn't. I saved the last burst for the bastard who was MVD in a pork-pie hat and who looked like a kid. A college boy. He was still alive when he stared into the flame that spit out of the muzzle only an inch away from his nose.

I cut her down carefully, dressed her, cradled her in my arms like a baby and knew that I was crying. Me. I could still do that. I felt her fingers come up and touch one of the wet spots on my cheek, heard her say the three words that blessed everything I did, then I went back to the path that led out into the night that was still cold and rainy, but still free to be enjoyed. There was a soft spot on the ground where I laid her with my coat under her head while I went back to do what I had to do. I went back to the room where death had visited and walked under the rafters until I reached the pork-pie hat that lay next to the remains of the thing that wore it. I lifted his wallet out of his back pocket and flipped his coat open so I could rip the inside lining pocket out along with some shreds of the coat fabric. That was all. Except for one thing. When I went down the stairs once more I found a drum of paint whose spilled contents made a sticky flow into some empty cans. When I built up a mound of old papers around the stuff I touched a match to it, stood there until I was satisfied with its flame, then went back to Velda. Her eyes were closed and her breathing heavy. She came up in my arms and I fixed my coat around her.

I carried her that way to my car and drove her home, and stayed while a doctor hovered above her. I prayed. It was answered when the doctor came out of the room and smiled. I said another prayer of thankfulness and did the things that had to be done to make her comfortable. When the nurse came to sit by her side I picked up my hat and went downstairs.

The rain came down steadily. It was clear and pure. It swept by the curb carrying the filth into the sewer.

We know now, don't we, Judge? We know the answer.

There were only a few hours left of the night. I drove to the office and opened the lamp. I took out the two envelopes in there and spread them out on my desk. The beginning and the end. The complexities and the simplicities. It was all so clever and so rotten.

And to think that they might have gotten away with it!

It was over and done with now. Miles away an abandoned paint factory would be a purgatory of flame and explosions that would leave only the faintest trace of what had been there. It was a hell that wiped away all sins leaving only the good and the pure. The faintest trace that it left would be looked into and expounded upon. There would be nothing left but wonder and the two big words, WHY and HOW. There were no cars at the scene. They wouldn't have been foolish enough to get there that way. The flames would char and blacken. They would leave remains that would take months to straighten out, and in that straightening they would come across melted leaden slugs and a twisted gun that was the property of the investigating bureau in Washington. There would be cover-up and more wonder and more specu-lation, then, eventually, someone would stumble on part of the truth. Yet even then, it was a truth only half-known and too big to be told.

Only I knew the whole thing and it was too big for me. I was going to tell it to the only person who would understand what it meant.

I picked up the phone.

CHAPTER ELEVEN

THE SIXTH time it rang I heard it come off the cradle. A sharp click was the light coming on then Lee Deamer's voice gave me a sleepy hello.

I said, "This is Mike Hammer, Lee." My voice had a tired drag too. "Hate to call you at this hour, but I have to speak to you."

"Well, that's all right, Mike. I was expecting you to call. My secretary told me you had called earlier."

"Can you get dressed?"

"Yes. Are you coming over here?"

"I'd rather not, Lee. I don't want to be cooped up right now. I need the smell of air. A hell of a lot has happened. It isn't anything I can broadcast and I can't keep it to myself. You're the only one I can talk to. I want to show you where it started and how it happened. I want you to see the works. I have something very special to show you."

"What Oscar left behind?"

"No, what somebody else did. Lee, you know those government documents that were copied?"

"Mike! It can't be!"

"It is."

"This is . . . why, it's. . . ."

"I know what you mean. I'll pick you up in a few minutes. Hurry up."

"I'll be ready by the time you get here. Really, Mike, I don't know what to say."

"Neither do I, that's why I want you to tell me what to do. I'll be right over."

I put the phone back slowly, then gathered the envelopes into a neat pack and stuck them in my pocket. I went downstairs and stood on the sidewalk with my face turned toward the sky.

It was still raining.

It was a night just like that first one.

The rain had a hint of snow in it.

Before I reached Lee's house I made a stop. The place was

a rooming house that had a NO VACANCY sign in front
and a row of rooms with private entrances. I went in and
knocked on the second door. I knocked again and a bed
squeaked. I knocked the third time and a muffled voice swore
and feet shuffled across the floor.

The door went open an inch and I saw one eye and part
of a crooked nose. "Hello, Archie," I said.

Archie threw the door open and I stepped in. Archie owed
me a lot of favors and now I was collecting one. I told him
to get dressed and it took him about two minutes to climb
into his clothes.

He waited until we were in the car before he opened his
yap. "Trouble?" That was all he said.

"Nope. All you're going to do is drive a car. No trouble."

We went over to Lee's place and I rang the bell. They have
one of those speaking-tube gadgets there and Lee said he'd
be right down. I saw him hurry through the lobby and open
the door.

He grinned when we shook hands. I was too tired to grin
back. "Is it pretty bad, Mike? You look like you're out on
your feet."

"I am. I'm bushed but I can't go to bed with this on my
mind. My car is out front."

The two of us went down the walk and I opened the door
for him. We got in the back together and I told Archie to
head for the bridge. Lee sat back and let his eyes ask me if
we could talk with Archie in the car. I shook my head no so
we just sat there watching the rain streak across the windows.

At the entrance to the bridge I passed Archie a half a buck
and he handed it to the cop on duty at the toll booth. We
started up the incline when I tapped him on the shoulder.

"Stop here, Archie. We're going to walk the rest of the
way. Go on over to Jersey and sop up some beer. Come back
in a half-hour. We'll be at the top of the hump on the other
side waiting for you." I dropped a fin on the seat beside him
to pay for the beer and climbed out with Lee behind me.

It was colder now and the rain was giving birth to a snow-
flake here and there. The steel girders of the bridge towered
into the sky and were lost, giant man-made trees that glis-
tened at the top as the ice started to form.

Our feet made slow clicking sounds against the concrete
of the walk and the boats on the river below called back to
them. I could see the red and green eyes staring at me.
They weren't faces this time.

"This is where it started, Lee," I said.

He glanced at me and his face was puzzled.

"No, I don't expect you to understand, because you don't know about it." We had our hands stuffed in our pockets against the cold, and our collars turned up to keep out the wet. The hump was ahead of us, rising high into the night.

"Right up there is where it happened. I thought I'd be alone that night, but there were two other people. One was a girl. The other was a little fat guy with a stainless-steel tooth. They both died."

I took the fat envelope out of my pocket and shook out the pages inside. "It's amazing, isn't it? Here the best minds in the country are looking for this and I fell right into it. It's the detailed plans of the greatest weapon ever made and I have it right here in my hand."

Lee's mouth fell open. He recovered and reached for it. "How, Mike? How could this come to you?"

There wasn't any doubting its authenticity. He shook his head, completely bewildered, and gave it back to me. "That's the story, Lee. That's what I wanted to tell you, but first I want to make sure this country has a secret that's safe."

I took my lighter out and spun the little wheel. There was a spark, then a blue flame that wavered in the wind. I touched it to the papers and watched them smolder and suddenly flame up. The yellow light reflected from our faces, dying down to a soft red glow. When there was nothing left but a corner that still held the remnants of the symbols and numbers, I flicked the papers over the edge and watched them go to the wind. That one corner I put in my pocket.

"If it had happened to anyone else, I wonder what the answer would have been?"

I shook my head and reached for a Lucky. "Nobody will ever know that, Lee." We reached the top of the hump and I stopped.

The winter was with us again. The girders were tall white fingers that grew from the floor of the bridge, scratching the sky open. Through the rift the snow sifted down and made wet patches on the ground.

I leaned on the handrail, looking out over the river. "It was the same kind of night: it was cold and wet and all alone. A girl came running up that ramp with a guy behind her who had a gun in his pocket. I shot the guy and the girl jumped over the railing. That's how simple it was. The only things they left behind were two green cards that identified them as members of the Communist Party.

"So I was interested. I was interested in anything that toted around a green card. That's how I got interested in Oscar. The guy he killed had a green card too. Hell, you know the rest of the story. There's a few things only I know and that's the main thing. I know how many people died tonight. I know what the papers will look like tomorrow and the month after. You know what, Lee, I killed more people tonight than I have fingers on my hands. I shot them in cold blood and enjoyed every minute of it. I pumped slugs in the nastiest bunch of bastards you ever saw and here I am calmer than I've ever been and happy too. They were Commies, Lee. They were red sons-of-bitches who should have died long ago, and part of the gang who are going to be dying in the very near future unless they get smart and take the gas pipe. Pretty soon what's left of Russia and the slime that breeds there won't be worth mentioning and I'm glad because I had a part in the killing.

"God, but it was fun! It was the way I liked it. No arguing, no talking to the stupid peasants. I just walked into that room with a tommy gun and shot their guts out. They never thought that there were people like me in this country. They figured us all to be soft as horse manure and just as stupid."

It was too much for Lee. He held onto the rail and looked sick.

I said, "What's the matter, Oscar?"

His eyes were glazed and he coughed. "You mean . . . Lee."

"No I don't. I mean Oscar. Lee's dead."

It was all there, the night, the cold and the fear. The unholy fear. He was looking at my face and he had the same look of unholy fear as the girl had that other night so long ago.

I said it slow. I let him hear every word. "The girl that died here that night was Paula Riis. She was a nurse in an asylum for the insane. I had it wrong . . . she didn't help Oscar to escape . . . she just quit and Oscar escaped later by himself. Paula came to New York and got tied up with a lot of crappy propaganda the Commies handed out and went overboard for it. She thought it was great. She worked like hell and wound up in a good spot.

"Then it happened. Somehow she saw the records or was introduced to the big boy in this country. She knew it was you. What happened, did she approach you thinking you were Oscar's brother? *Whatever happened she recognized you as Oscar and all her illusions were shattered. She knew you were Oscar Deamer and demented as hell!*

"That's why you were a Commie, Oscar, because you were batty. It was the only philosophy that would appeal to your crazy mind. It justified everything you did and you saw a chance of getting back at the world. You escaped from that sanitarium, took Lee's private papers and made yourself a name in the world while Lee was off in the woods where he never saw a paper of any kind and never knew what you did. You must have had an expert dummy the fingerprints on that medical record . . . but then, you had access to that kind of expert, didn't you?

"It was rough when Paula recognized you. She lost her ideals and managed to contact Lee. She told him to come East and expose you, but she did something else first. She had a boy friend in the party. His name was Charlie Moffit and she told him the story hoping to drag him out of the Commie net.

"Charlie was the stupid one. He saw a play of his own and made it. He saw how he could line you up for some ready cash and gave you the story over the phone. It was right after the Legion Parade, the 13th, that you had a heart attack according to your secretary . . . not because your brother contacted you because his ticket was dated the 15th, a Friday, and he didn't arrive until the day after. *You had a heart attack when Charlie Moffit called you!*

"You contacted the torpedo that went under the MVD title and you worried about it, but there was no out until Lee arrived himself and gave you a buzz. That was the best touch of all! Then you saw how you could kill Charlie yourself, have the blame shifted to your brother with a reasonable story that would make it look good. You knew you had a way to kill two birds with one stone . . . and get rid of a brother who could have stood in your way. There was only one thing you didn't foresee. Charlie Moffit was a courier in the chain that passed along those documents. During one of his more lucid moments he recognized that they were important and held on to them for life insurance. He mailed them to his girl friend, Paula, to take care of."

He was white. He hung on to the rail and shook. He was scared stiff.

"So you waited until Charlie called again and arranged to meet him. You had it all figured out beforehand and it looked good as gold. You got hold of an old actor and had him impersonate you while you went out and killed Charlie Moffit. The actor was good, too. He knew how to make speeches. You paid him off, but you didn't know then that he liked to drink. He never did before because he had no money. Later you found that he had a loose tongue when he drank and he had to go too. But that was an easy kill and it's getting ahead of the story.

"You killed Charlie, switched with the actor at the dinner meeting, and made yourself a wonderful alibi. It happened after the supper when you were going around speaking to the groups, a time when nobody would be conscious of the switch, especially since none of them knew you too well anyway.

"I don't know what the play was at your brother's place when Pat and I went after him, but I'll try to set it up. See if I'm right. Mr. MVD went there first and got him running. He got him in the subway and shoved him under the train so his identity would be washed out."

As casually as I could I took Velda's envelope from my pocket and fingered out the sheet inside. He didn't bother to look at it.

I said, "My secretary dug up this story. She went back to your home state and went through the records. She found out that you and your brother were twins, all right, but you weren't identical twins. *You were fraternal twins and he didn't look like you at all!*

"But to get back to the beginning. You knew when Lee called you that there was more to it than you thought. You knew Charlie wasn't smart enough to dig up the stuff by himself, so you and fat boy did some fast snooping and found out about Paula. During that time she saw you or the other guy and got scared. She wanted to talk and called the police, asking them to meet her on the bridge where they could be alone.

"Your MVD pal was a little shrewder. He tapped her phone line and moved in to intercept her, but she moved a little faster and got out of the house before he came around. She had just enough lead to make it to the top of the bridge right where we're standing when he arrived. It was pretty— you should have been here. You should have seen what I did to him. The sour note was Paula. She thought I was one of them looking for a cut of the loot or something, because she couldn't picture any decent person hauling out a rod just like that and blowing a guy's face off. She went over the bridge.

"It would have been so nice for you if I hadn't had a conscience and wanted to find out what the green card meant. You knew my reputation but never thought I could go that far. You hired me so you could keep tabs on me and now look what happened.

"Maybe nothing would have happened if those documents hadn't turned up missing. Those people would have died just to keep your identity a secret. But one of those dead men was a critical link connected with the missing documents, so you cooked up the story of your brother's having left something incriminating behind him, thinking that maybe I'd come across the documents and hand them over to you. Well, Oscar, I did. You had your boys try to run them down first, but they didn't quite make it.

"I got to be a very dangerous guy in your little game. I was all over the picture with my nose picking up a lot of smells. You passed the orders to get me out of the way at any price and damn near succeeded. Too bad your new MVD boy didn't get me instead of Ethel Brighton up in the cabin there. She was dangerous too. She finally got wise to how foolish she had been and talked to the right people. She was even going to turn me in, but your MVD boy stopped that.

"You know, I thought Ethel put the finger on me when she saw my identification in my wallet. But it wasn't Ethel, it was you. You fingered me because I was getting in there. You thought that I had gone too far already and didn't want to take any more chances. So out come the strong-arm boys and the MVD lad.

"He sure was a busy little beaver. He wanted to kill me in the worst way. When you guys discovered that I had those documents you must have gone nuts. Maybe it even occurred to you that in the process of getting them I would have uncovered all the angles to the thing. I did that, little man, I did just that.

"You got real gay at the end, though. You pulled a real smartie when you put the snatch on Velda. For that there was only one answer . . . I wanted to see you die. I saw them die. You should have seen what I saw and you would have died yourself even before a bullet reached you.

"But none of that is bad when you compare it to the big thing. That's you, Mr. Deamer. You, the little man whom the public loves and trusts . . . you who are to lead the people into the ways of justice . . . you who shouted against the diabolic policies of the Communists . . . you are the biggest Communist of them all!

"You know the theory . . . the ends justify the means. So you fought the Commie bastards and on the strength of that you hoped to be elected, and from there the Politburo took over. With you in where it counted you could appoint party members to key positions, right in there where they could wreck this country without a bit of trouble. Brother, that was a scheme. I bet the boys in the Kremlin are proud of you."

I saw the gun snake out of his pocket and I reached over and plucked it out of his fingers. Just like that. He stared after it as it arched out and down into the river.

"Tomorrow," I said, "the boys in the Kremlin are going to

be wondering what the hell happened. They'll wonder where their boys are and they'll put up a yell, but there will be fear behind that yell because when they learn what happened they'll have to revise their whole opinion of what kind of people are over here. They'll think it was a tough government that uncovered the thing secretly. They'll think it was one of Uncle's boys who chopped down that whole filthy mob, and they won't complain too much because they can't afford to admit those same boys who were here on diplomatic passes were actually spying. The Kremlin mob will really stand on their heads when they get my final touch. It's a beauty, Mr. Deamer. Do you know what I'm going to do?"

He was staring at my face. His eyes couldn't leave my eyes and his flesh was already dying with the fear inside him. He tried to talk and made only harsh breathing sounds. He raised his hands as if I were something evil and he had to keep me away. I was evil. I was evil for the good. I was evil and he knew it. I was worse than they were, so much worse that they couldn't stand the comparison. I had one, good, efficient, enjoyable way of getting rid of cancerous Commies. I killed them.

I said, "The touch is this, Oscar. You, the greatest Commie louse of them all, will be responsible for the destruction of your own party. You're going to die and the blame will go to the Kremlin. I'm going to stick a wallet and some shreds of cloth in your fist when you're dead. In your other hand will be the remains of those documents, enough to show what they were. Enough to make the coppers think that somehow you alone, in a burst of patriotic effort, managed to get hold of those important papers and destroyed them. It'll make them think that just as you were destroying them the killer came up and you fought it out. You came out second best, but in the struggle you managed to rip out the pocket that held his wallet and the cops will track it down thinking it came from your murderer, and what they find will be this . . . they'll find that it came from a guy who was an MVD man. He'll be dead, but that won't matter. If they manage to tie it in with the bodies in the paint shop they'll think that the killer went back to report without the papers he was sent after and the party, in their usual manner of not tolerating inefficiency, started to liquidate him and they smeared each other in the process. No, the Kremlin won't think that. They'll think it was all a very clever plan, an ingenious jumble that will never be straightened out, which it is. You're going to be a big hero. You saved the day and died in the saving. When the news is made public and the people know their favorite hero has been knocked off by the reds they'll go on a hunt that won't stop until the issue is decided, and brother, when the people in this country finally do get around to moving, they move fast!"

The irony of it brought a scream to his lips. He made a sudden mad lurch and tried to run, but the snow that came down so white and pure tripped him and I only had to reach out to get his throat in my hand.

I turned him around to face me, to let him look at what I was and see how I enjoyed his dying. The man who had thrown a lot of people on the long road to nowhere was a gibbering idiot slobbering at the mouth. I had his neck in my one hand and I leaned on the railing while I did it. I squeezed and squeezed and squeezed until my fingers were buried in the flesh of his throat and his hands clawed at my arm frantically, trying to tear me away.

I laughed a little bit. It was the only sound in the night. I laughed while his tongue swelled up and bulged out with his eyes and his face turned black. I held him until he was down on his knees and dead as he was ever going to be, then I took my hand away and watched while he fell forward into the snow. I had to pry his fingers apart to get the wallet in them. I made sure he had a good hold on the thing then I laughed again.

Maybe Archie would guess, I thought. He could guess all he wanted to, but he couldn't talk. I was holding a murder over his head, too. A justified killing that only he and I knew about. I saw the headlights of my car coming from the other end of the bridge and I walked across the steel walk to be there when Archie drove up.

The snow was coming down harder now. Soon that dark mass over there would be just a mound. And when the sun shone again the thaw would provide the deluge that would sweep everything into the sewer where it belonged.

It was lonely standing there. But I wouldn't be here long now. The car had almost reached the top of the ramp. I saw Archie bent over the wheel and took a last look around.

No, nobody ever walked across the bridge, especially not on a night like this.

Well, hardly nobody.

THE END

The
Twisted
Thing

To Sid Graedon

who saw the charred edges

Chapter One

The little guy's face was a bloody mess. Between the puff-balls of blue-black flesh that used to be eyelids, the dull gleam of shock-deadened pupils watched Dilwick uncomprehendingly. His lips were swollen things of lacerated skin, with slow trickles of blood making crooked paths from the corners of his mouth through the stubble of a beard to his chin, dripping onto a stained shirt.

Dilwick stood just outside the glare of the lamp, dangling like the Sword of Damocles over the guy's head. He was sweating too. His shirt clung to the meaty expanse of his back, the collar wilted into wrinkles around his huge neck. He pushed his beefy hand further into the leather glove and swung. The solid smack of his open hand on the little guy's jaw was nasty. His chair went over backward and his head cracked against the concrete floor of the room like a ripe melon. Dilwick put his hands on his hips and glared down at the caricature that once was human.

"Take him out and clean 'im up. Then get 'im back here." Two other cops came out of the darkness and righted the chair. One yanked the guy to his feet and dragged him to the door.

Lord, how I hated their guts. Grown men, they were supposed to be. Four of them in there taking turns pounding a confession from a guy who had nothing to say. And I had to watch it.

It was supposed to be a warning to me. Be careful, it said, when you try to withhold information from Dilwick you're looking for a broken skull. Take a look at this guy for example, then spill what you know and stick around so I, the Great Dilwick, can get at you when I want you.

I worked up a husky mouthful of saliva and spat it as close to his feet as I could. The fat cop spun on his heel and let his lips fold back over his teeth in a sneer. "You gettin' snotty, Hammer?"

9

I stayed slouched in my seat. "Any way you call it, Dil-wick," I said insolently. "Just sitting here thinking."

Big stuff gave me a dirty grimace. "Thinking . . . you?"

"Yeah. Thinking what you'd look like the next day if you tried that stuff on me."

The two cops dragging the little guy out stopped dead still. The other one washing the bloodstains from the seat quit swishing the brush over the wicker and held his breath. No-body ever spoke that way to Dilwick. Nobody from the biggest politician in the state to the hardest apple that ever stepped out of a pen. Nobody ever did because Dilwick would cut them up into fine pieces with his bare hands and enjoy it. That was Dilwick, the dirtiest, roughest cop who ever walked a beat or swung a nightstick over a skull. Crude, he was. Crude, hard and dirty and afraid of nothing. He'd sooner draw blood from a face than eat and everybody knew it. That's why nobody ever spoke to him that way. That is, nobody except me.

Because I'm the same way myself.

Dilwick let out his breath with a rush. The next second he was reaching down for me, but I never gave him the chance to hook his hairy paws in my shirt. I stood up in front of him and sneered in his face. Dilwick was too damn big to be used to meeting guys eye to eye. He liked to look down at them. Not this time.

"What do you think you'll do?" he snarled.

"Try me and see," I said.

I saw his shoulder go back and didn't wait. My knee came up and landed in his groin with a sickening smash. When he doubled over my fist caught him in the mouth and I felt his teeth pop. His face was starting to turn blue by the time he hit the floor. One cop dropped the little guy and went for his gun.

"Cut it, stupid," I said, "before I blow your goddamn head off. I still got my rod." He let his hand fall back to his side. I turned and walked out of the room. None of them tried to stop me.

Upstairs I passed the desk sergeant still bent over his paper. He looked up in time to see me and let his hand snake under the desk. Right then I had my own hand six inches from my armpit practically inviting him to call me. Maybe he had a family at home. He brought his hand up on top of the desk where I could see it. I've seen eyes like his peering out of a rathole when there was a cat in the room. He still had enough I AM THE LAW in him to bluster it out.

"Did Dilwick release you?" he demanded.

I snatched the paper from his hand and threw it to the

floor, trying to hold my temper. "Dilwick didn't release me," I told him. "He's downstairs vomiting his guts out the same way you'll be doing if you pull a deal like that again. Dilwick doesn't want *me*. He just wanted me to sit in on a cellar séance in legal torture to show me how tough he is. I wasn't impressed. But get this, I came to Sidon to legally represent a client who used his one phone call on arrest to contact me, not to be intimidated by a fat louse that was kicked off the New York force and bought his way into the cops in this hick town just to use his position for a rake-off."

The sergeant started to interrupt, licking his loose lips nervously, but I cut him short. "Furthermore, I'm going to give you just one hour to get Billy Parks out of here and back to his house. If you don't," and I said it slowly, "I'm going to call the State's Attorney and drop this affair in his lap. After that I'll come back here and mash your damn face to a pulp. Understand now? No habeas corpus, no nothing. Just get him out of here."

For a cop he stunk. His lower lip was trembling with fear. I pushed my hat on the back of my head and stamped out of the station house. My heap was parked across the street and I got in and turned it over. Damn, I was mad.

Billy Parks, just a nice little ex-con trying to go straight, but do you think the law would help him out? Hell no. Let one thing off-color pop up and they drag him in to get his brains kicked out because he had a record. Sure, he put in three semesters in the college on the Hudson, and he wasn't too anxious to do anything that would put him in his senior year where it took a lifetime to matriculate. Ever since he wrangled that chauffeur's job from Rudolph York I hadn't heard from him . . . until now, after York's little genius of a son had been snatched.

Rain started to spatter against the windshield when I turned into the drive. The headlights picked out the roadway and I followed it up to the house. Every light in the place was on as if the occupants were afraid a dark corner might conceal some unseen terror.

It was a big place, a product of wealth and good engineering, but in spite of its stately appearance and wrought-iron gates, somebody had managed to sneak in, grab the kid and beat it. Hell, the kid was perfect snatch bait. He was more than a son to his father, he was the result of a fourteen-year experiment. Then, that's what he got for bringing the kid up to be a genius. I bet he'd shell out plenty of his millions to see him safe and sound.

The front door was answered by one of those tailored flunkies who must always count up to fifty before they open up.

He gave me a curt nod and allowed me to come in out of the rain anyway.

"I'm Mike Hammer," I said, handing him a card. "I'd like to see your boss. And right away," I added.

The flunky barely glanced at the pasteboard. "I'm awfully sorry, sir, but Mr. York is temporarily indisposed."

When I shoved a cigarette in my mouth and lit it I said, "You tell him it's about his kid. He'll un-indispose himself in a hurry."

I guess I might as well have told him I wanted a ransom payment right then the way he looked at me. I've been taken for a lot of things in my life, but this was the first for a snatch artist. He started to stutter, swallowed, then waved his hand in the general direction of the living room. I followed him in.

Have you ever seen a pack of alley cats all set for a midnight brawl when something interrupts them? They spin on a dime with the hair still up their backs and watch the intruder through hostile eye slits as though they were ready to tear him so they could continue their own fight. An intense, watchful stare of mutual hate and fear.

That's what I ran into, only instead of cats it was people. Their expressions were the same. A few had been sitting, others stopped their quiet pacing and stood poised, ready. A tableau of hate. I looked at them only long enough to make a mental count of a round dozen and tab them as a group of ghouls whose morals had been eaten into by dry rot a long time.

Rudolph York was slumped in a chair gazing blankly into an empty fireplace. The photos in the rags always showed him to be a big man, but he was small and tired-looking this night. He kept muttering to himself, but I couldn't hear him. The butler handed him my card. He took it, not bothering to look at it.

"A Mr. Hammer, sir."

No answer.

"It . . . It's about Master Ruston, sir."

Rudolph York came to life. His head jerked around and he looked at me with eyes that spat fire. Very slowly he came to his feet, his hands trembling. "Have you got him?"

Two boys who might have been good-looking if it weren't for the nightclub pallor and the squeegy skin came out of a settee together. One had his fists balled up, the other plunked his highball glass on a coffee table. They came at me together. Saps. All I had to do was look over my shoulder and let them see what was on my face and they called it quits outside of swinging distance.

I turned my attention back to Rudolph York. "No."

"Then what do you want?"

"Look at my card."

He read, "Michael Hammer, Private Investigator," very slowly, then crushed the card in his hand. The contortions in his face were weird. He breathed silent, unspeakable words through tight lips, afraid to let himself be heard. One look at the butler and the flunky withdrew quietly, then he turned back to me. "How did you find out about this?" he charged.

I didn't like this guy. As brilliant a scientist as he might be, as wealthy and important, I still didn't like him. I blew a cloud of smoke in his direction. "Not hard," I answered, "not hard at all. I got a telephone call."

He kept beating his fist into an open palm. "I don't want the police involved, do you hear! This is a private matter."

"Cool off, doc. I'm not the police. However, if you try to keep me out of this I'll buzz one of the papers, then your privacy will really be shot to hell."

"Whom do you represent?" he asked coldly.

"Your chauffeur, Billy Parks."

"So?"

"So I'd like to know why you put the finger on him when you found out your kid was missing. I'd like to know why you let them mangle him without a formal charge even being lodged, and why you're keeping all this under your hat. And by damn you better start speaking and pretty loud at that."

"Please, Mr. Hammer."

A hand hit my shoulder and spun me, another came up from the side and cracked across my face. The punk said, "How dare you talk to Uncle like that!"

I let him get it out then backhanded him across the mouth with all I had. This time the other one grabbed my coat. He got a short jab in the ribs that bent him over, then the palm of my hand across his puss that straightened him up again. I shoved him away and got the punk's tie in my hand. When I was breathing in his face I twisted on the tie until the blue started running up his neck, then I smacked him on each side of that whisky-sodden face until my hand hurt. When I dropped him he lay on the floor crying, trying to cover his face with his hands.

I spoke to the general assembly rather than to him. "In case anyone else has ideas like that, he'd better have more in his hands than a whisky glass."

York hadn't missed a trick. He looked old again. The fire left his eyes and he groped for the arm of his chair. York was having a pretty rough time of it, but after having seen Billy I didn't feel sorry for him.

I threw my butt in the fireplace and parked in the chair opposite him. He didn't need any prompting. "Ruston was not in his bed in the morning. It had been slept in, but he was not there. We searched the house and the grounds for him, but found no trace of his presence. I must have become excited. The first thing that entered my head was that I had an ex-convict in my employ. I called the local police and reported what had taken place. They led Parks away. I've since regretted the incident."

"I imagine," I remarked dryly. "How much is it costing you to keep this quiet?"

He shuddered. "Nothing. I did offer them a reward if they could locate Ruston."

"Oh, swell. Great. That's all they needed. Cripes, you got a brain like a fly!" His eyes widened at that. "These local jokers aren't cops. Sure, they'd be quiet, who wouldn't? Do you think they'd split the kind of reward money you'd be offering if they could help it?"

I felt like rapping him in the teeth. "Throwing Billy to the wolves was stupid. Suppose he was an ex-con. With three convictions to his credit he wasn't likely to stick his neck out for that offence. He'd be the first suspect as it was. Damn, I'd angle for Dilwick before I would Billy. He's more the type."

York was sweating freely. He buried his face in his hands and swayed from side to side, moaning to himself. He stopped finally, then looked up at me. "What will I do, Mr. Hammer? What *can* be done?"

I shook my head.

"But something must be done! I must find Ruston. After all these years . . . I can't call the police. He's such a sensitive boy . . . I—I'm afraid."

"I merely represent Billy Parks, Mr. York. He called me because he was in a jam and I'm his friend. What I want from you is to give him back his job. Either that or I call the papers."

"All right. It really doesn't matter." His head dropped again. I put on my hat and stood up, then, "But you? Mr. Hammer, you aren't the police as you say. Perhaps you could help me, too."

I threw him a straw. "Perhaps."

He grabbed at it. "Would you? I need somebody . . . . who will keep this matter silent."

"It'll cost you."

"Very well, how much?"

"How much did you offer Dilwick?"

"Ten thousand dollars."

I let out a whistle, then told him, "Okay, ten G's plus expenses."

Relief flooded his face like sunlight. The price was plenty steep but he didn't bat an eye. He had been holding this inside himself too long and was glad to hand it to someone else.

But he still had something to say. "You drive a hard bargain, Mr. Hammer, and in my position I am forced, more or less, to accept. However, for my own satisfaction I would like to know one thing, how good a detective are you?"

He said it in a brittle tone and I answered him the same way. An answer that made him pull back away from me as though I had a contagious disease. I said, "York, I've killed a lot of men. I shot the guts out of two of them in Times Square. Once I let six hundred people in a nightclub see what some crook had for dinner when he tried to gun me. He got it with a steak knife. I remember because I don't want to remember. They were too nasty. I hate the bastards that make society a thing to be laughed at and preyed upon. I hate them so much I can kill without the slightest compunction. The papers call me dirty names and the kind of rats I monkey with are scared stiff of me, but I don't give a damn. When I kill I make it legal. The courts accuse me of being too quick on the trigger but they can't revoke my license because I do it right. I think fast, I shoot fast, I've been shot at plenty. And I'm still alive. That's how good a detective I am."

For a full ten seconds he stood speechless, staring at me with an undisguised horror. There wasn't a sound from the room. It isn't often that I make a speech like that, but when I do it must be convincing. If thoughts could be heard that house would be a babble of fearful confusion. The two punks I biffed looked like they had just missed being bitten by a snake. York was the first one to compose himself. "I suppose you'd like to see the boy's room?"

"Uh-uh."

"Why not? I thought . . ."

"The kid's gone, that's enough. Seeing the room won't do any good. I don't have the equipment to fool around with clues, York. Fingerprints and stuff are for technical men. I deal with motives and people."

"But the motive . . ."

I shrugged. "Money, probably. That's what it usually is. Let's start at the beginning first." I indicated the chair and York settled back. I drew up closer to him. "When did you discover him to be missing?"

"Yesterday morning. At eight o'clock, his regular rising hour, Miss Malcom, his governess, went into his room. He was not in bed. She looked for him throughout the house, then told me he could not be found. With the aid of the gardener and Parks we searched the grounds. He was not there."

"I see. What about the gatekeeper?"

"Henry saw nothing, heard nothing."

"Then you called the police, I suppose?" He nodded. "Why did you think he was kidnapped?"

York gave an involuntary start. "But what other reason could account for his disappearance?"

I leaned forward in my seat. "According to all I've ever read about your son, Mr. York, he is the most brilliant thing this side of heaven. Wouldn't a young genius be inclined to be highly strung?"

He gripped the arms of the chair until the veins stood out on the back of his hands. The fire was in his eyes again. "If you are referring to his mental health, you are mistaken. Ruston was in excellent spirits as he has been all his life. Besides being his father and a scientist, I am also a doctor."

It was easy to see that he didn't want any doubts cast upon the mind of one he had conditioned so carefully so long. I let it go for the time being.

"Okay, describe him to me. Everything. I have to start somewhere."

"Yes. He is fourteen. In appearance he is quite like other boys. By appearance I mean expressions, manners and attitudes. He is five feet one-inch tall, light brown hair, ruddy complexion. He weighs one hundred twelve pounds stripped. Eyes, brown, slight scar high on the left side of his forehead as the result of a fall when he was younger."

"Got a picture of him?" The scientist nodded, reached inside his jacket pocket and came out with a snapshot. I took it. The boy was evidently standing in the yard, hands behind his back in a typically shy-youth manner. He was a good-looking kid at that. A slight smile played around his mouth and he seemed to be pretty self-conscious. He had on shorts and a dark sweater. Romping in the background was a spotted spaniel.

"Mind if I keep it?" I asked.

York waved his hand. "Not at all. If you want them, there are others."

When I pocketed the snap I lit another cigarette. "Who else is in the house? Give me all the servants, where they sleep, anyone who has been here recently. Friends, enemies, people you work with."

"Of course." He cleared his throat and listed the household. "Besides myself, there is Miss Malcom, Parks, Henry, two cooks, two maids and Harvey. Miss Grange works for me as a laboratory assistant, but lives at home in town. As for friends, I have few left that I ever see since I stopped teaching at the university. No enemies I can think of. I believe the only ones who have been inside the gate the past few weeks were tradesmen from town. That is," he indicated the gang in the room with a thumb, "outside these, my closest relatives. They are here and gone constantly."

"You are quite wealthy?" The question was unnecessary, but I made my point.

York cast a quick look about him, then a grimace that was half disgust passed over him. "Yes, but my health is still good."

I let the ghouls hear it. "Too bad for them."

"The servants all sleep in the north wing. Miss Malcom has a room adjoining Ruston's and connected to it. I occupy a combination study and bedroom at the front of the house.

"I work with no one and for no one. The nature of my work you must be familiar with; it is that of giving my son a mind capable of greater thought and intelligence than is normally found. He may be a genius to you and others, but to me he is merely one who makes full use of his mind. Naturally, my methods are closely guarded secrets. Miss Grange shares them with me, but I trust her completely. She is as devoted to my son as I am. Since the death of my wife when the child was born, she has aided me in every way. I think that is all?"

"Yeah, I guess that'll do."

"May I ask how you will proceed?"

"Sure. Until we get a sign from whoever kidnapped your son I'm going to sit tight. The ones that grabbed the kid must think they know what they're doing, otherwise they wouldn't pick someone like your boy who is always in the public eye. If you wanted to you could have every cop in the state beating the bushes. I take it there was no note . . ."

"None at all."

". . . so they're playing it close to see what you'll do. Call the cops and they're liable to take a powder. Hold off a bit and they will contact you. Then I'll go to work . . . that is if it's really a snatch."

He bit into his lip and gave me another of those fierce looks. "You say that as though you don't think he was kidnapped."

"I say that because I don't *know* he was kidnapped. It could be anything. I'll tell you better when I see a ransom note."

York didn't get a chance to answer, for at that moment the butler reappeared, and between him and the luscious redhead they supported a bloody, limp figure. "It's Parks, sir. Miss Malcom and I found him outside the door!"

We ran to him together. York gasped when he saw Parks' face then sent the butler scurrying off for some hot water and bandages. Most of the gore had been wiped off, but the swellings were as large as ever. The desk sergeant had done as I told him, the hour wasn't up yet, but somebody was still going to pay for this. I carried Billy to a chair and sat him down gently.

I stepped back and let York go to work when the butler returned with a first-aid kit. It was the first good chance I had to give Miss Malcom the once-over all the way from a beautiful set of legs through a lot of natural curves to an extraordinarily pretty face. Miss Malcom they called her.

I call her Roxy Coulter. She used to be a strip artist in the flesh circuit of New York and Miami.

Chapter Two

But Roxy had missed her profession. Hollywood should have had her. Maybe she didn't remember Atlantic City or that New Year's Eve party in Charlie Drew's apartment. If she did she held a dandy deadpan and all I got in return for my stare was one of those go ahead peeks, but don't touch looks.

A peek was all I got, because Billy came around with a groan and made an effort to sit up. York put his hand against his chest and forced him down again. "You'll have to be quiet," he cautioned him in a professional tone.

"My face," his eyes rolled in his head, "jeez, what happened to my face?"

I knelt beside him and turned over the cold compress on his forehead. His eyes gleamed when he recognized me. "Hello, Mike. What happened?"

"Hi, Billy. They beat up on you. Feel any better?"

"I feel awful. Oh, that bastard. If only I was bigger, Mike . . . damn, why couldn't I be big like you? That dirty . . ."

"Forget about him, kid." I patted his shoulder. "I handed him a little of the same dish. His map'll never be the same."

"Cripes! I bet you did! I thought something funny happened down there. Thanks, Mike, thanks a lot."

"Sure."

Then his face froze in a frightened grimace. "Suppose . . . suppose they come back again? Mike . . . I—I can't stand that stuff. I'll talk, I'll say anything. I can't take it, Mike!"

"Ease off. I'm not going anywhere. I'll be around."

Billy tried to smile and he gripped my arm. "You will?"

"Yup. I'm working for your boss now."

"Mr. Hammer." York was making motions from the side of the room. I walked over to him. "It would be better if he didn't get too excited. I gave him a sedative and he should sleep. Do you think you can manage to carry him to his room? Miss Malcom will show you the way."

"Certainly," I nodded. "And if you don't mind, I'd like to do a little prowling afterward. Maybe question the servants."

"Of course. The house is at your disposal."

Billy's eyes had closed and his head had fallen on his chin when I picked him up. He'd had a rough time of it all right. Without a word Miss Malcom indicated that I was to follow her and led me through an arch at the end of the room. After passing through a library, a study and a trophy room that looked like something out of a museum, we wound up in a kitchen. Billy's room was off an alcove behind the pantry. As gently as I could I laid him under the covers. He was sound asleep.

Then I stood up. "Okay, Roxy, now we can say hello."

"Hello, Mike."

"Now why the disguise and the new handle? Hiding out?"

"Not at all. The handle as you call it is my real name. Roxy was something I used on the stage."

"Really? Don't tell me you gave up the stage to be a diaper changer. What are you doing here?"

"I don't like your tone, Mike. You change it or go to hell."

This was something. The Roxy I knew never had enough self-respect to throw her pride in my face. Might as well play it her way.

"Okay, baby, don't get teed off on me. I have a right to be just a little bit curious, haven't I? It isn't very often that you catch somebody jumping as far out of character as you have. Does the old man know about the old life?"

"Don't be silly. He'd can me if he did."

"I guessed as much. How did you tie up in this place?"

"Easy. When I finally got wise to the fact that I was getting my brains knocked out in the big city I went to an agency and signed up as a registered nurse. I was one before I got talked into tossing my torso around for two hundred a week. Three days later Mr. York accepted me to take care of his child. That was two years ago. Anything else you want to know?"

I grinned at her. "Nope. It was just funny meeting you, that's all."

"Then may I leave?"

I let my grin fade and eased her out through the door. "Look, Roxy, is there somewhere we can go talk?"

"I don't play those games anymore, Mike."

"Get off my back, will you? I mean talk."

She arched her eyebrows and watched me steadily a second, then seeing that I meant it, said, "My room. We can be alone there. But only talk, remember?"

"Roger, bunny, let's go."

This time we went into the outer foyer and up a stairway that seemed to have been carved out of a solid piece of mahogany. We turned left on the landing and Roxy opened the door for me.

"In here," she said.

While I picked out a comfortable chair she turned on a table lamp then offered me a smoke from a gold box. I took one and lit it. "Nice place you got here."

"Thank you. It's quite comfortable. Mr. York sees that I have every convenience. Now shall we talk?"

She was making sure I got the point in a hurry. "The kid. What is he like?"

Roxy smiled a little bit, and the last traces of hardness left her face. She looked almost maternal. "He's wonderful. A charming boy."

"You seem to like him."

"I do. You'd like him too." She paused, then, "Mike . . . do you really think he was kidnapped?"

"I don't know, that's why I want to talk about him. Downstairs I suggested that he might have become temporarily unbalanced and the old man nearly chewed my head off. Hell, it isn't unreasonable to figure that. He's supposed to be a genius and that automatically puts him out of the normal class. What do you think?"

She tossed her hair back and rubbed her forehead with one hand. "I can't understand it. His room is next door, and I heard nothing although I'm usually a light sleeper. Ruston was perfectly all right up to then. He wouldn't simply walk out."

"No? And why not?"

"Because he is an intelligent boy. He likes everyone, is satisfied with his environment and has been very happy all the time I've known him."

"Uh-huh. What about his training? How did he get to be a genius?"

"That you'll have to find out from Mr. York. Both he and Miss Grange take care of that department."

I squashed the butt into the ashtray. "Nuts, it doesn't seem likely that a genius can be made. They have to be born. You've been around him a lot. Tell me, just how much of a genius is he? I know only what the papers print."

"Then you know all I know. It isn't what he knows that makes him a genius, it's what he is capable of learning. In one week he mastered every phase of the violin. The next week it was the piano. Oh, I realize that it seems impossible, but it's quite true. Even the music critics accept him as a master of several instruments. It doesn't stop there, either. Once he showed an interest in astronomy. A few days later he exhausted every book on the subject. His father and I took him to the observatory where he proceeded to amaze the experts with his uncanny knowledge. He's a mathematical wizard besides. It doesn't take him a second to give you the cube root of a six-figure number to three decimal points. What more can I say? There is no field that he doesn't excel in. He grasps fundamentals at the snap of the fingers and learns in five minutes what would take you or me years of study. That, Mike, is the genius in a nutshell, but that's omitting the true boy part of him. In all respects he is exactly like other boys."

"The old man said that too."

"He's quite right. Ruston loves games, toys and books. He has a pony, a bicycle, skates and a sled. We go for long walks around the estate every once in a while and do nothing but talk. If he wanted to he could expound on nuclear physics in ten-syllable words, but that isn't his nature. He'd sooner talk football."

I picked another cigarette out of the box and flicked a match with my thumbnail. "That about covers it, I guess. Maybe he didn't go off his nut at that. Let's take a look at his room."

Roxy nodded and stood up. She walked to the end of the room and opened a door. "This is it." When she clicked on the light switch I walked in. I don't know what I expected, but this wasn't it. There were pennants on the walls and pictures tucked into the corners of the dresser mirror. Clothes were scattered in typical boyish confusion over the backs of chairs and the desk.

In one corner was the bed. The covers had been thrown to the foot and the pillow still bore the head print of its occupant. If the kid had really been snatched I felt for him. It was no night to be out in your pajamas, especially when you left the top of them hanging on the bedpost.

I tried the window. It gave easily enough, though it was evident from the dust on the outside of the sill that it hadn't been opened recently.

"Keep the kid's door locked at night?" I asked Roxy.

She shook her head. "No. There's no reason to."

"Notice any tracks around here, outside the door or window?"

Another negative. "If there were any," she added, "they would have been wiped out in the excitement."

I dragged slowly on the cigarette, letting all the facts sink in. It seemed simple enough, but was it? "Who are all the twerps downstairs, bunny?"

"Relatives, mostly."

"Know 'em?"

Roxy nodded. "Mr. York's sister and her husband, their son and daughter, and a cousin are his only blood relations. The rest are his wife's folks. They've been hanging around here as long as I've been here, just waiting for something to happen to York."

"Does he know it?"

"I imagine so, but he doesn't seem bothered by them. They try to outdo each other to get in the old boy's favor. I suppose there's a will involved. There usually is."

"Yeah, but they're going to have a long wait. York told me his health was perfect."

Roxy looked at me curiously, then dropped her eyes. She fidgeted with her fingernails a moment and I let her stew a bit before I spoke.

"Say it, kid."

"Say what?"

"What you have on your mind and almost said."

She bit her lip, hesitating, then, "This is between you and me, Mike. If Mr. York knew I told you this I'd be out of a job. You won't mention it, will you?"

"I promise."

"About the second week I was here I happened to overhear Mr. York and his doctor after an examination. Apparently Mr. York knew what had happened, but called in another doctor to verify it. For some time he had been working with special apparatus in his laboratory and in some way became over exposed to radiation. It was enough to cause some internal complications and shorten his life-span. Of course, he isn't in any immediate danger of dying, but you never can tell. He wasn't burned seriously, yet considering his age, and the fact that his injury has had a chance to work on him for two years, there's a possibility that any emotional or physical excitement could be fatal."

"Now isn't that nice," I said. "Do you get what that means, Roxy?" She shook her head. "It might mean that somebody else knows that too and tried to stir the old boy up by kidnapping the one closest to him in the hope that he kicks off during the fun. Great . . . that's a nice subtle sort of murder."

"But that's throwing it right on the doorstep of the beneficiary of his estate."

"Is it? I bet even a minor beneficiary would get enough of
the long green to make murder worthwhile. York has plenty."

"There are other angles too, Mike."

"Been giving it some thought, haven't you?" I grinned at
her. "For instance, one of the family might locate the kid
and thus become number-one boy to the old man. Or perhaps
the kid was the chief beneficiary and one of them wanted to
eliminate him to push himself further up the list. Yeah, kid,
there's a lot of angles, and I don't like any of 'em."

"It still might be a plain kidnapping."

"Roger. That it might. It's just that there're a lot more
possibilities to it that could make it interesting. We'll know
soon enough." I opened the door and hesitated, looking over
my shoulder. " 'Night, Roxy."

"Good night."

York was back by the fireplace again, still brooding. I
would have felt better if he had been pacing the floor. I
walked over and threw myself in a big chair. "Where'll I spend
the night?" I asked him.

He turned very slowly. "The guest room. I'll ring for Harvey."

"Never mind. I'll get him myself when I'm ready."

We sat in silence a few minutes then York began a nervous
tapping of his fingers. Finally, "When do you think we'll have
word?"

"Two, three days maybe. Never can tell."

"But he's been gone a day already."

"Tomorrow, then. I don't know."

"Perhaps I should call the police again."

"Go ahead, but you'll probably be burying the boy after
they find him. Those punks aren't cops, they're political ap-
pointees. You ought to know these small towns. They couldn't
find their way out of a paper bag."

For the first time he showed a little parental anxiety. His
fist came down on the arm of the chair. "Damn it, man, I
can't simply sit here! What do you think it's like for me?
Waiting. Waiting. He may be dead now for all we know."

"Perhaps, but I don't think so. Kidnapping's one thing,
murder's another. How about introducing me to those people?"

He nodded. "Very well." Every eye in the room was on
me as we made the rounds. I didn't suppose there would be
anyone too anxious to meet me after the demonstration a
little while ago.

The two gladiators were first. They were sitting on the love seat trying not to look shaky. Both of them still had red welts across their cheeks. The introduction was simple enough. York merely pointed in obvious disdain. "My nephews, Arthur and William Graham."

We moved on. "My niece, Alice Nichols." A pair of deep brown eyes kissed mine so hard I nearly lost my balance. She swept them up and down the full length of me. It couldn't have been any better if she did it with a wet paintbrush. She was tall and she had seen thirty, but she saw it with a face and body that were as fresh as a new daisy. Her clothes made no attempt at concealment; they barely covered. On some people skin is skin, but on her it was an invitation to dine. She told me things with a smile that most girls since Eve have been trying to put into words without being obvious or seeming too eager and I gave her my answer the same way. I can run the ball a little myself.

York's sister and her husband were next. She was a middle-aged woman with "Matron" written all over her. The type that wants to entertain visiting dignitaries and look down at "peepul" through a lorgnette. Her husband was the type you'd find paired off with such a specimen. He was short and bulgy in the middle. His single-breasted gray suit didn't quite manage to cross the equator without putting a strain on the button. He might have had hair, but you'd never know it now. One point of his collar had jumped the tab and stuck out like an accusing finger.

York said, "My sister, Martha Ghent, her husband, Richard." Richard went to stick out his hand but the old biddie shot him a hasty frown and he drew back, then she tried to freeze me out. Failing in this she turned to York. "Really, Rudolph, I hardly think we should meet this . . . this person."

York turned an appealing look my way, in apology. "I'm sorry, Martha, but Mr. Hammer considers it necessary."

"Nevertheless, I don't see why the police can't handle this."

I sneered at her in my finest manner. "I can't see why you don't keep your mouth shut, Mrs. Ghent."

The way her husband tried to keep the smile back, I thought he'd split a gut. Martha stammered, turned blue and stalked off. York looked at me critically, though approvingly.

A young kid in his early twenties came walking up as though the carpet was made of eggs. He had Ghent in his features, but strictly on his mother's side. A pipe stuck out of his pocket and he sported a set of thick-lensed glasses. The girl at his side didn't resemble anyone, but seeing the way she put her arm around Richard I took it that she was the daughter.

She was. Her name was Rhoda, she was friendly and smiled. The boy was Richard, Junior. He raised his eyebrows until they drew his eyes over the rims of his glasses and peered at me disapprovingly. He perched his hands on his hips and "Humphed" at me. One push and he would be over the line that divides a man and a pansy.

The introductions over, I cornered York out of earshot of the others. "Under the circumstances, it might be best if you kept this gang here until things settle down a bit. Think you can put them up?"

"I imagine so. I've been doing it at one time or another for the last ten years. I'll see Harvey and have the rooms made up."

"When you get them placed, have Harvey bring me a diagram showing where their rooms are. And tell him to keep it under his hat. I want to be able to reach anyone anytime. Now, is there anyone closely connected with the household we've missed?"

He thought a moment. "Oh, Miss Grange. She went home this afternoon."

"Where was she during the kidnapping?"

"Why . . . at home, I suppose. She leaves here between five and six every evening. She is a very reserved woman. Apparently has very little social activity. Generally she furthers her studies in the library rather than go out anywhere."

"Okay, I'll get to her. How about the others? Have they alibis?"

"Alibis?"

"Just checking, York. Do you know where they were the night before last?"

"Well . . . I can't speak for all of them, but Arthur and William were here. Alice Nichols came in about nine o'clock then left about an hour later."

This part I jotted down on a pad. "How did you collect the family . . . or did they all just drift in?"

"No, I called them. They helped me search, although it did no good. Mr. Hammer, what are we going to do? Please . . ."

Very slowly, York was starting to go to pieces. He'd stood up under this too calmly too long. His face was pale and withered-looking, drawn into a mask of tragedy.

"First of all, you're going to bed. It won't do any good for you to be knocking yourself out. That's what I'm here for." I reached over his shoulder and pulled a velvet cord. The flunky came in immediately and hurried over to us. "Take him upstairs," I said.

York gave the butler instructions about putting the family

up and Harvey seemed a little surprised and pleased that he'd be allowed in on the conspiracy of the room diagram.

I walked to the middle of the floor and let the funeral buzz down before speaking. I wasn't nice about it. "You're all staying here tonight. If it interferes with other plans you've made it's too bad. Anyone that tries to duck out will answer to me. Harvey will give you your rooms and be sure you stay in them. That's all."

Lady sex appeal waited until I finished then edged up to me with a grin. "See if you can grab the end bedroom in the north wing," she said, "and I'll get the one connected to it."

I said in mock surprise, "Alice, you can get hurt doing things like that."

She laughed. "Oh, I bruise easily, but I heal fast as hell."

Swell girl. I hadn't been seduced in a long time.

I wormed out through a cross fire of nasty looks to the foyer and winked at Richard Ghent on the way. He winked back; his wife wasn't looking.

I slung on my coat and hat and went out to the car. When I rolled it through the gate I turned toward town and stepped on the gas. When I picked up to seventy I held it there until I hit the main drag. Just before the city line I pulled up to a gas station and swung in front of a pump. An attendant in his early twenties came out of the miniature Swiss Alpine cottage that served as a service station and automatically began unscrewing the gas cap. "Put in five," I told him.

He snaked out the hose and shoved the nose in the tank, watching the gauge. "Open all night?" I quizzed.

"Yeah."

"On duty yourself?"

"Yup. 'Cept on Sundays."

"Don't suppose you get much to do at night around here."

"Not very much."

This guy was as talkative as a pea pod. "Say, was much traffic along here night before last?"

He shut off the pump, put the cap back on and looked at me coldly. "Mister, I don't know from nothing," he said.

It didn't take me long to catch on to that remark. I handed him a ten-spot and followed him inside while he changed it. I let go a flyer. "So the cops kind of hinted that somebody would be nosing around, huh?"

No answer. He rang the cash register and began counting out bills. "Er . . . did you happen to notice Dilwick's puss? Or was it one of the others?"

He glanced at me sharply, curiously. "It was Dilwick. I saw his face."

Instead of replying I held out my right hand. He peered at

it and saw where the skin had been peeled back off half the knuckles. This time I got a great big grin.

"Did you do that?"

"Uh-huh."

"Okay, pal, for that we're buddies. What do you want to know?"

"About traffic along here night before last."

"Sure, I remember it. Between nine o'clock and dawn the next morning about a dozen cars went past. See, I know most of 'em. A couple was from out of town. All but two belonged to the up-country farmers making milk runs to the separator at the other end of town."

"What about the other two?"

"One was a Caddy. I seen it around a few times. Remember it because it had one side dented in. The other was that Grange dame's two-door sedan. Guess she was out wolfing." He laughed at that.

"Grange?"

"Yeah, the old bag that works out at York's place. She's a stiff one."

"Thanks for the info, kid." I slipped him a buck and he grinned. "By the way, did you pass that on to the cops too?"

"Not me. I wouldn't give them the right time."

"Why?"

"Lousy bunch of bastards." He explained it in a nutshell without going into detail.

I hopped in and started up, but before I drove off I stuck my head out the window. "Where's this Grange babe live?"

"At the Glenwood Apartments. You can't miss it. It's the only apartment house in this burg."

Well, it wouldn't hurt to drop up and see her anyway. Maybe she had been on her way home from work. I gunned the engine and got back on the main drag, driving slowly past the shaded fronts of the stores. Just outside the business section a large green canopy extended from the curb to the marquee of a modern three-story building. Across the side in small, neat letters was GLENWOOD APARTMENTS. I crawled in behind a black Ford sedan and hopped out.

Grange, Myra, was the second name down. I pushed the bell and waited for the buzzer to unlatch the door. When it didn't come I pushed it again. This time there was a series of clicks and I shoved the door open. One flight of stairs put me in front of her apartment. Before I could ring, the metal peephole was pulled back and a pair of dark eyes threw insults at me.

"Miss Grange?"

"Yes."

"I'd like to speak to you if you can spare a few moments."

"Very well, go ahead." Her voice sounded as if it came out of a tree trunk. This made the third person I didn't like in Sidon.

"I work for York," I explained patiently, "I'd like to speak to you about the boy."

"There's nothing I care to discuss."

Why is it that some dames can work me up into a lather so fast with so little is beyond me, but this one did. I quit playing around. I pulled out the .45 and let her get a good look at it. "You open that door or I'll shoot the lock off," I said.

She opened it. The insults in her eyes turned to terror until I put the rod back under cover. Then I looked at her. If she was an old bag I was Queen of the May. Almost as tall as I was, nice brown hair cut short enough to be nearly mannish and a figure that seemed to be well molded, except that I couldn't tell too well because she was wearing slacks and a house jacket. Maybe she was thirty, maybe forty. Her face had a built-in lack of expression like an old painting. Wearing no makeup didn't help it any, but it didn't hurt, either.

I tossed my hat on a side table and went inside without being invited. Myra Grange followed me closely, letting her wooden-soled sandals drag along the carpet. It was a nice dump, but small. There was something to it that didn't sit right, as though the choice of furniture didn't fit her personality. Hell, maybe she just sublet.

The living room was ultramodern. The chairs and the couch were surrealist dreams of squares and angles. Even the coffee table was balanced precariously on little pyramids that served as legs. Two framed wood nymphs seemed cold in their nudity against the background of the chilled blue walls. I wouldn't live in a room like this for anything.

Myra held her position in the middle of the floor, legs spread, hands shoved in her side pockets. I picked a leather-covered ottoman and sat down.

She watched every move I made with eyes that scarcely concealed her rage. "Now that you've forced your way in here," she said between tight lips, "perhaps you'll explain why, or do I call the police?"

"I don't think the police would bother me much, kiddo." I pulled my badge from my pocket and let her see it. "I'm a private dick myself."

"Go on." She was a cool tomato.

"My name is Hammer. Mike Hammer. York wants me to find the kid. What do you think happened?"

"I believe he was kidnapped, Mr. Hammer. Surely that is evident."

"Nothing's evident. You were seen on the road fairly late the night the boy disappeared. Why?"

Instead of answering me she said, "I didn't think the time of his disappearance was established."

"As far as I'm concerned it is. It happened that night. Where were you?"

She began to raise herself up and down on her toes like a British major. "I was right here. If anyone said he saw me that night he was mistaken."

"I don't think he was." I watched her intently. "He's got sharp eyes."

"He was mistaken," she repeated.

"All right, we'll let it drop there. What time did you leave York's house?"

"Six o'clock, as usual. I came straight home." She began to kick at the rug impatiently, then pulled a cigarette from a pocket and stuck it in her mouth. Damn it, every time she moved she did something that was familiar to me but I couldn't place it. When she lit the cigarette she sat down on the couch and watched me some more.

"Let's quit the cat and mouse, Miss Grange. York said you were like a mother to the kid and I should suppose you'd like to see him safe. I'm only trying to do what I can to locate him."

"Then don't classify me as a suspect, Mr. Hammer."

"It's strictly temporary. You're a suspect until you alibi yourself satisfactorily then I won't have to waste my time and yours fooling around."

"Am I alibied?"

"Sure," I lied. "Now can you answer some questions civilly?"

"Ask them."

"Number one. Suspicious characters loitering about the house anytime preceding the disappearance."

She thought a moment, furrowing her eyebrows. "None that I can recall. Then again, I am inside all day working in the lab. I wouldn't see anyone."

"York's enemies. Do you know them?"

"Rudolph . . . Mr. York has no enemies I know of. Certain persons working in the same field have expressed what you might call professional jealousy, but that is all."

"To what extent?"

She leaned back against the cushions and blew a smoke ring at the ceiling. "Oh, the usual bantering at the clubs. Making light of his work. You know."

I didn't know anything of the kind, but I nodded. "Anything serious?"

"Nothing that would incite a kidnapping. There were heated discussions, yes, but few and far between. Mr. York was loathe to discuss his work. Besides, a scientist is not a person who would resort to violence."

"That's on the outside. Let's hear a little bit about his family. You've been connected with York long enough to pick up a little something on his relatives."

"I'd rather not discuss them, Mr. Hammer. They are none of my affair."

"Don't be cute. We're talking about a kidnapping."

"I still don't see where they could possibly enter into it."

"Damn it," I exploded, "you're not supposed to. I want information and everybody wants to play repartee. Before long I'm going to start choking it out of people like you."

"Please, Mr. Hammer, that isn't necessary."

"So I've been told. Then give."

"I've met the family very often. I know nothing about them although they all try to press me for details of our work. I've told them nothing. Needless to say, I like none of them. Perhaps that is a biased opinion but it is my only one."

"Do they feel the same toward you?"

"I imagine they are very jealous of anyone so closely connected with Mr. York as I am," she answered with a caustic grimace. "You might surmise that of any rich man's relatives. However, for your information and unknown to them, I enjoy a personal income outside the salary Mr. York pays me and I am quite unconcerned with the disposition of his fortune in the event that anything should happen to him. The only possession he has that I am interested in is the boy. I have been with him all his life, and as you say, he is like a son to me. Is there anything else?"

"Just what is York's work . . . and yours?"

"If he hasn't told you, I'm not at liberty to. Naturally, you realize that it centered around the child."

"Naturally." I stood up and looked at my watch. It was nine-fifteen. "I think that covers it, Miss Grange. Sorry to set you on your ear to get in, but maybe I can make it up sometime. What do you do nights around here?"

Her eyebrows went up and she smiled for the first time. It was more of a stifled laugh than a smile and I had the silly feeling that the joke was on me. "Nothing you'd care to do with me," she said.

I got sore again and didn't know why. I fought a battle with the look, stuck my hat on and got out of there. Behind me I heard a muffled chuckle.

The first thing I did was make a quick trip back to the filling station. I waited until a car pulled out then drove up to the door. The kid recognized me and waved. "Any luck?" he grinned.

"Yeah, I saw her. Thought she was an old bag?"

"Well, she's a stuffy thing. Hardly ever speaks."

"Listen," I said, "are you sure you saw her the other night?"

"Natch, why?"

"She said no. Think hard now. Did you see her or the car?"

"Well, it was her car. I know that. She's the only one that ever drives it."

"How would you know it?"

"The aerial. It's got a bend in it so it can only be telescoped down halfway. Been like that every since she got the heap."

"Then you can't be certain she was in it. You wouldn't swear to it?"

"Well . . . no. Guess not when you put it that way. But it was her car," he insisted.

"Thanks a lot." I shoved another buck at him. "Forget I was around, will you?"

"Never saw you in my life," he grinned. Nice kid.

This time I took off rather aimlessly. It was only to pacify York that I left the house in the first place. The rain had let up and I shut off the windshield wipers while I turned onto the highway and cruised north toward the estate. If the snatch ran true to form there would be a letter or a call sometime soon. All I could do would be to advise York to follow through to get the kid back again then go after the ones that had him.

If it weren't for York's damn craving for secrecy I could buzz the state police and have a seven-state alarm sent out, but that meant the house would crawl with cops. Let a spotter get a load of that and they'd dump the kid and that'd be the end of it until some campers came across his remains sometime. As long as the local police had a sizable reward to shoot for they wouldn't let it slip. Not after York told them not to.

I wasn't underestimating Dilwick any. I'd bet my bottom dollar he'd had York's lines tapped already, ready to go to town the moment a call came through. Unless I got that call at the same time I was liable to get scratched. Not me, brother. Ten G's was a lot of mazuma in any language.

The lights were still on en masse when I breezed by the estate. It was still too early to go back, and as long as I could keep the old boy happy by doing a little snooping I figured I was earning my keep, at least. About ten miles down the highway the town of Bayview squatted along the water's edge waiting for summer to liven things up.

A kidnap car could have gone in either direction, although this route was unlikely. Outside Bayview the highway petered off into a tar road that completely disappeared under drifting winter sands. Anything was worth trying, though. I dodged an old flivver that was standing in the middle of the road and swerved into the gravel parking place of a two-bit honky-tonk. The place was badly run down at the heels and sadly in need of a paint job. A good deodorant would have helped, too. I no sooner got my foot on the rail when a frowsy blonde sidled up to me and I got a quick once-over. "You're new around here ain't you?"

"Just passing through."

"Through to where? That road outside winds up in the drink."

"Maybe that's where I'm going."

"Aw now, Buster, that ain't no way to feel. We all got our troubles but you don't wanna do nothing like that. Lemme buy you a drink, it'll make you feel better."

She whistled through her teeth and when that got no response, cupped her hands and yelled to the bartender who was busy shooting crap on the bar. "Hey, Andy, get your tail over here and serve your customers."

Andy took his time. "What'll you have, pal?"

"Beer."

"Me too."

"You too nothing. Beat it, Janie, you had too much already."

"Say, see here, I can pay my own way."

"Not in my joint."

I grinned at the two of them and chimed in. "Give her a beer why don't you?"

"Listen, pal, you don't know her. She's half tanked already. One more and she'll be making like a Copa cutie. Not that I don't like the Copa, but the dames there are one thing and she's another, just like night and day. Instead of watching, my customers all get the dry heaves and trot down to Charlie's on the waterfront."

"Well, I like that!" Janie hit an indignant pose and waved her finger in Andy's face. "You give me my beer right now or I'll make better'n the Copa. I'll make like . . . like . . ."

"Okay, okay, Janie, one more and that's all."

The bartender drew two beers, took my dough instead of Janie's and rang it up. I put mine away in one gulp. Janie never reached completely around her glass. Before Andy could pick out the change Janie had spilled hers halfway down the bar.

Andy said something under his breath, took the glass away

then fished around under the counter for a rag. He started to mop up the mess.

I watched. In my head the little bells were going off, slowly at first like chimes on a cold night. They got louder and louder, playing another scrambled, soundless symphony. A muscle in my neck twitched. I could almost feel that ten grand in my pocket already. Very deliberately I reached out across the bar and gathered a handful of Andy's stained apron in my fist. With my other hand I yanked out the .45 and held it an inch away from his eye. He was staring death in the face and knew it.

I had trouble keeping my voice down. "Where did you get that bar rag, Andy?"

His eyes shifted to the blue-striped pajama bottoms that he held in his hand, beer soaked now, but recognizable. The other half to them were in Ruston York's bedroom hanging on the foot of the bed.

Janie's mouth was open to scream. I pointed the gun at her and said, "Shut up." The scream died before it was born. She held the edge of the bar with both hands, shaking like a leaf. Ours was a play offstage; no one saw it, no one cared. "Where, Andy?"

". . . Don't know, mister. Honest . . ."

I thumbed the hammer back. He saw me do it. "Only one more chance, Andy. Think hard."

His breath came in little jerks, fright thickened his tongue. "Some . . . guy. He brought it in. Wanted to know . . . if they were mine. It . . . was supposed to be a joke. Honest, I just use it for a bar rag, that's all."

"When?"

". . . 's afternoon."

"Who, Andy?"

"Bill. Bill Cuddy. He's a clam digger. Lives in a shack on the bay."

I put the safety back on, but I still held his apron. "Andy," I told him, "if you're leveling with me it's okay, but if you're not, I'm going to shoot your head off. You know that, don't you?"

His eyes rolled in his head then came back to meet mine. "Yeah, mister. I know. I'm not kidding. Honest, I got two kids . . ."

"And Janie here. I think maybe you better keep her with you for a while. I wouldn't want anyone to hear about this, understand?"

Andy understood, all right. He didn't miss a word. I let him go and he had to hang on to his bar to keep from crumbling. I slid the rod back under my coat, wrung out the pajamas and folded them into a square.

When I straightened my hat and tie I said, "Where is Cuddy's place?"

Andy's voice was so weak I could hardly hear it. "Straight . . . down the road to the water. Turn left. It's the deck . . . deckhouse of an old boat pulled up on the . . . beach."

I left them standing there like Hansel and Gretel in the woods, scared right down to their toes. Poor Andy. He didn't have anymore to do with it than I did, but in this game it's best not to take any chances.

As Janie had said, the road led right to the drink. I parked the car beside a boarded-up house and waded through the wet sand on foot. Ten feet from the water I turned left and faced a line of broken-down shacks that were rudely constructed from the junk that comes in on the tide. Some of them had tin roofs, with the advertisements for soft drinks and hot dogs still showing through.

Every once in a while the moon would shine through a rift in the clouds, and I took advantage of it to get a better look at the homemade village.

Cuddy's place was easier to find than I expected. It was the only dump that ever had seen paint, and on the south side hung a ship's name plate with CARMINE spelled out in large block letters. It was a deckhouse, all right, probably washed off during a storm. I edged up to a window and looked in. All I could see were a few vague outlines. I tried the door. It opened outward noiselessly. From one corner of the room came the raspy snore of a back-sleeper with a load under his belt.

A match lit the place up. Cuddy never moved, even when I put the match to the ship's lantern swinging from the center of the ceiling. It was a one-room affair with a few chairs, a table and a double-decker bed along the side. He had rigged up a kerosene stove with the pipe shooting through the roof and used two wooden crates for a larder. Beside the stove was a barrel of clams.

Lots of stuff, but no kid.

Bill Cuddy was a hard man to awaken. He twitched a few times, pawed the covers and grunted. When I shook him some more his eyelids flickered, went up. No pupils. They came down ten seconds later. A pair of bleary, bloodshot eyes moved separately until they came to an accidental focus on me.

Bill sat up. "Who're you?"

I gave him a few seconds to study me, then palmed my badge in front of his face. "Cop. Get up."

His legs swung to the floor, he grabbed my arm. "What's

the matter, officer? I ain't been poachin'. All I got is clams, go look." He pointed to the barrel. "See?"

"I'm no game warden," I told him.

"Then whatcha want of me?"

"I want you for kidnapping. Murder maybe."

"Oh . . . No!" His voice was a hoarse croak. "But . . . I ain't killed nobody atall. I wouldn't do that."

He didn't have to tell me that. There are types that kill and he wasn't one of them. I didn't let him know I thought so.

"You brought a set of pajamas into Andy's place this afternoon. Where did you get them?"

He wrinkled his nose, trying to understand what I was talking about. "Pajamas?"

"You heard me."

He remembered then. His face relaxed into a relieved grin. "Oh, that. Sure, I found 'em lying on Shore Road. Thought I'd kid Andy with 'em."

"You almost kidded him to death. Put on your pants. I want you to show me the spot."

He stuck his feet into a pair of dungarees and pulled the suspenders over his bony shoulders, then dragged a pair of boots out from under the bed. A faded denim shirt and a battered hat and he was dressed. He kept shooting me sidewise glances, trying to figure it out but wasn't getting anyplace.

"You won't throw me in the jug, will you?"

"Not if you tell the truth."

"But I did."

"We'll see. Come on." I let him lead the way. The sand had drifted too deep along the road to take the car so we plodded along slowly, keeping away from the other shacks. Shore Road was a road in name only. It was a strip of wet Sahara that separated the tree line from the water. A hundred yards up and the shacks had more room between them. Bill Cuddy pointed ahead.

"Up there is the cove where I bring the boat in. I was coming down there and where the old cistern is I see the pants lying right in the middle of the road."

I nodded. A few minutes later we had reached the cistern, a huge, barrel-shaped thing lying on its side. It was big enough to make a two-car garage. Evidently it, like everything else around here, had been picked up during a storm and deposited along the shore. Bill indicated a spot on the ground with a gnarled forefinger.

"Right here's the spot, officer, they was lying right here."

"Fine. See anyone?"

"Naw. Who would be out here? They was washed up, I guess."

I looked at him, then the water. Although the tide was high the water was a good forty yards from the spot. He saw what I meant and he shifted uneasily.

"Maybe they blew up."

"Bill?"

"Huh?"

"Did you ever see wet clothes blow along the ground? Dry clothes, maybe, but wet?"

He paused. "Nope."

"Then they didn't blow up or wash up. Somebody dropped them there."

He got jittery then, his face was worried. "But I didn't do it. No kidding, I just found them there. They was new-looking so I brung 'em to Andy's. You won't jug me, will you? I . . ."

"Forget it, Bill. I believe you. If you want to keep your nose clean turn around and trot home. Remember this, though. Keep your mouth shut, you hear?"

"Gee, yeah. Thanks . . . thanks, officer. I won't say nothing to nobody." Bill broke into a fast shuffle and disappeared into the night.

Alone like that you can see that what you mistook for silence was really a jungle of undertones, subdued, foreign, but distinct. The wind whispering over the sand, the waves keeping time with a steady lap, lap. Tree sounds, for which there is no word to describe bark rubbing against bark, and the things that lived in the trees. The watch on my wrist made an audible tick.

Somewhere oars dipped into the water and scraped in the oarlocks. There was no telling how far away it was. Sounds over water carry far on the wind.

I tried to see into the night, wondering how the pajamas got there. A road that came from the cove and went nowhere. The trees and the bay. A couple of shacks and a cistern.

The open end faced away from me, making it necessary to push through yards of saw grass to reach it. Two rats ran out making ugly squeaking noises. When I lit a match I seemed to be in a hall of green slime. Droplets of water ran down the curved sides of the cistern and collected in a stinking pool of scum in the middle. Some papers had blown in, but that was all. The only things that left their footprints in the muck had tails. When I couldn't hold my breath any longer I backed out and followed the path I had made to the road.

Right back where I started. Twenty-five yards away was the remains of a shack. The roof had fallen in, the sides bulged out like it had been squeezed by a giant hand. Further down was another. I took the first one. The closer I came to it the worse it looked. Holes in the side passed for windows, the door hung open on one hinge and was wedged that way by a pile of sand that had blown around the corner. No tracks, no nothing. It was as empty as the cistern.

Or so I thought.

Just then someone whimpered inside. The .45 leaped into my hand. I took a few wooden matches, lit them all together and threw them inside and went in after them.

I didn't need my gun. Ruston York was all alone, trussed up like a Christmas turkey over in the corner, his naked body covered with bruises.

In a moment I was on my knees beside him, working the knots loose. I took it easy on the adhesive tape that covered his mouth so I wouldn't tear the skin off. His body shook with sobs. Tears of fright and relief filled his large, expressive eyes, and when he had his arms free he threw them around my neck. "Go ahead and cry, kid," I said.

He did, then. Hard, body-racking gasps that must have hurt. I wiggled out of my jacket and put it around him, talking quickly and low to comfort him. The poor kid was a mess.

It came with jarring suddenness, that sound. I shoved the kid on his back and pivoted on my heels. I was shooting before I completed the turn. Someone let out a short scream. A heavy body crashed into my chest and slammed my back against the wall. I kicked out with both feet and we spilled to the floor. Before I could get my gun up a heavy boot ripped it out of my hand.

They were all over me. I gave it everything I had, feet, fingernails and teeth, there wasn't enough room to swing. Somehow I managed to hook my first two fingers in a mouth and yank, and I felt a cheek rip clear to the ear.

There was no more for me. Something smashed down on my skull and I stopped fighting. It was a peaceful feeling, as if I were completely adrift from my body. Feet thudded into my ribs and pounded my back raw, but there was no pain, merely vague impressions. Then even the impressions began to fade.

Chapter Three

I came back together like a squadron of flak-eaten bombers re-forming. I heard the din of their motors, a deafening, pulsating roar that grew louder and louder. Pieces of their skin, fragments of their armor drifted to earth and imbedded themselves in my flesh until I thought I was on fire.

Bombs thudded into the earth and threw great flashes of flame into my face and rocked my body back and forth, back and forth. I opened my eyes with an effort.

It was the kid shaking me. "Mister. Can you get up? They all ran away looking for me. If you don't get up they'll be back and find us. Hurry, please hurry."

I tried to stand up, but I didn't do too good a job. Ruston York got his arms around me and boosted. Between the two of us I got my feet in position where I could shove with my legs and raise myself. He still had on my coat, but that was all.

I patted his shoulder. "Thanks, kid. Thanks a lot."

It was enough talk for a while. He steered me outside and up into the bushes along the trees where we melted into the darkness. The sand muffled our footsteps well. For once I was grateful for the steady drip of rain from the trees; it covered any other noises we made.

"I found your gun on the floor. Here, do you want it?" He held the .45 out gingerly by the handle. I took it in a shaking hand and stowed it in the holster. "I think you shot somebody. There's an awful lot of blood by the door."

"Maybe it's mine," I grunted.

"No, I don't think so. It's on the wall, too, and there's a big hole in the wall where it looks like a bullet went through."

I prayed that he was right. Right now I half-hoped they'd show again so I could have a chance to really place a few where they'd hurt.

I don't know how long it took to reach the car, but it seemed like hours. Every once in a while I thought I could discern shouts and guarded words of caution. By the time Ruston helped slide me under the wheel I felt as though I had been on the Death March.

We sat there in silence a few moments while I fumbled for a cigarette. The first drag was worth a million dollars. "There's a robe in the back," I told the kid. He knelt on the seat, got it and draped it over his legs.

"What happened?"

"Gosh, mister, I hardly know. When you pushed me away I ran out the door. The man I think you shot nearly grabbed me, but he didn't. I hid behind the door for a while. They must have thought I ran off because when they followed me out one man told the others to scatter and search the beach, then he went away too. That's when I came in and got you."

I turned the key and reached for the starter. It hurt. "Before that. What happened then?"

"You mean the other night?"

"Yeah."

"Well, I woke up when the door opened. I thought maybe it was Miss Malcom. She always looks in before she goes to bed, but it wasn't her. It was a man. I wanted to ask him who he was when he hit me. Right here." Ruston rubbed the top of his head and winced.

"Which door did he come in?"

"The one off the hall, I think. I was pretty sleepy."

Cute. Someone sneaks past the guard at the gate, through a houseful of people and puts the slug on the kid and walks off with him.

"Go on." While he spoke I let in the clutch and swung around, then headed the car toward the estate.

"I woke up in a boat. They had me in a little room and the door was locked. I could hear the men talking in the stern and one called the man who was steering, Mallory. That's the only time I heard a name at all."

The name didn't strike any responsive chord as far as I was concerned, so I let him continue.

"Then I picked the lock and . . ."

"Wait a second, son." I looked at him hard. "Say that again."

"I picked the lock. Why?"

"Just like that you picked the lock. No trouble to it or anything?"

"Uh-uh." He flashed a boyish grin at me, shyly. "I learned all about locks when I was little. This one was just a plain lock."

He *must* be a genius. It takes me an hour with respectable burglar tools to open a closet door.

". . . and as soon as I got out I opened a little hatch and crawled up on the deck. I saw the lights from shore and jumped overboard. Boy, was that water cold. They never even heard me at all. I nearly made it at that. After I jumped the boat kept right on going and disappeared, but I guess they found the door open down below. I should have locked it again but I was sort of scared and forgot. Just when I got up on the shore some man came running at me and they had me again. He said he'd figured I'd head for the lights, then he slapped me. He was waiting for the others to come and he made me go into the shack with him. Seems like they tied up in the cove and had to wait awhile before they could take me back to the boat.

"He had a bottle and started drinking from it, and pretty

soon he was almost asleep. I waited until he was sort of dopey then threw my pajama pants out the window with a rock in them hoping someone would find them. He never noticed what I did. But he did know he was getting drunk, and he didn't have any more in the bottle. He hit me a few times and I tried to get away. Then he really gave it to me. When he got done he took some rope and tied me up and went down the beach after the others. That was when you came in."

"And I went out," I added.

"Gee, mister, I hope you didn't get hurt too badly." His face was anxious, truly anxious. It's been a long time since someone worried about me getting hurt. I ran my fingers through his hair and shook his head gently.

"It isn't too bad, kid," I said. He grinned again, pulled the robe tighter and moved closer to me. Every few seconds he'd throw me a searching glance, half curious, half serious.

"What's your name?"

"Mike Hammer."

"Why do you carry a gun?"

"I'm a detective, Ruston. A private detective."

A sigh of relief escaped him. He probably figured me for one of the mob who didn't like the game, I guess.

"How did you happen to find me?"

"I was looking for you."

"I'm . . . I'm glad it was you, Mr. Hammer, and not somebody else. I don't think anyone would have been brave enough to do what you did."

I laughed at that. He was a good kid. If any bravery was involved he had it all. Coming back in after me took plenty of nerve. I told him so, but he chuckled and blushed. Damn, you couldn't help but like him. In spite of a face full of bruises and all the hell he had been through he could still smile. He sat there beside me completely at ease, watching me out of the corner of his eye as though I was a tin god or something.

For a change some of the lights were off in the house. Henry, the gatekeeper, poked a flashlight in the car and his mouth fell open. All he got out was, "M . . . Master Ruston!"

"Yeah, it's him. Open the gates." He pulled a bar at the side and the iron grillwork rolled back. I pushed the buggy through, but by the time I reached the house Henry's call had the whole family waiting on the porch.

York didn't even wait until I stopped. He yanked the door open and reached for his son. Ruston's arms went around his neck and he kept repeating, "Dad . . . Dad."

I wormed out of the car and limped around to the other side. The family was shooting questions at the kid a mile a minute and completely ignored me, not that it mattered. I shoved them aside and took York by the arm. "Get the kid in the house and away from this mob. He's had enough excitement for a while."

The scientist nodded. Ruston said, "I can walk, Dad." He held the robe around himself and we went in together.

Before the others could follow, York turned. "If you don't mind, please go to your rooms. You will hear what happened in the morning."

There was no disputing who was master in that house. They looked at one another then slouched off in a huff. I drew a few nasty looks myself.

I slammed the door on the whole pack of them and started for the living room, but Harvey interrupted me en route. Having once disrupted his composure, events weren't likely to do it a second time. When he handed me the tray with the diagram of the bedroom layout neatly worked up he was the perfect flunky.

"The guest plan, sir," he said. "I trust it is satisfactory?"

I took it without looking at it and thanked him, then stuck it in my pocket.

York was in an anteroom with his son. The kid was stretched out on a table while his father went over each bruise carefully, searching for abrasions. Those he daubed with antiseptic and applied small bandages. This done he began a thorough examination in the most professional manner.

When he finished I asked, "How is he?"

"All right, apparently," he answered, "but it will be difficult to tell for a few days. I'm going to put him to bed now. His physical condition has always been wonderful, thank goodness."

He wrapped Ruston in a robe and rang for Harvey. I picked up the wreckage that was my coat and slipped into it. The butler came in and at York's direction, picked the kid up and they left the room. On the way out Ruston smiled a good-night at me over the butler's shoulder.

York was back in five minutes. Without a word he pointed at the table and I climbed on. By the time he finished with me I felt like I had been in a battle all over again. The open cuts on my face and back stung from iodine, and with a few layers of six-inch tape around my ribs I could hardly breathe. He told me to get up in a voice shaky from suppressed emotion, swallowed a tablet from a bottle in his kit and sat down in a cold sweat.

When I finished getting dressed I said, "Don't you think you ought to climb into the sack yourself? It's nearly daybreak."

He shook his head. "No. I want to hear about it. Everything. Please, if you don't mind . . . the living room."

We went in and sat down together. While I ran over the story he poured me a stiff shot of brandy and I put it away neat.

"I don't understand it. Mr. Hammer . . . it is beyond me."

"I know. It doesn't seem civilized, does it?"

"Hardly." He got up and walked over to a Sheraton secretary, opened it and took out a book. He wrote briefly and returned waving ten thousand dollars in my face. "Your fee, Mr. Hammer. I scarcely need say how grateful I am."

I tried not to look too eager when I took that check, but ten G's is ten G's. As unconcernedly as I could, I shoved it in my wallet. "Of course, I suppose you want me to put a report in to the state police," I remarked. "They ought to be able to tie into that crew, especially with the boat. A thing like that can't be hidden very easily."

"Yes, yes, they will have to be apprehended. I can't imagine why they chose to abduct Ruston. It's incredible."

"You are rich, Mr. York. That is the primary reason."

"Yes. Wealth does bring disadvantages sometimes, though I have tried to guard against it."

I stood up. "I'll call them then. We have one lead that might mean something. One of the kidnappers was called Mallory. Your boy brought that up."

"What did you say?"

I repeated it.

His voice was barely audible. "Mallory . . . No!"

As if in a trance he hurried to the side of the fireplace. A pressure on some concealed spring-activated hidden mechanism and the side swung outward. He thrust his hand into the opening. Even at this distance I could see him pale. He withdrew his hand empty. A muscular spasm racked his body. He pressed his hands against his chest and sagged forward. I ran over and eased him into a chair.

"Vest . . . pocket."

I poked my fingers under his coat and brought out a small envelope of capsules. York picked one out with trembling fingers and put it on his tongue. He swallowed it, stared blankly at the wall. Very slowly a line of muscles along his jaw hardened into knots, his lips curled back in an animal-like snarl. "The bitch," he said, "the dirty man-hating bitch has sold me out."

"Who, Mr. York? Who was it?"

He suddenly became aware of me standing there. The snarl faded. A hunted-quarry look replaced it. "I said nothing, you understand? Nothing."

I dropped my hand from his shoulder. I was starting to get a dirty taste in my mouth again. "Go to hell," I said, "I'm going to report it."

"You wouldn't dare!"

"Wouldn't I? York, old boy, that son of yours pulled me out of a nasty mess. I like him. You hear that? I like him more than I do a lot of people. If you want to expose him to more danger that's your affair, but I'm not going to have it."

"No . . . that's not it. This can't be made public."

"Listen, York, why don't you stow that publicity stuff and think of your kid for a change? Keep this under your hat and you'll invite another snatch and maybe you won't be so lucky. Especially," I added, "since somebody in your household has sold you out."

York shuddered from head to foot.

"Who was it, York? Who's got the bull on you?"

"I . . . have nothing to say."

"No? Who else knows you're counting your hours because of those radiation burns? What's going to happen to the kid when you kick off?"

That did it. He turned a sick color. "How did you find out about that?"

"It doesn't matter. If I know it others probably do. You still didn't tell me who's putting the squeeze on you."

"Sit down, Mr. Hammer. Please."

I pulled up a chair and parked.

"Could I," he began, "retain you as sort of a guardian instead of reporting this incident? It would be much simpler for me. You see, there are certain scientific aspects of my son's training that you, as a layman, would not understand, but if brought to light under the merciless scrutiny of the newspapers and a police investigation might completely ruin the chances of a successful result.

"I'm not asking you to understand, I'm merely asking that you cooperate. You will be well paid, I assure you. I realize that my son is in danger, but it will be better if we can repel any danger rather than prevent it at its source. Will you do this for me?"

Very deliberately I leaned back in my chair and thought it over. Something stunk. It smelled like Rudolph York. But I still owed the kid a debt.

"I'll take it, York, but if there's going to be trouble I'd like to know where it will come from. Who's the man-hating turnip that has you in a brace?"

His lips tightened. "I'm afraid I cannot reveal that, either. You need not do any investigating. Simply protect my interests, and my son."

"Okay," I said as I rose. "Have it your own way. I'll play dummy. But right now I'm going to beat the sheet. It's been a tough day. You'd better hit it yourself."

"I'll call Harvey."

"Never mind, I'll find it." I walked out. In the foyer I pulled the diagram out of my pocket and checked it. The directions were clear enough. I went upstairs, turned left at the landing and followed the hand-carved balustrade to the other side. My room was next to last and my name was on white cardboard, neatly typed, and framed in a small brass holder on the door. I turned the knob, reached for the light and flicked it on.

"You took long enough getting here."

I grinned. I wondered what Alice Nichols had used as a bribe to get Harvey to put me in next to her. "Hello, kitten."

Alice smiled through a cloud of smoke. "You were better-looking the last time I saw you."

"So? Do I need a shave?"

"You need a new face. But I'll take you like you are." She shrugged her shoulders and the spider web of a negligee fell down to her waist. What she had on under it wasn't worth mentioning. It looked like spun moonbeams with a weave as big as chicken wire. "Let's go to bed."

"Scram, kitten. Get back in your own hive."

"That's a corny line, Mike, don't play hard to get."

I started to climb out of my clothes. "It's not a line, kitten, I'm beat."

"Not that much."

I draped my shirt and pants over the back of the chair and flopped in the sack. Alice stood up slowly. No, that's not the word. It was more like a low-pressure spring unwinding. The negligee was all the way off now. She was a concert of savage beauty.

"Still tired?"

"Turn off the light when you go out, honey." Before I rolled over she gave me a malicious grin. It told me that there were other nights. The lights went out. Before I corked off one thought hit me. It couldn't have been Alice Nichols he had meant when he called some babe a man-hating bitch.

Going to sleep with a thought like that is a funny thing. It sticks with you. I could see Alice over and over again, getting up out of that chair and walking across the room, only this time she didn't even wear moonbeams. Her body was lithe, seductive. She did a little dance. Then someone else came into my dream, too. Another dame. This one was familiar, but I couldn't place her. She did a dance too, but a different kind. There was none of that animal grace, no fluid motion.

She took off her clothes and moved about stiffly, ill at ease. The two of them started dancing together, stark naked, and this new one was leading. They came closer, the mist about their faces parted and I got a fleeting glimpse of the one I couldn't see before.

I sat bolt upright in bed. No wonder Miss Grange did things that bothered me. It wasn't the woman I recognized in her apartment, it was her motions. Even to striking a match toward her the way a man would. Sure, she'd be a man-hater, why not? She was a Lesbian.

"Damn!"

I hopped out of bed and climbed into my pants. I picked out York's room from the diagram and tiptoed to the other side of the house. His door was partly opened. I tapped gently. No answer.

I went in and felt for the switch. Light flooded the room, but it didn't do me any good. York's bed had never been slept in. One drawer of his desk was half-open and the contents pushed aside. I looked at the oil blot on the bottom of the drawer. I didn't need a second look at the hastily opened box of .32 cartridges to tell me what had been in there. York was out to do murder.

Time, time, there wasn't enough of it. I finished dressing on the way out. If anyone heard the door slam after me or the motor start up they didn't care much. No lights came on at all. I slowed up by the gates, but they were gaping open. From inside the house I could hear a steady snore. Henry was a fine gatekeeper.

I didn't know how much of a lead he had. Sometime hours ago my watch had stopped and I didn't reset it. It could have been too long ago. The night was fast fading away. I don't think I had been in bed a full hour.

On that race to town I didn't pass a car. The lights of the kid's filling station showed briefly and swept by. The unlit head lamps of parked cars glared in the reflection of my own brights and went back to sleep.

I pulled in behind a line of cars outside the Glenwood Apartments, switched off the engine and climbed out. There wasn't a sign of life anywhere. When this town went to bed it did a good job.

It was one time I couldn't ring doorbells to get in. If Ruston had been with me it wouldn't have taken so long; the set of skeleton keys I had didn't come up with the right answer until I tried two dozen of them.

The .45 was in my fist. I flicked the safety off as I ran up the stairs. Miss Grange's door was closed, but it wasn't locked; it gave when I turned the knob.

No light flared out the door when I kicked it open. No sound broke the funeral quiet of the hall. I stepped in and eased the door shut behind me.

Very slowly I bent down and unlaced my shoes, then put them beside the wall. There was no sense sending in an invitation. With my hand I felt along the wall until I came to the end of the hall. A switch was to the right. Cautiously, I reached around and threw it up, ready for anything.

I needn't have been so quiet. Nobody would have yelled. I found York, all right. He sat there grinning at me like a blooming idiot with the top of his head holding up a meat cleaver.

Chapter Four

Now it was murder. First it was kidnapping, then murder. There seems to be no end to crime. It starts off as a little thing, then gets bigger and bigger like an over-inflated tire until it busts all to hell and gone.

I looked at him, the blood running red on his face, seeping out under the clots, dripping from the back of his head to the floor. It was only a guess, but I figured I had been about ten minutes too late.

The room was a mess, a topsy-turvy cell of ripped-up furniture and emptied drawers. The carpet was littered with trash and stuffing from the pillows. York still clutched a handful of papers, sitting there on the floor where he had fallen, staring blankly at the wall. If he had found what he was searching for it wasn't here now. The papers in his hand were only old receipted electric bills made out to Myra Grange.

First I went back and got my shoes, then I picked up the phone. "Give me the state police," I told the operator.

A Sergeant Price answered. I gave it to him briefly. "This is Mike Hammer, Sergeant," I said. "There's been a murder at the Glenwood Apartments and as far as I can tell it's only a few minutes old. You'd better check the highways. Look for a Ford two-door sedan with a bent radio antenna. Belongs to a woman named Myra Grange. Guy that's been bumped is Rudolph York. She works for him. Around thirty, I'd say, five, six or seven, short hair, well built. Not a bad-looking tomato. No, I don't know what she was wearing. Yeah ... yeah, I'll stay here. You want me to inform the city cops?"

The sergeant said some nasty things about the city boys and told me to go ahead.

I did. The news must have jarred the guy on the desk awake because he started yelling his fool head off all over the place. When he asked for more information I told him to come look for himself, grinned into the mouthpiece and hung up.

I had to figure this thing out. Maybe I could have let it go right then, but I didn't think that way. My client was dead, true, but he had overpaid me in the first place. I could still render him a little service gratis.

I checked the other rooms, but they were as scrambled as the first one. Nothing was in place anywhere. I had to step over piles of clothes in the bedroom that had been carefully, though hurriedly, turned inside out.

The kitchen was the only room not torn apart. The reason for that was easy to see. Dishes and pans crashing against the floor would bring someone running. Here York had felt around, moved articles, but not swept them clear of the shelves. A dumbwaiter door was built into the wall. It was closed and locked. I left it that way. The killer couldn't have left by that exit and still locked it behind him, not with a hook-and-eye clasp. I opened the drawers and peered inside. The fourth one turned up something I hadn't expected to see. A meat cleaver.

That's one piece of cutlery that is rarely duplicated in a small apartment. In fact, it's more or less outdated. Now there were two of them.

The question was: Who did York surprise in this room? No, it wasn't logical. Rather, who surprised York? It had to be that way. If York had burst in here on Grange there would have been a scene, but at least she would have been here too. It was hard picturing her stepping out to let York smash up the joint.

When York came in the place was empty. He came to kill, but finding his intended victim gone, forgot his primary purpose and began his search. Kill. Kill. That was it. I looked at the body again. What I looked for wasn't there anymore.

Somebody had swiped the dead man's gun.

Why? Damn these murderers anyway, why must they mess things up so? Why the hell can't they just kill and be done with it? York sat there grinning for all he was worth, defying me to find the answer. I said, "Cut it out, pal. I'm on your side."

Two cleavers and a grinning dead man. Two cleavers, one in the kitchen and one in his head. What kind of a killer would use a cleaver? It's too big to put in a pocket, too heavy to swing properly unless you had a fairly decent wrist. It would have to be a man, no dame likes to kill when there's a chance of getting spattered with blood.

But Myra Grange . . . the almost woman. She was more half man. Perhaps her sensibilities wouldn't object to crunching a skull or getting smeared with gore. But where the hell did the cleaver come from?

York grinned. I grinned back. It was falling into place now. Not the motive, but the action of the crime, and something akin to motive. The killer knew York was on his way here and knew Grange was out. The killer carried the cleaver for several reasons. It might have just been handy. Having aimed and swung it was certain to do the job. It was a weapon to which no definite personality could be attached.

Above all things, it was far from being an accidental murder. I hate premeditation. I hate those little thoughts of evil that are suppressed in the mind and are being constantly superimposed upon by other thoughts of even greater evil until they squeeze out over the top and drive a person to the depths of infamy.

And this murder was premeditated. Perhaps that cleaver was supposed to have come from the kitchen, but no one could have gone past York to the kitchen without his seeing him, and York had a gun. The killer had chosen his weapon, followed York here and caught him in the act of rifling the place. He didn't even have to be silent about it. In the confusion of tearing the place apart York would never have noticed little sounds . . . until it was too late.

The old man half-stooping over the desk, the upraised meat-ax, one stroke and it was over. Not even a hard stroke. With all that potential energy in a three-pound piece of razor-sharp steel, not much force was needed to deliver a killing blow. Instantaneous death, the body twisting as it fell to face the door and grin at the killer.

I got no further. There was a stamping in the hall, the door was pushed open and Dilwick came in like a summer storm. He didn't waste any time. He walked up to me and stood three inches away, breathing hard. He wasn't pretty to look at.

"I ought to kill you, Hammer," he grated.

We stood there in that tableau a moment. "Why don't you?"

"Maybe I will. The slightest excuse, any excuse. Nobody's going to pull that on me and get away with it. Not you or anybody."

I sneered at him. "Whenever you're ready, Dilwick, here or in the mayor's office, I don't care."

Dilwick would have liked to have said more, but a young

giant in the gray and brown leather of the state police strode over to me with his hand out. "You Mike Hammer?" I nodded.

"Sergeant Price," he smiled. "I'm one of your fans. I had occasion to work with Captain Chambers in New York one time and he spent most of the time talking you up."

The lad gave me a bone-crushing handshake that was good to feel.

I indicated the body. "Here's your case, Sergeant."

Dilwick wasn't to be ignored like that. "Since when do the state police have jurisdiction over us?"

Price was nice about it. "Ever since you proved your-selves to be inadequately supplied with material . . . and men." Dilwick flushed with rage. Price continued, addressing his remarks to me. "Nearly a year ago the people of Sidon petitioned the state to assist in all police matters when the town in general and the county in particular was being used as a rendezvous and sporting place by a lot of out-of-state gamblers and crooks."

The state cop stripped off his leather gloves and took out a pad. He noted a general description of the place, time, then asked me for a statement. Dilwick focused his glare on me, letting every word sink in.

"Mr. York seemed extremely disturbed after his son had been returned to him. He . . ."

"One moment, Mr. Hammer. Where was his son?"

"He had been kidnapped."

"So?" Price's reply was querulous. "It was never reported to us."

"It was reported to the city police." I jerked my thumb at Dilwick. "He can tell you that."

Price didn't doubt me, he was looking for Dilwick's re-action. "Is this true?"

"Yes."

"Why didn't we hear about it?"

Dilwick almost blew his top. "Because we didn't feel like telling you, that's why." He took a step nearer Price, his fists clenched, but the state trooper never budged. "York wanted it kept quiet and that's the way we handled it, so what?"

It came back to me again. "Who found the boy?"

"I did." Dilwick was closer to apoplexy than ever. I guess he wanted that ten grand as badly as I did. "Earlier this eve-ning I found the boy in an abandoned shack near the water-front. I brought him home. Mr. York decided to keep me handy in case another attempt was made to abduct the kid."

Dilwick butted in. "How did you know York was here?"

"I didn't." I hated to answer him, but he was still the police. "I just thought he might be. The boy had been kicked around and I figured that he wanted Miss Grange in the house."

The fat cop sneered. "Isn't York big enough to go out alone anymore?"

"Not in his condition. He had an attack of some sort earlier in the evening."

Price said, "How did you find out he was gone, Mr. Hammer?"

"Before I went to sleep I decided to look in to see how he was. He hadn't gone to bed. I knew he'd mentioned Miss Grange and, as I said, figured he had come here."

Price nodded. "The door . . . ?"

"It was open. I came in and found . . . this." I swept my hand around. "I called you, then the city police. That's all."

Dilwick made a face and bared what was left of his front teeth. "It stinks."

So it did, but I was the only one who was sure of it.

"Couldn't it have been like this, Mr. Hammer." Dilwick emphasized the *mister* sarcastically. "You find the kid, York doesn't like to pay out ten thousand for hardly any work, he blows after you threaten him, only you followed him and make good the threat."

"Sure, it could," I said, "except that it wasn't." I poked a butt in my mouth and held a match to it. "When I kill people I don't have to use a meat hatchet. If they got a gun, I use a gun. If they don't I use my mitts." I shifted my eyes to the body. "I could kill him with my fingers. On bigger guys . . . I'd use both hands. But no cleaver."

"How did York get here, Mr. Hammer?"

"Drove, I imagine. You better detail a couple of boys to lock up his car. A blue '64 Caddy sedan."

Price called a man in plain clothes over with his forefinger and repeated the instructions. The guy nodded and left.

The coroner decided that it was time to get there with the photo guys and the wicker basket. For ten minutes they went around dusting the place and snapping flashes of the remains from all positions until they ran out of bulbs. I showed Price where I'd touched the wall and the switch so there wouldn't be a confusion of the prints. For the record he asked me if I'd give him a set of impressions. It was all right with me. He took out a cardboard over which had been spread a light paraffin of some sort and I laid both hands on it and pressed. Price wrote my name on the bottom, took the number off my license and stowed it back in his pocket.

Dilwick was busy going through the papers York had scattered about, but finding nothing of importance returned his attention to the body. The coroner had spread the contents of the pockets out on an end table and Price rifled through them. I watched over his shoulder. Just the usual junk: a key ring, some small change, a wallet with two twenties and four threes and membership cards in several organizations. Under the wallet was the envelope with the capsules.

"Anything missing?" Price asked.

I shook my head. "Not that I know of, but then, I never went through his pockets."

The body was stuffed into a wicker basket, the cleaver wrapped in a towel and the coroner left with his boys. More troopers came in with a few city guys tagging along and I had to repeat my story all over again. Standing outside the crowd was a lone newspaperman, writing like fury in a note pad. If this was New York they'd have to bar the doors to hold back the press. Just wait until the story reached the wires. This town wouldn't be able to hold them all.

Price called me over to him. "You'll be where I'll be able to reach you?"

"Yeah, at York's estate."

"Good enough. I'll be out sometime this morning."

"I'll be with him," Dilwick cut in. "You keep your nose out of things, too, understand?"

"Blow it," I said. "I know my legal rights."

I shoved my hat on and stamped my butt out in an ashtray. There was nothing for me here. I walked to the door, but before I could leave Price hurried after me. "Mr. Hammer."

"Yeah, Sergeant?"

"Will I be able to expect some cooperation from you?"

I broke out a smile. "You mean, if I uncover anything will I let you in on it, don't you?"

"That covers it pretty well." He was quite serious.

"Okay," I agreed, "but on one condition."

"Name it."

"If I come across something that demands immediate action, I'm going to go ahead on it. You can have it too as soon as I can get it to you, but I won't sacrifice a chance to follow a lead to put it in your hands."

He thought a moment, then, "That sounds fair enough. You realize, of course, that this isn't a permit to do as you choose. The reason I'm willing to let you help out is because of your reputation. You've been in this racket longer than I have, you've had the benefit of wide experience and are familiar with New York police methods. I know your history, otherwise you'd be shut out of this case entirely. Shorthanded as we are, I'm personally glad to have you help out."

"Thanks, Sergeant. If I can help, I will. But you'd better not let Dilwick get wise. He'd do anything to stymie you if he heard about this."

"That pig," Price grunted. "Tell me, what are you going to do?"

"The same thing you are. See what became of the Grange dame. She seems to be the key figure right now. You putting out a dragnet?"

"When you called, a roadblock was thrown across the highways. A seven-state alarm is on the Teletype this minute. She won't get far. Do you know anything of her personally?"

"Only that she's supposed to be the quiet type. York told me that she frequents the library a lot, but I doubt if you'll find her there. I'll see what I can pick up at the house. If I latch on to anything about her I'll buzz you."

I said so long and went downstairs. Right now the most important thing in my life was getting some sleep. I felt like I hadn't seen a pillow in months. A pair of young troopers leaned against the fender of a blue Caddy sedan parked down further from my heap. They were comparing notes and talking back and forth. I'd better remind Billy to come get it.

The sun was thumbing its nose at the night when I reached the estate. Early-morning trucks that the gas station attendant had spoken of were on the road to town, whizzing by at a good clip. I honked my horn at the gate until Henry came out, still chewing on his breakfast.

He waved. "So it was you. I wondered who opened the gates. Why didn't you get me up?"

I drove alongside him and waited until he swallowed. "Henry, did you hear me go out last night?"

"Me? Naw, I slept like a log. Ever since the kid was gone I couldn't sleep thinking that it was all my fault because I sleep so sound, but last night I felt pretty good."

"You must have. Two cars went out, the first one was your boss."

"York? Where'd he go?"

"To town."

He shifted uneasily from one foot to the other. "Do . . . do you think he'll be sore because I didn't hear him?"

I shook my head. "I don't think so. In fact, I don't think he wanted to be heard."

"When's he coming back?"

"He won't. He's dead." I left him standing there with his mouth open. The next time he'd be more careful of those gates.

I raced the engine outside the house and cut it. If that didn't wake everyone in the house the way I slammed the door did. Upstairs I heard a few indignant voices sounding off behind closed doors. I ran up the stairs and met Roxy at the top, holding a quilted robe together at her middle.

She shushed me with her hand. "Be quiet, please. The boy is still asleep." It was going to be hard on him when he woke up.

"Just get up, Roxy?"

"A moment ago when you made all the noise out front. What are you doing up?"

"Never mind. Everybody still around?"

"How should I know? Why, what's the matter?"

"York's been murdered."

Her hand flew to her mouth. For a long second her breath caught in her throat. "W . . . who did it?" she stammered.

"That's what I'd like to know, Roxy."

She bit her lip. "It . . . it was like we were talking about, wasn't it?"

"Seems to be. The finger's on Myra Grange now. It happened in her apartment and she took a powder."

"Well, what will we do?"

"You get the gang up. Don't tell them anything, just that I want to see them downstairs in the living room. Go ahead."

Roxy was glad to be doing something. She half ran to the far end of the hall and threw herself into the first room. I walked around to Ruston's door and tried it. Locked. Roxy's door was open and I went in that way, closing it behind me, then stepped softly to the door of the adjoining room and went in.

Ruston was fast asleep, a slight smile on his face as he played in his dreams. The covers were pulled up under his chin making him look younger than his fourteen years. I blew a wisp of hair away that had drifted across his brow and shook him lightly. "Ruston."

I rocked him again. "Ruston."

His eyes came open slowly. When he saw me he smiled. "Hello, Mr. Hammer."

"Call me Mike, kid, we're pals, aren't we?"

"You bet . . . Mike." He freed one arm and stretched. "Is it time to get up?"

"No, Ruston, not yet. There's something I have to tell you." I wondered how to put it. It wasn't easy to tell a kid that the father he loved had just been butchered by a blood-crazy killer.

"What is it? You look awfully worried, Mike, is something wrong?"

"Something is very wrong, kid, are you pretty tough?"

Another shy smile. "I'm not tough, not really. I wish I were, like people in stories."

I decided to give it to him the hard way and get it over with. "Your dad's dead, son."

He didn't grasp the meaning of it at first. He looked at me, puzzled, as though he had misinterpreted what I had said.

"Dead?"

I nodded. Realization came like a flood. The tears started in the corners. One rolled down his cheek. "No . . . he can't be dead. He can't be!" I put my arms around him for a second time. He hung on to me and sobbed.

"Oh . . . Dad. What happened to him, Mike? What happened?"

Softly, I stroked his head, trying to remember what my own father did with me when I hurt myself. I couldn't give him the details. "He's . . . just dead, Ruston."

"Something happened, I know." He tried to fight the tears, but it was no use. He drew away and rubbed his eyes. "What happened, Mike, please tell me?"

I handed him my handkerchief. He'd find out later, and it was better he heard it from me than one of the ghouls. "Someone killed him. Here, blow your nose." He blew, never taking his eyes from mine. I've seen puppies look at me that way when they've been kicked and didn't understand why.

"Killed? No . . . nobody would kill Dad . . . not my dad."

I didn't say a word after that. I let it sink in and watched his face contort with the pain of the thought until I began to hurt in the chest myself.

For maybe ten minutes we sat like that, quietly, before the kid dried his eyes. He seemed older now. A thing like that will age anyone. His hand went to my arm. I patted his shoulder.

"Mike?"

"Yes, Ruston?"

"Do you think you can find the one who did it?"

"I'm going to try, kid."

His lips tightened fiercely. "I want you to. I wish I were big enough to. I'd shoot him, that's what I'd do!" He broke into tears again after that outburst. "Oh . . . Mike."

"You lay there, kid. Get a little rest, then when you feel better get dressed and come downstairs and we'll have a little talk. Think of something, only don't think of . . . that. It takes time to get over these things, but you will. Right now it hurts worse than anything in the world, but time will fix it up. You're tough, Ruston. After last night I'd say that you were the toughest kid that ever lived. Be tough now and don't cry anymore. Okay?"

"I'll try, Mike, honest, I'll try."

He rolled over in the bed and buried his face in the pillow. I unlocked his door to the hall and went out. I had to stick around now whether I wanted to or not. I promised the kid. And it was a promise I meant to keep.

Once before I made a promise, and I kept it. It killed my soul, but I kept it. I thought of all the blood that had run in the war, all that I had seen and had dripped on me, but none was redder or more repulsive than that blood I had seen when I kept my last promise.

Chapter Five

Their faces were those that stare at you from the walls of a museum; severe, hostile, expectant. They stood in various attitudes waiting to see what apology I had to offer for dragging them from their beds at this early hour.

Arthur Graham awkwardly sipped a glass of orange juice between swollen lips. His brother puffed nervously at a cigarette. The Ghents sat as one family in the far corner, Martha trying to be aloof as was Junior. Rhoda and her father felt conspicuous in their hurried dressing and fidgeted on the edge of their chairs.

Alice Nichols was . . . Alice. When I came into the living room she threw an eyeful of passion at me and said under her breath, "Lo, lover." It was too early for that stuff. I let the bags under my eyes tell her so. Roxy, sporting a worried frown, stopped me to say that there would be coffee ready in a few minutes. Good. They were going to need it.

I threw the ball from the scrimmage line before the opposition could break through with any bright remarks. "Rudolph York is dead. Somebody parted his hair with a cleaver up in Miss Grange's apartment."

I waited.

Martha gasped. Her husband's eyes nearly popped out. Junior and Rhoda looked at each other. Arthur choked on his orange juice and William dropped his cigarette. Behind me Alice said, "Tsk, tsk."

The silence was like an explosion, but before the echo died away Martha Ghent recovered enough to say coldly, "And where was Miss Grange?"

I shrugged. "Your guess is as good as mine." I laid it on the table then. "It's quite possible that she had nothing to do with it. Could be that someone here did the slaughtering. Before long the police are going to pay us a little visit. It's kind of late to start fixing up an alibi, but if you haven't any, you'd better think of one, fast."

While they swallowed that I turned on my heel and went out to the kitchen. Roxy had the coffee on a tray and I lifted a cup and carried it into Billy's room. He woke up as soon as I turned the knob.

"Hi, Mike." He looked at the clock. "What're you doing up?"

"I haven't been to bed yet. York's dead."

"What!"

"Last night. Got it with a cleaver."

"Good night! What happens now?"

"The usual routine for a while, I guess. Listen, were you in the sack all this time?"

"Hell, yes. Wait a minute, Mike, you . . ."

"Can you prove it? I mean did anyone see you there?"

"No. I've been alone. You don't think . . ."

"Quit worrying, Billy. Dilwick will be on this case and he's liable to have it in for you. That skunk will get back at you if he can't at me. He's got what little law there is in this town on his side now. What I want to do is establish some way you can prove you were here. Think of any?"

He put his finger to his mouth. "Yeah, I might at that. Twice last night I thought I heard a car go out."

"That'd be York then me."

"Right after the first car, someone came downstairs. I heard 'em inside, then there was some funny sound like somebody coughing real softly, then it died out. I couldn't figure out what it was."

"That might do it if we can find out who came down. Just forget all about it until you're asked, understand?"

"Sure, Mike. Geez, why did this have to happen? I'll be out on my ear now." His head dropped into his hands. "What'll I do?"

"We'll think of something. If you feel okay you'd better get dressed. York's car is still downtown, and when the cops get done with it you'll have to drive it back."

I handed him the coffee and he drank it gratefully. When he finished I took it away and went into the kitchen. Harvey was there drying his eyes on a handkerchief. He saw me and sniffed, "It's terrible, sir. Miss Malcom just told me. Who could have done such a thing?"

"I don't know, Harvey. Whoever it was will pay for it.

Look, I'm going to climb into bed. When the police come, get me up, will you?"

"Of course, sir. Will you eat first?"

"No thanks, later."

I skirted the living room and pushed myself up the stairs. The old legs were tired out. The bedclothes were where I had thrown them, in a heap at the foot of the bed. I didn't even bother to take off my shoes. When I put my head down I didn't care if the house burned to the ground as long as nobody awakened me.

The police came and went. Their voices came to me through the veil of sleep, only partially coherent. Voices of insistence, voices of protest and indignation. A woman's voice raised in anger and a meeker man's voice supporting it. Nobody seemed to care whether I was there or not, so I let the veil swirl into a gray shroud that shut off all sounds and thoughts.

It was the music that woke me. A terrible storm of music that reverberated through the house like a hurricane, shrieking in a wonderful agony. There had never been music like that before. I listened to the composition, wondering. For a space of seconds it was a song of rage, then it dwindled to a dirge of sorrow. No bar or theme was repeated.

I slipped out of the bed and opened the door, letting the full force of it hit me. It was impossible to conceive that a piano could tell such a story as this one was telling.

He sat there at the keyboard, a pitiful little figure clad in a Prussian blue bathrobe. His head was thrown back, the eyes shut tightly as if in pain, his fingers beating notes of anguish from the keys.

He was torturing himself with it. I sat beside him. "Ruston, don't."

Abruptly, he ceased in the middle of the concert and let his head fall to his chest. The critics were right when they acclaimed him a genius. If only they could have heard his latest recital.

"You have to take it easy, kid. Remember what I told you."

"I know, Mike, I'll try to be better. I just keep thinking of Dad all the time."

"He meant a lot to you, didn't he?"

"Everything. He taught me so many things, music, art . . . things that it takes people so long to get to know. He was wonderful, the best dad ever."

Without speaking I walked him over to the big chair beside the fireplace and sat down on the arm of the chair beside him. "Ruston," I started, "your father isn't here anymore, but he wouldn't want you to grieve about it. I think he'd rather you went on with all those things he was teaching you, and be what he wanted you to be."

"I will be, Mike," he said. His voice lacked color, but it rang earnestly. "Dad wanted me to excel in everything. He often told me that a man never lived long enough to accomplish nearly anything he was capable of because it took too long to learn the fundamentals. That's why he wanted me to know all these things while I was young. Then when I was a doctor or a scientist maybe I would be ahead of myself, sort of."

He was better as long as he could talk. Let him get it out of his system, I thought. It's the only way. "You've done fine, kid. I bet he was proud of you."

"Oh, he was. I only wish he could have been able to make his report."

"What report?"

"To the College of Scientists. They meet every five years to turn in reports, then one is selected as being the best one and the winner is elected President of the College for a term. He wanted that awfully badly. His report was going to be on me."

"I see," I said. "Maybe Miss Grange will do it for him."

I shouldn't have said that. He looked up at me woefully. "I don't think she will, not after the police find her."

It hit me right between the eyes. "Who's been telling you things, kid?"

"The policemen were here this morning. The big one made us all tell where we were last night and everything. Then he told us about Miss Grange."

"What about her?"

"They found her car down by the creek. They think she drowned herself."

I could have tossed a brick through a window right then. "Harvey!" I yelled. "Hey, Harvey."

The butler came in on the double. "I thought I asked you to wake me up when the police got here. What the hell happened?"

"Yes, sir. I meant to, but Officer Dilwick suggested that I let you sleep. I'm sorry, sir, it was more an order than a request."

So that was how things stood. I'd get even with that fat slob. "Where is everybody?"

"After the police took their statements he directed the family to return to their own homes. Miss Malcom and Parks are bringing Mr. York's car home. Sergeant Price wished me to tell you that he will be at the headquarters on the highway this evening and he would like to see you."

"I'm glad someone would like to see me," I remarked. I turned to Ruston. "I'm going to leave, son. How about you going to your room until Roxy . . . I mean Miss Malcom gets here? Okay?"

"All right, Mike. Why did you call her Roxy?"

"I have pet names for everybody."

"Do you have one for me?" he asked, little lights dancing in his eyes.

"You bet."

"What?"

"Sir Lancelot. He was the bravest of the brave."

As I walked out of the room I heard him repeat it softly. "Sir Lancelot, the bravest of the brave."

I reached the low fieldstone building set back from the road at a little after eight. The sky was threatening again, the air chilly and humid. Little beads of sweat were running down the windshield on the side. A sign across the drive read, STATE POLICE HEADQUARTERS, and I parked beside it.

Sergeant Price was waiting for me. He nodded when I came in and lay down the sheaf of papers he was examining. I threw my hat on an empty desk and helped myself to a chair. "Harvey gave me your message," I said. "What's the story?"

He leaned back in the swivel seat and tapped the desk with a pen. "We found Grange's car."

"So I heard. Find her yet?"

"No. The door was open and her body may have washed out. If it did we won't find it so easily. The tide was running out and would have taken the body with it. The river runs directly into the bay, you know."

"That's all supposition. She may not have been in the car."

He put the pencil between his teeth. "Every indication points to the fact that she was. There are clear tire marks showing where the car was deliberately wrenched off the road before the guardrails to the bridge. The car was going fast, besides. It landed thirty feet out in the water."

"That's not what you wanted to see me about?" I put in.

"You're on the ball, Mr. Hammer."

"Mike. I hate titles."

"Okay, Mike. What I want is this kidnapping deal."

"Figuring a connection?"

"There may be one if Grange was murdered."

I grinned. "You're on the ball yourself." Once again I went over the whole story, starting with Billy's call when he was arrested. He listened intently without saying a word until I was finished.

"What do you think?" he asked.

"Somebody's going to a lot of trouble."

"Do you smell a correlation between the two?"

I squinted at him. "I don't know . . . yet. That kidnapping came at the wrong time. A kidnapper wants money. This one never got away with his victim. Generally speaking, it isn't likely that a second try would be made on the same person, but York wanted the whole affair hushed up ostensibly for fear of the publicity it would bring. That would leave the kid open again. It is possible that the kidnapper, enraged at having his deal busted open, would hang around waiting to get even with York and saw his chance when he took off at that hour of the morning to see Grange."

Price shook out a cig from his pack and offered me one. "If that was the case, money would not have been the primary motive. A kidnapper who has muffed his snatch wants to get far away fast."

I lit up and blew a cloud of smoke at the ceiling. "Sounds screwed up, doesn't it?" He agreed. "Did you find out that York didn't have long to live anyway?"

He seemed startled at the change of subject. "No. Why?"

"Let's do it this way," I said. "York was on the list. He had only a few years at best to live. At the bottom of every crime there's a motive no matter how remote, and nine times out of ten that motive is cold, hard cash. He's got a bunch of relations that have been hanging around waiting for him to kick the bucket for a long time. One of them might have known that his condition was so bad that any excitement might knock him off. That one arranges a kidnapping, then when it fails takes direct action by knocking off York, making it look like Grange did it, then kills Grange to further the case by making it appear that she was a suicide in a fit of remorse."

Price smiled gently. "Are you testing me? I could shoot holes in that with a popgun. Arranging for a kidnapping means that you invite blackmail and lose everything you tried to get. York comes into it somewhere along the line because he was searching for something in that apartment. Try me again."

I laughed. "No good. You got all the answers."

He shoved the papers across the desk to me. "There are the statements of everybody in the house. They seem to support each other pretty well. Nobody left the house according to them so nobody had a chance to knock off York. That puts it outside the house again."

I looked them over. Not much there. Each sheet was an individual statement and it barely covered a quarter of the page. Besides a brief personal history was the report that once in bed, each person had remained there until I called them into the living room that morning.

I handed them back. "Somebody's lying. Is this all you got?"

"We didn't press for information although Dilwick wanted to. Who lied?"

"Somebody. Billy Parks told me he heard someone come downstairs during the night."

"Could it have been you?"

"No, it was before I followed York."

"He made no mention of it to me."

"Probably because he's afraid somebody will refute it if he does just to blacken him. I half promised him I'd check on it first."

"I see. Did York take you into his confidence at any time?"

"Nope. I didn't know him that long. After the snatch he hired me to stick around until he was certain his son was safe."

Price threw the pencil on the desk. "We're climbing a tree," he said tersely. "York was killed for a reason. Myra Grange was killed for the same reason. I think that for the time being we'll concentrate our efforts on locating Grange's body. When we're sure of her death we can have something definite to work on. Meanwhile I'm taking it for granted that she is dead."

I stood up to leave. "I'm not taking anything for granted, Sergeant. If she's dead she's out of it; if not the finger is still on her. I'm going to play around a little bit and see what happens. What's Dilwick doing?"

"Like you. He won't believe she's dead until he sees her either."

"Don't underestimate that hulk," I told him. "He's had a lot of police work and he's shrewd. Too shrewd, in fact, that's why he was booted off the New York force. He'll be looking out for himself when the time comes. If anything develops I'll let you know."

"Do that. See you later."

That ended the visit. I went out to the car and sat behind the wheel a while, thinking. Kidnapping, murder, a disappearance. A house full of black sheep. One nice kid, an ex-stripper for a nurse and a chauffeur with a record. The butler, maybe the butler did it. Someday a butler would do it for a change. A distraught father who stuck his hand in a hole in the fireplace and found something gone. He sets out to kill and gets killed instead. The one he wanted to kill is gone, perhaps dead too. Mallory. That was the name that started the ball of murder rolling. But Mallory figured in the kidnapping.

Okay, first things first. The kidnapping was first and I'd take it that way. It was a hell of a mess. The only thing that could make it any worse was to have Grange show up with an airtight alibi. I hated to hold out on Price about Mallory, but if he had it Dilwick would have to get it too, and that would put the kibosh on me. Like hell. I promised the kid.

I shoved the car in gear and spun out on the highway. Initial clue, the cops call it, the hand that puts the hound on the trail, that's what I had to have. York thought it was in Grange's apartment. Find what he was searching for and you had the answer. Swell, let's find it.

This time I parked around the block. The rain had started again, a light mist that you breathed into your lungs and dampened matches in your pocket. From the back of the car I pulled a slicker and climbed into it, turning the collar up high. I walked back to Main Street, crossed over to the side of the street opposite the apartment and joined the few late workers in their dash toward home.

I saw what I was looking for, a black, unmarked sedan occupied by a pair of cigar-smoking gentlemen who were trying their best to remain unnoticed. They did a lousy job. I circled the block until I was behind the apartment. A row of modest one-family houses faced me, their windows lighted with gaiety and cheer. Each house was flanked by a driveway.

Without waiting I picked the right one and turned down the cinder drive, staying to the side in the shadow of a hedgerow where the grass partially muffled my feet. Somehow I slipped between the garage and the hedges to the back fence without making too much of a racket. For ten minutes I stood that way, motionless. It wasn't a new experience for me. I remembered other pits of blackness where little brown men waited and threw jeers into our faces to draw us out. That was a real test of patience. This guy was easier. When another ten minutes passed the match lit his face briefly, then subsided into the ill-concealed glow of a cigarette tip.

Dilwick wasn't taking any chances on Myra Grange slipping back to her apartment. Or anyone else for that matter.

Once I had him spotted I kept my eyes a few feet to the side of him so I wouldn't lose him. Look directly at an object in the dark and you draw a blank spot. I went over the fence easily enough, then flanked the lookout by staying in the shadows again. By the time I reached the apartment building I had him silhouetted against the lights of another house. The janitor had very conveniently left a row of ash barrels stacked by the cellar entrance. I got up that close, at least. Six feet away on the other side of the gaping cavern of the entrance the law stood on flat feet, breathing heavily, cursing the rain under his breath.

My fingers snaked over the lip of a barrel, came away with a piece of ash the size of a marble. I balanced it on my thumb, then flipped it. I heard nothing, but he heard it and turned his head, that was all. I tried again with the same results. The next time I used a bigger piece. I got better results, too. He dropped the butt, ground it under his heel and walked away from the spot.

As soon as he moved I ducked around the barrels and down the stairs, then waited again, flattened against the wall. Finding nothing, the cop resumed his post. I went on tiptoes down the corridor, my hand out in front like a sleepwalker.

This part was going to take clever thinking. If they had both exits covered it was a sure bet that the apartment door was covered, too. I came to a bend in the tunnel and found myself in the furnace room. Overhead a dim bulb struggled against dust and cobwebs to send out a feeble glow. On the other side of the room a flight of metal steps led to the floor above. Sweet, but not practical. If I could make the roof I might be able to come down the fire escape, but that meant a racket or being seen by the occupants.

Right then I was grateful to the inventor of the dumbwaiter. The empty box yawned at me with a sleepy invitation. The smell was bad, but it was worth it. I climbed aboard and gave the rope a tentative pull to see if the pulleys squealed. They were well oiled. *Danke schön,* janitor. You get an *A*.

When I passed the first floor I was beginning to doubt whether I could make it all the way. Crouching there like that I had no leverage to bear on the ropes. It was all wrist motion. I took a hitch in the rope around the catch on the sliding door and rested a second, then began hauling away again. Somewhere above me voices passed back and forth. Someone yelled, "Put it on the dumbwaiter."

I held my breath. Let them catch me here and I was sunk. Dilwick would like nothing better than to get me on attempted burglary and work me over with a few of his boys.

A moment went by, two, then, "Later, honey, it's only half-full."

Thanks, pal. Remind me to scratch your back. I got another grip on the rope and pulled away. By the time I reached Myra's door I was exhausted. Fortunately, one of the cops had forgotten to lock it after taking a peek down the well, not that it mattered. I didn't care whether anyone was inside or not. I shoved the two-bit door open and tumbled to the floor. I was lucky. The house was quiet as a tomb. If I ever see that trick pulled in a movie and the hero steps out looking fresh as a daisy I'll throw rocks at the screen. I lay there until I got my wind back.

The flash I used had the lens taped, so the only light it shed was a round disk the size of a quarter. I poked around the kitchen a bit taking it all in. Nobody had cleaned up since the murder as far as I could see. I went into the living room, avoiding the litter on the floor. The place was even worse than it was before. The police had finished what York had started, pulling drawers open further, tearing the pictures from the walls and scuffling up the rug.

But they hadn't found it. If they had I wouldn't've had to use the dumbwaiter to get in. Dilwick was better than shrewd. He was waiting for Grange to come back and find it for him.

Which meant that he was pretty certain Grange was alive. Dilwick knew something that Price and I didn't know, in that case.

In the first half hour I went through every piece of junk that had been dragged out without coming across anything worthwhile. I kicked at the pile and tried the drawers in the desk again. My luck stunk; Grange didn't go in for false bottoms or double walls. I thought of every place a dame hides things, but the cops had thought of them too. Every corner had been poked into, every closet emptied out. Women think of cute places like the hollows of bedposts and the inside of lamps, but the bedposts turned out to be solid and the lamps of modern transparent glass.

Hell, she had to have important things around. College degrees, insurance policies and that sort of stuff. I finally realized what was wrong. My psychology. Or hers. She only resembled a woman. She looked like one and dressed like one, physically, she was one, but Myra Grange had one of those twisted complexes. If she thought it was like a man. That was better. Being partially a woman she would want to secrete things; being part man she would hide them in a place not easily accessible, where it would take force, and not deduction to locate the cache.

I started grinning then. I pulled the cabinets away from the walls and tried the sills of the doors. When I found a hollow behind the radiator I felt better. It was dust-filled and hadn't been used for some time, mainly because a hand reaching in there could be burned if the heat was on, but I knew I was on the right track.

It took time, but I found it when I was on my hands and knees, shooting light along the baseboards under the bed. It wasn't even a good job of concealment. I saw where a claw hammer had probably knocked a hole in the plaster behind it.

A package of envelopes held together by a large rubber band was the treasure. It was four-inches thick, at least, with corners of stock certificates showing in the middle. A nice little pile.

I didn't waste time going through them then. I stuck the package inside my coat and buttoned the slicker over it. I had one end of the baseboard in place when I thought what a fine joke it would be to pull on slobbermouth to leave a calling card. With a wrench I pulled it loose, laid it on the floor where it couldn't be missed and got out to the kitchen. Let my fat friend figure that one out. He'd have the jokers at the doors shaking in their shoes by the time he was done with them.

The trip down was better. All I had to do was hang on and let the rope slide through my hands. Between the first floor and the basement I tightened up on the hemp and cut down the descent. It was a good landing, just a slight jar and I walked away from there. Getting out was easier than coming in. I poked my head out the cellar window on the side where the walk led around to the back and the concrete stared me in the face, gave a short whistle and called, "Hey, Mac."

It was enough. Heavy feet came pounding around the side and I made a dash up the corridor, out the door and dived into the bushes before the puzzled cop got back to his post scratching his head in bewilderment. The fence, the driveway, and I was in my car pulling up the street behind a trailer truck.

The package was burning a hole in my pocket. I turned down a side street where the neon of an open diner provided a stopping-off place, parked and went in and occupied a corner booth. When a skinny waiter in an oversized apron took my order I extracted the bundle. I rifled through the deck, ignoring the bonds and policies. I found what I was after.

It was York's will, made out two years ago, leaving every cent of his dough to Grange. If that female was still alive this put her on the spot for sure. Here was motive, pure, raw motive. A several-million-dollar motive, but it might as well be a can tied to her tail. She was a lucky one indeed if she lived to enjoy it.

Sloppy Joe came back with my hamburgers and coffee.

I shelved the package while he dished out the slop, then forced it down my gullet, with the coffee as a lubricant. I was nearly through when I noticed my hands. They were dusty as hell. I noticed something else, too. The rubber band that had been around the package lay beside my coffee cup, stiff and rotted, and in two pieces.

Then I didn't get it after all, at least not what York was searching for. This package hadn't been opened for a hell of a long time, and it was a good bet that whatever had been in the fireplace had been there until the other night. The will had been placed in the package years ago.

Damn. Say it again, Mike, you outsmarted yourself that time. Damn.

Chapter Six

I set my watch by the clock on the corner while I waited for the light to change. Nine-fifteen, and all was far from well. Just what the hell was it that threw York into a spasm? I knew damn well now that whatever it was, either Grange had it with her or she never had it at all. I was right back where I started from. Which left two things to be done. Find Mallory, or see who came downstairs the night of the murder and why that movement was denied in the statements. All right, let it be Mallory. Maybe Roxy could supply some answers. I pulled the will from the package and slipped it inside my jacket, then tossed the rest of the things in the back of the glove compartment.

Henry had the gates open as soon as I turned off the road. When he shut them behind me I called him over. "Anyone been here while I was gone?"

"Yes, sir. The undertaker came, but that was all."

I thanked him and drove up the drive. Harvey nodded solemnly when he opened the door and took my hat. "Have there been any developments, sir?"

"Not a thing. Where's Miss Malcom?"

"Upstairs, I believe. She took Master Ruston to his room a little while ago. Shall I call her for you?"

"Never mind, I'll go up myself."

I rapped lightly and opened the door at the same time. Roxy took a quick breath, grabbed the negligee off the bed and held it in front of her. That split second of visioning nudity that was classic beauty made the blood pound in my ears. I shut my eyes against it. "Easy, Roxy," I said, "I can't see so don't scream and don't throw things. I didn't mean it."

She laughed lightly. "Oh, for heaven's sake, open them up. You've seen me like this before." I looked just as she tied the wrapper around her. That kind of stuff could drive a guy bats.

"Don't tempt me. I thought you'd changed?"

"Mike . . . don't say it that way. Maybe I have gone modest, but I like it better. In your rough way you respected it too, but I can't very well heave things at you for seeing again what you saw so many times before."

"The kid asleep?"

"I think so." The door was open a few inches, the other room dark. I closed it softly, then went back and sat on the edge of the bed. Roxy dragged the chair from in front of her vanity and set it down before me.

"Do I get sworn in first?" she asked with a fake pout.

"This is serious."

"Shoot."

"I'm going to mention a name to you. Don't answer me right away. Let it sink in, think about it, think of any time since you've been here that you might have heard it, no matter when. Roll it around on your tongue a few times until it becomes familiar, then if you recognize it tell me where or when you heard it and who said it . . . if you can."

"I see. Who is it?"

I handed her a cigarette and plucked one myself. "Mallory," I said as I lit it for her. I hooked my hands around my knee and waited. Roxy blew smoke at the floor. She looked up at me a couple of times, her eyes vacant with thought, mouthing the name to herself. I watched her chew on her lip and suck in a lungful of smoke.

Finally she rubbed her hand across her forehead and grimaced. "I can't remember ever having heard it," she told me. "Is it very important?"

"I think it might be. I don't know."

"I'm sorry, Mike." She leaned forward and patted my knee.

"Hell, don't take it to heart. He's just a name to me. Do you think any of the characters might know anything?"

"That I couldn't say. York was a quiet one, you know."

"I didn't know. Did he seem to favor any of them?"

She stood up and stretched on her toes. Under the sheer fabric little muscles played in her body. "As far as I could see, he had an evident distaste for the lot of them. When I first came here he apparently liked his niece, Rhoda. He remembered her with gifts upon the slightest provocation. Expensive ones, too. I know, I bought them for him."

I snubbed my butt. "Uh-huh. Did he turn to someone else?"

"Why, yes." She looked at me in faint surprise. "The other niece, Alice Nichols."

"I would have looked at her first to begin with."

"Yes, you would," she grinned. "Shall I go on?"

"Please."

"For quite a while she got all the attention which threw the Ghents into an uproar. I imagine they saw Rhoda being his heir and didn't like the switch. Mr. York's partiality to Alice continued for several months then fell off somewhat. He paid little attention to her after that, but never forgot her on birthdays or holidays. His gifts were as great as ever. And that," she concluded, "is the only unusual situation that ever existed as far as I know."

"Alice and York, huh? How far did the relationship go?"

"Not that far. His feelings were paternal, I think."

"Are you sure?"

"Pretty sure. Mr. York was long past his prime. If sex meant anything to him it was no more than a biological difference between the species."

"It might mean something to Alice."

"Of that I'm sure. She likes anything with muscles, but with Mr. York she didn't need it. She did all right without it. I noticed that she cast a hook in your direction."

"She didn't use the right bait," I stated briefly. "She showed up in my room with nothing on but a prayer and wanted to play. I like to be teased a little. Besides, I was tired. Did York know she acted that way?"

Roxy plugged in a tiny radio set and fiddled with the dial. "If he did he didn't care."

"Kitten, did York ever mention a will?"

An old Benny Goodman tune came on. She brought it in clearer and turned around with a dance step. "Yes, he had one. He kept the family on the verge of a nervous breakdown every time he alluded to it, but he never came right out and said where his money would go."

She began to spin with the music. "Hold still a second will you. Didn't he hand out any hints at all?"

The hem of her negligee brushed past my face, higher than any hem had a right to be. "None at all, except that it would go where it was most deserving."

Her legs flashed in the light. My heart began beating faster again. They were lovely legs, long, firm. "Did Grange ever hear that statement?"

She stopped, poised dramatically and threw her belt at me.

"Yes." She began to dance again. The music was a rhumba now and her body swayed to it, jerking rhythmically. "Once during a heated discussion Mr. York told them all that Miss Grange was the only one he could trust and she would be the one to handle his estate."

There was no answer to that. How the devil could she handle it if she got it all? I never got a chance to think about it. The robe came off and she used it like a fan, almost disclosing everything, showing nothing. Her skin was fair, cream-colored, her body graceful. She circled in front of me, letting her hair fall to her shoulders. At the height of that furious dance I stood up.

Roxy flew into my arms. "Kiss me . . . you thing."

I didn't need any urging.

Her mouth melted into mine like butter. I felt her nails digging into my arms. Roughly, I pushed her away, held her there at arm's length. "What was that for?"

She gave me a delightfully evil grin. "That is because I could love you if I wanted to, Mike. I did once, you know."

"I know. What made you stop?"

"You're Broadway, Mike. You're the bright lights and big money . . . sometimes. You're bullets when there should be kisses. That's why I stopped. I wanted someone with a normal life expectancy."

"Then why this?"

"I missed you. Funny as it sounds, someplace inside me I have a spot that's always reserved for you. I didn't want you to ever know it, but there it is."

I kissed her again, longer and closer this time. Her body was talking to me, screaming to me. There would have been more if Ruston hadn't called out.

Roxy slipped into the robe again, the cold static making it snap. "Let me go," I said. She nodded.

I opened the door and hit the light switch. "Hello, Sir Lancelot." The kid had been crying in his sleep, but he smiled at me.

"Hello, Mike. When did you come?"

"A little while ago. Want something?"

"Can I have some water, please? My throat's awfully dry."

A pitcher half-full of ice was on the desk. I poured it into a glass, and handed it to him and he drank deeply. "Have enough?"

He gave the glass back to me. "Yes, thank you."

I gave his chin a little twist. "Then back to bed with you. Get a good sleep."

Ruston squirmed back under the covers. "I will. Good night, Mike."

"'Night, pal." I closed the door behind me. Roxy had changed into a deep maroon quilted job and sat in the chair smoking a cigarette. The moment had passed. I could see that she was sorry, too. She handed me my deck of butts and I pocketed them, then waved a good-night. Neither of us felt like saying anything.

Evidently Harvey had retired for the night. The staircase was lit only by tiny night-lights shaped to resemble candle flames, while the foyer below was a dim challenge to the eyesight. I picked my way through the rooms and found Billy's without upsetting anything. He was in bed, but awake. "It's Mike, Billy," I said.

He snapped on the bed lamp. "Come on in."

I shut the door and slumped in a chair next to him. "More questions. I know it's late, but I hope you don't mind."

"Not at all, Mike. What's new?"

"Oh, you know how these things are. Haven't found Miss Grange yet and things are settling around her. Dilwick's got his men covering her place like a blanket."

"Yeah? What for? Ain't she supposed to be drowned?"

"Somebody wants it to look that way, I think. Listen, Billy, you told me before that you heard someone come downstairs between York and me the night of the murder. It wasn't important before except to establish an alibi for you if it was needed, but now what you heard may have a bearing on the case. Go over it again, will you? Do it in as much detail as you can."

"Let's see. I didn't really hear York leave, I just remember a car crunching the gravel. It woke me up. I had a headache and a bad taste in my mouth from something York gave me. Pills, I think."

"It was supposed to keep you asleep. He gave you a sedative."

"Whatever it was I puked up in bed, that's why it didn't do me any good. Anyway, I lay here half-awake when I heard somebody come down the last two stairs. They squeak, they do. This room is set funny, see. Any noise outside the room travels right in here. They got a name for it."

"Acoustics."

"Yeah, that's it. That's why nobody ever used this room but me. They couldn't stand the noise all the time. Not only loud noises, any kind of noises. This was like whoever it was didn't want to make a sound, but it didn't do any good because I heard it. Only I thought it was one of the family trying to be quiet so they wouldn't wake anyone up and I didn't pay any attention to it. About two or three minutes after that comes this noise like someone coughing with their head under a coat and it died out real slow and that's all. I was just getting back to sleep when there was another car tearing out the drive. That was you, I guess."

"That all?"

"Yeah, that's all, Mike. I went back to sleep after that."

This was the ace. It had its face down so I couldn't tell whether it was red or black, but it was the ace. The bells were going off in my head again, those little tinkles that promised to become the pealing of chimes. The cart was before the horse, but if I could find the right buckle to unloosen I could put them right back.

"Billy, say nothing to nobody about this, understand? If the local police question you, say nothing. If Sergeant Price wants to know things, have him see me. If you value your head, keep your mouth shut and your door locked."

His eyes popped wide open. "Geez, Mike, is it that important?"

I nodded. "I have a funny feeling, Billy, that the noises you heard were made by the murderer."

"Good Golly!" It left him breathless. Then, "You . . . you think the killer . . ." he swallowed, ". . . might make a try for me?"

"No, Billy, not the killer. You aren't that important to him. Someone else might, though. I think we have a lot more on our hands than just plain murder."

"What?" It was a hoarse whisper.

"Kidnapping, for one thing. That comes in somewhere. You sit tight until you hear from me." Before I left I turned with my hand on the knob and looked into his scared face again. "Who's Mallory, Billy?"

"Mallory who?"

"Just Mallory."

"Gosh, I don't know."

"Okay, kid, thanks."

Mallory. He might as well be Smith or Jones. So far he was just a word. I navigated the gloom again half consciously, thinking of him. Mallory of the kidnapping; Mallory whose very name turned York white and added a link to the chain of crime. Somewhere Mallory was sitting on his fanny getting a large charge out of the whole filthy mess. York knew who he was, but York was dead. Could that be the reason for his murder? Likely. York, by indirect implication and his peculiar action intimated that Myra Grange knew of him too, but she was dead or missing. Was that Mallory's doing? Likely. Hell, I couldn't put my finger on anything more definite than a vague possibility. Something had to blow up, somebody would have to try to take the corners out of one of the angles. I gathered all the facts together, but they didn't make sense. A name spoken, the speaker unseen; someone who came downstairs at night, unseen too, and denying it; a search for a stolen something-or-other, whose theft was laid at the feet of the vanished woman. I muttered a string of curses under my breath and kicked aimlessly at empty air. Where was there to start? Dilwick would have his feelers out for Grange and so would Price. With that many men they could get around much too fast for me. Besides, I had the feeling that she was only part of it all, not the key figure that would unlock the mystery, but more like one whose testimony would cut down a lot of time and work. I still couldn't see her putting the cleaver into York then doing the Dutch afterward. If she was associated with him professionally she would have to be brilliant, and great minds either turn at murder or attempt to conceive of a flawless plot. York's death was brutal. It was something you might find committed in a dark alley in a slum section for a few paltry dollars, or in a hotel room when a husband returns to find his woman in the arms of her lover. A passion kill, a revenge kill, a crude murder for small money, yes, but did any of these motives fit here? For whom did York hold passion . . . or vice versa? Roxy hit it when she said he was too old. Small money? None was gone from his wallet apparently. That kind of kill would take place outside on a lonely road or on a deserted street anyway. Revenge . . . revenge. Grange said he had no enemies. That was now. Could anything have happened in the past? You could almost rule that out too, on the basis of precedent. Revenge murders usually happen soon after the event that caused the desire for revenge. If the would-be murderer has time to think he realizes the penalty for murder and it doesn't happen. Unless, of course, the victim, realizing what might happen, keeps on the move. That accentuates the importance of the event to the killer and spurs him on. Negative. York was a public figure for years. He had lived in the same house almost twenty years. Big money, a motive for anything. Was that it? Grange came into that. Why did she have the will? Those things are kept in a safe deposit box or lawyer's files. The chief beneficiary rarely ever got to see the document much less have it hidden among her personal effects for so long a time. Damn, Grange had told me she had a large income aside from what York gave her. She didn't care what he did with his money. What a very pretty attitude to take, especially when you know where it's going. She could afford to be snotty with me. I remembered her face when she said it, aloof, the hell-with-it attitude. Why the act if it·wasn't important then? What was she trying to put across?

Myra Grange. I didn't want it to, but it came back to her every time. Missing the night of the kidnapping; seen on the road, but she said no. Why? I started to grin a little. An unmarried person goes out at night for what reason? Natch . . . a date. Grange had a date, and her kind of dates had to be kept behind closed doors, that's why she was rarely seen about. York wouldn't want it to get around either for fear of criticism, that's why he was nice about it. Grange would deny it for a lot of reasons. It would hurt her professionally, or worse, she might lose a perfectly good girl friend. It was all supposition, but I bet I was close.

The night air hit me in the face. I hadn't realized I was standing outside the door until a chilly mist ran up the steps and hugged me. I stuck my hands in my pockets and walked down the drive. Behind me the house watched with staring eyes. I wished it could talk. The gravel path encircled the gloomy old place with gray arms and I followed it aimlessly, trying to straighten out my thoughts. When I came to the fork I stood motionless a moment then followed the turn off to the right.

Fifty yards later the colorless bulk of the laboratory grew out of the darkness like a crypt. It was a drab cinder-block building, the only incongruous thing on the estate. No windows broke the contours of the walls on either of the two sides visible, no place where prying eyes might observe what occurred within. At the far end a thirty-foot chimney poked a skinny finger skyward, stretching to clear the treetops. Upon closer inspection a ventilation system showed just under the eaves, screened air intakes and outlets above eye level.

I went around the building once, a hundred-by-fifty-foot structure, but the only opening was the single steel door in the front, a door built to withstand weather or siege. But it was not built to withstand curiosity. The first master key I used turned the lock. It was a laugh. The double tongue had prongs as thick as my thumb, but the tumbler arrangement was as uncomplicated as a glass of milk.

Fortunately, the light pulls had tiny phosphorescent tips that cast a greenish glow. I reached up and yanked one. Overhead a hundred-watt bulb flared into daylight brilliance. I checked the door and shut it, then looked about me. Architecturally, the building was a study in simplicity. One long corridor ran the length of it. Off each side were rooms, perhaps sixteen in all. No dirt marred the shining marble floor, no streaks on the enameled white walls. Each door was shut, the brass of the knobs gleaming, the woodwork smiling in. varnished austerity. For all its rough exterior, the inside was spotless.

The first room on the one side was an office, fitted with a desk, several filing cabinets, a big chair and a water cooler. The room opposite was its mate. So far so good. I could tell by the pipe rack which had been York's.

Next came some sort of supply room. In racks along the walls were hundreds of labeled bottles, chemicals unknown to me. I opened the bins below. Electrical fittings, tubes, meaningless coils of copper tubing lay neatly placed on shelves alongside instruments and parts of unusual design. This time the room opposite was no mate. Crouched in one corner was a generator, snuggling up to a transformer. Wrist-thick power lines came in through the door, passed through the two units and into the walls. I had seen affairs like this on portable electric chairs in some of our more rural states. I couldn't figure this one out. If the education of Ruston was York's sole work, why all the gadgets? Or was that merely a shield for something bigger?

The following room turned everything into a cockeyed mess. Here was a lounge that was sheer luxury. Overstuffed chairs, a seven-foot couch, a chair shaped like a French curve that went down your back, up under your knees and ended in a cushioned foot rest. Handy to everything were magazine racks of popular titles and some of more obscure titles. Books in foreign languages rested between costly jade bookends. A combination radio-phonograph sat in the corner, flanked by cabinets of symphonic and pop records. Opposite it at the other end of the room was a grand piano with operatic scores concealed in the seat. Cleverly contrived furniture turned into art boards and reading tables. A miniature refrigerator housed a bottle of ice water and several frosted glasses. Along the wall several Petri dishes held agar—agar with yellow bacteria cultures mottling the tops. Next to them was a double-lensed microscope of the best manufacture.

What a playpen. Here anyone could relax in comfort with his favorite hobby. Was this where Ruston spent his idle hours? There was nothing here for a boy, but his mind would appreciate it.

It was getting late. I shut the door and moved on, taking quick peeks into each room. A full-scale lab, test tubes, retorts, a room of books, nothing but books, then more electrical equipment. I crossed the corridor and stuck my head in. I had to take a second look to be sure I was right. If that wasn't the hot seat standing in the middle of the floor it was a good imitation.

I didn't get a chance to go over it. Very faintly I heard metal scratching against metal. I pulled the door shut and ran down the corridor, pulling at the light cords as I went. I wasn't the only one that was curious this night.

Just as I closed the door of Grange's office behind me the outside door swung inward. Someone was standing there in the dark waiting. I heard his breath coming hard with an attempt to control it. The door shut, and a sliver of light ran along the floor, shining through the crack onto my shoes. The intruder wasn't bothering with the overheads, he was using a flash.

A hand touched the knob. In two shakes I was palming my rod, holding it above my head ready to bring it down the second he stepped in the door. It never opened. He moved to the other side and went into York's office instead.

As slowly as I could I eased the knob around, then brought it toward my stomach. An inch, two, then there was room enough to squeeze out. I kept the dark paneling of the door at my back, stood there in the darkness, letting my breath in and out silently while I watched Junior Ghent rifle York's room.

He had the flashlight propped on the top of the desk, working in its beam. He didn't seem to be in a hurry. He pulled out every drawer of the files, scattering their contents on the floor in individual piles. When he finished with one row he moved to another until the empty cabinet gaped like a toothless old man.

For a second I thought he was leaving and faded to one side, but all he did was turn the flash to focus on the other side of the room. Again, he repeated the procedure. I watched.

At the end of twenty minutes his patience began to give out. He yanked things viciously from place and kicked at the chair, then obviously holding himself in check tried to be calm about it. In another fifteen minutes he had circled the room, making it look like a bomb had gone off in there. He hadn't found what he was after.

That came by accident.

The chair got in his way again. He pushed it so hard it skidded along the marble, hit an empty drawer and toppled over. I even noticed it before he did.

The chair had a false bottom.

Very clever. Search a room for hours and you'll push furniture all over the place, but how often will you turn up a chair and inspect it. Junior let out a surprised gasp and went down on his knees, his fingers running over the paneling. When his fingernails didn't work he took a screwdriver from his pocket and forced it into the wood. There was a sharp snap and the bottom was off.

A thick envelope was fastened to a wire clasp. He smacked his lips and wrenched it free. With his forefinger he lifted the flap and drew out a sheaf of papers. These he scanned quickly, let out a sarcastic snort, and discarded them on the floor. He dug into the envelope and brought out something else. He studied it closely, rubbing his hand over his stomach. Twice he adjusted his glasses and held them closer to the light. I saw his face flush. As though he knew he was being watched he threw a furtive glance toward the door, then shoved the stuff back in the envelope and put it in his side pocket.

I ducked back in the corridor while he went out the door, waited until it closed then snapped the light on and stepped over the junk. One quick look at the papers he had found in the envelope told me what it was. This will was made out only a few months ago, and it left three-quarters of his estate to Ruston and one-quarter to Alice. York had cut the rest out with a single buck.

Junior Ghent had something more important, though. I folded the will into my pocket and ran to the door. I didn't want my little pal to get away.

He didn't. Fifty yards up the drive he was getting the life beat out of him.

I heard his muffled screams, and other voices, too. I got the .45 in my hand and thumbed the safety off and made a dash for them.

Maybe I should have stayed on the grass, but I didn't have that much time. Two figures detached themselves from the one on the ground and broke for the trees. I let one go over their heads that echoed over the grounds like the rolling of thunder, but neither stopped. They went across a clearing and I put on speed to get free of the brush line so I could take aim. Junior stopped that. I tripped over his sprawled figure and went flat on my kisser. The pair scrambled over the wall before I was up. From the ground I tried a snap shot that went wild. On the other side of the wall a car roared into life and shot down the road.

A woman's quick, sharp scream split the air like a knife and caught me flat-footed. Everything happened at once. Briars ripped at my clothes when I went through the brush and whipped at my face. Lights went on in the house and Harvey's voice rang out for help. By the time I reached the porch Billy was standing beside the door in his pajamas.

"Upstairs, Mike, it's Miss Malcom. Somebody shot her!"

Harvey was waving frantically, pointing to her room. I

raced inside. Roxy was lying on the floor with blood making a bright red picture on the shoulder of her nightgown. Harvey stood over me, shaking with fear as I ripped the cloth away. I breathed with relief. The bullet had only passed through the flesh under her arm.

I carried her to bed and called to the butler over my shoulder. "Get some hot water and bandages. Get a doctor up here."

Harvey said, "Yes, sir," and scurried away.

Billy came in. "Can I do anything, Mike? I . . . I don't want to be alone."

"Okay, stay with her. I want to see the kid."

I opened the door to Ruston's room and turned on the light. He was sitting up, holding himself erect with his hands, his eyes were fixed on the wall in a blank stare, his mouth open. He never saw me. I shook him, he was stiff as a board, every muscle in his body as rigid as a piece of steel. He jerked convulsively once or twice, never taking his eyes from the wall. It took a lot of force to pull his arms up and straighten him out.

"Harvey, did you call that doctor?"

Billy sang out, "He's doing it now, Mike."

"Damn it, tell him to hurry. The kid's having a fit or something."

He hollered down the stairs to Harvey; I could hear the excited stuttering over the telephone, but it would be awhile before a medic would reach the house. Ruston began to tremble, his eyes rolled back in his head. Leaning over I slapped him sharply across the cheek.

"Ruston, snap out of it." I slapped him again. "Ruston."

This time his eyelids flickered, he came back to normal with a sob. His mouth twitched and he covered his face with his hands. Suddenly he sat up in bed and shouted, "Mike!"

"I'm right here, kid," I said, "take it easy." His face found mine and he reached for my hand. He was trembling from head to foot, his body bathed in cold sweat.

"Miss Malcom . . . ?"

"Is all right," I answered. "She just got a good scare, that's all." I didn't want to frighten him anymore than he was. "Did someone come in here?"

He squeezed my hand. "No . . . there was a noise, and Miss Malcom screamed. Mike, I'm not very brave at all. I'm scared."

The kid had a right to be. "It was nothing. Cover up and be still. I'll be in the next room. Want me to leave the door open?"

"Please, Mike."

I left the light on and put a rubber wedge under the door to keep it open. Billy was standing by the bed holding a handkerchief to Roxy's shoulder. I took it away and looked at it. Not much of a wound, the bullet was of small caliber and had gone in and come out clean. Billy poked me and pointed to the window. The pane had spider-webbed into a thousand cracks with a neat hole at the bottom a few inches above the sill. Tiny glass fragments winked up from the floor. The shot had come in from below, traveling upward. Behind me in the wall was the bullet hole, a small puncture head high. I dug out the slug from the plaster and rolled it over in my hand. A neat piece of lead whose shape had hardly been deformed by the wall, caliber .32. York's gun had found its way home.

I tucked it in my watch pocket. "Stay here, Billy, I'll be right back."

"Where are you going?" He didn't like me to leave.

"I got a friend downstairs."

Junior was struggling to his feet when I reached him. I helped him with a fist in his collar. This little twerp had a lot of explaining to do. He was a sorry-looking sight. Pieces of gravel were imbedded in the flesh of his face and blood matted the hair of his scalp. One lens of his specs was smashed. I watched him while he detached his lower lip from his teeth, swearing incoherently. The belting he took had left him half-dazed, and he didn't try to resist at all when I walked him toward the house.

When I sat him in a chair he shook his head, touching the cut on his temple. He kept repeating a four-letter word over and over until realization of what had happened hit him. His head came up and I thought he was going to spit at me.

"You got it!" he said accusingly on the verge of tears now.

"Got what?" I leaned forward to get every word. His eyes narrowed.

Junior said sullenly, "Nothing."

Very deliberately I took his tie in my hand and pulled it. He tried to draw back, but I held him close. "Little chum," I said, "you are in a bad spot, very bad. You've been caught breaking and entering. You stole something from York's private hideaway and Miss Malcom has been shot. If you know what's good for you, you'll talk."

"Shot . . . killed?"

There was no sense letting him know the truth. "She's not dead yet. If she dies you're liable to face a murder charge."

"No. No. I didn't do it. I admit I was in the laboratory, but I didn't shoot her. I . . . I didn't get a chance to. Those men jumped on me. I fought for my life."

"Did you? Were you really unconscious? Maybe. I went after them until I heard Miss Malcom scream. Did she scream because you shot her, then faked being knocked out all the while?"

He turned white. A little vein in his forehead throbbed, his hands tightened until his nails drew blood from the palms. "You can't pin it on me," he said. "I didn't do it, I swear."

"No? What did you take from the room back there?"

A pause, then, "Nothing."

I reached for his pockets, daring him to move. Each one I turned inside out, dumping their contents around the bottom of the chair. A wallet, theater stubs, two old letters, some keys and fifty-five cents in change. That was all.

"So somebody else wanted what you found, didn't they?" He didn't answer. "They got it, too."

"I didn't have anything," he repeated.

He was lying through his teeth. "Then why did they wait for you and beat your brains out? Answer that one." He was quiet. I took the will out and waved it at him. "It went with this. It was more important than this, though. But what would be more important to you than a will? You're stupid, Junior. You aren't in this at all, are you? If you had sense enough to burn it you might have come into big dough when the estate was split up, especially with the kid under age. But no, you didn't care whether the will was found and probated or not, because the other thing was more important. It meant more money. How, Junior, how?"

For my little speech I had a sneer thrown at me. "All right," I told him, "I'll tell you what I'm going to do. Right now you look like hell, but you're beautiful compared to what you'll look like in ten minutes. I'm going to slap the crap out of you until you talk. Yell all you want to, it won't do any good."

I pulled back my hand. Junior didn't wait, he started speaking. "Don't. It was nothing. I . . . I stole some money from my uncle once. He caught me and made me sign a statement. I didn't want it to be found or I'd never get a cent. That was it."

"Yes? What made it so important that someone else would want it?"

"I don't know. There was something else attached to the statement that I didn't look at. Maybe they wanted that."

It could have been a lie, but I wasn't sure. What he said made sense. "Did you shoot Miss Malcom?"

"That's silly." I tightened up on the tie again. "Please, you're choking me. I didn't shoot anyone. I never saw her. You can tell, the police have a test haven't they?"

"Yes, a paraffin test. Would you submit to it?"

Relief flooded his face and he nodded. I let him go. If he had pulled the trigger he wouldn't be so damn anxious. Besides, I knew for sure that he hadn't been wearing gloves.

A car pulled up outside and Harvey admitted a short, stout man carrying the bag of his profession. They disappeared upstairs. I turned to Junior. "Get out of here, but stay where you can be reached. If you take a powder I'll squeeze your skinny neck until you turn blue. Remember one thing, if Miss Malcom dies you're it, see, so you better start praying."

He shot out of the chair and half ran for the door. I heard his feet pounding down the drive. I went upstairs.

"How is she?" The doctor applied the last of the tape over the compress and turned.

"Nothing serious. Fainted from shock." He put his instruments back in his bag and took out a notebook. Roxy stirred and woke up.

"Of course you know I'll have to report this. The police must have a record of all gunshot wounds. Her name, please."

Roxy watched me from the bed. I passed it to her. She murmured, "Helen Malcom."

"Address?"

"Here." She gave her age and the doctor noted a general description then asked me if I had found the bullet.

"Yeah, it was in the wall. A .32 lead-nose job. I'll give it to the police." He snapped the book shut and stuck it in his bag. "I'd like you to see the boy, too, Doctor," I mentioned. "He was in a bad way."

Briefly, I went over what had happened the past few days. The doctor picked his bag up and followed me inside. "I know the boy," he said. "Too much excitement is bad for any youngster, particularly one as finely trained as he is."

"You've seen him before? I thought his father was his doctor."

"Not the boy. However I had occasion to speak to his father several times in town and he spoke rather proudly of his son."

"I should imagine. Here he is."

The doctor took his pulse and I winked over his shoulder. Ruston grinned back. While the doctor examined him I sat at the desk and looked at nine-by-twelve photos of popular cowboy actors Ruston had in a folder. He was a genius, but the boy kept coming out around the seams. A few of the books in the lower shelves were current Western novels and some books on American geography in the 1800s. Beside the desk was a used ten-gallon hat and lariat with the crown of the skimmer autographed by Hollywood's foremost heroic cattle hand. I don't know why York didn't let his kid alone to enjoy himself the way boys should. Ruston would rather be a cowboy than a child prodigy any day, I'd bet. He saw me going over his stuff and smiled.

"Were you ever out West, Mike?" he asked.

"I took some training in the desert when I was with Uncle Whiskers."

"Did you ever see a real cowboy?"

"Nope, but I bunked with one for six months. He used to wear high-heeled boots until the sergeant cracked down on him. Some card. Wanted to wear his hat in the shower. First thing he'd do when he'd get up in the morning was to put on his hat. He couldn't get used to one without a six-inch brim and was forever wanting to tip his hat to the Lieutenant instead of saluting."

Ruston chuckled. "Did he carry a six-shooter?"

"Naw, but he was a dead shot. He could pick the eyes out of a beetle at thirty yards."

The doctor broke up our chitchat by handing the kid some pills. He filled a box with them, printed the time to take them on the side and dashed off a prescription. He handed it to me. "Have this filled. One teaspoonful every two hours for twenty-four hours. There's nothing wrong with him except a slight nervous condition. I'll come back tomorrow to see Miss Malcom again. If her wound starts bleeding call me at once. I gave them both a sedative so they should sleep well until morning."

"Okay, Doctor, thanks." I gave him over to Harvey who ushered him to the door.

Roxy forced a smile. "Did you get them, Mike?"

"Forget about it," I said. "How did you get in the way?"

"I heard a gun go off and turned on the light. I guess I shouldn't have done that. I ran to the window but with the light on I couldn't see a thing. The next thing I knew something hit me in the shoulder. I didn't realize it was a bullet until I saw the hole in the window. That's when I screamed," she added sheepishly.

"I don't blame you, I'd scream too. Did you see the flash of the gun?"

Her head shook on the pillow. "I heard it I think, but it sounded sort of far off. I never dreamed . . ."

"You weren't hurt badly, that's one thing."

"Ruston, how . . ."

"Okay. You scared the hell out of him when you yelled.

He's had too much already. That set him off. He was stiff as a fence post when I went in to him."

The sedative was beginning to take effect. Roxy's eyes closed sleepily. I whispered to Billy, "Get me a broom handle or something long and straight, will you?"

He went out and down the corridor. While I waited I looked at the hole the bullet had made, and in my mind pictured where Roxy had stood when she was shot. Billy came in with a long brass tube.

"Couldn't find a broom, but would this curtain rod do?"

"Fine," I said softly. Roxy was asleep now. "Stand over here by the window."

"What you going to do?"

"Figure out where that shot came from."

I had him hold the rod under his armpit and I sighted along the length of it, lining the tube up with the hole in the wall and the one in the window. This done I told him to keep it that way then threw the window up. More pieces of glass tinkled to the floor. I moved around behind him and peered down the rod.

I was looking at the base of the wall about where the two assailants had climbed the top. That put Junior out of it by a hundred feet. The picture was changing again, nothing balanced. It was like trying to make a mural with a kaleidoscope. Hell's bells. Neither of those two had shot at me, yet that was where the bullet came from. A silencer maybe? A wild shot at someone or a shot carefully aimed. With a .32 it would take an expert to hit the window from that range much less Roxy behind it. Or was the shot actually aimed at her?

"Thanks, Billy, that's all."

He lowered the rod and I shut the window. I called him to one side, away from the bed. "What is it, Mike?"

"Look, I want to think. How about you staying up here in the kid's room tonight. We'll fix some chair cushions up on the floor."

"Okay, if you say so."

"I think it will be best. Somebody will have to keep an eye on them in case they wake up, and Ruston has to take his medicine," I looked at the box, "every three hours. I'll give Harvey the prescription to be filled. Do you mind?"

"No, I think I'll like it here better'n the room downstairs."

"Keep the doors locked."

"And how. I'll push a chair up against them too."

I laughed. "I don't think there will be any more trouble for a while."

His face grew serious. "You can laugh, you got a rod under your arm."

"I'll leave it here for you if you want."

"Not me, Mike. One more strike and I'm out. If I get caught within ten feet of a heater they'll toss me in the clink. I'd sooner take my chances."

He began pulling the cushions from the chairs and I went out. Behind me the lock clicked and a chair went under the knob. Billy wasn't kidding. Nobody was going to get in there tonight.

Chapter Seven

Downstairs I dialed the operator and asked for the highway patrol. She connected me with headquarters and a sharp voice crackled at me. "Sergeant Price, please."

"He's not here right now, is there a message?"

"Yeah, this is Mike Hammer. Tell him that Miss Malcom, the York kid's nurse, was shot through the shoulder by a thirty-two-caliber bullet. Her condition isn't serious and she'll be able to answer questions in the morning. The shot was fired from somewhere on the grounds but the one who fired it escaped."

"I got it. Anything else?"

"Yes, but I'll give it to him in person. Have they found any trace of Grange yet?"

"They picked up her hat along the shore of the inlet. Sergeant Price told me to tell you if you called."

"Thanks. They still looking for her?"

"A boat's grappling the mouth of the channel right now."

"Okay, if I get time I'll call back later." The cop thanked me and hung up. Harvey waited to see whether I was going out or not, and when I headed for the door got my hat.

"Will you be back tonight, sir?"

"I don't know. Lock the door anyway."

"Yes, sir."

I tooled my car up the drive and honked for Henry to come out and open the gates. Although there was a light on in his cottage, Henry didn't appear. I climbed out again and walked in the place. The gatekeeper was sound asleep in his chair, a paper folded across his lap.

After I shook him and swore a little his eyes opened, but not the way a waking person's do. They were heavy and dull, he was barely able to raise his head. The shock of seeing me there did more to put some life in him than the shaking. He blinked a few times and ran his hand over his forehead.

"I'm . . . sorry, sir. Can't understand myself . . . lately. These awful headaches, and going to sleep like that."

"What's the matter with you, Henry?"

"It's . . . nothing, sir. Perhaps it's the aspirin." He pointed to a bottle of common aspirin tablets on the table. I picked it up and looked at the label. A well-known brand. I looked again, then shook some out on my palm. There were no manufacturer's initials on the tablets at all. There were supposed to be, I used enough of them myself.

"Where did you get these, Henry?"

"Mr. York gave them to me last week. I had several fierce headaches. The aspirin relieved me."

"Did you take these the night of the kidnapping?"

His eyes drifted to mine, held. "Why, yes. Yes, I did."

"Better lay off them. They aren't good for you. Did you hear anything tonight?"

"No, I don't believe I did. Why?"

"Oh, no reason. Mind if I take some of these with me?" He shook his head and I pocketed a few tablets. "Stay here," I said, "I'll open the gates."

Henry nodded and was asleep before I left the room. That was why the kidnapper got in so easily. That was why York left and the killer left and I left without being heard at the gate.

It was a good bet that someone substituted sleeping tablets for the aspirins. Oh, brother, the killer was getting cuter all the time.

But the pieces were coming together one by one. They didn't fit the slots, but they were there, ready to be assembled as soon as someone said the wrong word, or made a wrong move. The puzzle was closer to the house now, but it was outside, too. Who wanted Henry to be asleep while Ruston was snatched? Who wanted it so bad that his habits were studied and sleeping pills slipped into his aspirin bottle? If someone was that thorough they could have given him something to cause the headaches to start with. And who was in league with that person on the outside?

A wrong move or a wrong word. Someone would slip sometime. Maybe they just needed a little push. I had Junior where the hair was short now, that meant I had the old lady, too. Jump the fence to the other side now. Alice. She said *tsk, tsk* when I told them York was dead. Sweet thing.

I had to make another phone call to trooper headquarters

to collect the list of addresses from the statements. Price still hadn't come in, but evidently he had passed the word to give me any help I needed, for there was no hesitation about handing me the information.

Alice lived west of town in a suburb called Wooster. It was little less than a crossroad off the main highway, but from the size of the mansions that dotted the estates it was a refuge of the wealthy. The town itself boasted a block of storefronts whose windows showed nothing but the best. Above each store was an apartment. The bricks were white, the metal work bright and new. There was an aura of dignity and pomp in the way they nestled there. Alice lived above the fur shop, two stores from the end.

I parked between a new Ford and a Caddy convertible. There were no lights on in Alice's apartment, but I didn't doubt that she'd want to see me. I slid out and went into the tiny foyer and looked at the bell. It was hers. For a good five seconds I held my finger on it, then opened the door and went up the steps. Before I reached the top, Alice, in the last stages of closing her robe, opened the door, sending a shaft of light in my face.

"Well, I'll be damned," she exclaimed. "You certainly pick an awful time to visit your friends."

"Aren't you glad to see me?" I grinned.

"Silly, come on in. Of course I'm glad to see you."

"I hate to get you up like this."

"You didn't. I was lying in bed reading, that's all." She paused just inside the door. "This isn't a professional visit, is it?"

"Hardly. I finally got sick and tired of the whole damn setup and decided to give my mind a rest."

She shut the door. "Kiss me."

I pecked her on the nose. "Can't I even take my hat off?"

"Oooo," she gasped, "the way you said that!"

I dropped my slicker and hat on a rack by the door and trailed her to the living room. "Have a drink?" she asked me.

I made with three fingers together. "So much, and ginger."

When she went for the ice I took the place in with a sweep of my head. Swell, strictly swell. It was better than the best Park Avenue apartment I'd ever been in, even if it was above a store. The furniture cost money and the oils on the wall even more. There were books and books, first editions and costly manuscripts. York had done very well by his niece.

Alice came back with two highballs in her hand. "Take one," she offered. I picked the big one. We toasted silently, she with the devil in her eyes, and drank.

"Good?"

I bobbed my head. "Old stuff, isn't it?"

"Over twenty years. Uncle Rudy gave it to me." She put her drink down and turned off the overhead lights, switching on a shaded table lamp instead. From a cabinet she selected an assortment of records and put them in the player. "Atmosphere," she explained impishly.

I didn't see why we needed it. When she had the lamp at her back the robe became transparent enough to create its own atmosphere. She was all woman, this one, bigger than I thought. Her carriage was seduction itself and she knew it. The needle came down and soft Oriental music filled the room. I closed my eyes and visualized women in scarlet veils dancing for the sultan. The sultan was me. Alice said something I didn't catch and left.

When she came back she was wearing the cobwebs. Nothing else.

"You aren't too tired tonight?"

"Not tonight," I said.

She sat down beside me. "I think you were faking the last time, and after all my trouble."

Her skin was soft and velvety-looking under the cobwebs, a vein in her throat pulsed steadily. I let my eyes follow the contours of her shoulders and down her body. Impertinent breasts that mocked my former hesitance, a flat stomach waiting for the touch to set off the fuse, thighs that wanted no part of shielding cloth.

I had difficulty getting it out. "I *had* to be tired."

She crossed her legs, the cobwebs parted. "Or crazy," she added.

I finished the drink off in a hurry and held out the glass for another. I needed something to steady my nerves.

Ice clinked, glass rang against glass. She measured the whisky and poured it in. This time she pulled the coffee table over so she wouldn't have to get up again. The record changed and the gentle strains of a violin ran through the *Hungarian Rhapsody*. Alice moved closer to me. I could feel the warmth of her body through my clothes. The drinks went down. When the record changed again she had her head on my shoulder.

"Have you been working hard, Mike?"

"No, just legwork."

Her hair brushed my face; soft, lovely hair that smelled of jasmine. "Do you think they'll find her?"

I stroked her neck, letting my fingers bite in just a little. "I think so. Sidon is too small a town to try to hide in. Did you know her well?"

"Ummm. What? Oh, no. She was very distant to all of us."

More jasmine. She buried her face in my shoulder. "You're a thing yourself," I grinned. "Shouldn't you be wearing black?"

"No. It doesn't become me."

I blew in her ear. "No respect for the dead."

"Uncle never liked all those post-funeral displays anyway."

"Well, you should do something since you were his favorite niece. He left you a nice lump of cash."

She ran her fingers through my hair, bending my head close to hers. "Did he?" Lightly, her tongue ran over her lips, a pink, darting temptation.

"Uh-huh." We rubbed noses, getting closer all the time. "I saw his will. He must have liked you."

"Just you like me, Mike, that's all I want." Her mouth opened slightly. I couldn't take anymore. I grabbed her in my arms and crushed her lips against mine. She was a living heartbeat, an endless fire that burned hot and deep. Her arms went about me, holding tightly. Once, out of sheer passion, she bit me like a cat would bite.

She tore her mouth away and pressed it against my neck, then rubbed her shoulders from side to side against my chest until the cobwebs slipped down her arms and pinioned them there. I touched her flesh, bruised her until she moaned in painful ecstasy, demanding more. Her fingers fumbled with the buttons of my coat. Somehow I got it off and draped it over a chair, then she started on my tie. "So many clothes, Mike, you have so many clothes." She kissed me again.

"Carry me inside." I scooped her off the couch, cradling her in my arms, the cobwebs trailing beneath her. She pointed with her finger, her eyes almost closed. "In there."

No lights. The comforter was cool and fluffy. She told me to stay there and kissed my eyes shut. I felt her leave the bed and go into the living room. The record changed and a louder piece sent notes of triumph cascading into the room. Agonizing minutes passed waiting until she returned, bearing two half-full glasses on a tray like a gorgeous slave girl. Gone now were even the cobwebs.

"To us, Mike, and this night." We drank. She came to me with arms outstretched. The music came and went, piece after piece, but we heard nothing nor cared. Then there was no sound at all except the breathing.

It was well into morning before we stirred. Alice said no, but I had to leave. She coaxed, but now the sight of her meant less and I could refuse. I found my shoes, laced them, and tucked the covers under her chin.

"Kiss me." She held her mouth up.

"No."

"Just one?"

"All right, just one." She wasn't making it any too easy. I pushed her back against the pillows and said good night.

"You're so ugly, Mike. So ugly you're beautiful."

"Thanks, so are you." I waved and left her. In the living room I picked my coat up from the floor and dusted it off. My aim was getting worse, I thought I had it on the chair.

On the way out I dropped the night latch and shut the door softly. Alice, lovely, lovely Alice. She had a body out of this world. I ran down the stairs pulling on my slicker. Outside the sheen of the rain glimmered from the streets. I gave the brim of my hat a final tug and stepped out.

There were no flashes of light, no final moments of distortion. Simply that one sickening, hollow-sounding smash on the back of the head and the sidewalk came up and hit me in the face.

I was sick. It ran down my chin and wet my shirt. The smell of it made me sicker. My head was a huge balloon that kept getting bigger and bigger until it was taut and ready to burst into a thousand fragments. Something cold and metallic jarred my face repeatedly. I was cramped, horribly cramped. Even when I tried to move I stayed cramped. Ropes bit into my wrists leaving hempen splinters imbedded under the skin, burning like darts. Whenever the car hit a bump the jack on the floor would slam into my nose.

No one else was with me back there. The empty shoulder holster bit into my side. Nice going, I thought, you walked into that with your mouth open and your eyes shut. I tried to see over the back of the seat, but I couldn't raise myself that far. We turned off the smooth concrete of the highway and the roadway became sloshy and irregular. The jack bounced around more often. First I tried to hold it down with my forehead, but it didn't work, then I drew back from it. That was worse. The muscles in my back ached with the torture of the rack.

I got mad as hell. Sucker. That's what I was. Sucker. Someone was taking me for a damn newcomer at this racket. Working me over with a billy then tossing me in the back of a car. Just like the prohibition days, going for a ride. What the hell did I look like? I had been tied up before and I had been in the back of a car before, but I didn't stay there long. After the first time I learned my lesson. Boy Scout stuff, be prepared. Some son of a bitch was going to get his brains kicked out.

The car skidded to a stop. The driver got out and opened the door. His hands went under my armpits and I was thrown into the mud. Feet straddled me, feet that merged into a dark overcoat and a masked face, and a hand holding my own gun so that I was looking down the muzzle.

"Where is it?" the guy said. His voice carried an obvious attempt at disguise.

"What are you talking about?"

"Damn you anyway, what did you do with it? Don't try to stall me, what did you do with it? You hid it somewhere, you bastard, it wasn't in your pocket. Start talking or I'll shoot your head off!"

The guy was working himself up into a kill-crazy mood. "How do I know where it is if you won't tell me what you want," I snarled.

"All right, you bastard, get smart. You stuck your neck out once too often. I'll show you." He stuck the gun in his pocket and bent over, his hands fastening in my coat collar and under my arm. I didn't help him any. I gave him damn near two hundred pounds of dead weight to drag into the trees.

Twice the guy snagged himself in the brush and half-fell. He took it out on me with a slap in the head and a nasty boot in the ribs. Every once in a while he'd curse and get a better grip on my coat, muttering under his breath what was going to happen to me. Fifty yards into the woods was enough. He dropped me in a heap and dragged the rod out again, fighting for his breath. The guy knew guns. The safety was off and the rod was ready to spit.

"Say it. Say it now, damn you, or you'll never say it. What did you do with them . . . or should I work you over first?"

"Go to hell, you pig."

His hand went up quickly. The gun described a chopping arc toward my jaw. That was what I was waiting for. I grabbed the gun with both hands and yanked, twisting at the same time. He screamed when his shoulder jumped out of the socket, screamed again when I clubbed the edge of my palm against his neck.

Feet jabbed out and ripped into my side, he scrambled to get up. In the middle of it I lost the gun. I held on with one arm and sank my fist into him, but the power of the blow was lost in that awkward position.

But it was enough. He wrenched away, regained his feet and went scrambling through the underbrush. By the time I found the gun he was gone. Time again. If I had had only a minute more I could have chased him, but I hadn't had time to cut my feet loose. Yeah, I'd been on the floor of a car before with my hands tied behind my back. After that first

time I have always carried a safety-razor blade slipped
through the open seam into the double layer of cloth under
my belt. It works nice, very handy. Someday I'd get tied up
with my hands in front and I'd be stuck.

The knots were soft. A few minutes with them and I was on
my feet. I tried to follow his tracks a few yards, but gave it
up as a bad job. He had fallen into a couple of soft spots and
left hunks of his clothes hanging on some tree limbs. He
didn't know where he was going and didn't care. All he knew
was that if he stopped and I caught him he'd die in that
swamp as sure as he was born. It was almost funny. I turned
around and waded back through the tangled underbrush,
dodging snaky low-hanging branches that tried to whip my
eyes out.

At least I had the car. My erstwhile friend was going to
have to hoof it back to camp. I walked around the job, a late
Chevvy sedan. The glove compartment was empty, the interior in need of a cleaning. Wrapped around the steering
post was the ownership card with the owner's name: Mrs.
Margaret Murphy, age fifty-two, address in Wooster, occupa-
tion, cook. A hell of a note, lifting some poor servant's buggy.
I started it up. It would be back in town before it was missed.

When I turned around I plowed through the ruts of a country road for five minutes before reaching the main highway.
My lights hit a sign pointing north to Wooster. I must have
been out some time, it was over fifteen miles to the city. Once
on the concrete I stepped on the gas. More pieces of the puzzle. I had something. I felt in my pocket; the later will was
still there. Then what the hell was it? What was so almighty
important that I'd been taken for a ride and threatened to
make me talk?

Ordinarily I'm not stupid, on the contrary, my mind can
pick up threads and weave them into whole cloth, but now I
felt like putting on the dunce cap and sitting in the corner.

Nuts.

Twenty minutes to nine I was on the outskirts of Wooster.
I turned down the first side street I came to, parked and got
out of the car after wiping off any prints I might have made.
I didn't know just how the local police operated, but I wasn't
in the mood to do any explaining. I picked up the main road
again and strode uphill toward Alice's. If she was up there
was no indication of it. I recovered my hat from the foyer,
cast one look up to the shuttered window and got in my own
car. Things were breaking all around my head and I couldn't
make any sense out of anything. It was like taking an exam
with the answer sheet in front of you and failing because
you forgot your glasses.

Going back to Sidon I had time to think. No traffic, just the steady hum of the engine and the sharp whirr of the tires. I was supposed to have something. I didn't have it. Yet certain parties were so sure I did have it they put the buzz on me. *It, it,* for Pete's sake, why don't they name the name? I had two wills and some ideas. They didn't want the wills and they didn't know about the ideas. Something else I might have picked up . . . or didn't pick up.

Of course. Of all the potted, tin-headed fools, I took the cake. Junior Ghent got more than the one will. That was all he had left after the two boys got done with him. They took something else, but whatever it was Junior didn't want me messing in his plans by telling me about it. They took it all right, but somewhere between me and the wall they dropped that important something, and figuring me to be smarter than I should have been, thought I must have found it.

I grinned at myself in the rearview mirror. I'm thick sometimes, but hit me often enough and I get the idea. I didn't even have to worry about Junior beating me to it. He *knew* they had it . . . he wouldn't plan on them dropping it. My curiosity was getting tired of thinking in terms of *its*. This had better be good or I was going to be pretty teed off.

Nice, sweet little case. Two hostile camps. Both fighting each other, both fighting me. In between a lot of people getting shot at and Ruston kidnapped to boot. Instead of a logical starting place it traveled in circles. I kicked the gas pedal a little harder.

Harvey was waiting with the door open when I turned up the drive. I waved him inside and followed the gravel drive to the spot where Junior had taken his shellacking. After a few false starts, I picked out the trail the two had taken across the yard and began tracking. Here and there a footprint was still visible in the soft sod; a twig broken off, flower stalks bent, a stone kicked aside. I let my eyes read over every inch of the path and six feet to the sides, too. If I knew what I was looking for it wouldn't have been so bad. As it was, it took me a good twenty minutes to reach the wall.

That was where it was. Lying face up in full view of anybody who cared to look. A glaring white patch against the shrubbery, a slightly crinkled, but still sealed envelope.

The IT.

Under my fingers I felt a handful of what felt like postcards. With a shrug I shoved the envelope unopened into my pocket. Item one. I poked around in the grass and held the shrubs aside with my feet. Nothing. I got down on the ground and looked across the grass at a low angle, hoping to catch the sunlight glinting off metal. The rough calculations I took from

Roxy's room showed this to be the point of origin of the bullet, but nowhere could I see an empty shell. Hell, it could have been a revolver, then there would be no ejected shell. Or it could have been another gun instead of York's. Nuts there. A .32 is a defensive weapon. Anybody who wants to kill uses a .38 or better, especially at that range. I checked the distance to Roxy's window again. Just to hit the house would mean an elevation of thirty degrees. The lad who made the window was good. Better than that, he was perfect. Only he must have fired from a hole in the ground, because there was no place he could have hidden in this area. That is, if it wasn't one of the two who went over the wall.

I gave up and went back to the car and drove around to the front of the house.

Dutiful Harvey stared at the dirt on my clothes and said, "There's been an accident, sir?"

"You might call it that," I agreed pleasantly. "How is Miss Malcom?"

"Fine, sir. The doctor was here this morning and said she was not in any danger at all."

"The boy?"

"Still quite agitated after his experience. The doctor gave him another sedative. Parks has remained with them all this while. He hasn't set foot out of the room since you left."

"Good. Has anyone been here at all?"

"No, sir. Sergeant Price called several times and wants you to call him back."

"Okay, Harvey, thanks. Think you can find me something to eat? I'm starved."

"Certainly, sir."

I trotted upstairs and knocked on the door. Billy's voice cautiously inquired who it was, and when I answered pulled a chair away from the door and unlocked it.

"Hi, Billy."

"Hello, Mike . . . what the hell happened?"

"Somebody took me for a ride."

"Cripes, don't be so calm about it."

"Why not? The other guy has to walk back."

"Who?"

"I don't know yet."

Roxy was grinning at me from the bed. "Come over and kiss me, Mike." I gave her a playful tap on the jaw.

"You heal fast."

"I'll do better if you kiss me." I did. Her mouth was a field of burning poppies.

"Okay?"

"I want more."

"When you get better." I squeezed her hand. Before I went into Ruston's room I dusted myself off in front of the mirror. He had heard me come in and was all smiles.

"Hello, Mike. Can you stay here awhile this time?"

"Oh, maybe. Feeling good?"

"I feel all right, but I've been in bed too long. My back is tired."

"I think you'll be able to get up today. I'll have Billy take you for a stroll around the house. I'd do it myself only I have some work to clean up."

"Mike . . . how is everything coming? I mean . . ."

"Don't think about it, Ruston."

"That's all I can do when I lie here awake. I keep thinking of that night, and Dad and Miss Grange. If only there was something I could do I'd feel better."

"The best you can do is stay right here until everything's settled."

"I read in books . . . they were books of no account . . . but sometimes in cases like this the police used the victim as bait. That is, they exposed a person to the advantage of the criminal to see if the criminal would make another attempt. Do you think . . ."

"I think you have a lot of spunk to suggest a thing like that, but the answer is no. You aren't being the target for another snatch, not if I can help it. There're too many other ways. Now how about you hopping into your clothes and getting that airing." I peeled the covers back and helped him out of bed. For a few seconds he was a bit unsteady, but he settled down with a grin and went to the closet. I called Billy in and told him what to do. Billy wasn't too crazy about the idea, but it being daylight, and since I said that I'd stick around, he agreed.

I left the two of them there, winked at Roxy and went downstairs in time to lift a pair of sandwiches and a cup of coffee from Harvey's tray. Grunting my thanks through a mouthful of food I went into the living room and parked in the big chair. For the first time since I had been there a fire blazed away in the fireplace. Good old Harvey. I wolfed down the first sandwich and drowned it in coffee. Only then did I take the envelope out of my pocket. The flap was pasted on crooked, so it had to be the morning dew that had held it shut. I remembered that look on Junior's face when he had seen what was in it. I wondered if *it* was so good mine would look the same way.

I ran my finger under the flap and drew out six pictures.

Now I saw why Junior got so excited. Of the two women in the photos, the only clothes in evidence were shoes. And Myra

Grange only had one on at that. Mostly, she wore a leer. A big juicy leer. Alice Nichols looked expectant. The pictures were pornography of the worst sort. Six of them, every one different, both parties fully recognizable, yet the views were of a candid sort, not deliberately posed. No, that wasn't quite it, they were posed, yet unposed . . . at least Myra Grange wasn't posing.

I had to study the shots a good ten minutes before I got the connection. What I had taken to be a border around the pictures done in the printing was really part of the shot. These pics were taken with a hidden camera, one concealed behind a dresser, with the supposed border being some books that did the concealing. A hidden camera and a time arrangement to trip it every so often.

No, Myra Grange wasn't posing, but Alice Nichols was. She had deliberately maneuvered for position each time so Grange was sure to be in perfect focus.

How nice, Alice. How very nicely you and York framed Grange. A frame to neutralize another frame. So?

I fired up a butt and shoved the pics back in my pocket. The outer rim of the puzzle was falling into the grooves in my mind now. Grange had an old will. Why? Would York have settled his entire estate on her voluntarily? Or could he have been forced into it? If Grange had something on her boss . . . something big . . . it had to be big . . . then she could call the squeeze play, and be reasonably sure of making a touchdown, especially when York didn't have long to go anyway. But sometime later York had found out about Grange and her habits and saw a way out. Damn, it was making sense now. He played up to Rhoda Ghent, plied her with gifts, then asked her to proposition Grange. She refused and he dropped her like a hot potato then started on Alice. York should have talked to her first. Alice had no inhibitions anyway, and a cut of York's will meant plenty of action to her. She makes eyes at Grange, Grange makes eyes at Alice and the show is on with the lights properly fed and the camera in position. Alice hands York the negatives, York has a showdown with Grange, threatening to make the pictures public and Grange folds up, yet holds onto the old will in the hope something would happen to make York change his mind. Something like a meat cleaver perhaps? It tied in with what Roxy told me. It could even explain the big play after the pictures. Junior had found out about them somehow, possibly from his sister. If he could get the shots in a law court he could prove how Alice came by her share and get her kicked right out of the show. At least then the family might have some chance to split the quarter of the estate. One hostile camp taken care of. Alice had to be the other. She had to have the pictures before Junior could get them . . . or anybody else for that matter. What could be better than promising a future split of her quarter if they agreed to get the pictures for her? That fit, too. Except that they came too late and saw Junior, knew that he had beaten them to it, so they waylay him, take the stuff and blow. Only I happened in at the wrong time and in the excitement the package gets lost.

I dragged heavily on the cigarette and ran over it again, checking every detail. It stayed the same way. I liked it. Billy and Ruston yelled to me on their way out, but I only waved to them. I was trying to reason out what it was that Grange had on York in the beginning to start a snowball as big as this one rolling downhill.

Flames were licking the top of their sooty cavern. Dante's own inferno, hot, roasting, destroying. It would have been so nice if I could only have known what York had hidden in the pillar of the fireplace. York's secret hiding place, that and the chair bottom. Why two places unless he didn't want to have all his eggs in one basket. Or was it another case of first things first? He could have put something in the fireplace years ago and not cared to change it.

With a show of impatience I flipped the remains of the butt into the flames, then stretched my legs out toward the fireplace. Secrets, secrets, so damn many secrets. I moved my head to one side so I could see the brick posts on the end of the smoke-blackened pit. It was well concealed, that cache. Curiosity again. I got up and looked it over more closely. Not a brick out of line, not a seam visible. Unless you saw it open you would never guess it to be there.

I went over every inch of it, rapping the bricks with my bare knuckles, but unlike wood, they gave off no sound. There had to be a trip for it somewhere. I looked again where the stone joined the wall. One place shoulder-high was smudged. I pressed.

The tiny door clicked and swung open.

Nice. It was faced with whole brick that joined with a fit in a recess of the concrete that the eye couldn't discern. To get my hand in I had to hold the door open against the force of a spring. I fished around, but felt nothing except cold masonry until I went to take my hand out. A piece of paper caught in the hinge mechanism brushed my fingers. I worked it out slowly, because at the first attempt to dislodge it, part of the paper crumbled to dust. When I let the door go it snapped shut, and I was holding a piece of an ancient newspaper.

It was brown with age, ready to fall apart at the slightest pressure. The print was faded, but legible. It bore the dateline of a New York edition, one that was on the stands October 9, fourteen years ago. What happened fourteen years ago? The rest of the paper had been stolen, this was a piece torn off when it was lifted from the well in the fireplace. A dateline, nothing but a fourteen-year-old dateline.

I'm getting old, I thought. These things ought to make an impression sooner. Fourteen years ago Ruston had been born.

Chapter Eight

Somehow, the library had an unused look. An ageless caretaker shuffled up the aisle carrying a broom and a dustpan, looking for something to sweep. The librarian, untrue to type, was busy painting her mouth an unholy red, and never looked up until I rapped on the desk. That got me a quick smile, a fast once-over, then an even bigger smile.

"Good morning. Can I help you?"

"Maybe. Do you keep back copies of New York papers?"

She stood up and smoothed out her dress around her hips where it didn't need smoothing at all. "This way, please."

I followed her at a six-foot interval, enough so I could watch her legs that so obviously wanted watching. They were pretty nice legs. I couldn't blame her a bit for wanting to show them off. We angled around behind ceiling-high bookcases until we came to a stairwell. Legs threw a light switch and took me downstairs. A musty odor of old leather and paper hit me on the last step. Little trickles of moisture beaded the metal bins and left dark stains on the concrete walls. A hell of a place for books.

"Here they are." She pointed to a tier of shelves, stacked with newspapers, separated by layers of cardboard. Together we located the old *Globe* editions then began peeling off the layers. In ten minutes we both looked like we had been playing in coal. Legs threw me a pout. "I certainly hope that whatever you're after is worth all this trouble."

"It is, honey," I told her, "it is. Keep your eyes open for October 9."

Another five minutes, then, "This it?"

I would have kissed her if she didn't have such a dirty face. "That's the one. Thanks."

She handed it over. I glanced at the dateline, then at the one in my hand. They matched. We laid the paper out on a reading desk and pulled on the overhead light. I thumbed through the leaves, turning them over as I scanned each column. Legs couldn't stand it any longer. "Please . . . what are you looking for?"

I said a nasty word and tapped the bottom of the page. "This."

"But . . ."

"I know. It's gone. Somebody ripped it out."

She said the same nasty word, then asked, "What was it?"

"Beats me, honey. Got any duplicates around?"

"No, we only keep one copy. There's rarely any call for them except from an occasional high-school history student who is writing a thesis on something or other."

"Uh-huh." Tearing that spot out wasn't going to do any good. There were other libraries. Somebody was trying to stall me for time. Okay, okay, I have all the time in the world. More time than you have, brother.

I helped her stack the papers back on their shelves before going upstairs. We both ducked into washrooms to get years of dust off our skin, only she beat me out. I half expected it anyway.

When we were walking toward the door I dropped a flyer. "Say, do you know Myra Grange?" Her breath caught and held. "Why . . . no. That is, isn't she the one . . . I mean with Mr. York?"

I nodded. She had made a good job of covering up, but I didn't miss that violent blush of emotion that surged into her cheeks at the mention of Grange's name. So this was why the vanishing lady spent so many hours in the library. "The same," I said. "Did she ever go down there?"

"No." A pause. "No, I don't think so. Oh, yes. She did once. She took the boy . . . Mr. York's son down there, but that was when I first came here. I went with them. They looked over some old manuscripts, but that was all."

"When was she here last?"

"Who are you?" She looked scared.

My badge was in my hand. She didn't have to read it. All she needed was the sight of the shield to start shaking. "She was here . . . about a week ago."

Very carefully, I looked at her. "No good. That was too long ago. Let's put it this way. When did you *see* her last?" Legs got the point. She knew I knew about Myra and guessed as much about her. Another blush, only this one faded with the fear behind it.

"A . . . a week ago, I told you." I thanked her and went out. Legs was lying through her teeth and I couldn't blame her.

The water was starting to bubble now. It wouldn't be long before it started to boil. Two things to do before I went to New York, one just for the pleasure of it. I made my first stop at a drugstore. A short, squat pharmacist came out from behind the glass partition and murmured his greetings. I threw the pills I had taken from Henry's bottle on the counter in front of me.

"These were being taken for aspirin," I said. "Can you tell me what they are?"

He looked at me and shrugged, picking up one in his fingers. He touched a cautious tongue to the white surface, then smelled it. "Not aspirin," he told me. "Have you any idea what they might be?"

"I'd say sleeping pills. One of the barbiturates." The druggist nodded and went back behind his glass. I waited perhaps five minutes before he came back again.

"You were right," he said. I threw two five-dollar bills on the counter and scooped up the rest of the pills. Very snazzy, killer, you got a lot of tricks up your sleeve. A very thorough guy. It was going to be funny when I had that killer at the end of my rod. I wondered if he was thorough enough to try to get rid of me.

Back and forth, back and forth. Like a swing. From kidnapping to murder to petty conniving and back to the kidnapping again. Run, run, run. Shuttle train stuff. Too many details. They were like a shroud that the killer was trying to draw around the original motive. That, there had to be. Only it was getting lost in the mess. It could have been an accident, this eruption of pointless crimes, or they might have happened anyway, or they could have been foreseen by the killer and used to his own advantage. No, nobody could be that smart. There's something about crime that's like a disease. It spreads worse than the flu once it gets started. It already had a good start when Ruston was kidnapped. It seemed like that was months ago, but it wasn't . . . just a few short days.

I reviewed every detail on my way to Wooster, but the answer always came up the same. Either I was dumb or the killer was pretty cagey. I had to find Mallory, I had to find Grange, I had to find the killer if he wasn't one of those two. So far all I found was a play behind the curtain.

Halfway there I gave up thinking and concentrated on the road. With every mile I'd gotten madder until I was chain-smoking right through my deck of butts. Wooster was alive this time. People walked along the streets in noisy contentment, limousines blared indignantly at lesser cars in front of them, and a steady stream of traffic went in and out of the shop doors. There was plenty of room in front of Alice's house. I parked the car and went into the foyer, remembering vividly the crack on my skull.

This time the buzz was a short one. I took the stairs fast, but she was faster. She stood in the door with a smile, ready to be kissed. I said, "Hello, Alice," but I didn't kiss her. Her smile broke nervously.

"What's the matter, Mike?"

"Nothing, kid, nothing at all. Why?"

"You look displeased about something." That was putting it mildly.

I went inside without lifting my hat. Alice went to reach for the decanter, but I stopped her by throwing the envelope on the coffee table. "You were looking for these, I think."

"I?" She pulled one of the pictures out of the wrapper, then shoved it back hastily, her face going white. I grinned.

Then I got nasty. "In payment for last night."

"You can go now."

"Uh-uh. Not yet." Her eyes followed mine to the ashtray. There were four butts there, two of them had lipstick on them and the other two weren't my brand.

Alice tried to scream a warning, but it never got past her lips. The back of my hand caught her across the mouth and she rolled into the sofa, gasping with the sting of the blow. I turned on my heels and went to the bedroom and kicked the door open. William Graham was sitting on the edge of the bed as nice as you please smoking a cigarette. His face was scratched in a dozen places and hunks torn out of his clothes from the briars in the woods.

Every bit of color drained out of his skin. I grabbed him before he could stand up and smashed him right in the nose. Blood spurted all over my coat. His arms flailed out, trying to push me away, but I clipped him again on the nose, and again, until there was nothing but a soggy, pulpy mass of flesh to hit. Then I went to work on the rest of his puss. Slapping, punching, then a nasty cut with the side of my hand. He was limp in my grasp, his head thrown back and his eyes wide open. I let him go and he sagged into a shapeless heap on the floor. It was going to take a thousand dollars worth of surgery to make his face the same.

Alice had seen and heard. When I went into the living room she was crouched in terror behind a chair. That didn't stop me. I yanked her out; her dress split down the middle. "Lie to me, Alice," I warned, "and you'll look just like him. Maybe worse. You put him up to bumping me, didn't you?"

All she could do was nod soundlessly.

"You told him he wasn't in the will, but if he and his brother found the pictures and gave them to you you'd cut them in for your share?"

She nodded again. I pushed her back. "York made the will," I said. "It was his dough and I don't care what he did with it. Take your share and go to hell with it. You probably will anyway. Tell Arthur I'll be looking for him. When I find him he's going to look like his brother."

I left her looking eighty years old. William was moaning through his own blood when I went out the door. Good party. I liked it. There would be no more rides from that enemy camp. The redskins have left, vamoosed, departed.

There was only one angle to the Graham boys that I couldn't cover. Which one of them took the shot at Roxy and why? I'll be damned if I heard a shot. They didn't stop long enough to say boo far less than snap off a quickie. And they certainly would have shot at me, not toward the window. I wasn't sure of anything, but if there was money on the table I'd say that neither one had used a gun at all that night. It was details like that that creased me up. I had to make a choice one way or the other and follow it to a conclusion. All right, it was made. The Graham boys were out. Someone else fired it.

New York was a dismal sight after the country. I hadn't thought the grass and the trees with their ugly bilious color of green could have made such an impression on me. Somehow the crowded streets and the endless babble of voices gave me a dirty taste in my mouth. I rolled into a parking lot, pocketed my ticket, then turned into a chain drugstore on the stem. My first call was back to Sidon. Harvey answered and I told him to keep the kid in the room with Roxy and Billy until I got back and take any calls that came for me. My next dime got Pat Chambers, Captain of Homicide.

"Greetings, chum," I said, "this is Uncle Mike."

"It's about time you buzzed me. I was beginning to think you cooled off another citizen and were on the fly. Where are you?"

"Right off Times Square."

"Coming down?"

"No, Pat. I have some business to attend to. Look, how about meeting me on the steps of the library. West Forty-third Street entrance. It's important."

"Okay. Say in about half an hour. Will that do?"

I told him fine and hung up. Pat was tops in my book. A careful, crafty cop, and all cop. He looked more like a gentleman-about-town, but there it ended. Pat had a mind like an adding machine and a talent for police work backed up by the finest department in the world. Ordinarily a city cop has no truck with a private eye, but Pat and I had been buddies a long time with one exception. It was a case of mutual respect, I guess.

At a stand-up-and-eat joint I grabbed a couple dogs and a lemonade then beat it to the library in time to see Pat step out of a prowl car. We shook hands and tossed some remarks back and forth before Pat asked, "What's the story?"

"Let's go inside where we can talk."

We went through the two sets of doors and into the reading room. Holding my voice down I said, "Ever hear of Rudolph York, Pat?"

"So?" He had.

I gave him the story in brief, adding at the end, "Now I want to see what was attached to the rest of this dateline. It'll be here somewhere, and it's liable to turn up something you can help me with."

"For instance?"

"I don't know yet, but police records go back pretty far, don't they? What I want to know may have happened fourteen years ago. My memory isn't that good."

"Okay, let's see what we can dig up."

Instead of going through the regular library routine, Pat flashed his shield and we got an escort to where the papers were filed. The old gentleman in the faded blue serge went unerringly to the right bin, pulled out a drawer and selected the edition I wanted all on the first try. He pointed to a table and pulled out chairs for us. My hands were trembling with the excitement of it when I opened the paper.

It was there. Two columns right down the side of the page. Two columns about six-inches long with a photo of York when he was a lot younger. Fourteen years younger. A twenty-four-point heading smacked me between the eyes with its implications.

FATHER ACCUSES SCIENTIST OF BABY SWITCH

Herron Mallory, whose wife gave birth to a seven-pound boy that died two days later, has accused Rudolph York, renowned scientist, of switching babies. Mallory alleged that it was York's son, not his, who died. His claim is based on the fact that he saw his own child soon after birth, and recognized it again when it was shown to York, his own having been pronounced dead earlier. Authorities denied that such a mistake could have happened. Head Nurse, Rita Cambell, verified their denials by assuring both York and Mallory that she had been in complete charge during the two days, and recognized both babies by sight, confirming identification by their bracelets. Mrs. York died during childbirth.

I let out a long, low whistle. The ball had moved up to mid-field. Pat suggested a follow-up and we brought out the following day's sheet. On page four was a small, one-column spread. It was stated very simply. Herron Mallory, a small-time petty thief and former bootlegger, had been persuaded to drop the charges against Rudolph York. Apparently it was suspected that he couldn't make any headway against a solid citizen like York in the face of his previous convictions. That was where it ended. At least for the time being.

York had a damn good reason then to turn green when Mallory's name was mentioned. Pat tapped the clipping. "What do you think?"

"It might be the real McCoy . . . then again it might be an accident. I can't see why York would pull a stunt like that."

"There're possibilities here. York was no young man when his son was born. He might have wanted an heir awfully bad."

"I thought of that, Pat, but there's one strike against it. If York was going to pull a switch, with his knowledge of genetics he certainly would have taken one with a more favorable family history, don't you think?"

"Yes, if he made the switch himself. But if it were left up to someone else . . . the nurse, for instance, the choice might have been pretty casual."

"But the nurse stated . . ."

"York was very wealthy, Mike."

"I get it. But there's another side too. Mallory, being a cheap chiseler, might have realized the possibilities in setting up a squawk after his own child died, and picked on York. Mallory would figure York would come across with some hard cash just to keep down that kind of publicity. How does that read?"

"Clever, Mike, very clever. But which one do you *believe?*"

The picture of York's face when he heard the name Mallory flashed across my mind. The terror, the stark terror; the hate. York the strong. He wouldn't budge an inch if Mallory had simply been trying some judicious blackmail. Instead, he would have been the one to bring the matter to the police. I said: "It was a switch, Pat."

"That puts it on Mallory."

I nodded. "He must have waited a long time for his chance. Waited until the kid was worth his weight in gold to York and the public, then put the snatch on him. Only he underesti-mated the kid and bungled the job. When York went to Grange's place, Mallory followed him, thinking that York might have figured where the kidnapping came from and split his skull."

"Did you try to trace the cleaver, Mike?"

"No, it was the kind you could buy in any hardware store, and it was well handled, besides. A tool like that would be nearly impossible to trace. There was no sense in my fooling around with it. Price will track it down if it's possible. Frankly, I don't think it'll work. What's got me now is why someone ripped out this clipping in the Sidon library. Even as a stall it wouldn't mean much."

"It's bound to have a bearing."

"It'll come, it'll come. How about trying to run down Mallory for me? Think you can find anything on him?"

"We should, Mike. Let's go down to headquarters. If he was pinched at all we'll have a record of it."

"Roger." We were lucky enough to nab a cab waiting for the red light on the corner of Fifth and Forty-second. Pat gave him the downtown address and we leaned back into the cushions. Fifteen minutes later we got out in front of an old-fashioned red brick building and took the elevator to the third floor. I waited in an office until Pat returned bearing a folder under his arm. He cleared off the desk with a sweep of his hand and shook the contents out on the blotter.

The sheaf was fastened with a clip. The typewritten notation read, Herron Mallory. As dossiers go, it wasn't thick. The first page gave Mallory's history and record of his first booking. Age, 20 in 1927; born in New York City of Irish-Russian parents. Charged with operating a vehicle without a license. That was the starter. He came up on bootlegging, petty larceny; he was suspected of participating in a hijack-killing and a holdup. Plenty of charges, but a fine list of cases suspended and a terse "not convicted" written across the bottom of the page. Mr. Mallory either had a good lawyer or friends where it counted. The last page bore his picture, a profile and front view shot of a dark fellow slightly on the thin side with eyes and mouth carrying an inbred sneer.

I held it under the light to get a better look at it, studying it from every angle, but nothing clicked.

Pat said, "Well?"

"No good, chum. Either I never saw him before or the years have changed him a lot. I don't know the guy from Adam."

He held out a typewritten report. One that had never gotten past a police desk. I read it over. In short, it was the charges that Mallory had wanted filed against York for kidnapping his kid. No matter who Mallory was or had been, there was a note of sincerity in that statement. There was also a handwritten note on hospital stationery from Head Nurse Rita Cambell briefly decrying the charge as absolutely false. There was no doubt about it. Rita Cambell's note was aggressive and assuring enough to convince anyone that Mallory was all wet. Fine state of affairs. I had never participated in the mechanics of becoming a father, but I did know that the male parent was Johnny-the-Gom as far as the hospital was concerned. He saw his baby maybe once for two minutes through a tiny glass plate set in the door. Sure, it would be possible to recognize your child even in that time, but all babies do look alike in most ways. To the nurse actually in charge of the child's entire life, however, each one has the separate identity of a person. It was unlikely that she would make a mistake . . . unless paid for it. Damn, it *could* happen unless you knew nurses. Doubt again. Nurses had a code of ethics as rigid as a doctor's. Any woman who gave her life to the profession wasn't the type that would succumb to a show of long green.

Hell, I was getting all balled up. First I was sure it was a switch, now I wasn't so sure. Pat had seen the indecision in my face. He can figure things, too. "There it is, Mike. I can't do anything more because it's outside my jurisdiction, but if I can help you in any way, say the word."

"Thanks, kid. It really doesn't make much difference whether it was a switch or not. Someplace Mallory figures in it. Before I can go any further I'll have to find either Mallory or Grange, but don't ask me how. If Price turns up Grange I'll get a chance to talk to her, but if Dilwick is the one I'll be out in the cold."

Pat looked sour. "Dilwick ought to be in jail."

"Dilwick ought to be dead. He's a bastard."

"He's still the law, though, and you know what that means."

"Yeah."

Pat started stuffing the papers back in the folder, but I stopped him. "Let me take another look at them, will you?"

"Sure."

I rifled through them quickly, then shook my head.

"Something familiar?"

"No . . . I don't think so. There's something in there that's ringing a bell, but I can't put my finger on it. Oh, nuts, put 'em away."

We went downstairs together and shook hands in the doorway. Pat hailed a cab and I took the next one up to Fifty-fourth and Eighth, then out over to the parking lot. The day was far from being wasted; I was getting closer to the theme of the thing. On top of everything else there was a possible baby switch. It was looking up now. Here was an underlying motive that was as deep and unending as the ocean. The groping, the fumbling after ends that led nowhere was finished. This was meat that could be eaten. But first it had to be chewed; chewed and ground up fine before it could be swallowed.

My mind was hammering itself silly. The dossier. What was in the dossier? I saw something there, but what? I went over it carefully enough; I checked everything against everything else, but what did I forget?

The hell with it. I shoved the key in the ignition and stepped on the starter.

Chapter Nine

Going back to Sidon I held it down to a slow fifty, stopping only once for a quick bite and a tank of gas. Someday I was going to get me a decent meal. Someday. Three miles from the city I turned off the back road to a clover leaf, then swung onto the main artery. When I reached the state police headquarters I cut across the concrete and onto the gravel.

For once Price was in when I wanted him.

So was Dilwick.

I said hello to Price and barely nodded to Dilwick.

"You lousy slob!" he muttered softly.

"Shut up, pig."

"Maybe you both better shut up," Price put in quietly. I threw my hat on the desk and pushed a butt between my lips. Price waited until I lit it, then jerked his thumb toward the fat cop.

"He wants words with you, Mike."

"Let's hear 'em," I offered.

"Not here, wise guy. I think you'd do better at the station. I don't want to be interrupted."

That was a nasty dig at Price, and the sergeant took it right up. "Forget that stuff," he barked, "while he's here he's under my jurisdiction. Don't forget it."

For a minute I thought Dilwick was going to swing and I was hoping he would. I'd love to be in a two-way scramble over that guy. The odds were too great. He looked daggers at Price. "I won't forget it," he repeated.

Price led off. "Dilwick says you broke into the Grange

apartment and confiscated something of importance. What about it, Mike?"

I let Dilwick have a lopsided grin. "Did I?"

"You know damn well you did! You'd better . . ."

"How do you know it was important?"

"It's gone, that's reason enough."

"Hell."

"Wait a minute, Mike," Price cut in. "What did you take?"

I saw him trying to keep his face straight. Price liked this game of baiting Dilwick.

"I could say nothing, pal, and he couldn't prove a thing. I bet you never found any prints of mine, did you, Dilwick?" The cop's face was getting redder. ". . . and the way you had that building bottled up nobody *should* have been able to get in, should they?" Dilwick would split his seams if I kept it up any longer. "Sure, I was there, so what? I found what a dozen of you missed."

I reached in my pocket and yanked out the two wills. Dilwick reached a shaking hand for them but I passed them to Price. "This old one was in Grange's apartment. It isn't good because this is the later one. Maybe it had better be filed someplace."

Dilwick was watching me closely. "Where did the second one come from?"

"Wouldn't you like to know?"

I was too slow. The back of Dilwick's hand nearly rocked my head off my shoulders. The arm of a chair hit my side and before I could spill over into it Dilwick had my shirt front. Price caught his hand before he could swing again.

I kicked the chair away and pulled free as Price stepped between us. "Let me go, Price!" I yelled.

"Damn it, I said to turn it off!"

Dilwick backed off reluctantly. "I'll play that back to you, Dilwick," I said. Nobody was pulling that trick on me and getting by with it. It's a wonder he had the nerve to start something after that last pasting I gave him. Maybe he was hoping I'd try to use my rod . . . that would be swell. He could knock me off as nice as anything and call it police business.

"Maybe you'll answer the next time you're spoken to, Hammer. You've pulled a lot of shady deals around here lately and I'm sick of it. As for you, Price, you're treating him like he's carrying a badge. You've got me hogtied, but that won't last long if I want to work on it."

The sergeant's voice was almost a whisper. "One day you're going to go too far. I think you know what I mean."

Evidently Dilwick did. His lips tightened into a thin line

and his eyes blazed, but he shut up just the same. "Now if you have anything to say, say it properly."

With an obvious attempt at controlling his rage, Dilwick nodded. He turned to me again. "Where did you get the other will?"

"Wouldn't you like to know?" I repeated.

"You letting him get away with this, Price?"

The trooper was on the spot. "Tell him, Mike."

"I'll tell you, Price. He can listen in. I found it among York's personal effects."

For a full ten minutes I stood by while the two of them went over the contents of the wills. Price was satisfied with a cursory examination, but not so Dilwick. He read every line, then reread them. I could see the muscles of his mouth twitch as he worked the thing out in his mind. No, I was not underestimating Dilwick one bit. There wasn't much that went on that he didn't know about. Twice, he let his eyes slide off the paper and meet mine. It was coming. Any minute now.

Then it was here. "I could read murder into this," he grated.

Price turned sharply. "Yes?"

"Hammer, I think I'm going to put you on the spot."

"Swell. You'd like that. Okay, go ahead."

"Pull up your ears and get a load of this, Price. This punk and the Nichols dame could make a nice team. Damn nice. You didn't think I'd find out about those pictures, did you, Hammer? Well, I did. You know what it looks like to me? It looks like the Nichols babe blackmailed Grange into making York change his will. Let York see those shots and Grange's reputation would be shot to hell, she'd be fired and lose out on the will to boot. At least if she came through on the deal, all she'd lose was the will."

I nodded. "Pretty, but where do I come in?"

"Right now. Grange got hold of those pictures somehow. Only Nichols pulls a fast one and tells York that Grange was the one who was blackmailing her. York takes off for Grange's apartment in a rage because he had a yen for his pretty little niece, only Grange bumps him. Then Nichols corners you and you bump Grange and get the stuff off her, and the will. Now you turn it up, Nichols comes into a wad of cash and you split it."

It wasn't as bad as I thought. Dilwick had squeezed a lot of straight facts out of somebody, only he was putting it together wrong. Yeah, he had gotten around, all right. He had reached a lot of people to get that much and he'd like to make it stick.

Price said, "What about it, Mike?"

I grinned. "He's got a real sweet case there." I looked at the cop. "How're you going to prove it?"

"Never mind," he snarled, "I will, I will. Maybe I ought to book you right now on what I have. It'll hold up and Price knows it, too."

"Uh-uh. It'll hold up . . . for about five minutes. Did you find Grange yet?"

He said nothing.

"Nuts," I laughed, "no corpus delicti, no Mike Hammer."

"Wrong, Hammer. After a reasonable length of time and sufficient evidence to substantiate death, a corpse can be assumed."

"He's right, Mike."

"Then he's got to shoot holes in my alibi, Price. I have a pretty tight one."

"Where did you go after you left Alice's apartment the other night?" Brother, I should have guessed it. Dilwick had put the bee on the Graham kid and the bastard copped a sneak. It was ten to one he told Dilwick he hadn't seen me.

That's what I get for making enemies. If the Graham kid thought he could put me on the spot he'd do it. So would Alice for that matter.

But there were still angles. "Go ahead and work on my alibi, Dilwick. You know what it is. Only I'll give you odds that I can make your witness see the light sooner than you can."

"Not if you're in the can."

"First get me there. I don't think you can. Even if you did a good lawyer could rip those phonies apart on the stand and you know it. You're stalling, Dilwick. What're you scared of? Me? Afraid I'll put a crimp in your doings?"

"You're asking for it, punk."

Price came back into the argument. "Skip it, Dilwick. If you have the goods on him then present it through the regular channels, only don't slip up. Let you and your gang go too far and there'll be trouble. I'm satisfied to let Mr. Hammer operate unhampered because I'm familiar with him . . . and you, too."

"Thanks, pal."

Dilwick jammed his hat on and stamped out of the room. If I wanted to get anywhere I was going to have to act fast, because my fat friend wasn't going to let any grass grow under his feet finding enough dope to toss me in the clink. When the door slammed I let Price have my biggest smile. He smiled right back.

"Where've you been?"

"New York. I tried to get you before I left but you weren't around."

"I know. We've had a dozen reports of Grange being seen and I've been running them down."

"Any luck?"

"Nothing. A lot of mistaken identities and a few cranks who wanted to see the police in action. What did you get?"

"Plenty. We're back to the kidnapping again. This whole pot of stew started there and is going to end there. Ruston wasn't York's kid at all. His died in childbirth and another was switched to take its place. The father of the baby was a small-time hoodlum and tried to make a complaint but was dissuaded along the line. All very nicely covered up, but I think it's a case of murder that's been brewing for fourteen years."

During the next half hour I gave him everything I knew, starting with my trip to the local library. Price was a lot like Pat. He sat there saying nothing, taking it all in and letting it digest in his mind. Occasionally he would nod, but never interrupted until I had finished.

He said: "That throws the ball to this Mallory character."

"Roger, and the guy is completely unknown. The last time he showed up was a few days after the switch took place."

"A man can change a lot in fourteen years."

"That's what I'm thinking," I agreed. "The first thing we have to do is concentrate on locating Grange. Alive or dead she can bring us further up to date. She didn't disappear for nothing."

"All right, Mike, I'll do my share. I still have men dragging the channel and on the dragnet. What are you going to do?"

"There are a few members of the loyal York clan that I'd like to see. In the meantime do you think you can keep Dilwick off my neck?"

"I'll try, but I can't promise much. Unfortunately, the law is made up of words which have to be abided more by the letter than the spirit therein, so to speak. If I can sidetrack him I will, but you had better keep him under observation if you can. I don't have to tell you what he's up to. He's a stinker."

"Twice over. Okay, I'll keep in touch with you. Thanks for the boost. The way things are I'm going to have to be sharp on my end to beat Dilwick out of putting me up at the expense of the city."

Dusk had settled around the countryside like a gray blanket when I left headquarters. I stepped into the car and rolled out the drive to the highway. I turned toward the full glow that marked the lights of Sidon and pulled into the town at suppertime. I would have gone straight to the estate if I hadn't passed the library which was still lit up.

It was just an idea, but I've had them before and they'd paid off. I slammed the brakes on, backed up and parked in front of the building. Inside the door I noticed the girl at the desk, but she wasn't the same one I had spoken to before. This one had legs like a bridge lamp. Thinking that perhaps Legs was in one of the reading rooms, I toured the place, but aside from an elderly gentleman, two schoolteacher types and some kids, the place was empty.

Just to be sure I checked the cellar, too, but the light was off and I didn't think she'd be down there in the dark even if Grange was with her. Not with that musty-tomb odor anyway.

The girl at the desk said, "Can I help you find something, sir?"

"Maybe you can."

"What book was it?"

I tried to look puzzled. "That is what I forgot. The girl that was here this morning had it all picked out for me. Now I can't find her."

"Oh, you mean Miss Cook?"

"Yeah," I faked, "that's the one. Is she around now?"

This time the girl was the one to be puzzled. "No, she isn't. She went home for lunch this afternoon and never returned. I came on duty early to replace her. We've tried to locate her all over town, but she seems to have dropped from sight. It's so very strange."

It was getting hot now, hotter than ever. The little bells were going off inside my skull. Little bells that tinkled and rang and chimed and beat themselves into shattered pieces of nothing. It was getting hotter, this broth, and I was holding onto the handle.

"This Miss Cook. Where does she live?"

"Why, two blocks down on Snyder Avenue. Shall I call her apartment again? Perhaps she's home now."

I didn't think she'd have any luck, but I said, "Please do."

She lifted the receiver and dialed a number. I heard the buzz of the bell on the other end, then the voice of the land-lady answering. No, Miss Cook hadn't come in yet. Yes, she would tell her to call as soon as she did. Yes. Yes. Good night.

"She isn't there."

"So I gathered. Oh, well, she's probably had one of her boy friends drop in on her. I'll come back tomorrow."

"Very well, I'm sorry I couldn't help you."

Sorry, everybody was being sorry. Pretty soon somebody

was going to be so sorry they died of it. Snyder Avenue was a quiet residential section of old brownstone houses that had undergone many a face-lifting and emerged looking the same as ever. On one corner a tiny grocery store was squeezed in between buildings. The stout man in the dirty white apron was taking in some boxes of vegetables as he prepared to close up shop. I drew abreast of him and whistled.

When he stopped I asked, "Know a Miss Cook? She's the librarian. I forgot which house it was."

"Yeah, sure." He pointed down the block. "See that car sitting under the streetlight? Well the house just past it and on the other side is the one. Old Mrs. Baxter is the landlady and she don't like noise, so you better not honk for her."

I yelled my thanks and went up the street and parked behind the car he had indicated. Except for the light in the first floor front, the place was in darkness. I ran up the steps and looked over the doorbell. Mrs. Baxter's name was there, along with four others, but only one bell.

I pushed it.

She must have been waiting for me to make up my mind, because she came out like a jack-in-the-box.

"Well?"

"Mrs. Baxter?"

"That's me."

"I'm looking for Miss Cook. They . . ."

"Who ain't been looking for her. All day long the phone's been driving me crazy, first one fellow then another. When she gets back here I'm going to give her a good piece of my mind."

"May I come in, Mrs. Baxter?"

"What for? She isn't home. If she didn't leave all her things here I'd say she skipped out. Heaven only knows why."

I couldn't stand there and argue with her. My wallet slipped into my palm and I let her see the glint of the metal. Badges are wonderful things even when they don't mean a thing. Her eyes went from my hand to my face before she moistened her lips nervously and stood aside in the doorway.

"Has . . . has there been trouble?"

"We don't know." I shut the door and followed her into the living room. "What time did she leave here today?"

"Right after lunch. About a quarter to one."

"Does she always eat at home?"

"Only her lunch. She brings in things and . . . you know. At night she goes out with her boy friends for supper."

"Did you see her go?"

"Yes. Well, no. I didn't see her, but I heard her upstairs and heard her come down. The way she always takes the stairs two at a time in those high heels I couldn't very well not hear her."

"I see. Do you mind if I take a look at her room? There's a chance that she might be involved in a case we're working on and we don't want anything to happen to her."

"Do you think . . ."

"Your guess is as good as mine, Mrs. Baxter. Where's her room?"

"Next floor in the rear. She never locks her door so you can go right in."

I nodded and went up the stairs with the old lady's eyes boring holes in my back. She was right about the door. It swung in when I turned the knob. I shut the door behind me and switched on the light, standing there in the middle of the room for a minute taking it all in. Just a room, a nice, neat girl's room. Everything was in its place, nothing was disarranged. The closet was well stocked with clothes including a fairly decent mink coat inside a plastic bag. The drawers in the dresser were the same way. Tidy. Nothing gone.

Son of a bitch, *she* was snatched too! I slammed the drawer shut so hard a row of bottles went over. Why didn't I pick her up sooner. She was Myra Grange's alibi! Of course! And somebody was fighting pretty hard to keep Myra Grange's face in the mud. She didn't skip out on her own . . . not and leave all her clothes here. She went out that front door on her way back to work and she was picked up somewhere between here and the library. Fine, swell. I'd made a monkey of myself by letting things slide just a little longer. I wasn't the only one who knew that she and Grange were on more than just speaking terms. That somebody was either following me around or getting there on his own hook.

A small desk and chair occupied one corner of the room beside the bed. A small letter-writing affair with a flap front was on the desk. I pulled the cover down and glanced at the papers neatly placed in the pigeonholes. Bills, receipted bills. A few notes and some letters. In the middle of the blotter a writing tablet looked at me with a blank stare.

The first three letters were from a sailor out of town. Very factual letters quite unlike a sailor. Evidently a relative. Or a sap. The next letter was the payoff. I breezed through it and felt the sweat pop out on my face. Paragraph after paragraph of lurid, torrid love . . . words of endearment . . . more love, exotic, fantastic.

Grange had signed only her initials at the bottom.

When I slid the letter back I whistled through my teeth. Grange had certainly gone whole hog with her little partner. I would have closed the desk up after rifling through the rest of the stuff if I hadn't felt that squeegy feeling crawling around my neck. It wasn't new. I had had it in Pat's office.

Something I was supposed to remember. Something I was supposed to see. Damn. I went back through the stuff, but as far as I could see there wasn't anything there that I had seen before I came into the room. Or was there?

Roger . . . there was! It was in my hand. I was staring at Grange's bold signature. It was the handwriting that I had recognized. The first time I had seen it was on some of her papers I had taken from that little cache in her apartment. The next time I had seen it was on the bottom of a statement certifying that Ruston was York's son and not Mallory's, only that time the signature read *Rita Cambell.*

It hit me like a pile driver, hard, crushing. It had been dangling in front of my face all this time and I hadn't seen it. But I wasn't alone with the knowledge, hell no. Somebody else had it too, that's why Grange was dead or missing and Cook on the lam.

Motive, at last the motive. I stood alone in the middle of the room and spun the thing around in my mind. This was raw, bitter motive. It was motive that incited kidnapping and caused murder and this was proof of it. The switch, the payoff. York taking Grange under his wing to keep the thing quiet. Crime that touched off crime that touched off more crime like a string of firecrackers. When you put money into it the thing got bigger and more scrambled than ever.

I had gotten to the center of it. The nucleus. Right on the target were Ruston and Grange. Somebody was aiming at both of them. Winged the kid and got Grange. Mallory, but who the hell was he? Just a figure known to have existed, and without doubt still existing.

I needed bait to catch this fish, yet I couldn't use the kid; he had seen too much already. That is, unless he was willing. I felt like a heel to put it up to him. But it was that or try to track Grange down. Senseless? I didn't know. Maybe a dozen cops *had* dragged the river, and maybe the dragnet *was* all over the state, but maybe they were going at it the wrong way. Sure, maybe it would be best to try for Grange. She was bound to have the story if anyone had, and I wouldn't be taking a chance with the kid's neck either.

Mrs. Baxter was waiting for me at the foot of the stairs, wringing her hands like a nervous hen. "Find anything?" she asked.

I nodded. "Evidence that she expected to come back here. She didn't just run off."

"Oh, dear."

"If anyone calls, try to get their names, and keep a record

of all calls. Either Sergeant Price of the state police will check on it or me personally. Under no conditions give out the information to anyone else, understand?"

She muttered her assent and nodded. I didn't want Dilwick to pull another fasty on me. As soon as I left, all the lights on the lower floor blazed on. Mrs. Baxter was the scary type, I guess.

I swung my heap around in a U-turn, then got on the main street and stopped outside a drugstore. My dime got me police headquarters and headquarters reached Price on the radio. We had a brief chitchat through the medium of the desk cop and I told him to meet me at the post in fifteen minutes.

Price beat me there by ten feet and came over to see what was up.

"You have the pictures of Grange's car after it went in the drink?"

"Yeah, inside, want to see them?"

"Yes."

On the way in I told him what had happened. The first thing he did was go to the radio and put out a call on the Cook girl. I supplied the information the best I could, but my description centered mainly about her legs. They were things you couldn't miss. For a few minutes Price disappeared into the back room and I heard him fiddling around with a filing cabinet.

He came out with a dozen good shots of the wrecked sedan. "If you don't mind, tell me what you're going to do with these?"

"Beats me," I answered. "It's just a jumping-off place. Since she's still among the missing she can still be found. This is where she was last seen apparently."

"There've been a lot of men looking for her."

I grinned at him. "Now there's going to be another." Each one of the shots I went over in detail, trying to pick out the spot where it went in, and visualizing just how it turned in the air to land like it did. Price watched me closely, trying to see what I was getting at.

"Price . . ."

"Yes."

"When you pulled the car out, was the door on the right open?"

"It was, but the seat had come loose and was jammed in the doorway. She would have had some time trying to climb out that way."

"The other door was open too?"

His head bobbed. "The lock had snapped when the door

was wrenched open, probably by the force of hitting the water, although being on the left, it could have happened when her car was forced off the road."

"Think she might have gotten out that way?"

"Gotten out . . . or floated out?"

"Either one."

"More like it was the other way."

"Was the car scratched up much?"

The sergeant looked thoughtful. "Not as much as it should have been. The side was punched in from the water, and the front fender partially crumpled where it hit the bottom, but the only new marks were short ones along the bottom of the door and on the very edge of the fender, and at that we can't be sure that they didn't come from the riverbed."

"I get it," I said. "You think that she was scared off the road. I've seen enough women drivers to believe that, even if she was only half a dame. Why not? Another car threatening to slam into her would be reason enough to make her jump the curb. Well, it's enough for me. If she was dead there wouldn't be much sense keeping her body hidden, and if it weren't hidden it would have shown up by now, so I'm assuming that Grange is still alive somewhere and if she's alive she can be found."

I tossed the sheaf of pictures back to Price. "Thanks, chum. No reflection on any of you, but I think you've been looking for Grange the wrong way. You've been looking for a body."

He smiled a bit and we said good night. What had to be done had to wait until morning . . . the first thing in the morning. I tooled my car back to town and called the estate. Harvey was glad to hear from me, yes, everything was all right. Billy had been in the yard with Ruston all day and Miss Malcom had stayed in her room. The doctor had been there again and there was nothing to worry about. Ruston had been asking for me. I told Harvey to tell the kid I'd drop up as soon as I could and not to worry. My last instructions still went. Be sure the place was locked up tight, and that Billy stayed near the kid and Roxy. One thing I did make sure of. Harvey was to tell the gatekeeper what was in the bottle that he thought contained aspirin.

When I hung up I picked up another pack of butts, a clean set of underwear, shirt and socks in a dry goods store, then threw the stuff in the back of the car and drove out around town until I came to the bay. Under the light of the half-moon it was black and shimmering, an oily, snaky tongue that searched the edges of the shore with frightened, whimpering sounds. The shadows were black as pitch, not a soul was on the streets. Three-quarters of a mile down the road one lone window winked with a yellow, baleful eye.

I took advantage of the swath Grange had cut in the restraining wire and pulled up almost to the brink of the dropoff, changed my mind, pulled out and backed in, just in case I had to get out of there in a hurry. When I figured I was well set I opened my fresh deck of butts, chain-smoked four of them in utter silence, then closed up the windows to within an inch of the top, pulled my hat down over my eyes and went to sleep.

The sun was fighting back the night when I woke up. Outside the steamed-up windows a gray fog was drifting up from the waters, coiling and uncoiling until the tendrils blended into a low-hanging blanket of haze that hung four feet over the ground.

It looked cold. It was cold. I was going to be kicking myself a long time if nothing came of this. I stripped off my clothes throwing them into the car until I was standing shivering in my underwear. Well, it was one way to get a bath, anyway. I could think of better ways.

A quick plunge. It had to be quick or I would change my mind. I swam out to the spot I had fixed in my mind; the spot where Grange's car had landed. Then I stopped swimming. I let myself go as limp as possible, treading water just enough to keep my head above the surface. You got it. I was supposed to be playing dead, or almost dead. Half knocked out maybe. The tide was the same, I had checked on that. If this had been just another river it wouldn't have mattered, but this part was more an inlet than anything else. It emptied and filled with the tides, having its own peculiarities and eddies. It swirled and washed around objects long sunk in the cove of the bottom. I could feel it tug at my feet, trying to drag me down with little monkey hands, gentle, tugging hands that would mean nothing to a swimmer, but could have a noticeable effect on someone half dazed.

Just a few minutes had passed and I was already out of sight of the car around the bend. Here the shores drew away as the riverbed widened until it reached the mouth of the inlet opening into the bay. I thought that I was going to keep right on drifting by, and had about made up my mind to quit all this damn foolishness when I felt the first effect of the eddy.

It was pulling me toward the north shore. A little thrill of excitement shot through me, and although I was numb I felt an emotional warmth dart into my bones. The shore was closer now. I began to spin in a slow, tight circle as something underneath me kicked up a fuss with the water. In another moment I saw what was causing the drag. A tiny U-bend in the shoreline jutted out far enough to cause a suction in the main flow and create enough disturbance to pull in anything not too far out.

Closer . . . closer . . . I reached out and got hold of some finger-thick reeds and held on, then steadied myself with one hand in the mud and clambered up on the shore. There were no tracks save mine, but then again there wouldn't be. Behind me the muck was already filling in the holes my feet had made. I parted the reeds, picking my way through the remains of shellfish and stubble. They were tough reeds, all right. When I let them go they snapped back in place like a whip. If anyone had come out of the river it would have been here. It *had* to be here!

The reeds changed into scrub trees and thorny brush that clawed at my skin, raking me with their needlepoints. I used a stick as a club and beat at them, trying to hold my temper down. When they continued to eat their way into my flesh I cursed them up and down.

But the next second I took it all back. They were nice briars. Beautiful briars. The loveliest briars I had ever seen, because one of them was sporting part of a woman's dress.

I could have kissed that torn piece of fabric. It was stained, but fresh. And nobody was going to go through those reeds and briars except the little sweetheart I was after. This time I was gentler with the bushes and crawled through them as best I could without getting myself torn apart. Then the brush gave way to grass. That green stuff felt better than a Persian rug under my sore feet. I sat down on the edge of the clearing and picked the thorns out of my skin.

Then I stood up and shoved the tail end of my T-shirt down into my shorts. Straight ahead of me was a shack. If ever there was an ideal hiding place, this was it, and as long as I was going to visit its occupant I might as well look my charming best.

I knocked, then kicked the door open. A rat scurried along the edge of the wall and shot past my feet into the light. The place was as empty as a tomb. But it *had* been occupied. Someone had turned the one room into a shambles. A box seat was freshly splintered into sharp fragments on the floor, and the makeshift stove in the middle of the room lay on its side. Over in the corner a bottle lay smashed in a million pieces, throwing jagged glints of light to the walls. She had been here. There was no doubt of it. Two more pieces of the same fabric I held in my hand were caught on the frayed end of the wooden table. She had put up a hell of a fight, all right, but it didn't do her any good.

When the voice behind me said, "Hey, you!" I pivoted on my heel and my hand clawed for the gun I didn't have. A little old guy in baggy pants was peering at me through the one lens of his glasses, wiping his nose on a dirty hunk of rag at the same time.

"That's not healthy, Pop."

"You one of them there college kids?" he asked.

I eased him out the door and came out beside him. "No, why?"

"Always you college kids what go around in yer shorts. Seed some uptown once." He raised his glasses and took a good look at my face. "Say . . . you ain't no college kid."

"Didn't say I was."

"Well, what you guys joining? I seed ya swimming in the crick, just like the other one."

I went after that *other one* like a bird after a bug. "What other one?" My hands were shaking like mad. It was all I could do to keep my hands off his shirt and shake the facts out of him.

"The one what come up t'other day. Maybe it was yesterday. I disremember days. What ya joining?"

"Er . . . a club. We have to swim the river then reach the house without being seen. Guess they won't let me join now that somebody saw me. Did you see the other guy too?"

"Sure. I seed him, but I don't say nothing. I seed lotta funny things go on and I don't ask no questions. It's just that this was kinda funny, that's all."

"What did he look like?"

"Well, I couldn't see him too good. He was big and fat. I heered him puffing plenty after he come out of the weeds. Yeah, he was a big feller. I didn't know who he was so I went back through the woods to my boat."

"Just the other guy, that's all you saw?"

"Yep."

"Nobody else?"

"Nope."

"Anybody live in that shack?"

"Not now. Comes next month and Pee Wee'll move in. He's a tramp. Don't do nothing but fish and live like a pig. He's been living there three summers now."

"This other one you saw, did he have a mean-looking face, sort of scowling?"

"Ummmm. Now that you mention it, he looked kinda mad. Guess that was one reason why I left."

Dilwick. It was Dilwick. The fat slob had gotten the jump

on me again. I knew he was smart . . . he had to be to get along the way he did, but I didn't think he was that smart. Dilwick had put the puzzle together and come out on top. Dilwick had found Grange in the shack and carted her off. Then why the hell didn't he produce her? Maybe the rest of the case stunk, but this part raised a putrid odor to high heaven. Everybody under the sun wanted in on the act, now it was Dilwick. Crime upon crime upon crime upon crime. Wasn't it ever going to end? Okay, fat boy, start playing games with me. You think you pulled a quickie, don't you? You think nobody knows about this . . . T.S., junior, I know about it now, and brother, I think I'm beginning to see where I'm going.

"How can I get back to the bridge without swimming, Pop?"

He pointed a gnarled finger toward the tree line. "A path runs through there. Keeps right along the bank, but stick to it and nobody'll see ya in ya jeans. Hope they let ya join that club."

"I think I can fix it." I batted away the bugs that were beginning to swarm around me and took off for the path. Damn Dilwick anyway.

Chapter Ten

Going back was rough. My feet were bleeding at the end of the first hundred yards and the blue-tailed flies were making my back a bas-relief of red lumps. Some good samaritan had left a dirty burlap bag that reeked of fish and glinted with dried scales in the path and I ripped it in half and wrapped the pieces over my instep and around my ankles. It wasn't so bad after that.

By the time I reached the bridge the sun was hanging well up in the sky and a few office workers were rolling along the road on their way to town. I waited until the road was clear, then made a dash across the bridge to the car and climbed into some dry clothes. My feet were so sore I could hardly get into my shoes, but leaving the laces open helped a little. I threw the wet shorts in the back with the rest of the junk and reached for a butt. There are times when a guy wants a cigarette in the worst way, and this was one of them.

I finished two, threw the car in gear and plowed out to the

concrete. Now the fun began. Me and Dilwick were going to be as inseparable as clamshells. Grange was the key to unlock this mess. Only Dilwick had Grange. Just to be certain I pulled into a dog wagon and went to the pay phone. Sergeant Price was in again. It was getting to be a habit.

I said hello, then: "Get a report on Grange yet, Sergeant?"

He replied in the negative.

"How about the city cops?"

"Nothing there either. I thought you were looking for her?"

"Yeah . . . I am. Look, do me a favor. Buzz the city bulls and see if they've turned up anything in the last few hours. I'll hold on."

"But they would have called me if . . ."

"Go on, try it anyway."

Price picked up another phone and dialed. I heard him ask the cop on the desk the question, then he slammed the receiver down. "Not a thing, Mike."

"Okay, that's all I want to know." I grinned to myself. It was more than a feud between the city and the state police; it was monkey business. But it was all right with me. In fact, I was happier about it than I should have been. I was looking forward to kicking Dilwick's teeth right down his big fat yap.

But before I did anything I was going to get some breakfast. I went through my first order, had seconds, then went for another round. By that time the counterman was looking at the stubble of the beard on my face and wondering whether or not I was a half-starved tramp filling my belly then going to ask to work out the check.

When I threw him a ten his eyes rolled a little. If he didn't check the serial number of that bill to see if it was stolen I didn't know people. I collected my change and glanced at the time. Ten-fifteen. Dilwick would be getting to his office about now. Swell.

This time I found a spot on the corner and pulled in behind a pickup truck. I shut off the motor then buried my nose in a magazine with one eye on the station house across the street. Dilwick came waddling up five minutes later. He disappeared inside and didn't show his face for two hours. When he did come out he was with one of the boys that had worked over Billy that night.

The pair stepped into an official car and drove down the street, turning onto Main. I was two cars behind. A half mile down they stopped, got out and went into a saloon. I took up a position where I could cover the entrance.

That was the way the day went; from one joint to another. By five o'clock I was dying for a short beer and a sandwich, and the two decided to call it quits. Dilwick dumped his partner off in front of a modern, two-story brick building, then cut across town, beating out a red light on the way. By the time I had caught up with him he was locking the car up in front of a trim duplex. He never saw me, not because I slouched down in my seat as I shot by, but because he was waving to a blonde in the window.

I only got a glimpse of her well-rounded shoulders and ample bust, but the look on her face told me that I had might as well go home because this was going to be an all-night affair.

No sense taking any chances. I bought a container of coffee and some sandwiches in a delicatessen then circled the block until I eased into the curb across the street and fifty yards behind the police buggy. The sandwiches went in a hurry. On top of the dash I laid out my cigs and a pack of matches, then worked the seat around until I was comfortable. At nine o'clock the lights went out in the duplex. Twenty cigarettes later they were still out. I curled up on the seat and conked off.

I was getting to hate the morning. My back ached from the swim yesterday and the cramped position behind the wheel. I opened the door and stretched my legs, getting a peek at myself in the rear-vision mirror. I didn't look pretty. Dilwick's car was still in front of the duplex.

"Have a rough night?"

I raised my eyebrows at the milkman. He was grinning like a fool.

"See a lot of you guys around this morning. Want a bottle of milk? It's good and cold."

"Hell yeah, hand one over." I fished in my pocket and threw him a half.

"Someday," he said, "I'm going to sell sandwiches on this route. I'll make a million."

He walked off whistling as I yanked the stopper out and raised the bottle to my lips. It was the best drink I ever had. Just as I reached the bottom the door opened in the duplex. A face came out, peered around, then Dilwick walked out hurriedly. I threw the empty bottle to the grass beside the curb then waited until the black sedan had turned the corner before I left my position. When I reached the intersection Dilwick was two blocks ahead. Tailing him was too easy. There were no cars out that early to screen me. When he stopped at a diner I kept right on going to the station house and got my old spot back, hoping that I hadn't made a mistake in figuring that Dilwick would come back to his castle after he had breakfast.

This time I was lucky. He drove up a half hour later.

Forcing myself to be patient was brutal. For four solid hours Dilwick went through the saloon routine solo, then he picked up his previous companion. At two in the afternoon he acquired another rummy and the circus continued. I was never far behind. Twice, I hopped out and followed them on foot, then scrambled for my heap when they came out of a joint. Six o'clock they stopped in a chop suey joint for supper and I found a chance to get a shave and watch them at the same time from a spot on the other side of the avenue. If this kept up I'd blow my top. What the hell was Dilwick doing with Grange anyway? What goes on in a town where all the cops do is tour the bars and spend their nights shacking up with blondes? If Grange was such a hot potato why wasn't Dilwick working on her? Or did he have her stashed away somewhere . . . or what could be worse, maybe I was all wet in thinking Dilwick had her in the first place.

Nuts.

I had a coffee and was two cigarettes to the good when the trio came out of the restaurant, only this time they split up in front of the door, shaking hands all around. Dilwick got in the car, changed his mind and walked down to a liquor store. When he came out with a wrapped bottle under his arm the other two were gone. Good, this was better. He slid under the wheel and pulled out. I let a convertible get between us and went after him. No blonde tonight. Dilwick went through town taking his time until he reached the highway, stopped at one of those last chance places for a beer while I watched from the spacious driveway, unwrapped his bottle before he started again and had a swig.

By the time he was on the highway it was getting dark. What a day. Five miles out of Sidon he turned right on a black macadam road that wound around the fringes of some good-sized estates and snapped on his lights. I left mine off. Wherever he was going, he wasn't in a hurry. Apparently the road went nowhere, twisting around hills and cutting a swath through the oaks lining the roads. After a while the estates petered out and the countryside, what was visible of it, became a little wild.

Ahead of me his taillight was a red eye, one that paced itself at an even thirty-five. On either side of me were walls of Stygian blackness, and I was having all I could do to stay on the road. I had to drive with one eye on the taillight and the other on the macadam, but Dilwick was making it easy for me by taking it slow.

Too easy. I was so busy driving I didn't see the other car

slide up behind me until it was too late. They had their lights out too.

I hit the brakes as they cut across my nose, my hand fumbling for my rod. Even before I stopped the guy had leaped out of the car and was reaching through my window for me. I batted the hand away from my neck then got slammed across my eyes with a gun barrel. The door flew open. I kicked out with my feet and somebody grunted. Somehow I got the gun in my hand, but another gun lashed out of the darkness and smashed across my wrist.

Damn, I was stupid! I got mousetrapped! Somehow I kicked free of the car and swung. A formless shape in front of me cursed and grunted. Then a light hit me full in the face. I kicked it out of a hand, but the damage had been done. I couldn't see at all. A fist caught me high on the head as a pair of arms slipped around my waist and threw me into a fender. With all my strength I jerked my head back and caught the guy's nose. The bone splintered and hot blood gushed down my collar.

It was kick and gouge and try to get your teeth in something. The only sounds were of fists on flesh and feet on the road. Heavy breathing. I broke free for a moment, ducked, and came in punching. I doubled one up when I planted my knuckles in his belly up to the wrist. A billy swooshed in the air, missed and swooshed again. I thought my shoulder was broken. I got so damn mad I let somebody have it in the shins and he screamed in pain when I nearly busted the bone with my toe. The billy caught me in the bad shoulder again and I hit the ground, stumbling over the guy who was holding his leg. He let go long enough to try for my throat, but I brought my knee up and dug it in his groin.

All three of us were on the ground, rolling in the dirt. I felt cold steel under my hand and wrapped my fingers around a gun butt as a foot nearly ripped me in half. The guy with the billy sent one tearing into my side that took the breath out of my lungs. He tried again as I rolled and grazed me, then landed full on my gut with both his knees. Outlined against the sky I could see him straddling me, the billy raised in the air, ready to crush in my skull. Little balls of fire were popping in my brain and my breath was still a tight knot in my belly when that shot-weighted billy started to come down.

I raised the gun and shot him square in the face, blowing his brains all over the road.

But the billy was too much to stop. It was pulled off course yet it managed to knock me half-senseless when it grazed my temple. Before I went completely out I heard feet pounding on the road and an engine start up. The other guy wasn't taking any chances. He was clearing out.

I lay there under a corpse for three-quarters of an hour before I had enough strength to crawl away. On my hands and knees I reached my car and pulled myself erect. My breath came in hot, jerky gasps. I had to bend to one side to breathe at all. My face felt like a truck went over it and I was sticky with blood and guts, but I couldn't tell how much of it was my own. From the dash I pulled a flashlight and played its beam over the body in the road. Unless he had some identifying scars, nobody would ever be able to tell who he was. Ten feet away from his feet his brainpan lay like a gooey ashtray on the road.

His pockets held over a hundred bucks in cash, a wallet with a Sidon police shield pinned to it and a greasy deck of cards. The billy was still in his hand. I found my own gun, cleaned off the one I had used and tossed it into the bushes. It didn't matter whether they found it or not. I was going to be number-one client in a murder case.

Lousy? It was stinking. I was supposed to have been rubbed out. All very legal, of course. I was suspiciously tailing a cop down a dark road with my lights out, and when ordered to halt put up a fight and during it got myself killed. Except it didn't happen that way. I nailed one and the other got away to tell about it. Maybe Dilwick would like it better this way.

So they caught me. They knew I was trailing them all day and laid a lot of elaborate plans to catch me in the trap. I had to get out of there before that other one got back with reinforcements. I let the body stay as it was, then crawled under the wheel and drove onto the grass, swinging around the corpse, then back on the highway. This time I used my lights and the gas pedal, hightailing it away as fast as I could hold the turns. Whenever I reached an intersection I cut off on it, hoping it wasn't a dead end. It took me a good two hours to circle the town and come out in the general vicinity of York's place, but I couldn't afford using the highway.

The car was in my way now; it could be spotted too easily. If they saw me it would be shoot to kill and I didn't have the kind of artillery necessary to fight a gang war. Dilwick would have every cop in town on the lookout, reporting the incident to Price only after they cornered me somewhere and punched me full of holes, or the death of the cop was printed in the papers.

There was only one reason for all the hoodah . . . Grange was still the key, and Dilwick knew I knew he had her.

Trusting luck that I wasn't too far from home, I ran the car off the road between the trees, pulling as far into the bushes as I could get. Using some cut branches for camouflage I covered up the hood and any part that could be seen by casual observation from the road. When I was satisfied I stepped out and began walking in a northerly direction.

A road finally crossed the one I was on with phone wires paralleling it. A lead from a pole a hundred yards down left the main line and went into the trees. When I reached it I saw the sleepy little bungalow hidden in the shadows. If my feet on the pavement didn't wake the occupants, my sharp rapping did.

Inside someone said, "George . . . the door."

Bedsprings creaked and the guy mumbled something then crossed the room to the door. A light went on overhead and when the guy in the faded bathrobe took a look at me he almost choked.

"I had an accident. Do you have a phone?"

"Accident? Yeah . . . yeah. Come in."

He gulped and glancing at me nervously, called, "Mary. It's a man who's had an accident. Anything I can do for you, mister? Anybody else hurt?"

The guy back there would never feel anything again. "No, nobody else is hurt."

"Here's the phone." His wife came out while I dialed Price's number. She tried to fuss around with a wet rag, wiping the blood off my face, but I waved her off. Price wasn't there, but I got his home number. He wasn't there either, he had left for headquarters. The woman was too excited. I insisted that I didn't need a doctor, but let her go over my battered face with the rag, then dialed headquarters again.

Price was there. He nearly exploded when he heard my voice. "What the hell happened? Where are you?"

"Out of town. What are you doing up at this hour?"

"Are you kidding? A police reporter slipped me the news that a cop was killed south of town. I got the rest from Dilwick. You're in a jam now."

"You're not telling me anything new," I said. "Has he got the police combing the town for me?"

"Everyone on the force is out. I had to put you on the Teletype myself. All the roads are blocked and they have a cordon around York's house. Are you giving yourself up?"

"Don't be silly. I'd be sticking my head in a noose. As far as Dilwick is concerned I have to be knocked off. It's a screw pitch, pal, and I'm in it deep, but don't believe all you hear."

"You killed him, didn't you?"

"You're damn right. If I hadn't it would have been me lying back there with my head in sections all over the ground.

They squeezed me good. I was tailing Dilwick, but they got wise and tailed me. Like a damn fool I let Dilwick lead me out in the sticks and they jumped me. What was I supposed to do, take it lying down? They didn't have orders to pick me up, they were supposed to knock me off."

"Where are you? I'll come out and get you."

"No dice, buddy, I have work to do."

"You'd better give yourself up, Mike. You'll be safer in the custody of the law."

"Like hell. Dilwick will have me held under his jurisdiction and that's what he wants. He'll be able to finish the job then."

"Just the same, Mike . . ."

"Say, whose side are you on?"

He didn't say a word for a full minute. "I'm a policeman, Mike. I'll have to take you in."

He was making it hard for me. "Listen, don't be a sap, Price, something's come up that I have to follow."

"What?"

I glanced at the two faces that were taking in every word. "I can't tell you now."

"The police can handle it."

"In a pig's eye. Now listen. If you want to see this case solved you'll have to stay off my back as much as you can. I know something that only the killer knows and I have to use it while it's hot. If you take me in it'll be too late for both of us. You know what Dilwick and his outfit are like. So I shot one of them. That's hardly killing a cop, is it? Then don't get so upset about me blasting a cheap crook. Do you want to see this case wrapped up or not?"

"Of course."

"Then keep your boys out of this. I'm not worried about the rest."

There was another silent period while he thought it over, then he spoke. "Mike, I shouldn't do this; it's against all rules and regulations. But I know how things stand and I still want to be a good cop. Sometimes to do that you have to fall in line. I'll stay off you. I don't know how long it will be before the pressure gets put on me, but until then I'll do what I can."

"Thanks, pal. I won't run out on you."

"I know that."

"Expect to hear from me every once in a while. Just keep the calls under your hat. If I need you I'll yell for help."

"I'll be around, Mike. You'd better steer clear of York's place. That place is alive with city cops."

"Roger . . . and thanks again."

When I cradled the phone I could see a thousand questions getting ready to come my way. The guy and his wife were all eyes and ears and couldn't make sense out of my conversation. It had to be a good lie to be believed.

I shoved my badge under their noses. "You've overheard an official phone conversation," I said brusquely. "Under no circumstances repeat any part of it. A band of thieves has been operating in this neighborhood under the guise of being policemen and we almost got them. Unfortunately one got away. There's been difficulty getting cooperation from the local police, and we have been operating under cover. In case they show up here you saw nothing, heard nothing. Understand?"

Wide-eyed, their heads bobbed in unison and I let myself out through the door. If they believed that one they were crazy.

As soon as I was in the shadows I turned up the road toward York's estate. Cops or no cops I had to get in there someway. From the top of a knoll I looked down the surrounding countryside. In the distance the lights of Sidon threw a glow into the sky, and here and there other lights twinkled as invisible trees flickered between us in the night breeze. But the one I was interested in was the house a bare mile off that was ablaze with lights in every window and ringed with the twin beams of headlights from the cars patroling the grounds. Occasionally one would throw a spotlight into the bushes, a bright finger of light trying to pin down a furtive figure. Me.

The hell with them. This was one time I couldn't afford a run-in with the bulls. I cut across the fields until the dark shape of a barn loomed ahead. Behind it was a haystack. It was either one or the other. I chose the stack and crawled in. It would take longer for the cows to eat me out than it would for some up-with-the-sun farmer to spot me shacking up with bossy. Three feet into the hay I shoved an armload of the stuff into the tunnel I had made, kicked my feet around until I had a fair-sized cave and went to sleep.

The sun rose, hit its midpoint then went down before I moved. My belly was rumbling with hunger and my tongue was parched from breathing chaff. If a million ants were inside my shirt I couldn't have felt more uncomfortable. Keeping the stack between me and the house, I crawled through the grass to the watering trough and brushed away the dirt that had settled on top of the water. If I thought that last bottle of milk was the best drink I ever had, I was wrong. When I could hold no more I splashed my face and neck, letting it soak my shirt, grinning with pleasure.

I heard the back door of the house slam and took a flying dive to the other side of the trough. Footsteps came closer, heavy, boot-shod feet. When I was getting set to make a jump I noticed that the steps were going right on by. My breath came a little easier. Sticking my head out from behind the trough I saw the broad back of my host disappearing into the barn. He was carrying a pail in either hand. That could mean he was coming over to the trough. I had it right then. Trying to step softly, I ducked into a crouch and made a dash for the darkness of the tree line.

Once there I stripped to the skin and dusted myself off with my shirt. Much better. A bath and something to eat and I would feel almost human. Sometime during the night my watch had stopped and I could only guess at the time. I put it at an arbitrary nine-thirty and wound it up. Still too early. I had one cigarette left, the mashed, battered remains of a smoke. Shielding the match I fired it up and dragged it down to my fingernails. For two hours I sat on a stump watching a scud of clouds blot out the stars and feeling little crawling things climb up my pants leg.

The bugs were too much. I'd as soon run the risk of bumping into a cordon of Dilwick's thugs. When my watch said ten after eleven I skirted the edge of the farm and got back on the road. If anyone came along I'd see them a mile away. I found my knoll again. The lights were still on in York's house, but not in force like they had been. Only one pair of headlights peered balefully around the grounds.

An hour later I stood opposite the east wall leaning over the edge of a five-foot drainage ditch with my watch in my hands. At regular six-minute intervals the outlines of a man in a slouch hat and raincoat would drift past. When he reached the end of the wall he turned and came back. There were two of them on this side. Always, when they met at the middle of the wall, there would be some smart retort that I couldn't catch. But their pacing was regular. Dilwick should have been in the Army. A regular beat like that was a cinch to sneak through. Once a car drove by checking up on the men and tossing a spot into the bushes, but from that angle the ditch itself was completely concealed by the foot-high weeds that grew along its lip.

It had to be quick. And noiseless.

It took the guy three minutes to reach the end of the wall, three minutes to get back to me again. Maybe three-quarters of a minute if he ran. When he passed the next time I checked my watch, keeping my eyes on the second hand. One, two, two and a half. I gripped the edge of the ditch. Ten seconds, five . . . I crouched . . . now! Vaulting the ditch I ducked across the road to the wall. Ten feet away, the tree I had chosen waved to me with leafy fingers. I jumped, grabbed the lowest limb and swung up, then picked my way up until I was even with the wall. My clothes caught on spikelike branches, ripped loose, then caught again.

Feet were swishing the grass. Feet that had a copper over them. This was the second phase. If he looked up and saw me outlined against the sky I was sunk. I palmed the .45 and threw the safety off, waiting. They came closer. I heard him singing a tuneless song under his breath, swearing at briars that bit at his ankles.

He was under the tree now, in the shadows. The singing stopped. The feet stopped. My hand tightened around the butt of the gun, aiming it where his head would be. If he saw me he was held in his tracks. I would have let one go at him if I didn't see the flare of the match in time. When his butt was lit he breathed the smoke in deeply then continued on his rounds. I shoved the gun back and put the watch on him again until it read another three minutes.

Button your coat . . . be sure nothing was going to jingle in your pockets . . . keep your watch face blacked out . . . hold tight . . . get ready . . . and jump. For one brief moment I was airborne before my fingers felt the cold stone wall. The corner caught me in the chest and I almost fell. Somehow I kicked my feet to the top and felt broken glass cemented in the surface shatter under my heels. Whether or not anybody was under me, I had to jump, I was too much of a target there on the wall. Keeping low I stepped over the glass and dropped off.

I landed in soft turf with hardly a sound, doubled up and rolled into a thorny rosebush. The house was right in front of me now; I could pick out Roxy's window. The pane was still shattered from the bullet that had pierced it and nicked her.

Ruston's window was lit, too, but the shade was drawn. Behind the house the police car stopped, some loud talking ensued, then it went forward again. No chance to check schedules now. I had to hope that I wasn't seen. Just as soon as the car passed I ran for the wall of the building, keeping in whatever cover the bushes and hedgerows afforded. It wasn't much, but I made the house without an alarm going off. The wrist-thick vine that ran up the side wasn't as good as a ladder, but it served the purpose. I went up it like a monkey until I was just below Roxy's window.

I reached up for the sill, grabbed it and as I did the damn brick pulled loose and tumbled down past me landing with a raucous clatter in the bushes below and then bounced sickeningly into other bricks with a noise as loud as thunder in my ears. I froze against the wall, heard somebody call out, then saw a bright shaft of light leap out from a spot in someone's hand below and watched it probe the area where the brick had landed.

Whoever he was didn't look up, not expecting anyone above him. His stupidity was making me feel a little better and I figured I had it made. I wasn't that lucky. There was too much weight on the vine and I felt it beginning to pull loose from wherever it was anchored in the wall above my head.

I didn't bother trying to be careful. Down below a couple of voices were going back and forth and their own sounds covered mine. I scrambled up, reached and got hold of an awning hook imbedded in the concrete of the exterior frame of the window and hung on with one hand, my knee reaching for the sill before I could pull the hook out of the wall.

Down below everybody was suddenly satisfied and the lights went out. In the darkness I heard feet taking up the vigil again. I waited a full minute, tried the window, realized that it was locked then tapped on the pane. I did it again, not a frantic tapping, but a gentle signaling that got a response I could hear right through the glass. I hoped she wouldn't scream, but would think it out long enough to look first.

She did.

There was enough reflected light from a bed lamp to highlight my face and I heard her gasp, reach for the latch and ease the window up. I rolled over the sill, dropped to the floor and let her shut the window behind me and pull down the blind. Only then did she snap on the light.

"Mike!"

"Quiet, kid, they're all over the place downstairs."

"Yes, I know." Her eyes filled up suddenly and she half-ran to me, her arms folding me to her.

Behind us there was a startled little gasp. I swung, pushed Roxy away from me, then grinned. Ruston was standing there in his pajamas, his face a dead white. "Mike!" he started to say, then swayed against the doorjamb. I walked over, grabbed him and rubbed his head until he started to smile at me.

"You take it easy, little buddy . . . you've had it rough. How about letting me be the only casualty around here. By the way, where is Billy?"

Roxy answered. "Dilwick took him downstairs and is making him stay there."

"Did he get rough with him?"

"No . . . Billy said he'd better lay off or he'd get a lawyer that would take care of that fat goon and Dilwick didn't touch him. For once Billy stood up for himself."

Ruston was shaking under my hand. His eyes would dart from the door to the window and he'd listen attentively to the heavy footsteps wandering down in the rooms below. "Mike, why did you come? I don't want them to see you. I don't care what you did, but you can't let them get you."

"I came to see you, kid."

"Me?"

"Uh-huh."

"Why?"

"I have something big to ask you."

The two of them stared at me, wondering what could be so great as to bring me through that army of cops. Roxy, quizzically; Ruston with his eyes filled with awe. "What is it, Mike?"

"You're pretty smart, kid, try to understand this. Something has come up, something that I didn't expect. How would you like to point out the killer for me? Be a target. Lead the killer to you so I can get him?"

"Mike, you can't!"

I looked at Roxy. "Why not?"

"It isn't fair. You can't ask him to do that!"

I slumped in a chair and rubbed my head. "Maybe you're right. It is a lot to expect."

Ruston was tugging at my sleeve. "I'll do it, Mike. I'm not afraid."

I didn't know what to say. If I missed I'd never be able to look at myself in the face again, yet here was the kid, ready and trusting me not to miss. Roxy sank to the edge of the bed, her face pale, waiting for my answer. But I couldn't let a killer run around loose.

"Okay, Lancelot, it's a deal." Roxy was hating me with her eyes. "Before we go over it, do you think you can get me something to eat?"

"Sure, Mike. I'll get it. The policemen won't bother me." Ruston smiled and left. I heard him going down the stairs, then tell the cop he was hungry and so was his governess. The cop growled and let him go.

Roxy said, "You're a louse, Mike, but I guess it has to be that way. We almost lost Ruston once, and it's liable to happen again if somebody doesn't think of something. Well, you did. I just hope it works, that's all."

"So do I, kid."

Ruston came running up the stairs and slipped into the room, bearing a pair of enormous sandwiches. I all but snatched them out of his hand and tore into them wolfishly. Once, the cop came upstairs and prowled past the door and I almost choked. After he went by, the two of them laughed silently at me standing there with my rod in my hand and the remains of a sandwich sticking out of my mouth.

Roxy went over and pressed her ear to the door, then slowly turned the key in the lock. "I suppose you'll leave the same way you came in, Mike, so maybe that'll give you more time if you have to go quickly."

"Gee, I hope nothing happens to you, Mike. I'm not afraid for myself, I'm just afraid what those policemen will do. They say you shot a cop and now you have to die."

"Lancelot, you worry too much."

"But even if you find out who's been causing all the trouble the police will still be looking for you, won't they?"

"Perhaps not," I laughed. "They're going to be pretty fed up with me when I bust this case."

The kid shuddered, his eyes closed tightly for a second. "I keep thinking of that night in the shack. The night you shot one of those men that kidnapped me. It was an awful fight."

I felt as though a mule had kicked me in the stomach. "What did you say?"

"That night . . . you remember. When you shot that man and . . ."

I cut him off. "You can get off that target, Ruston," I said softly. "I won't need you for a decoy after all."

Roxy twisted toward me, watching the expression in my eyes. "Why, Mike?"

"I just remembered that I shot a guy, that's why. I had forgotten all about it." I jammed on my hat and picked up a pack of Roxy's butts from the dresser. "You two stay here and keep the door locked. I can get the killer, now, by damn, and I won't have to make him come to me either. Roxy, turn that light off. Give me five minutes after I leave before you turn it on again. Forget you ever saw me up here or Dilwick will have your scalp."

The urgency in my voice moved her to action. Without a word in reply she reached out for the light and snapped it off. Ruston gasped and moved toward the door, with the slightest tremor of excitement creeping into his breathing. I saw him silhouetted there for an instant, a floor lamp right in front of him. Before I could caution him the shade struck him in the face. His hand went out . . . hit the lamp and it toppled to the floor with the popping of the bulb and the crash of a fallen tree. Or so it seemed.

Downstairs a gruff voice barked out. Before it could call again I threw the window up and went out, groping for the vine. Someplace in the house a whistle shrilled and angry fists beat at the door. Half-sliding, half-climbing, I went down the side of the building. Another whistle and somebody got nervous and let a shot blast into the confusion. From every side came the shouts and the whistles. Just before I reached the ground a car raced up and two figures leaped out. But I was lucky. The racket was all centered on the inside of the house and the coppers were taking it for granted that I was trapped there.

As fast as I could go, I beat it across the drive to the lawn, then into the trees. Now I knew where I was. One tree ahead formed the perfect ladder over the wall. I had my gun out now in case that patrol was waiting. There would be no command to halt, just a volley of shots until one of us dropped. All right, I was ready. Behind me a window smashed and Roxy screamed. Then there was a loud "There he goes!" and a pair of pistols spit fire. With the trees in the way and the distance opening between us, I wasn't concerned about getting hit.

The tree was a godsend. I went up its inclined trunk thanking whatever lightning bolt had split it in such a handy fashion, made the top of the wall and jumped for the grass. The sentries weren't there anymore. Probably trying to be in on the kill.

A siren screamed inside the wall and the chase was on, but it would be a futile chase now. Once in the tree line on the other side of the road I took it easy. They'd be looking for a car and the search would be along the road. So long, suckers!

Chapter Eleven

I slept in my car all night. It wasn't until noon that I was ready to roll. Now the streets would be packed with traffic and my buggy would be just another vehicle. There were hundreds like it on the road. Superficially it was a five-year-old heap that had seen plenty of service, but the souped-up motor under the hood came out of a limousine that had packed a lot of speed and power. Once on the road nothing the city cops had was going to catch me.

Good old Ruston. If my memory had been working right I wouldn't have forgotten my little pal I plugged. Guys who are shot need doctors, and need them quick, and in Sidon there wouldn't be that many medics that I couldn't run them all down. A crooked doc, that's what I wanted. If a gunshot had been treated Price would have known about it and told me, but none had been entered in the books. Either a crooked doc or a threatened doc. He was the one to find.

I stripped the branches from the fenders and cleared a path to the road, and then eased out onto the macadam. At the first crossroad a sign pointed to the highway and I took the turn. Two miles down I turned into a stream of traffic, picked out a guy going along at a medium clip and nosed in behind him.

We both turned off into the city, only I parked on a side street and went into a candy store that had a public phone. Fiddling through the Yellow Pages, I ripped out the sheet of doctors listed there, and went through the motions of making a phone call. Nobody bothered to so much as glance at me.

Back in the car I laid out my course and drove to the first on my list. It wasn't an impressive list. Seven names. Dr. Griffin was stepping out of his car when I pulled in.

"Doctor . . ."

"Yes?"

His eyes went up and down the ruin of my suit. "Don't mind me," I said. "I've been out all night chasing down the dick that shot that cop. I'm a reporter."

"Oh, yes, I heard about that. What can I do for you?"

"The police fired several shots at him. There's a chance that he might have been hit. Have you treated any gunshot wounds lately?"

He drew himself up in indignant pride. "Certainly not! I would have reported it immediately had I done so."

"Thank you, Doctor."

The next one wasn't home, but his housekeeper was. Yes, she knew all about the doctor's affairs. No, there had been no gunshot wounds since Mr. Dillon shot himself in the foot like a silly fool when loading his shotgun. Yes, she was very glad to be of service.

Dr. Pierce ushered me into his very modern office personally. I pulled the same reporter routine on him. "A gunshot wound, you say?"

"Yes. It wasn't likely that he'd treat it himself."

He folded his hands across his paunch and leaned back in his chair. "There was one the day before yesterday, but I reported that. Certainly you know about it. A .22-caliber bullet. The man was hit while driving out in the country. Said he didn't know where it came from."

I covered up quickly. "Oh, that one. No, this would have been a larger shell. The cops don't pack .22's these days."

"I expect not," he laughed.

"Well, thanks anyway, Doctor."

"Don't mention it."

Four names left. It was past three o'clock. The next two weren't home, but the wife of one assured me that her husband would not have treated any wounds of the sort because he had been on a case in the hospital during the entire week.

The other one was in Florida on a vacation.

Dr. Clark had offices a block away from police headquarters, a very unhealthy place right now. Cars drove up and away in a constant procession, but I had to chance it. I parked pointing away from the area, making sure I had plenty of room to pull out, my wheels turned away from the curb. A woman came out of the office holding a baby. Then a man walking on a cane. I didn't want to enter an office full of people if I could help it, but if he didn't get rid of his patients in a hurry I was going to have to bust in anyway. A boy went in crying, holding his arm. Damn it, I was losing time!

As I went to reach for the ignition switch another guy came out, a four-inch wide bandage going from the corner of his mouth to his ear. The bells again. They went off all at once inside my skull until I wanted to scream. The bandage. The hell with the gunshot wound, he was probably dead. The bandage. My fingers hooking in a mouth and ripping the skin wide open. Of course, he'd need a doctor too! You wouldn't find two freak accidents like that happening at once. He was a ratty-looking guy dressed in a sharp gray suit with eyes that were everywhere at once. He went down the steps easily and walked to a car a couple ahead of me. I felt my heart beginning to pound, beating like a heavy hammer, an incredible excitement that made my blood race in my veins like a river about to flood.

He pulled out and I was right behind him, our bumpers almost touching. There was no subtlety about this tail job, maybe that's why I got away with it so long. He didn't notice me until we were on the back road six miles out of town ripping off seventy miles an hour. Just the two of us. We had left all other traffic miles behind. I saw his eyes go to the rearvision mirror and his car spurted ahead. I grinned evilly to myself and stepped down harder on the accelerator until I was pushing him again.

His eyes hardly left the mirror. There was fright in them now. A hand went out and he signaled me to pass. I ignored it. Eighty-five now. A four-store town went by with the wind. I barely heard the whistle of the town cop blast as I passed him. Eighty-seven. The other car was having trouble holding the turns. It leaned until the tires screamed as the driver jerked it around. I grinned again. The frame of my car was rigged for just such emergencies. Ninety. Trees shot by like a huge picket fence. Another town. A rapid parade of identical billboards advertising a casino in Brocton. Ninety-five. A straightaway came up lined with more billboards. A nice flat stretch was ahead, he would have opened up on it if he could have, but his load was doing all it could. At the end of the straightaway was the outline of a town.

My little friend, you have had it, I said to myself. I went down on the gas, the car leaped ahead, we rubbed fenders. For a split second I was looking into those eyes and remembering that night, before I cut across his hood. He took to the shoulder, fought the wheel furiously but couldn't control it. The back end skidded around and the car went over on its side like a pinwheel. I stood on the brake, but his car was still rolling as I stopped.

I backed up and got out without shutting the engine off. The punk was lucky, damn lucky. His car had rolled but never up-ended, and those steel turret top jobs could take it on a roll in soft earth. He was crawling out of the door reaching under his coat for a rod when I jumped him. When I slapped him across that bandage he screamed and dropped the gun. I straddled him and picked it up, a snub-nosed .38, and thrust it in my waistband.

"Hello, pal," I said.

Little bubbles of pink foam oozed from the corners of his mouth, "Don't . . . don't do nothing . . ."

"Shut up."

"Please . . ."

"Shut up." I looked at him, looked at him good. If my face said anything he could read it. "Remember me? Remember that night in the shack? Remember the kid?"

Recognition dawned on him. A terrible, fearful recognition and he shuddered the entire length of his body. "What're ya gonna do?"

I brought my hand down across his face as hard as I could. He moaned and whimpered, "Don't!" Blood started to seep through the bandage, bright red now.

"Where's the guy I shot?"

He breathed, "Dead," through a mouthful of gore. It ran out his mouth and dribbled down his chin.

"Who's Mallory?"

He closed his eyes and shook his head. All right, don't talk. Make me make you. This would be fun. I worked my nails under the adhesive of the bandage and ripped it off with one tug. Clotted blood pulled at his skin and he screamed again. A huge half-open tear went from the corner of his mouth up his jawline, giving him a perpetual grin like a clown.

"Open your eyes." He forced his lids up, his chest heaved for air. Twitches of pain gripped his face. "Now listen to me, chum. I asked you who Mallory was. I'm going to put my fingers in your mouth and rip out those stitches one by one until you tell me. Then I'm going to open you up on the other side. If you'd sooner look like a clam, don't talk."

"No! I . . . I don't know no Mallory."

I slapped him across the cheek, then did as I promised. More blood welled out of the cut. He screamed once more, a short scream of intolerable agony. "Who's Mallory?"

"Honest . . . don't know . . ."

Another stitch went. He passed out cold.

I could wait. He came to groaning senselessly. I shook his head until his eyes opened. "Who do you work for, pal?"

His lips moved, but no sound came forth. I nudged him again. "The boss . . . Nelson . . . at the casino."

Nelson. I hadn't heard it before. "Who's Mallory?"

"No more. I don't know . . ." His voice faded out to nothing and his eyes shut. Except for the steady flow of blood seeping down his chin he looked as dead as they come.

It was getting dark again. I hadn't noticed the cars driving up until the lights of one shone on me. People were piling out of the first car and running across the field, shouting at each other and pointing to the overturned car.

The first one was all out of breath when he reached me. "What happened, mister? Is he dead? God, look at his face!"

"He'll be all right," I told him. "He just passed out." By that time the others were crowded around. One guy broke through the ring and flipped his coat open to show a badge.

"Better get him to a hospital. Ain't none here. Nearest one's in Sidon." He yanked a pad out of his pocket and wet the tip of a pencil with his tongue. "What's your name, mister?"

I almost blurted it out without thinking. If he heard it I'd be under his gun in a second, and there wasn't much I could do with this mob around. I stood up and motioned him away from the crowd. On the other side of the upturned car I looked him square in the eye.

"This wasn't an accident," I said, "I ran him off the road."

"You what?"

"Keep quiet and listen. This guy is a kidnapper. He may be a killer. I want you to get to the nearest phone and call Sergeant Price of the state police, understand? His headquarters is on the highway outside of Sidon. If you can't get him, keep trying until you do."

His hands gripped my lapels. "Say, buster, what are you trying to pull? Who the hell are you, anyway?"

"My name is Mike . . . Mike Hammer. I'm wanted by

every crooked cop in this part of the state and if you don't get your paws off me I'll break your arm!"

His jaw sagged, but he let go my coat, then his brows wrinkled. "I'll be damned," he said. "I always did want to meet you. Read all the New York papers y' know. By damn. Say, you *did* kill that Sidon cop, didn't you?"

"Yes, I did."

"By damn, that's good. He put a bullet into one of our local lads one night when he was driving back from the casino. Shot him while he was dead drunk because he didn't like his looks. He got away with it too, by damn. What was that you wanted me to tell the police?"

I breathed a lot easier. I never thought I'd find a friend this far out. "You call Price and tell him to get out to the casino as fast as his car will bring him. And tell him to take along some boys."

"Gonna be trouble?"

"There's liable to be."

"Maybe I should go." He pulled at his chin, thinking hard. "I don't know. The casino is all we got around here. It ain't doing us no good, but the guy that runs it runs the town."

"Stay out of it if you can help it. Get an ambulance if you want to for that guy back there, but forget the hospital. Stick him in the cooler. Then get on the phone and call Price."

"Okay, Mike. I'll do that for you. Didn't think you shot that cop in cold blood like the notices said. You didn't, did you?"

"He was sitting on top of me about to bash my brains out with a billy when I shot the top of his head off."

"A good thing, by damn."

I didn't hang around. Twenty pairs of eyes followed me across the field to my car, but if there was any explaining to be done the cop was making a good job of it. Before I climbed under the wheel he had hands helping to right the car and six people carrying the figure of The Face to the road.

Nelson, the Boss. Another character. Where did he come in? He wasn't on the level if rat-puss was working for him. Nelson, but no Mallory. I stepped on the starter and ran the engine up. Nelson, but no Mallory. Something cold rolled down my temple and I wiped it away. Sweat. Hell, it couldn't be true, not what I was thinking, but it made sense! Oh, hell, it was impossible, people just aren't made that way! The pieces didn't have to be fitted into place any longer . . . they were being drawn into a pattern of murder as if by a magnet under the board, a pattern of death as complicated as a Persian tapestry, ugly enough to hang in Hitler's own parlor.

Nelson, but no Mallory. The rest would be only incidental, a necessary incidental. I sweated so freely that my shirt was matted to my body.

I didn't have to look for the killer any longer. I knew who the killer was now.

The early crowd had arrived at the casino in force. Dozens of cars with plates from three states were already falling into neat rows at the direction of the attendant and their occupants in evening dress and rich business clothes were making their way across the lawn to the doors. It was an imposing place built like an old colonial mansion with twenty-foot pillars circling the entire house. From inside came the strains of a decent orchestra and a lot of loud talk from the bar on the west side. Floodlights played about the grounds, lighting up the trees in the back and glancing off the waters of the bay with sparkling fingers. The outlines of a boathouse made a dark blot in the trees, and out in the channel the lights from some moored yachts danced with the roll of the ships.

For five minutes I sat in the car with a butt hanging between my lips, taking in every part of the joint. When I had the layout pretty well in my mind I stepped out and flipped the attendant a buck. The guy's watery eyes went up and down my clothes, wondering what the hell I was doing there.

"Where'll I find Nelson, friend?"

He didn't like my tone, but he didn't argue about it. "What do you want him for?"

"We got a load of special stuff coming in on a truck and I want to find out what he wants done with it."

"Booze?"

"Yeah."

"Hell, ain't he taking the stuff off Carmen?"

"This is something special, but I'm not jawing about it out here. Where is he?"

"If he ain't on the floor he'll be upstairs in his office."

I nodded and angled over to the door. Two boys in shabby tuxedos stood on either side throwing greetings to the customers. They didn't throw any to me. I saw them exchange glances when they both caught the outlines of the rod under my coat. One started drifting toward me and I muttered, "I got a truckload of stuff for the boss. When it comes up get it around the back. We had a police escort all the way out of Jersey until we lost them."

The pair gave me blank stares wondering what I was talking about, but when I brushed by them they fingered me an okay thinking I was on the in. Bar noises came from my left, noises you couldn't mistake. They were the same from the crummiest joint in the Bronx to the swankiest supper club uptown. I went in, grabbed a spot at the end and ordered a brew. The punk gave me a five-ounce glass and soaked me six bits for it. When he passed me my change I asked for the boss.

"Just went upstairs a minute ago." I downed the drink and threaded my way out again. In what had been the main living room at one time were the bobbing heads of the dancers, keeping time to the orchestra on the raised dais at one end. Dozens of white-coated waiters scurried about like ants getting ready for winter, carrying trays loaded to the rims with every size glass there was. A serving bar took up one whole end of the corridor with three bartenders passing out drinks. This place was a gold mine.

I went up the plush-carpeted stairs with traffic. It was mostly male. Big fat guys chewing on three-buck cigars carrying dough in their jeans. An occasional dame with a fortune in jewelry dangling from her extremities. At the top of the landing the whir of the wheels and the click of the dice came clearly over the subdued babble of tense voices seated around the tables. Such a beautiful setup. It would be a shame to spoil it. So this was what Price had referred to. Protected gambling. Even with a hundred-way split to stay covered the boss was getting a million-dollar income.

The crowd went into the game rooms, but I continued down the dimly lit hallway past the rest rooms until I reached another staircase. This one was smaller, less bright, but just as plush and just as well used. Upstairs someone had a spasm of coughing and water splashed in a cooler.

I looked around me, pressing flat against the wall, then ducked around the corner and stood on the first step. The gun was in my hand, fitting into its accustomed spot. One by one I went up the stairs, softly, very softly. At the top, light from a doorway set into the wall threw a yellow light on the paneling opposite it. Three steps from the landing I felt the board drop a fraction of an inch under my foot. That was what I was waiting for.

I hit the door, threw it open and jammed the rod in the face of the monkey in the tux who was about to throw the bolt. "You should have done that sooner," I sneered at him.

He tried to bluff it out. "What the hell do you think you're doing?"

"Shut up and lay down on the floor. Over here away from the door."

I guess he knew what would happen if he didn't. His face

went white right down into his collar and he fell to his knees then stretched out on the floor like he was told. Before he buried his map in the nap of the carpet he threw me one of those "you'll-be-sorry" looks.

Like hell I'd be sorry. I wasn't born yesterday. I turned the gun around in my hand and got behind the door. I didn't have long to wait. The knob turned, a gun poked in with a guy behind it looking for a target, a leer of pure sadistic pleasure on his face. When I brought the butt of the .45 across his head the leer turned to amazement as he spilled forward like a sack of wet cement. The skin on his bald dome was split a good three inches from the thong hook on the handle and pulled apart like a gaping mouth. He would be a long time in sleepy town.

"You ought to get that trip fixed in the stairs," I said to the fancy boy on the floor. "It drops like a trapdoor."

He looked back at me through eyes that seemed to pulse every time his heart beat. Both his hands were on the floor, palms down, his body rising and falling with his labored breathing. Under a trim moustache his chin fell away a little, quivering like the rest of him. A hairline that had once swept across his forehead now lay like low tide on the back of his head, graying a little, but not much. There was a scar on one lip and his nose had been twisted out of shape not too long ago, but when you looked hard you could still see through the wear of the years.

He was just what I expected. "Hello, Mallory," I said, "or should I say, Nelson?"

I could hardly hear his voice. "W . . . who are you?"

"Don't play games, sucker. My name is Mike Hammer. You ought to know me. I bumped one of your boys and made a mess of the other awhile back. You should see him now. I caught up with him again. Get up."

"What . . . are you going . . . to do?" I looked down at the .45. The safety was off and it was the nastiest-looking weapon in existence at that moment. I pointed it at his belly.

"Maybe I'll shoot you. There." I indicated his navel with the muzzle.

"If it's money you want, I can give it to you, Hammer. Please, get the rod off me."

Mallory was the tough guy. He edged away from me, holding his hands out in a futile attempt to stop a bullet if it should come. He stopped backing when he hit the edge of the desk. "I don't want any of your dough, Mallory," I said, "I want you." I let him look into the barrel again. "I want to hear something you have to say."

"I . . ."

"Where's Miss Grange . . . or should I say Rita Cambell?"

He drew his breath in a great swallow and before I could move swung around, grabbed the pen set from the desk and sent the solid onyx base crashing into my face.

Fingers clawed at my throat and we hit the floor with a tangle of arms and legs. I brought my knee up and missed, then swung with the gun. It landed on the side of his neck and gave me a chance to clear my head. I saw where the next punch was going. I brought it up from the floor and smacked him as hard as I could in the mouth. My knuckles pushed back his lips and his front teeth popped like hollow things under the blow.

The bastard spit them right in my face.

He was trying to reach my eyes. I tossed the rod to one side and laughed long and loud. Only for that one moment did he possess any strength at all, just that once when he was raging mad. I got hold of both his arms and pinned them down, then threw him sideways to the floor. His feet kicked out and kicked again until I got behind him. With his back on the floor I straddled his chest and sat on his stomach, both his hands flat against his sides, held there by my legs. He couldn't yell without choking on his own blood and he knew it, but he kept trying to spit at me nevertheless.

With my open palm I cracked him across the cheek. Right, left, right, left. His head went sideways with each slap, but my other hand always straightened it up again. I hit him until the palms of my hands were sore and his cheek split in a dozen places from my ring. At first he flopped and moaned for me to stop, then fought bitterly to get away from the blows that were tearing his face to shreds. When he was almost out, I quit.

"Where's Grange, Mallory?"

"The shed." He tried to plead with me not to hit him, but I cracked him one anyway.

"Where's the Cook girl?"

No answer. I reached for my rod and cradled it in my hand.

"Look at me, Mallory."

His eyes opened halfway. "My hand hurts. Answer me or I use this on you. Maybe you won't live through it. Where's the Cook girl?"

"Nobody else. Grange . . . is the . . . only one."

"You're lying, Mallory."

"No . . . just Grange."

I couldn't doubt but what he was telling the truth. After what I gave him he was ready to spill his guts. But that still didn't account for Cook. "Okay, who does have her then?"

Blood bubbled out of his mouth from his split gums. "Don't know her."

"She was Grange's alibi, Mallory. She was with the Cook dame the night York was butchered. She would have given Grange an out."

His eyes came open all the way. "She's a bitch," he mouthed. "She doesn't deserve an alibi. They kidnapped my kid, that's what they did!"

"And you kidnapped him back . . . fourteen years later."

"He was mine, wasn't he? He didn't belong to York."

I gave it to him slowly. "You didn't really want him, did you? You didn't give a damn about the kid. All you wanted was to get even with York. Wasn't that it?"

Mallory turned his head to one side. "Answer me, damn you!"

"Yes."

"Who killed York?"

I waited for his answer. I had to be sure I was right. This was one time I had to be sure.

"It . . . it wasn't me."

I raised the gun and laid the barrel against his forehead. Mallory was staring into the mouth of hell. "Lie to me, Mallory," I said, "and I'll shoot you in the belly, then shoot you again a little higher. Not where you'll die quick, but where you'll wish you did. Say it was you and you die fast . . . like you don't deserve. Say it wasn't you and I may believe you and I may not . . . only don't lie to me because I know who killed York."

Once more his eyes met mine, showing pain and terror. "It . . . wasn't me. No, it wasn't me. You've got to believe that." I let the gun stay where it was, right against his forehead. "I didn't even know he was dead. It was Grange I wanted."

Even with his shattered mouth the words were coming freely as he begged for his life. "I got the news clipping in the mail. The one about the trouble in the hospital. There was no signature, but the letter said that Grange was Rita Cambell and she was a big shot now and if I kidnapped the kid, instead of ransom I could get positive information from York that his kid was my son. I wouldn't have snatched him if it wasn't so easy. The letter said the watchman on the gate would be drugged and the door to the house open on a certain night. All I had to do to get the kid was go in after him. I was still pretty mad at York and the letter made it worse. I wanted Myra Grange more than the old man, that's why when those crazy lugs I sent after the kid lost him I made a try for her. I followed her from her house to another place then waited for her to come out before I grabbed her. She was in there when York was killed and I was waiting outside. Honest, I didn't kill him. She didn't know who I was until I told her. Ever since that time when York stole my kid I used the name Nelson. She started to fight with me in the car and hit me over the head with the heel of her shoes. While I was still dizzy she beat it and got in her car and scrammed. I chased her and forced her off the road by the river and she went in. I thought she was dead. . . ."

The footsteps coming up the stairs stopped him. I whipped around and sent a shot crashing through the door. Somebody swore and yelled for reinforcements. I prodded Mallory with the tip of the rod. "The window and be quick."

He didn't need any urging. The gun in his back was good incentive. That damn warning trip. Either it went off someplace else or the boys on the doors got suspicious. Egghead was starting to groan on the floor. "Get the window up."

Mallory opened the catch and pushed. Outside the steel railings of the fire escape were waiting. I thanked the good fathers who passed the law making them compulsory for all three-story buildings. We went out together, then down the metal stairs without trying to conceal our steps. If I had a cowbell around my neck I couldn't have made more noise. Mallory kept spitting blood over the side, trying to keep his eyes on me and the steps at the same time. Above us heavy bodies were ramming the door. The lock splintered and someone tripped over the mug on the floor, but before they could get to the window we were on the ground.

"The boathouse. Shake it, Mallory, they won't care who they hit," I said.

Mallory was panting heavily, but he knew there was wisdom in my words. A shot snapped out that was drowned in a sudden blast from the orchestra, but I saw the gravel kick up almost at my feet. We skirted the edge of cars and out in between the fenders, then picked an opening and went through it to the boathouse. The back of it was padlocked.

"Open it."

"I . . . I don't have the key."

"That's a quick way to get yourself killed," I reminded him.

He fumbled for a key in his pocket, brought it out and inserted it in the padlock. His hands were shaking so hard that he couldn't get it off the hasp. I shoved him away and ripped it loose myself. The door slid sideways, and I thumbed him in, closing the door behind us. With the gun in the small of his back I flicked a match with my fingernail.

Grange and Cook were lying side by side in a pile of dirt at the far end of the boathouse. Both were tied up like Thanksgiving turkeys with a wad of cloth clamped between their jaws. They were out cold. Mallory's mouth dropped to his chin and he pointed a trembling finger at Cook. "She's here!"

"What the hell did you expect?"

His face grew livid until blood flowed afresh from his mouth. Mallory might have said something in anger if the match had not scorched my finger. I dropped it and cursed. He pulled away from the gun at the same time and ran for it. I took four steps toward the door, my arms outstretched to grab him, but he wasn't there. At the other end of the room one of the girls started to moan through her gag. A knob turned and for a second I saw stars in the sky at the side of the wall. My first shot got him in the leg and he fell to the floor screaming. In the half-light of the match I hadn't seen that side door, but he knew it was there. I ran over and yanked him back by the foot, mad enough to send a bullet into his gut.

I never had the chance. There was a blast of gunfire and my rod was torn from my grasp. The beam of a spotlight hit me in the eyes as Dilwick's voice said, "Freeze, Hammer. You make one move and I'll shoot hell out of you."

The light moved over to the side, never leaving me. Dilwick snapped on the overhead; one dim bulb that barely threw enough light to reach both ends. He was standing there beside the switch with as foul a look as I ever hope to see on a human face and murder in his hands. He was going to kill me.

It might have ended then if Mallory hadn't said, "You lousy rat. You stinking, lousy rat. You're the one who's been bleeding me. You son of a bitch."

Dilwick grinned at me, showing his teeth. "He's a wise guy, Hammer. Listen to him bawl."

I didn't say a word.

Dilwick went over and got my gun from the floor, using his handkerchief on the butt, never taking his eyes from either of us. He looked at me, then Mallory, and before either of us could move sent a shot smashing into Mallory's chest from my .45. The guy folded over in a quarter-roll and was still. Dilwick tossed the still-smoking gun down the room. "It was nice while it lasted," he said, "but now it will be even better."

I waited.

"The boss had a swell racket here. A perfect racket. He paid us off well, but I'm going to take over now. The hell with being a cop. It'll make a pretty story, don't you think? I come in here and see you shoot him, then shoot you. Uh-huh, a very pretty story and nobody will blame me. You'll be wrapped up cold for a double murder, first that copper and now him."

"Sure," I said, "but what are you going to do about Grange and her pal?"

Dilwick showed his teeth again. "She's wanted for York's murder, isn't she? Wouldn't it be sweet if they were found dead in a love tryst? The papers would love that. Boy, what a front-page story if *you* don't crowd them off. Grange and her sweetie doing the double Dutch in the drink instead of her cooking for the York kill. That would put a decent end to this mess. I got damn sick and tired of trying to cover up for the boss anyway, and you got in my hair, Hammer."

"Did I?"

"Don't get smart. If I had any sense I would have taken care of you myself instead of letting that dumb bunny of a detective bollix up things when you were tailing me on that back road."

"You wouldn't have done any better either," I spat out.

"No? But I will now." He raised the gun and took deliberate aim at my head.

While he wasted time thumbing back the hammer I tugged the snub-nosed .38 from my waistband that I had taken from the punk with the wrecked face and triggered one into his stomach. His face froze for an instant, the gun sagged, then with all the hatred of his madness he stumbled forward a step, raising his gun to fire.

The .38 roared again. A little blue spot appeared over the bridge of his nose and he went flat on his face.

Mine wasn't the only gun to speak. Outside there was a continual roar of bullets; screams from the house and commands being shouted into the dark. A car must have tried to pull away and smashed into another. More shots and the tinkling of broken glass. A man's voice screamed in agony. A tommy went off in short burps blasting everything in its path. Through the door held open by Mallory's body the brilliant white light of a spotlight turned the night to day and pairs of feet were circling the boathouse.

I shouted, "Price, it's me, Mike. I'm in here!"

A light shot in the door as hands slid the other opening back. A state trooper with a riot gun pointed at me slid in and I dropped the .38. Price came in behind him. "Damn, you still alive?"

"I look it, don't I?" Laughing almost drunkenly I slapped him on the shoulder. "Am I glad to see you! You sure took long enough to get here." Price's foot stretched out and pushed the body on the floor.

"That's . . ."

"Dilwick," I finished. "The other one over there is Mallory."

"I thought you were going to keep me informed on how things stood," he said.

"It happened too fast. Besides, I couldn't be popping in places where I could be recognized."

"Well, I hope your story's good, Mike. It had better be. We're holding people out there with enough influence to swing a state legislature, and if the reason is a phony or even smells like one, you and I are both going to be on the carpet. You for murder."

"Nuts, what was all the shooting about outside?"

"I got your message such as it was and came up here with three cars of troopers. When we got on the grounds a whole squad of mugs with guns in their hands came ripping around the house. They let go at us before we could get out of the cars and there was hell to pay. The boys came up expecting action and they got it."

"Those mugs, chum, were after me. I guess they figured I'd try to make a break for it and circled the house. Dilwick was the only one who knew where we'd be. Hell, he should have. I was after Grange and the Cook girl and he had them in here."

"Now you tell me. Go on and finish it."

I brought him up to date in a hurry. "Dilwick's been running cover for Mallory. When you dig up the books on this joint you're going to see a lot of fancy figures. But our boy Dilwick got ideas. He wanted the place for himself. He shot Mallory with my gun and was going to shoot me, only I got him with the rod I took off the boy whose car I flipped over. Yeah, Dilwick was a good thinker all right. When Grange didn't show up he did what I did and floated down the river himself and found how the eddies took him to the shore. At that time both he and Mallory were figuring on cutting themselves a nice slice of cash from the York estate. Grange was the only one who knew there was evidence that Ruston wasn't York's son and they were going to squeeze it out of her or turn her over to the police for the murder of York."

Price looked at the body again, then offered me a cigarette. "So Grange really did bump her boss. I'll be a so-and-so."

I lit the butt slowly, then blew the smoke through my nostrils. "Grange didn't bump anybody."

The sergeant's face wrinkled. He stared at me queerly.

"This is the aftermath, Price," I reflected. "It's what happens when you light the fuse."

"What the hell are you talking about?"

I didn't hear him. I was thinking about a kidnapping. I was thinking about a scientist with a cleaver in his skull and the chase on for his assistant. I was thinking about Junior Ghent rifling York's office and coming up with some dirty pictures, and then getting beat up. I was thinking about a shot nicking Roxy and a night with Alice Nichols that might have been fun if it hadn't been planned so my clothes could be searched and my skull cracked afterward. I was thinking about a secret cache in the fireplace, a column in the paper, a cop trying to kill me and some words Mallory told me. I was thinking how all this might have been foreseen by the killer when the killer planned the first kill. I was thinking of the face of the killer.

It was a mess. I had said that a hundred times now, but what a beautiful mess it was. There had never been a mess as nasty as this. Nope, not a dull moment. Every detail seemed to overlap and prod something bigger to happen until you were almost ready to give up, and the original murder was obscured by the craziest details imaginable. Rah, rah, sis boom bah, with a fanfare of trumpets as the police come in and throw bullets all over the place. Was it supposed to end like this? I knew one thing. I was supposed to have died someplace along the line. The killer must be fuming now because I was very much alive. What makes people think they can get away with murder? Some plan it simple, some elaborately extreme, but this killer let things take care of themselves and they wound up better than anyone could have hoped for.

"Don't keep secrets, Mike, who did it?"

I threw the butt down, stamped on it. "I'll tell you tomorrow, Price."

"You'll tell me now, Mike."

"Don't fight me, kid. I appreciate all that you did for me, but I don't throw anyone to the dogs until I'm sure."

"You've killed enough people to be sure. Who was it?"

"It still goes. I have to check one little detail."

"What?"

"Something that makes a noise like a cough."

Price thought I was crazy. "You tell me now or I'll hold you until you do. I can't stick my neck out any further. I'll have hot breaths blowing on my back too, and they'll be a lot hotter if I can't explain this mix-up!"

I was tired. I felt like curling up there with Dilwick and going to sleep. "Don't squeeze, Price. I'll tell you tomorrow. When you take this little package home . . ." I swept my hand around the room, ". . . you'll get a commendation." Over in the corner a trooper was taking the bonds from the girls. Grange was moaning again. "You can get her side of the story anyway, and that will take care of your superiors until you hear from me."

The sergeant waited a long moment then shrugged his

shoulders. "You win. I've waited this long . . . I guess tomorrow will be all right. Let's get out of here."

We carried Grange out together with the other trooper lug-
ging the Cook girl over his shoulder. Myra Grange's pupils
were big black circles, dilated to the utmost. She was hopped
up to the ears. We got them into one of the police cars then
stood around until the casino gang was manacled to each
other and the clientele weeded out. I grinned when I spotted
a half-dozen Sidon cops in the group. They had stopped bel-
lowing long ago, and from the worried looks being passed
around it was going to be a race to see who could talk the
loudest and the fastest. There would be a new police force in
Sidon this time next week. The public might be simple enough
to let themselves be bullied around and their government
rot out from underneath them, but it would only go so far.
An indignant public is like a mad bull. It wouldn't stop until
every tainted employee on the payroll was in a cell. Maybe
they'd even give me a medal. Yeah, maybe.

I was sick of watching. I called Price over and told him I
was going back. His face changed, but he said nothing. There
was a lot he wanted to say, but he could tell how it was with
me. Price nodded and let me climb into my car. I backed it
up and turned around in the drive. Tomorrow would be a
busy day. I'd have to prepare my statements on the whole
affair to hand over to a grand jury, then get set to prove it. You
don't simply kill people and walk away from it. Hell, no.
Righteous kill or not the law had to be satisfied.

Yes, tomorrow would be a busy day. Tonight would be
even busier. I had to see a killer about a murder.

Chapter Twelve

It was ten after eleven when I reached the York estate.
Henry came out of his gatehouse, saw me and gaped as
though he were looking at a ghost. "Good heavens, Mr. Hammer. The police are searching all over for you! You . . . you
killed a man."

"So I did," I said sarcastically. "Open the gates."

"No . . . I can't let you come in here. There'll be trouble."

"There will if you don't open the gates." His face seemed
to sag and his whole body assumed an air of defeat. Disgust
was written in the set of his mouth, disgust at having to look
at a man who shot a fellowman. I drove through and stopped.

"Henry, come here."

The gatekeeper shuffled over reluctantly. "Yes, sir?"

"I'm not wanted any longer, Henry. The police have settled the matter up to a certain point."

"You mean you didn't . . ."

"No, I mean I shot him, but it was justified. I've been
cleared, understand?"

He smiled a little, not quite understanding, but he breathed
a sigh of relief. At least he knew he wasn't harboring a fugi-
tive in me. I pulled up the driveway to the house, easing
around the turns until the beams of my brights spotlighted
the house. Inside I saw Harvey coming to the door. Instead of
parking in front of the place I rolled around to the side and
nosed into the open door of the garage. A big six-car affair,
but now there were only two cars in it, counting mine. A long
time ago someone started using it for a storeroom and now
one end was cluttered with the junk accumulated over the
years. Two boys' bicycles were hanging from a suspension
gadget set in the ceiling and underneath them a newer model
with a small one-cylinder engine built into the frame. Hanging from a hook screwed into an upright were roller skates
and ice skates, but neither pair had been used much. Quite
a childhood Ruston had.

I shut the door of the garage and looked up. The rain had
started. The tears of the gods. Of laughter or sorrow? Maybe
the joke was on me, after all.

Harvey was his usual, impeccable, unmoving self as he
took my hat and ushered me into the living room. He made no
mention of the affair whatsoever, nor did his face reveal any
curiosity. Even before he announced me, Roxy was on her
way down the stairs with Ruston holding her arm. Billy
Parks came out of the foyer grinning broadly, his hand outstretched. "Mike! You sure got your nerve. By gosh, you're
supposed to be Public Enemy Number One!"

"Mike!"

"Hello, Lancelot. Hello, Roxy. Let me give you a hand."

"Oh, I'm no cripple," she laughed. "The stairs get me a
little, but I can get around all right."

"What happened, Mike?" Ruston smiled. "The policemen
all left this evening after they got a phone call and we
haven't seen them since. Golly, I was afraid you'd been shot
or something. We thought they caught you."

"Well, they came close, kid, but they never even scratched
me. It's all finished. I'm in the clear and I'm about ready to go
home."

Billy Parks stopped short in the act of lighting a cigarette.

His hands began to tremble slightly and he had trouble finding the tip of the butt.

Ruston said, "You mean the police don't want you any
longer, Mike?" I shook my head. He gave a little cry of glad-
ness and ran to me, throwing his arms about me in a tight
squeeze. "Gee, Mike, I'm so happy."

I patted his arm and smiled crookedly. "Yep, I'm almost
an honest man again."

"Mike . . ."

Roxy's voice was the hoarse sound of a rasp on wood. She
was clutching the front of her negligee with one hand, trying
to push a streamer of hair from her eyes with the other. A
little muscle twitched in her cheek. "Who . . . did it, Mike?"

Billy was waiting, Roxy was waiting. I heard Harvey pause
outside the door. Ruston looked from them to me, puzzled.
The air in the room was charged, alive. "You'll hear about
it tomorrow," I said.

Billy Parks dropped his cigarette.

"Why not now?" Roxy gasped.

I took a cigarette from my pocket and stuffed it between my
lips. Billy fumbled for his on the floor and held the lit tip to
mine. I dragged the smoke in deeply. Roxy was beginning to
go white, biting on her lip. "You'd better go to your room,
Roxy. You don't look too good."

"Yes . . . yes. I had better. Excuse me. I really don't feel
too well. The stairs . . ." She let it go unfinished. While Ruston helped her up I stood there in silence with Billy. The kid
came down again in a minute.

"Do you think she'll be all right, Mike?"

"I think so."

Billy crushed his cig out in an ashtray. "I'm going to bed,
Mike. This day has been tough enough."

I nodded. "You going to bed, too, Ruston?"

"What's the matter with everybody, Mike?"

"Nervous, I guess."

"Yes, that's it, I suppose." His face brightened. "Let me
play for them. I haven't played since . . . that night. But I
want to play. Will it be all right?"

"Sure, go ahead."

He grinned and ran out of the room. I heard him arrange
the seat, then lift the lid of the piano, and the next moment
the heavy melody of a classical piece filled the house. I sat
down and listened. It was gay one moment, serious the next.
He ran up and down the keys in a fantasy of expression. Good
music to think by. I chain-lit another cigarette, wondering
how the music was affecting the murderer. Did it give him a
creepy feeling? Was every note part of his funeral theme?

Three cigarettes gone in thought and still I waited. The music had changed now, it was lilting, rolling in song. I put the butt out and stood up. It was time to see the killer.

I put my hand on the knob and turned, stepped in the room and locked the door behind me. The killer was smiling at me, a smile that had no meaning I could fathom. It was a smile of neither defeat nor despair, but nearer to triumph. It was no way for a murderer to smile. The bells in my head were rising in a crescendo with the music.

I said to the murderer, "You can stop playing now, Ruston."

The music didn't halt. It rose in spirit and volume while Ruston York created a symphony from the keyboard, a challenging overture to death, keeping time with my feet as I walked to a chair and sat down. Only when I pulled the .45 from its holster did the music begin to diminish. My eyes never left his face. It died out in a crashing maze of minor chords that resounded from the walls with increased intensity.

"So you found me out, Mr. Hammer."

"Yes."

"I rather expected it these last few days." He crossed his legs with complete nonchalance and barely a glance at the gun in my hand. I felt my temper being drawn to the brink of unreason, my lips tightening.

"You're a killer, little buddy," I said. "You're a blood-crazy, insane little bastard. It's so damn inconceivable that I can hardly believe it myself, but it's so. You had it well planned, chum. Oh, but you would, you're a genius. I forgot. That's what everyone forgot. You're only fourteen but you can sit in with scientists and presidents and never miss a trick."

"Thank you."

"You have a hair-trigger mind, Ruston. You can conceive and coordinate and anticipate beyond all realm of imagination. All the while I was batting my brains out trying to run down a killer you must have held your sides laughing. You knew pretty well what killing York would expose . . . a series of crimes and petty personalities scrambled together to make the dirtiest omelet ever cooked. But *you'd* never cook for it. Oh, no . . . not you. If . . . if you were found out the worst that could happen would be that you'd face a juvenile court. That's what you thought, didn't you? Like hell.

"Yes, you're only a child, but you have a man's mind. That's why I'm talking to you like I would to a man. That's why I can kill you like I would a man."

He sat there unmoving. If he knew fear he showed it only

in the tiny blue vein that throbbed in his forehead. The smile still played around his mouth. "Being a genius, I guess you thought I was stupid," I continued. With every word my heart beat harder and faster until I was filled with hate. "It was getting so that I thought I was stupid myself. Why wouldn't I? Every time I turned around something would happen that was so screwy that it didn't have any place in the plot, yet in a way it was directly related. Junior Ghent and Alice. The Graham boys. Each trying to chop off a slice of cash for themselves. Each one concerned with his own little individual problem and completely unknowing of the rest. It was a beautiful setup for you.

"But please don't think I was stupid, Ruston. The only true stupidity I showed was in calling you Lancelot. If I ever meet the good knight somewhere I'll beg him to forgive me. But I wasn't so stupid otherwise, Ruston. I found out that Grange had something on York . . . and that something was the fact that she was the only one who knew that he was a kidnapper in a sense. York . . . an aging scientist who wanted an heir badly so he could pass on his learning to his son . . . but his son died. So what did he do? He took a kid who had been born of a criminal father and would have been reared in the gutter, and turned him into a genius. But after a while the genius began to think and hate. Why? Hell, only you know that.

"But somewhere you got hold of the details concerning your birth. You knew that York had only a few years to live and you knew, too, that Grange had threatened to expose the entire affair if he didn't leave his money to her. Your father (should I call him that?) was a thinker too. He worked out a proposition with Alice to have an affair with his Lesbian assistant and hold that over her head as a club, and it worked, except that Junior Ghent learned of the affair when his sister told him that York had proposed the same deal to her, too, and Junior wanted to hold that over Grange's head, and Alice's, too, so that he could come in for part of the property split. Man, what a scramble it was after that. Everybody thought I had the dope when it was lying beside the wall out there. Yeah, the wall. Remember the shot you took at Roxy? You were in your room. You tossed that lariat that was beside your bed around the awning hook outside her window, swung down and shot at her through the glass. She had the light on and couldn't see out, but she was a perfect target. You missed at that range only because you were swinging. That really threw me off the track. Nice act you put on when I brought the doctor in. You had him fooled too. I didn't get that until a little while ago.

"Now I know. You, as an intelligent, emotional man were

in love. What a howl. In love with your nurse." His face darkened. The vein began to throb harder than ever and his hands clenched into a tight knot. "You shot at her because you saw me and Roxy in a clinch and were jealous. Brother, how happy you must have been when the cops were on my back with orders to shoot to kill. I thought you were simply surprised to see me when I climbed in the window that time. Your face went white, remember? For one second there you thought I came back to get you. That was it, wasn't it?"

His head nodded faintly, but still he said nothing. "Then you saw your chance of bringing the cops charging up by knocking over the lamp. Brilliant mind again. You knew the bulb breaking would sound like a shot. Too bad I got away, wasn't it?

"If I wasn't something of a scientist myself I never would have guessed it. Let me tell you how confounded smart I am. Your time doesn't matter much anyway. I caught up with one of your playmates that snatched you. I beat the living hell out of him and would have done worse to make him talk and he knew it. I'm a scientist at that kind of stuff. He would have talked his head off, only he didn't have anything to say. You know what I asked him? I asked him who Mallory was and he didn't know any Mallory. Good reason too, because ever since you were yanked out of his hands, your father went by the name of Nelson.

"No, he didn't know any Mallory, yet you came home after the kidnapping and said . . . you . . . heard . . . the . . . name . . . Mallory . . . mentioned. When I finally got it I knew who the killer was. Then I began to figure how you worked it. Someplace in the house, and I'll find it later, you have the information and Grange's proof that you were Mallory's son. Was it a check that York gave Myra Grange? Somehow you located Mallory and sent him the clipping out of the back issue in the library and the details on how to kidnap you. That was why the clipping was gone. You set yourself up to be snatched hoping that the shock would kill York. It damn near did. You did it well, too, even to the point of switching Henry's aspirins to sleeping tablets. You set yourself up knowing you could outthink the ordinary mortals on the boat and get away. You came mighty close to failing, pal. I wish you had.

"But when that didn't do it you resorted to murder . . . and what a murder. No sweeter deal could have been cooked up by anyone. You knew that when York heard Mallory's name brought into it he'd think Grange had spilled the works and go hunting up his little pet. You thought correctly. York went out there with a gun, but I doubt if he intended to use it. The rod was supposed to be a bluff. Billy heard York leave, and he heard me leave, but how did you reach the apartment? Let me tell you. Out in the garage there's a motorbike. Properly rigged they can do sixty or seventy any day. The noise like a cough that Billy heard was you, Ruston. The sound of the motorbike, low and throaty. I noticed it had a muffler on it. Yeah, York had a gun, and you had to take along a weapon too. A meat cleaver. When I dreamed up all this I wondered why nobody spotted you going or coming, but it wouldn't be too hard to take to the back roads.

"Ruston, you were born under an evil, lucky star. Everything that happened after you surprised York in that room and split his skull worked in your favor. Hell seemed to break loose with everybody trying to cut in on York's dough. Even Dilwick. A crooked copper working for Mallory. Your real father needed that protection and Dilwick fitted right in. Dilwick must have guessed at part of the truth without ever really catching on, and he played it to keep Mallory clear and in a good spot to call for a rake-off, but he got too eager. Dilwick's dead and the rest of his lousy outfit are where they're supposed to be, cooling their heels in a cell.

"But where are you? You . . . the killer. You're sitting here listening to me spiel off everything you already know about and you're not a bit worried. Why should you be? Three or four years in an institution for the criminally insane . . . then prove yourself normal and go back into the world to kill again. You have ethics like Grange. There was a woman who probably loved her profession. She loved it so much she saw a chance to further her career by aiding York, then using it as a club to gain scientific recognition for herself.

"But you . . . hell." I spit the word out. "You banked on getting away scot-free first, then as a second-best choice facing a court. Maybe you'd even get a suspended sentence. Sure, why not? Any psychiatrist would see how that could happen. Under the pressure of your studies your mind snapped. Boy, have you got a brain! No chair, not for you. Maybe a couple of years yanked from your life-span, but what did it matter? You were twenty years ahead of yourself anyway. That was it, wasn't it? Ha!

"Not so, little man. The game just doesn't go that way. I hate to go ex post facto on you, but simply because you're nicely covered by the law doesn't mean you'll stay that way. I'm making up a new one right now. Know what it is?"

He still smiled, no change of expression. It was almost as if he were watching one of his experiments in the rabbit cage.

"Okay," I said, "I'll tell you. All little geniuses . . . or is it genii? . . . who kill and try to get away with it get it in the neck anyway."

Very deliberately I let him see me flick the safety catch on the .45. His eyes were little dark pools that seemed to swim in his head.

I was wondering if I were going to like this.

I never killed a little genius before.

For the first time, Ruston spoke. "About an hour ago I anticipated this," he smiled. I tightened involuntarily. I didn't know why, but I almost knew beforehand what he'd say.

"When I threw my arms around you inside there feigning happiness over your miraculous reappearance, I removed the clip from your gun. It's a wonder you didn't notice the difference in weight."

Did you ever feel like screaming?

My hand was shaking with rage. I felt the hollow space where the clip fitted and swore. I was so damn safety conscious I didn't jack a shell into the chamber earlier either.

And Ruston reached behind the music rack on the piano and came out with the .32.

He smiled again. He knew damn well what I was thinking. Without any trouble I could make the next corpse. He fondled the gun, clicking the hammer back. "Don't move too quickly, Mike. No, I'm not going to shoot you, not just yet. You see, my little knowledge of sleight of hand was quite useful . . . as handy as to know how to open locks. The Normanic sciences weren't all I studied. Anything that presented a problem afforded me the pleasure of solving it in my spare time.

"Move your chair a little this way so I can see you to the best advantage. Ah . . . yes. Compliments are in order, I believe. You were very right and very clever in your deductions. Frankly, I didn't imagine anyone would be able to wade through the tangle that the murder preceded. I thought I did quite well, but I see I failed, up to a certain point. Look at it from my point of view before you invite any impetuous ideas. If you turned me over to the police and proved your case, I would, as you say, stand before a juvenile court. Never would I admit my actual adulthood to them, and I would be sent away for a few years, or perhaps not at all. You see, there's a side to my story too, one you don't know about.

"Or, Mike, and this is an important 'or' . . . I may kill you and claim self-defense. You came in here and in a state of extreme nervous tension hit me. I picked up a gun that dropped out of your pocket . . ." he held up the .32, ". . . and shot you. Simple? Who would disbelieve it, especially with your temperament . . . and my tender years. So sit still and I don't think I'll shoot you for a little while, at least. Before I do anything, I want to correct some erroneous impressions you seem to have.

"I am not a 'few' years ahead of my time . . . the difference is more like thirty. Even that is an understatement. Can you realize what that means? Me. Fourteen years old. Yet I have lived over fifty years! God, what a miserable existence. You saw my little, er, schoolhouse, but what conclusion did you draw? Fool that you were, you saw nothing. You saw no electrical or mechanical contrivances that had been developed by one of the greatest scientific minds of the century. No, you merely saw objects, never realizing what they were for." He paused, grinning with abject hatred. "Have you ever seen them force-feed ducks to enlarge their livers to make better sausages? Picture that happening to a mind. Imagine having the learning processes accelerated through pain. Torture can make the mind do anything when properly presented.

"Oh, I wasn't supposed to actually feel any of all that. It was supposed to happen while I was unconscious, with only the subconscious mind reacting to the incredible pressures being put upon it to grasp and retain the fantastic array of details poured into it like feed being forced through a funnel down a duck's gullet into its belly whether it wants it or not.

"Ah, but who is to say what happens to the mind when such a development takes place? What may happen to the intricate mechanism of the human mind under such stimulation? What new reactions will it develop . . . what new outlets will it seek to repel the monster that is invading it?

"That is how I became what I am . . . but what I learned! I went even farther than was expected of me . . . much farther than the simple sciences and mathematics *he* wanted me to absorb. I even delved into criminology, Mr. Hammer, going over thousands of case histories of past crimes, and when this little . . . circumstance . . . came to my attention, I knew what I had to do . . . then figured out how I could do it.

"I researched, studied and very unobtrusively collected my data, putting myself not *ahead* of you in the commission and solution of criminal actions, but on an approximate level. With your mind highly tuned to absorb, analyze and reconstruct criminal ways, your close association with the police and past experience, you have been able to run a parallel course with me and arrive at the destination at the same time."

He gave me a wry grin. "Or should I say a little behind me?" With his head he indicated the gun in his hand, ". . . seeing that at present I hold the most advantageous position."

I started to rise, but his gun came up. "Remain seated,

please. I only said I didn't *think* I would shoot you. Hear me out."

I sat down again.

"Yes, Mr. Hammer, if I had but given it a few days more study your case would have been a hopeless one. Yet you did find me out with all my elaborate precautions, but I still have a marvelous chance to retain my life and liberty. Don't you think?"

I nodded. He certainly would.

"But what good would it do me? Answer me that? What good would it do me? Would I ever have the girl I love . . . or would she have me? She would vomit at the thought. Me, a boy with an adult mind, but still a boy's body. What woman would have me? As the years passed my body would become mature, but the power of my mind would have increased ten-fold. Then I would be an old man within the physical shell of a boy. And what of society? You know what society would do . . . it would treat me as a freak. Perhaps I could get a position as a lightning calculator in a circus. That's what that man did to me! That's what he did with his machines and brilliant thoughts. He crumpled my life into a little ball and threw it in the jaws of science. How I hated him. How I wish I could have made him suffer the way he made me suffer!

"To be twisted on the rack is trivial compared to the way one can be tortured through the mind. Has your brain ever been on fire? Have you ever had your skull probed with bolts of electrical energy while strapped to a chair? Of course not! You can remain smug and commonplace in your normal life and track down criminals and murderers. Your one fear is that of dying. Mine was of not dying soon enough!

"You can't understand how much the human body can suffer punishment. It's like a giant machine that can feed itself and heal its own wounds, but the mind is even greater. That simple piece of sickly gray matter that twists itself into gentle shapes under a thin layer of bone and looks so disarming lying in a bottle of formaldehyde is a colossus beyond conception. It thinks pain! Imagine it . . . it thinks pain and the body screams with the torture of it, yet there is nothing you can call physical in the process. It can conceive of things beyond normal imagination if it is stirred to do so. That is what mine did. Things were forced into it. Learning, he called it, but it might as well have been squeezed into my brain with a compressor, for it felt that way. I knew pain that was not known by any martyr . . . it was a pain that will probably never be known again.

"Your expression changes, Mr. Hammer. I see you believe what I say. You should . . . it is true. You may believe it, but you will never understand it. Right now I can see you change your mind. You condone my actions. I condone them. But would a jury if they knew? Would a judge . . . or the public? No, they couldn't visualize what I have undergone."

Something was happening to Ruston York even as he was speaking. The little-boy look was gone from his face, replaced by some strange metamorphosis that gave him the facial demeanor I had seen during the wild mouthings of dictators. Every muscle was tense, veins and tendons danced under the delicate texture of his skin and his eyes shone with the inward fury that was gnawing at his heart.

He paused momentarily, staring at me, yet somehow I knew he wasn't really seeing me at all. "You were right, Mr. Hammer," he said, a new, distant note in his voice now. "I *was* in love with my nurse. Or better . . . I am in love with . . . Miss Malcom. From the moment she arrived here I have been in love with her."

The hard, tight expression seemed to diminish at the thought and a smile tugged faintly at the corners of his mouth. "Yes, Mr. Hammer, love. Not the love a child would give a woman, but a man's love. The kind of love you can give a woman . . . or any other normal man."

Suddenly the half-smile vanished and the vacant look came back again. "That's what that man did to me. He made an error in his calculations, or never expected his experiment to reach such a conclusion, but that man did more than make me a mental giant. He not only increased my intellectual capacity to the point of genius . . . but in the process he developed my emotional status until I was no longer a boy.

"I am a man, Mr. Hammer. In every respect except this outer shell, and my chronological age, I am a man. And I am a man in love, trapped inside the body of a child. Can you imagine it? Can you think of me presenting my love to a woman like Roxy Malcom? Oh, she might understand, but never could she return that love. All I would get would be pity. Think of that . . . pity. That's what that bastard did to me!"

He was spitting the words out now, his face back in the contours of frustration and hatred, his eyes blankly looking at me, yet through me. It had to be like this, I thought, when he was on the brink of the deep end. It was the only chance I had. Slowly, I tucked my feet under me, the movement subtle so as not to distract him. I'd probably take a slug or two, but I'd lived through them before and if I managed it right I might be able to get my hands on his gun before he could squeeze off a fatal one. It was the only chance I had. My fingers were tight on the arms of the chair, the muscles in my shoulders bunched to throw myself forward . . . and all the time my guts were churning because I knew what I could expect before I could get all the way across that room to where he was sitting.

"I have to live in a world of my own, Mr. Hammer. No other world would accept me. As great a thing, a twisted thing that I am, I have no world to live in."

The blankness suddenly left his eyes. He was seeing me now, seeing what I was doing and knowing what I was thinking. His thumb pulled back the hammer on the .32 to make it that much easier to trigger off. Behind the now almost colorless pupils of his eyes some crazy thought was etching itself into his mind.

Ruston York looked at me, suddenly with his boy-face again. He even smiled a tired little smile and the gun moved in his hand. "Yes," he repeated, "as great as I am, I am useless."

Even while he had talked, he had done something he had never done before. He exposed himself to himself and for the first time saw the futility that was Ruston York. Once again he smiled, the gun still on me.

There was no time left at all. It had to be now, *now!* Only a second, perhaps, to do it in.

He saw me and smiled, knowing I was going to do it. "Sir Lancelot," he said wistfully.

Then, before I could even get out of the chair, Ruston York turned the gun around in his hand, jammed the muzzle of it into his mouth and pulled the trigger.